After studying English at Oxford, Phillipa Ashley worked as a copywriter and journalist. Her first novel, *Decent Exposure*, won the RNA New Writers Award and was made into a TV movie called *12 Men of Christmas* starring Kristin Chenoweth and Josh Hopkins. Phillipa lives in a Staffordshire village and has an engineer husband and a scientist daughter who indulge her arty whims. She runs a holiday-let business in the Lake District, but a big part of her heart belongs to Cornwall. She visits the county several times a year for 'research purposes', an arduous task that involves sampling cream teas, swimming in wild Cornish coves, and following actors around film shoots in a camper van. Her hobbies include watching *Poldark*, Earl Grey tea, prosecco-tasting, and falling off surfboards in front of RNLI lifeguards.

You can discover more about the author at http://phillipa-ashley.com

CONFETTI AT THE CORNISH CAFE

Cal and Demi are preparing to launch their beloved Kilhallon resort as a wedding venue. Cakes are baking, Cornish flowers are blooming, and fairy lights are twinkling. It's the perfect place for a magical marriage ceremony. But their first clients are no ordinary couple. The bride and groom are internationally famous actors Lily Craig and Ben Trevone. Kilhallon is about to host a celebrity wedding . . . With the pressure on, Demi and Cal are doing all they can to keep their guests happy and avoid any wedding disasters. But is the unpredictable weather the only thing standing in the way of the Big Day? As secrets surface and truths are told, can Demi and Cal ensure that Kilhallon's first wedding is a success? One thing's for sure — this will be a Cornish celebration to remember . . .

Books by Phillipa Ashley
Published by Ulverscroft:

WISH YOU WERE HERE
IT SHOULD HAVE BEEN ME
SUMMER AT THE CORNISH CAFE
CHRISTMAS AT THE CORNISH CAFE

PHILLIPA ASHLEY

CONFETTI AT THE CORNISH CAFE

Complete and Unabridged

CHARNWOOD
Leicester

First published in Great Britain in 2017 by
Avon
A Division of HarperCollins*Publishers*
London

First Charnwood Edition
published 2018
by arrangement with
HarperCollins*Publishers*
London

A catalogue record for this book is available from the British Library.

ISBN 978-1-4448-3734-6

Published by
F. A. Thorpe (Publishing)
Anstey, Leicestershire

Set by Words & Graphics Ltd.
Anstey, Leicestershire
Printed and bound in Great Britain by
T. J. International Ltd., Padstow, Cornwall

This book is printed on acid-free paper

For John,
Happy 30th wedding anniversary

'My heart is, and always will be, yours.'
    Jane Austen — *Sense and Sensibility*

Prologue

Kilhallon Park, Cornwall
Late February

'Good morning and . . . '
I reach out my hand to turn off the radio alarm and I hit something else. Not the cold metal of the radio, but warm skin . . . *hairy* skin . . . and I know it's not my dog, Mitch, because the skin next to me has smooth, firm muscle beneath it: human, not canine.

'Are you awake, Demi?'
At the sound of his voice, I open my eyes and Cal's face comes into focus in the dim light of this late February morning. Propped up on one elbow, he smiles down at me as I slowly surface from a deep sleep in our bed. Yes, *our* bed. Mine and Cal's. It's been over eight weeks since I moved into the main farmhouse with him but I still have to pinch myself when I think of all that's happened since I arrived at Kilhallon Park last Easter.

Cal Penwith was — still is — my boss, but he's also now, my . . . 'boyfriend'? That makes him sound like we're still at school and 'partner' sounds as if we're sharing an office in an accountancy firm. 'Lover'? Definitely, but also much more than that. I suppose we're officially 'a couple'. Christmas marked the turning point in our relationship and we not only share the

1

same bed now but the same home and, perhaps, some of the same hopes and fears.

'Were you dreaming?' Cal asks, amusement glinting in his deep brown eyes. That look may seem charming and sexy but I know it hides a world of danger. You might as well bathe in the still waters of Kilhallon Cove on a summer's day and think they could never rise up and batter you onto the rocks as believe that Cal Penwith isn't trouble.

'Um, I thought I was back in the cottage, and that the alarm had gone off.'

He smiles a mischievous smile. 'Ah, but I'm your alarm now.' He dances his fingers towards the top of the duvet. 'And I'm a lot more fun to wake up with than Radio St Trenyan.'

I huff and hesitate before replying, to tease him, although he knows that I know that he's totally right. 'Mmm. Maybe. Just a little bit.'

'More than a little bit, I hope.' Cal peels back the duvet and plants a kiss on my shoulder. The warmth of his lips combats the instant chill of the air hitting my skin. The seventeenth-century farmhouse's central heating hasn't been upgraded for thirty years because Cal's ploughed any spare cash into turning Kilhallon from a rusty old caravan site into a 'boutique eco resort'. Our guests pad about barefoot on their underfloor heating while we grab another blanket, but that's fine by me. The business comes first and I don't mind, especially when I have Cal here by my side.

'Brrr.'

Sleet rattles against the sash window, driven by

a wind straight off the Atlantic Ocean. I'm shivering, although that might not be *totally* down to the sub-zero temperatures. I snatch the duvet up to my chin.

'I'll keep you warm, if you want me to,' says Cal with a wicked grin, pulling the cover back again. He raises his eyebrow at the sight and, in return, my body tingles as my eyes adjust to being awake and I appreciate the view of him in our bed. Even after a Cornish winter there are still tan lines at his neck and arms, a hint of summer gold lingers on his skin. He spends most of his time outdoors, working on the cottages and campsite in all weathers. Of *course* I want him to keep me warm. Leaving the heat of my bed and Cal's body to head out into the winter sleet is about as appealing as mucking out Cal's 'lively' horse, Dexter, but work comes first, doesn't it?

'We have tons to do today. Haven't you forgotten this is the most important day ever for Kilhallon Park and Demelza's Cafe?' I say.

Reminding myself about our big — make that humungous — day sends a shiver down my spine. Demelza's Cafe is my responsibility: it was my idea to set it up on the coast path as part of Kilhallon, Cal's new boutique holiday resort on the far west Cornish coast. Cal invested a pot of money in it and named it after me. No pressure there, then . . . Not that I don't love running it more than anything I've ever done in my life.

We weathered some almighty storms last year while we were fighting to get the resort and cafe off the ground. Sometimes I still have to pinch

3

myself when I stand behind the counter, knowing I'm the manager of my own cafe. The day I first met Cal, I'd just lost my job at a cafe in our local town, St Trenyan. I had no job, no home and I'd become estranged from my family. I'd no idea what I was going to do next, then I heard of a job going as an 'assistant' at a new holiday resort up the coast . . .

Now, here I am, less than a year later, about to show two famous actors around as we launch Kilhallon as an 'alternative' wedding venue.

I take a deep breath. 'Our VIP visitors are coming and I want everything to be perfect. You can call me paranoid but I'm desperate to make sure everything goes well.'

Cal strokes my cheek. 'I know you are. I know how much Demelza's means to you and how hard you've fought to make it a success but it's ages until they arrive and I'll be there to meet them with you.'

'Technically, they're your responsibility anyway,' I tease. 'Lily Craig and Ben Trevone are friends of Isla's.'

Cal tuts while dancing his fingers down my chest. 'Don't play the Isla card,' he warns, risking a joke about his ex-girlfriend. Cal used to be an aid worker in Syria and returned to Kilhallon Park last Easter after a series of traumatic events. He was devastated to find Isla was engaged to Luke, although he assures me he's over her now and I think I believe him. Isla is a glamorous TV producer and she persuaded her actor friends, Ben and Lily, to hold their wedding at Kilhallon Park to help boost our profile. They've been so busy filming and doing publicity that they haven't had time to visit Kilhallon yet or set a date but I *really* hope they confirm the wedding day while they're here. It's our first event of the kind and will mean massive kudos for the resort and cafe, *if* it all goes well.

'Like I said, I'll be there to meet them with you. You're worrying way too much and besides, nothing's as important as keeping your boss happy,' Cal says, cheekily.

'You promised never to play the boss card.'

'No more often than strictly necessary.' He lifts a lock of my hair from my face. I catch a glimpse of it in the rust-mottled mirror on the dressing table. I definitely have morning hair.

'Have I ever told you you look incredibly sexy when you've just woken up? Sort of rumpled and wild and up for it . . . ' He lets my hair fall and kisses the hollow at the top of my breastbone.

'Only when you want something . . . ' I murmur, unable to keep still. 'Mitch will want his morning run in a minute . . . ' I say feebly.

Cal trails a warm tongue down my cleavage. 'All the more reason to make hay while the sun shines . . . '

'There's no sun,' I murmur.

Scratching and whining from outside the door tells me that Mitch is awake and restless already. Crows caw loudly from the trees behind the farmhouse, as if to warn me. Cal disappears under the duvet, his voice muffled. 'Mitch will be fine and as for the sun,' he says as I squirm in pure, wicked pleasure, 'I'll make sure things get hot in here.'

5

So I ignore my dog and the fact we need to get ready for this important day in Kilhallon's history and give in to some activities that involve shared body heat. After all, I'm only human, and I told you Cal is dangerous.

1

'Oi! Demi, I think they're coming.'

Polly's shout reaches me as I'm trying to stuff a king-size duvet into its cover in the bedroom of Kilhallon House. Our PA/resort manager has worked for the Penwiths for decades and lives in a cottage behind the main farmhouse. It's now almost ten a.m. and I've been up since seven, trying to fit in a list of jobs as long as my arm — including the half-hour first thing this morning that didn't count as work but did involve getting hot, sweaty and pleasantly tired with Cal.

'Demi! Get in here!'

The latch door bangs against the oak frame, making me jump. Polly has a voice that can shake walls that have stood for three hundred years but I don't think she caused this particular earthquake. Abandoning the duvet — I'd got it the wrong way round anyway, I'm so wound up — I hurry across the landing and into the spare bedroom. The window is wide open and Polly is leaning out, a pair of binoculars clamped to her eyes. She obviously hasn't noticed the wind howling around the house and driving sleet onto the window ledge.

Shivering, I join her at the window. 'What are you doing?'

'Looking out for *them*. Like you should be.'

'Well, *they're* not due for ages and it's freezing in here.'

Lowering the binoculars, Polly turns away from the window, red marks around her eyes. 'You youths. No hardiness. Generation snowflake.'

'Give me the binoculars. *Please*,' I say, grabbing them from Polly and risking being turned into a slush puppy as I lean out of the window for a better look.

'Oh sh — '

'Told you,' she declares behind me.

A large black 4×4 with darkened windows rattles over the cattle grid at the top of the track that leads from the main road down to Kilhallon Park. At least it's not a flashy sports car so it shouldn't get stuck in the giant pothole that opened up during the Christmas floods. Cal still hasn't had time to fill it in yet . . . I'll have to text him to let him know our wedding couple are early.

'It must be them: *Bonnie and Clyde*,' says Polly, using the codenames she coined for Lily and Ben.

My heart sinks. 'Not yet. I'm not ready.' Through the binoculars, I spot the personalised number plate and the driver in the front seat. He has a buzz cut, is built like a rugby player and is definitely not Ben. The passenger seat is empty and I can't make out anything through the blacked-out rear windows but I bet the stars are in there. It's not one of our half-term guests' cars and my cafe, Demelza's, isn't open to the public today. And while I was expecting a frozen shellfish delivery later, I don't think the fishmonger has swapped his van for a personalised BMW 4×4 yet.

I lower the binoculars, trying to tame the butterflies — make that the fat, furry moths — beating their wings inside my stomach. 'I suppose it could be someone on business, or a potential guest wanting to look around, but I don't recognise the car.'

Polly huffs. 'Bet you a tenner it's Bonnie and Clyde.'

'You don't have to call them Bonnie and Clyde when it's just us around. You can use their real names.'

Polly has her hands on her hips. She's not a big woman and her ash-blonde bob makes her look younger than her fifty-six years but there's something solid about her that can be very intimidating if you don't know her. Or even if you *do*. 'They'll always be Bonnie and Clyde to me,' she declares. 'I can't think of them as anyone else — and why they want to hold their wedding here is beyond me. They'll doubtless take one look at the place in this weather and decide to head straight back to London.'

'Thanks for the vote of confidence.'

'I speak as I find.'

'It's not really a wedding. Lily and Ben are calling it a 'hand-fasting' because we don't have a civil wedding licence for Kilhallon. They're going to make things legal at their local register office when all the media fuss has died down.'

'Hmm. Right funny way of going about things if you ask me.' Polly carries on muttering as she wrestles with closing the window against the gale. She works hard and genuinely cares about me and Cal, sometimes *too* much, to the point of interfering. She also has no problem with voicing her opinions, whether we like it or not.

The howls of the wind die down and Polly throws me a grim but encouraging smile, as if I'm off to get my head chopped off. 'You'd better go and meet them, but I shouldn't bring them into reception. That stray cat that keeps hanging around decided to use the floor as a litter tray earlier and I haven't had chance to clean up yet, what with looking out for these actors.'

I wrinkle my nose. 'Any idea where Cal's got to?'

Polly drills me with one of her 'looks'. 'I don't know. I haven't seen him since last night. You should know his whereabouts more than I do, anyway . . .'

I should say now that Polly doesn't entirely approve of Cal and me living together. Not, I think, because he's my boss and the owner of Kilhallon. Not for any moral reasons either — Polly's no churchgoer — but she seems to have some nutty idea that 'it' — i.e. *us* — will end in tears one day. She's also taken it upon herself to act as Cal's mum since his own mother passed away years ago. And, in a roundabout way, she's become a bit of a surrogate mother figure to me as well, though I never asked her to. My mum passed away and I was cut adrift from the rest of my family for a while. I know she's only being kind and she does have a heart of gold but . . .

Maybe it will end in tears, and maybe it won't. Cal and I don't discuss the long term. We've both had things happen in our lives that have

10

taught us to be wary of planning too far ahead and making promises we can't keep.

And for now, everything's going fine.

Or will be, if I can track him down.

'I haven't seen him since he went off to the waste site after breakfast. He promised he'd be back at Kilhallon to meet Bonnie and Clyde — gah, I mean Lily and Ben, you've got me at it now.'

Polly smirks in satisfaction at my slip-up.

'Do you mind making sure Mitch stays in the farmhouse while I meet Lily and Ben?' I say, feeling annoyed with myself and with Cal. 'He's had his walk and breakfast so he should be happy to stay in the warm until they've gone.'

Not everyone likes dogs and I don't want Mitch greeting our guests too 'enthusiastically' or going AWOL like he did in a fog last autumn. That was terrifying and both Mitch and I ended up falling down one of the old mine working holes on the cliffs. Luckily, we both escaped with nothing more than sore legs, although it could have been much worse.

'I suppose I could keep an eye on the hound alongside my other jobs,' Polly grumbles.

'Thanks!'

Leaving Polly muttering about 'pampered pooches and celebrities', I skip downstairs and grab an old waxed jacket from the vestibule. I whizz out to the car park via the reception area at the front of Kilhallon House, ready to greet the VIPs. The wind whistles around the farmhouse and cuts through me. Tiny pools of slush lie in hollows in the gravel and hailstones pile up against the former farm buildings that we now use for storage. I wouldn't be surprised if Polly's chickens are wearing thermal undies. Lily and Ben could hardly have picked a worse time to visit. I only hope they have good imaginations.

While I wait for them to roll into the car park, I have a quick glance around the yard outside our reception. Cal must be around somewhere because his battered old Land Rover is parked in its usual place in front of the barn that serves as our storage and maintenance shed. Then again, I suspect he might be trying to avoid this meeting. Celebrities and their lives hold about as much interest for him as a tractor engine does for me. I mean, can you believe he hadn't even *heard* of Lily Craig and Ben Trevone?

Then again, Cal hasn't seen a lot of TV or films over the past few years. He was involved in his own real-life drama in Syria, one that had a tragic ending for his friend Soraya and her daughter, Esme. At Christmas, Cal finally opened up to me about the terrible events that led to Soraya's death and the disappearance of Esme in the conflict. I was shocked but I think sharing the burden has brought us closer.

In fact, everyone at Kilhallon and in the local area had to pull together over the Christmas and New Year period after a tidal surge destroyed many homes in the nearby village of St Trenyan. We provided temporary accommodation for some of the homeless families, including my dad, his partner, Rachel, and their brand-new baby, Freya. They're living in a rented flat in St Trenyan at the moment while their own home is repaired after the floods.

That disaster was such an awful business but the silver lining was that it put me back in contact with my estranged father. Freya has given us all the chance to meet up since then and rebuild some bridges. She's just adorable and it's strange — in a good way — to see my dad so besotted with her. I keep wondering if he was like that with me once, before everything went downhill for us all. I've also made contact again with my older brother, Kyle. He's in the army and I hadn't seen him for ages, but we've now exchanged emails so the ice is broken.

We've moved on in other ways over the winter. Cal has completed the renovation of our final set of cottages so now we have eight in total, plus eight yurts which we'll pitch again in our glamping field ready for Easter. Our main camping field has another thirty pitches and will also open again at Easter. It's strange to see the cottage I used to live in redecorated in a simple but contemporary style. The flowery 1970s decor has been painted over with neutral tones and the creaking furniture replaced with inky blue sofas and functional wood. Cal's done a great job on a budget but I can't help feeling he's removed a little too much of the quirky personality of what was my first real home for years. Moving out of it and into the farmhouse with Cal was a big step for me as it meant losing some of my hard-won independence.

The BMW rolls into the car park and there's still no sign of Cal and no answers to my frantic texts. Luckily, I know that Nina, one of my staff, has arrived early at the cafe to help with the refreshments so Cal and I can focus on looking after Ben and Lily. I've texted her to warn her they're early so at least we'll have a cosy welcome ready for them in Demelza's.

There's still not a whiff of Cal so it looks like I'm on my own — again. *Breathe.*

The gleaming BMW comes to a halt next to Cal's dilapidated Defender. Fixing on my cheeriest, sunniest smile, I march over as a man mountain with a shaved head eases out of the driver's seat.

He opens the rear passenger door wide and stands back.

Two long, slim legs encased in black skinny jeans emerge from the door and a guy a few years older than me drops neatly down to the gravel. He wears a black leather jacket over a black sweater, with Stan Smiths on his feet that are almost as white as his teeth. He glances around him. I can't see his eyes because of his Aviators but I can see myself reflected in them: my hair's a wild tangle, my face as pale as the moon framed by the furry trim of my hood.

Pushing the hood off my hair, I come face to face with Ben Trevone, the ludicrously handsome action-hero lead of *Knife Edge*, heart-throb star of *Desperate Poets* and voice of a heroic sea otter in the Oscar-nominated animation *Ocean Furries*. Unlike Cal, I do go to the cinema with my mates, although I admit I borrowed *Ocean Furries* from one of the kids who was evacuated here after the Christmas floods so I could swot up on Ben Trevone's latest film.

With a smile that makes my jaw ache, I hold out my hand. 'Welcome to Kilhallon!'

Ignoring my hand, Ben looks around him. His dazzling teeth gleam against a tan he definitely didn't get on a Cornish beach. He *is* very handsome in a smooth, 'boy band' way, though not as hunky as he looked in *Knife Edge*. On the other hand, I'm glad he isn't armed to the teeth with an AK-47 and a selection of knives.

'So this is, like, *it*?' he asks in an accent that's a mix of his native Cornish and an American twang — which you don't hear every day, especially not in St Trenyan.

Panicking inside, I shove my hands in my pockets. 'Well, er . . . like, yes.'

He switches his focus from me to the farmhouse and the barn and Cal's Land Rover. We've done a *lot* of work on Kilhallon but suddenly every slightly wonky plank, moss-covered roof and rusty bumper pops out at me.

'Uh huh,' he says.

'Are we there yet, Ben?' a thin, small voice pipes up from the far rear passenger seat. Oh, so maybe Lily Craig isn't with him after all and he's decided to bring his little sister.

'Seems like it,' he says, without turning around as their minder toes a puddle with his biker boot.

'Can I come out now, then?' the little voice trills from the depths of the car.

'If you want, babe, but it's enough to freeze your bollocks off,' Ben calls back, craning his neck to look beyond me towards the sea.

'It is very cold today. There's been a storm, you see, but in summer, it's gorgeous up here

15

and I'm sure the weather will be fantastic for your wedding.'

'Handfasting.' Ben spits out the word in his *Knife Edge* voice. Given that he played a robotic ex-soldier primed to wreak revenge on his enemies, I find this slightly disturbing.

'Handfasting. Of course. As it's a bit . . . um . . . chilly, why don't we go straight to Demelza's, our onsite catering centre?' I babble, making it up as I go along. 'My team will have hot chocolate and cakes waiting.'

'Tell her I don't do dairy,' the voice pipes up.

Oh God, it *must* be Lily.

'Lily doesn't do dairy,' says Ben solemnly.

'I know and I've planned for that. There are plenty of dairy-free alternatives at the cafe and we can also discuss the menus and decorations for your celebration. We'll be much cosier there. You don't even have to get out of the car, I can show you the way,' I call above a fresh gust of wind so that the little voice can hear me.

Ben glances over my head towards the track that leads down to Demelza's, then at his minder.

'That OK, Harry?'

Harry, the minder, nods slowly. His head is shaven like Jake Gyllenhaal's in *Jarhead* but he's at least a head taller and three stone heavier than Jake must be. The material of his long-sleeved grey T-shirt strains over his huge biceps as if he has a grapefruit stuffed down there. He makes Ben look like a Munchkin.

'OK, guys, let's do this,' says Ben as if he's about to confront the forces of darkness rather

16

than a hot chocolate and one of my scones.

Ben climbs back inside the BMW and Harry shuts the door, leaving me shivering on the gravel. Harry then opens the passenger side door. He says nothing but nods at me through his own black shades, which must surely be illegal for driving in our dark Cornish winters. Mind you, for all I know he could be wearing eyeliner and false lashes under them, which would be very, very funny.

Squashing down a giggle, which is definitely from nerves not excitement, I take the hint and climb inside the BMW. I sink into the leather seats and Harry points a single finger at the track that leads from the side of the car park down to the cafe. Why doesn't he speak? Maybe he can't speak? Feeling slightly guilty in case he really is a mute, I nod vigorously and point in the same direction.

And we're off, bumping gently down the short track to the cafe. No one says a word but I'm thinking plenty of them. One, Cal had better turn up pretty soon or I will kill him, and two, when he does turn up I will kill him anyway for getting us into this totally weird wedding situation.

Crossing my fingers, toes and any other bits, I tell myself that the only way is up from this beginning. Demelza's has been closed for a few days as it's our quietest time of year. Thank goodness I laid out the wedding presentation last night and didn't leave it until today. Beyond that, I'm praying that Nina and Shamia have had time to get the food on as I promised our guests.

Lights glow in the windows of the cafe, which was converted from an old storage barn last summer. Its stone walls look strong and welcoming against the backdrop of crashing waves and the wild Atlantic swell. Harry stops the car and jumps out. He holds a huge umbrella over Ben and Lily as they make the dash from the car to the cafe in the driving sleet. I hope Demelza's can work its magic on our frosty couple, as it has on so many people, but I have a feeling these two will be *much* tougher nuts to crack.

2

'Please, make yourselves comfortable. We'll have the coffee and refreshments ready in no time. Sorry, we didn't expect you quite so soon, but it's fine. We're delighted you could make it because Isla told us how busy you are.' Yes, I know I'm babbling as we walk into the cafe and wildly over compensating but it's not been the best start to the meeting — *and where the hell is Cal?*

'We're usually really late, aren't we, babe?' says Ben, allowing Lily to skip ahead of him into the cafe. She's not much over five feet tall and her massive silver Puffa coat brushes her toes. Add a pair of dainty pointy boots and she reminds me of a very glamorous pixie. Her fur-trimmed hood hides her features but she's definitely smiling.

She giggles. 'Always. We're notorious for our lateness but we thought we'd surprise everyone today.'

Lucky me, I think, but I can't help liking Lily's sense of humour, which gives me hope she's possibly as human as the rest of us.

Yes, I know Demelza's is my cafe but even after six months, I always think walking inside is like stepping into a cosy, delicious haven. We've pulled out the stops to make it welcoming this cold spring morning, arranging early narcissi in stone jars on the window ledges to add a pop of yellow sunshine. Confetti-coloured freesias have

19

been placed on every table and we've laid the two tables closest to the window with the vintage china I found at Kilhallon House last summer. Lily and Ben should be able to enjoy the view over the sea from there. The coffee machine is already burbling and the room is filled with the smell of freshly baked pastries. In the background, Cornish folk songs are playing softly. Mentally, I cross my fingers and hope they like the fresh and welcoming atmosphere we've tried to create.

Ben plonks himself down at a table and picks up a teacup as if he's never seen one before. Lily lingers in the middle of the room. She pulls off her hood and a mane of glossy red hair falls down her back. Although she wears very little make-up, and is swamped by the shiny coat, she's still stunning. Not like a real human, but a fairy in a children's storybook. She turns around slowly, and lifts her arms, as if the cafe might revolve around her if she so wills.

I hold my breath. She could quite easily turn round this second and head out of Kilhallon and that would be that. Because we're not glamorous, though we'll bust a gut to be our very best. At the end of the day, we're only a cosy little place in a wild and beautiful corner of Cornwall.

Lily sighs deeply as if she's just finished a particularly hard yoga session. My heart thumps madly. I avoid a strong urge to wipe my palms on my jeans, waiting for this big star's verdict on my little Cornish cafe.

Lily stares straight at me, a sad but sweet smile on her face.

'This place is very . . . *soothing*. Like being wrapped in a big squishy duvet. It's very authentic. Yes, I like it. I like it a lot.'

It's hard not to let out a huge sigh of relief, even if part of me already wishes that Lily, Ben and Harry would get straight back into their 'actor mobile' and drive out of Kilhallon. Yes, it's exciting to have them here and it would be amazing publicity for the park and cafe but I already can't stand the tension of trying to live up to their expectations. *Calm down*, Cal would say, *just be yourself*.

But he's not here, is he?

Lily perches on one of our old oak settles next to Ben. She picks up one of the vintage tapestry cushions I 'recycled' from the farmhouse and hugs it. Ben is on his phone. Harry is sitting at a nearby table with his arms folded. He makes the chair look an infant's school chair.

'What can we get you all, then, before we discuss menus and food? I thought we'd warm up in here before we take a tour of the rest of the park and the wedding . . . '

'Handfasting,' Ben mutters without glancing up from his phone. 'We're going to do the legal bit at the register office near our house a few weeks later. No one will be looking for that once we've had the ceremony here.'

'Isla said you want a simple ceremony in a natural setting?' I say.

'Oh yes, we don't want a fuss, do we, Ben? I can't stand all those weddings with zillions of people where the bride and groom sit on thrones and everyone arrives by helicopter.'

21

'Is there a helipad?' Ben chimes in.

'Sorry, no. There's a field behind us that the emergency services could use at a push but no helipad.'

'Oh.' He goes back to his phone.

Lily smooths down her skirt. 'Isla said we'd never find a more beautiful setting, especially if the sun comes out.'

'I hope so. We'll have a marquee, though, so we'll be fine.' Fingers crossed again, I think, remembering how Isla's own engagement party was almost washed out by a summer storm. I won't forget that day for all kinds of reasons; I had to rescue Cal from the sea after he'd been drowning his sorrows as he watched Isla and his best friend, Luke, celebrate their happiness. It was barely eight months ago and so much has changed. I truly believe Cal is over Isla now, though he said he could never 'unlove' her.

Nina hovers behind the counter, staring at the guests as if she's in the middle of a dream.

'So, what drinks can I get you?' I say with a smile, dying to call Cal again but not wanting to let our guests know I'm ever so slightly panicking.

Lily orders a camomile tea, while Ben opts for a double espresso.

'How about you, Harry?' I ask. He has to speak now, he *has* to.

He grunts.

'He'll have an Earl Grey with lemon. No milk,' says Ben, still tapping on his phone.

'Oh . . . Okayy,' I say, surprised Harry doesn't drink liquefied girders. 'Nina? Would you mind making up the order, please?'

Nina seems frozen to the spot for a second then scuttles off behind the counter. She turns up the music a little and that, combined with the hiss and sputter of the coffee machine, makes the atmosphere seem far more like a 'normal' cafe day.

I chat to Lily about her journey here while Ben studies his phone and Harry flicks through a copy of a Cornish lifestyle magazine. Harry was sent on ahead by road ready to pick them up from Newquay airport this morning, though they didn't use Flybe. They chartered a private plane from an airfield in the Cotswolds where they're renting what Lily describes as a 'cute little cottage' but which sounds more like a mini stately home. She seems interested in the doggy treats cookbook I've been writing over the winter — not that I've had that much to do with it as my co-author, Eva Spero, and her team have taken over a lot of the writing. She's been to Eva's restaurant in Brighton once and seems impressed that I have a celebrity connection.

I'm not sure how much of Lily's breezy girly chat is really her, and how much is just her image. She has an Instagram account with hundreds of thousands of followers. Her fingers hover over a crystal-embellished iPhone. I bet she's dying to update her Instagram right now so I break off to help Nina serve the drinks and coffee-time treats.

As soon as I return to the table with a laden cake stand, Lily puts her phone down. 'There's a selection of mini pastries and tasters of our cakes. Of course, you'll have a tailor-made menu on the day and we can work with a local catering firm who have won tons of awards for their wedding food. But for today I thought you might enjoy some of the best of our home-cooked fare.'

Harry selects a slice of curranty pastry dredged in sugar. He observes it and his nose twitches as if he's inhaling the scent. Please don't say he's going to taste our guests' food for them . . . He wouldn't go that far, would he? He bites off a piece, chews, swallows and lets out a sigh of pleasure.

'Do you mind telling me what this is? It's really rather good,' he says, with an extremely posh lilt.

So amazed am I that he has a voice at all, let alone *that* particular voice, that I struggle to get my reply out. 'Um . . . it's figgy 'obbin.'

'Foggy *what*?'

'Figgy 'obbin — layers of feather-light puff pastry crammed with juicy raisins, lemon juice and sugar. That's the traditional recipe but I also added a few dried cranberries for extra crunch and to brighten it up. It's a real Cornish winter warmer.'

'It certainly is. It's delicious. Reminds me of Nanny's strudel.'

'Your gran was a keen baker?' I ask, still amazed at his accent. That voice could have come straight out of the drawing room of Polly's favourite series, *Downton Abbey*.

He laughs. 'Oh gosh, Granny never baked. I don't think she knew what an oven was and she rarely ventured into the kitchens. She had a cook and housekeeper for that sort of thing. No, our nanny used to bake us treats in the school holidays or when we had an exeat. She was from Salzburg and was an incredible pastry cook. Her strudel was my favourite but this is a delicious twist.'

Harry takes off his shades. He doesn't need false lashes or eyeliner. His eyes are striking enough: sea green with natural lashes to die for. Wow. My mind works overtime, trying to work out why a man who once had a nanny is working as minder to a celebrity couple.

'May I have another slice, please?'

I like him already. 'Of course,' I say, and hand him another plate.

While Harry tucks in to the figgy 'obbin, Lily nibbles a morsel of a mini cinnamon scone. I hold my breath, waiting for the verdict. She puts the rest on her plate and pushes it away from her as if it might bite her back. Oh dear, this isn't going well, but after dabbing her mouth with a serviette, she smiles.

'Yum. That was delicious, but I daren't have any more. I'm getting so fat, aren't I, Ben?'

'I dunno. You look all right to me.' Ben crunches a fairing without glancing up from his screen.

'Do you want the rest of this yummy scone, Harry?'

Holding the handle of the cup with his little finger crooked, Harry sips his tea. 'Thanks.'

Lily brings the plate over and puts it in front of him. 'Now you can get fat like me, can't you?'

Harry puts his shades back on. 'You're not fat,' he mutters and studies a Demelza's menu

25

while devouring the scone in one bite.

Ben is still swiping his phone. I hope he's on Instagram not Tinder.

Nina finds the courage to emerge from the counter for a chat with Lily who suggests she has a selfie with her and Ben. This gives me a welcome chance to escape outside to try and get Cal on my phone. Mobile coverage is patchy at Kilhallon, so I'm not surprised when his answer phone kicks in. Not surprised but pissed off.

'My partner, Cal, seems to be tied up with an urgent matter at the moment but he'll be along as soon as possible. I know he's dying to show you the wonderful space that Kilhallon has for your ceremony. I think it's drying up outside so while we wait for Cal and the sun to arrive, would you like to run through some menu ideas? We can have all the taster samples ready for you on your next visit and it will be spring then.'

'That sounds lovely, doesn't it, Ben?'

Finally, Ben puts down his phone and bends down to kiss Lily's head. 'Anything you want, babe. Harry, can you fetch Lily's scarf from the car? If we're going outside, I don't want her shivering, do I, babe?'

'I'll be OK, really, Ben.'

'Harry doesn't mind. That's what he's here for,' Ben says.

Without a word, Harry leaves the cafe with the remains of a figgy 'obbin in his huge hand.

'Harry's ex-military. Paras. His family once owned a huge dump in the Cotswolds but they fell on hard times,' Ben tells me, sitting next to Lily again.

Lily tuts. 'It isn't a dump. It's a beautiful old place.'

'Yeah, but he doesn't own it now, does he? They had to sell it when his granddad blew his brains out after he'd gone bankrupt. It's a boutique hotel,' Ben says to me. 'Quirky great pile, not my thing. Can I have some more coffee?' He holds up his mug.

'Of course.' I spring up, eager to help in any way I can. Still, I can't help feeling sorry for Harry, losing his family home and having to wait on Ben and Lily. I wonder how he stands being ordered around by Ben, to be honest.

'Cal should be here any time. Shall we talk about the type of food you'd like for your ceremony and reception?'

While we chat through the menus, Harry returns and stations himself in a corner, leafing through a guidebook on Cornish dog walks. Lily and Ben have been here half an hour and I'm urging Cal to put in an appearance. He may claim to be no PR man, but he can turn on the charm when he wants to and it often seems to have an effect on people. I'm hoping he'll work his magic on Lily, if not on Ben.

There's still no sign of Cal but the sun has moved around and is now shining full-on through the windows of the cafe. It may still be February but it's one of those days when you first feel some real, if faint, warmth in the sun's rays. The clouds have cleared away to bother people further east, leaving us with a beautiful sky the colour of forget-me-nots. Cal or no Cal, I sense this is the moment to show off Kilhallon

27

while I can. I hope that even sophisticated Lily will be charmed by the setting. I don't know about Ben but I suspect he'll go along with anything she wants, which would definitely make things easier for me.

'Would you like to see the view from the cafe now the rain has stopped and the wind has died down a little bit?'

Lily claps her hands in delight. 'Oh, I'd love to.'

Having returned with the wrap, Harry offers it to Lily and she fastens it around her neck, under her coat. I zip up my own jacket and we say goodbye and thanks to Nina, telling her we'll be back later for lunch. Harry and Ben decide to brave the great outdoors without extra layers. I'm not sure even a Cornish gale could blow Harry over anyway.

We step out onto the terrace of the cafe, bracing ourselves against the Atlantic wind. The heavy tables and chairs have survived the winter and are beginning to look weathered, but that's not a bad thing. We walk through the gap in the low stone wall around the terrace and stand outside on a strip of grass between Kilhallon land and the coastal path. Large pale-grey clouds tear across the sky. Lily's hair whips across her face and she pulls the strands out of her eyes. I can taste the salt on my lips.

'Wow.'

Lily takes a deep breath, just like she did when she stepped into Demelza's.

'It's an amazing view. I love the view from Ben's parents' house over Mounts Bay but the north west is so wild.'

'It's hard to decide which is better,' I say, aware of Ben standing next to us, not that he seems too bothered as he's still scrolling through his phone.

'Is there a signal up here?' he says, holding the handset up.

'It's patchy,' I admit. 'But there's Wi-Fi in the cafe and cottages. We plan to offer Wi-Fi all over the glamping field and events area before your wedding.'

He doesn't answer me but hmmphs and shoves his phone in his jacket. He joins Lily who has walked the few yards from our land to the coastal path. It's still windy but I think she'll be OK.

'This looks like a scene from *The French Lieutenant's Woman*, doesn't it, Ben?'

'Yeah,' he says, standing behind her with his arms around her waist.

'I haven't heard of that,' I say.

'It's a book and it was a film before I was born. Isla wants to do a remake but it's set in Lyme Regis not Cornwall. There's a scene where the heroine stands in a howling gale almost being blown off the Cobb. I'm hoping Ben will play the hero in it.'

Wow. I think Ben may have actually smiled. Maybe his grouchiness is from pre-wedding nerves or the pressure of his job. I wouldn't want to live my life under the microscope like they do, even though they're meant to live for the publicity. I bet they have to do a lot of things they don't want to as well.

The publisher of our canine cookbook wants my co-author, Eva Spero, and me to do some radio and TV appearances when it comes out later this year. To be honest, the idea makes me go weak at the knees but I guess I'll get used to it. Cal and I still haven't quite got over being featured in a Sunday lifestyle magazine last autumn, thanks to Eva who was impressed by our set-up when she turned up to Kilhallon's launch party last year.

'Shall we move on to the wedding glade? It's more sheltered down there,' I ask, seeing Ben shivering in the wind blowing off the sea.

Lily slots her arm through his. 'Are you cold?'

'Freezing my rocks off,' Ben mutters.

'Let's get out of the wind,' I say, wishing Ben had come equipped for the weather.

On our way to the glade, Harry walks to the left and a little behind, checking around him at intervals. Maybe he thinks an assassin might be hiding behind the cafe bins or the high-banked hedges that protect the camping field from the worst of the Atlantic wind.

Clumps of snowdrops nod their delicate heads in the breeze and early primroses dot the banks that line the lane to the cottages and the edge of the copse. I love the first signs of spring. When I spent a stint sleeping rough, all I cared about was a warm place to stay, but now I'm lucky enough to appreciate the seasons changing from a warm bed and home.

A boy waving a plastic cutlass shoots out of the copse next to us onto the path.

'Wooo hoooo! Watch out! I'm a pirate!'

'Jesus! What the — ' Ben steadies Lily as the boy clips her arm.

'Sorry!' the boy shouts but races off down the slope towards the yurt field, waving his sword cutlass. He's wearing a pirate hat and an eye patch but I'm sure I know him.

'Are you OK, baby?' Ben asks Lily.

Lily smiles. 'I'm fine. I'm fine.'

'Quick! Blackbeard's after us!' A little girl in pirate gear shoots out of the copse and clips Ben. He tries to stay upright but slips on the damp turf and lands smack on his bum in a puddle.

The girl shouts 'Sorry!' but she's already on her way, racing down the slope after her pirate friend.

'Fuck,' Ben growls, scrambling out of the puddle. 'You little sods!' he calls after them, trying to scramble to his feet.

'Are you OK, Ben?' Lily reaches down to help him up.

He shakes it off. 'My jeans are ruined. Little brats could have done me some serious damage.'

I wince. 'I'm sorry. I'm sure it was an accident.'

'Whose kids are they?' he snaps.

'They're from St Trenyan.' I'm in despair wondering why they are here and to be honest more pissed off at the way Ben's spoken about the children. I recognise them, of course: they're members of the families who were evacuated here after the flooding. They moved out of Kilhallon last month and into temporary accommodation so I've no idea why they're chasing around the site dressed as pirates today.

31

'They didn't do it on purpose, sweetheart,' Lily says, taking Ben's elbow as he gets to his feet. I swallow hard. His designer jeans are soaked with mud and his Stan Smiths are ruined. Where the hell is Cal?

My answer comes a split second later as Blackbeard himself, complete with tricorn and eye patch, jogs out of the copse shouting: 'Come here, you scurvy knaves. I'll make you walk the plank!'

3

'Sorry, mate!'

Cal screeches to a halt inches from Ben. Lily lets out a giggle but Ben glares at him with open contempt.

'Are those your kids? You should control the little sods,' he snaps.

Cal's smile vanishes and he pushes his eye patch over his forehead. 'They're not little sods. They're playing at pirates.'

Ben snorts. 'Pirates? They could have broken my neck. And look at my jeans. These were made specially for me by the designer. They're unique.'

'Well, they definitely are now, mate.' Cal frowns at the mud-spattered denim while I die a little inside. 'And they're not my children but I'll pass on your parenting advice to their mums and dads. I'm sure they'll *appreciate* it.'

'Cal!' I cut in, cringing at the naked menace in his voice while wanting to sink through the ground. 'This is Ben Trevone and Lily Craig. Our VIP guests.'

Cal glances from Ben to Lily then sucks in a breath before thrusting out his muddy hand. 'Oh, right. Well, good to meet you both. Sorry the kids were a bit over enthusiastic with their pirate raiding.'

Ignoring Cal's hand, Ben snorts. 'Over enthusiastic? They've ruined my jeans, not that I care, of course, or about being dumped on my arse in the mud, but Lily was almost knocked flying.'

'No, I wasn't. I'm fine and so are you. Ben's jeans will recover. I never liked them anyway,' Lily trills. 'You must be Cal. Why are you dressed as a pirate?' Lily asks him, clearly intrigued.

'I promised the children they could come to Kilhallon to play pirates. I just didn't realise they'd turn up today.'

Ben is speechless, which is a relief, but Cal gives Lily one of his bone-melting smiles. 'Apologies for my lateness. The children turned up for a half-term visit and I totally lost track of the time. They're a bit wild, but they've had a shitty time recently — their families were flooded out of their homes over Christmas by a tidal surge.'

Lily wrinkles her nose. 'Oh my God. How horrible for them. We did hear about it. Ben went to school in Penzance, you know.'

'Yes, I do,' I say. 'So I'm sure he can understand how terrible the storm was for the area.'

'We saw it on the news, didn't we, Ben? My cousins had to leave their house and Ben paid for them to go to a hotel for a few weeks. He's very thoughtful like that, aren't you, Ben?'

Ben manages a smile and puts his arm around Lily's shoulders. 'Anything to make you happy.'

'I bet Polly would wash your jeans, mate, and you can borrow an old pair of mine in the meantime,' Cal says.

Ben curls his lip. 'Thanks, but don't bother.'

'We've got a change of clothes in the car,' Lily

says. 'We're visiting Ben's mum in Penzance after we've left here. That's one of the reasons we wanted the ceremony at Kilhallon, because Ben's family live locally and mine are scattered over the South West so it's not so very far for them to come.'

She kisses Ben and he grunts.

'Would you like to come up to the house to change your clothes?' I ask him.

'No. I'd rather keep them on until we've finished yomping around this field . . . in case anyone else wants to knock me over,' he says.

'Probably a wise decision,' says Cal. 'Do you want me to fetch you some wellies?' he directs this to both of them.

'I'll be fine,' Lily says with a smile that would melt the hardest heart and I think has even melted Cal's. Her black leather pixie boots should be OK despite the wet conditions.

'I'll stay as I am,' says Ben, who I think would rather jump off a cliff than be seen in wellies.

Lily slips her arm through his and kisses him. 'I rather like you all muddy and wet.'

Finally, Ben smiles.

'Your eye patch has slipped,' I whisper to Cal while Ben helps Lily down the slope towards the 'events space'.

Cal lifts off the tricorn and pulls the eye patch over his head before pecking me on the cheek. 'Sorry I'm late. I bet you've been climbing the walls having to look after those two on your own.'

'I didn't even notice you weren't around.'

Cal sucks in a breath. 'That bad, eh? I didn't

know the kids would be here today but their parents turned up with them. They came to say thanks and I didn't want to turn them away. Then I kind of got involved in a pirate raid and lost all track of time.'

'A pirate raid? Great. At least you have your priorities right.'

He grins. 'You're not *too* pissed off, are you?'

While I shake my head at him, I can't help but smile. Cal likes kids, probably because he's still about twelve inside. He also spent a lot of time helping them during his time in Syria as an aid worker. He grew especially close to Esme and her mother, Soraya. Soraya's death in an attack on the city caused Cal a lot of pain, and I know he feels partly responsible. Although he told me about it over Christmas, we've not spoken about it since, but I know he thinks about Esme constantly and wonders whether she survived.

We rejoin Lily and Ben and pause halfway down the gentle slope that leads to a circular patch of grass at the bottom of a hollow. To the left is the far edge of the little copse where the yurts are pitched during our camping season. Below us the young pirates are now sitting on one of the log seats we've placed in our 'wedding glade'. The area is available for use by the yurt guests and campers when it's not booked for a wedding or party.

'This is the space where you'll be holding your . . . um . . . handfasting ceremony.' Cal puts his hand to his ear. 'Shh. Listen.'

The wind has dropped enough for us to hear the faint roar of the sea breaking on the rocks below the cliffs. Gulls wheel above us, gliding on the breeze, crying against the spring sky.

'Imagine it on a glorious summer's day — that hollow down there is where we would hold the ceremony,' I say, relieved that Kilhallon is finally hinting at how beautiful it can be. 'We're thinking of having a luxury events tepee for the reception in case the weather turns slightly cooler,' I say, recalling the storm we had last June. 'You can have drinks outside in the sun, and in the evening we can light braziers or campfires and decorate the tepee and wedding area however you like . . . Chinese lanterns, a fairy grotto, Moroccan themed . . . '

'Sounds amazing,' says Lily with a sigh.

'Let's take a closer look,' says Cal, subtly leading her down to the centre of the hollow. Even I'm impressed by what we can do at Kilhallon and I know the yurts looked amazing on our launch day last September. Now the sun's out and Cal's here, I feel more confident that we could put on a show that might even please Ben. Fingers crossed that soon we'll have found a wedding planner to help us so I can concentrate on the catering. The kids run into the woods, whooping, as we approach, which is probably a good thing for all of us.

Ben and I join Cal and Lily in the hollow. Cal sits on a log seat with Lily and they start to chat about a production she worked on with Isla.

'Have you got any ideas for themes yet?' I ask Ben, who keeps glancing at his phone.

'I dunno. I leave that sort of thing up to Lily.'
He pulls a face as he sidesteps a puddle.

'That's OK. We can talk more about it when we go back to the cafe. I think we should put some plans in place because the wedding date is the last Saturday in May — that isn't very far away.' I'm already crossing my fingers that they don't want anything unusual that has to be booked years in advance.

'Harry will need to talk about security,' Ben says airily.

'Oh, right. Of course,' I say, realising I hadn't thought about that side of things. Luckily we've blocked off the entire weekend for Lily and Ben's use, and they're paying us very well so we don't mind. I'll have to shut the cafe that weekend too and possibly for a couple of days beforehand.

After we've shown them the event space, we take a little walk to the boundary of the holiday park and stop to take in the view. The camping field is empty, of course, and looks stark after a winter. The hedgerows are still bare twigs although a few green buds are popping out among the brown. Beyond the stone walls, the sea glitters in the sunlight. The waves look like lacy frills from up here but I can tell there's a huge swell. I wouldn't like to be out on the water today, that's for sure.

'We can also offer the services of a freelance wedding planner, though I expect you'll have your own?' I say to Lily as we reach the hollow where the yurts are pitched.

'No, happy to leave ourselves in your capable hands.' She beams. 'I'm sure you've got a truly fabulous planner already lined up.'

An actual chill runs down my spine. We're going to have to get a wedding organiser fast. 'Do you have an idea of your theme yet?' I ask, hoping she won't ask the truly fabulous planner's name.

'Well . . . ' She glances at Ben briefly. 'This is the kind of story we want to create around our celebrations. A wild and windswept country ceremony, though not too windswept, I hope,' she says as a gust of wind whips her long red hair around her face. 'But a natural and totally relaxed affair, as if we just rocked up here with a bunch of mates and decided to hold the ceremony on the spur of the moment with everyone mucking in and throwing it all together.'

As my stomach churns like a cake mixer, I fix a smile on my face. 'Thrown together? Oh, I definitely think we can achieve that.'

'Lovely. You see, we'd like the whole day to look as if I'd simply picked a bunch of gorgeous wildflowers and tied them up with a ribbon and made a circlet for my hair. And that the girls had all picked flowers for the decorations and the boys had made a beautiful wedding arch with branches they'd found lying around in the woods. And that everyone had brought some food along: you know, clean eating, healthy stuff plus lots of yummy wicked treats like you see in old-fashioned tearooms. And we can have cider too along with the Krug of course . . . ' Lily sighs. 'So something super natural, not compli-cated and very un-starry.'

'Not complicated . . . No problem,' I say in a

strangled voice. 'Um. On a country theme, you could have straw bale seating and a fire pit in the evening, with an evening supper served out of wicker picnic baskets in the open if it's fine. Which of course, it will be,' I say, channelling any ideas I've seen on Pinterest and wedding sites. 'The grove here would look amazing with lanterns in the shape of woodland animals: hedgehogs, rabbits and badgers. I saw some online.'

Lily squeaks in delight. 'Hedgehog lanterns? How cute. I love that idea.'

'Why not go the whole hog, or hedgehog, and have real animals?' Cal says. 'You could even have an owl deliver the ring.'

We all stare at him for this totally random statement.

'An *owl*? You mean an actual feathered owl delivering the wedding rings?' Ben repeats.

'That's a very original idea . . . ' I manage.

'It's barking mad,' says Ben.

'Oh. But no . . . ' Lily trills. 'No, it's *not* because I've actually seen something like that before in a magazine. Oh, yes. That would be amazing. Imagine a real owl flying down the grove here and landing on Ben's arm.'

'No way. I'm not having a bird land on me, with its talons and beaky thing.' Ben shudders.

'Oh, Ben, you'd love it if you tried it. Please let us have an owl, for me?' Lily grabs Ben's arm. 'Please. It would be *so* perfect.'

I catch Cal's eye and glare at him and he mouths back 'sorry' and shrugs.

Lily kisses Ben and he forces a fleeting smile.

'I'll see. Like I say, anything for you, babe.'

'Come back 'ere, you horror!'

The owl is forgotten as we're all distracted by the sight of Polly hurrying down the slope towards us, shouting. Mitch lopes ahead of her and, oh my God, he's making a beeline for Ben and Lily.

'Mitch! Heel!'

I dash forward, hoping to intercept him before he leaps up and slobbers over Ben's designer clothes. Drool is not a good look on anyone. Fortunately, Mitch changes course at the last minute and screeches to a halt at my feet, tongue lolling.

'Good boy. Good boy,' I tell him, giving him a cuddle while keeping a firm hold on his collar.

'What a lovely boy he is,' Lily walks towards Mitch. 'He is friendly?'

'Yes, he's the biggest softy you can imagine.'

'I have a dog called Louie. He's the sweetest little French bulldog. He's such an angel but I can't always bring him away with me so my mum takes care of him for me.' Lily crouches down and fusses Mitch who is immediately smitten. He rolls over and invites a belly rub, a sure sign he likes someone.

Polly isn't so delighted, judging by the grim line of her mouth. She huffs towards us, waving a lead in the air. 'He ran off. I tried to keep him in but the moment I opened that door, he shot out like a bullet from a gun. You terror!' she calls to Mitch, who is snickering in pleasure as Lily tickles his tum.

'I adore Louie,' Lily says to Cal. 'Ben's not a

41

doggy person but he makes an exception for Louie, don't you, Ben?'

'Anything to make you happy, baby.'

Harry bends down to ruffle Mitch's ears and Mitch licks his hand. 'You're a very fine fellow, aren't you?' he says in a way that reminds me of some of the quirkier contestants on *University Challenge*, not that I watch it much but Polly's a fan and it's often on in the background.

'I'm sorry he's escaped,' Polly says to me.

'It's fine. He's not doing any harm. Lily has a dog of her own.'

Polly's face is red. 'That doesn't mean she wants that one leaping all over her.'

'We wouldn't have minded, would we, Ben?'

'It wouldn't make any difference to me,' he says, pointing to his muddy jeans.

Polly stares at his trousers. 'What on earth happened to you?'

'Some kids knocked me over,' Ben says.

'Kids? Not that terror who keeps tormenting my chickens? Max? Short for Maximum Trouble, I say.'

'It was Max, and his sister, Laura,' Cal cuts in. 'And we've apologised but Ben is OK now, aren't you? Polly, this is Lily Craig and Ben . . . our very special wedding guests.'

Polly's brow creases then her mouth forms an 'o' as she belatedly realises who she's been talking to. 'Oh . . . er. Right. Pleased to meet you . . . um . . . I just wanted a word with Cal and Demi. Excuse me.'

However, instead of asking for permission to take a selfie, she turns her back on them and pulls me aside. Cal talks to Ben while Lily plays tug-of-war with Mitch and a stick. Harry stands a few yards away by a granite monument.

Polly takes me out of earshot. 'We've got a visitor,' she says, lowering her voice.

'Right . . . ' So Polly must have needed an excuse to interrupt our meeting with Ben and Lily. She needn't have worried, I would have introduced her anyway. 'Can you deal with them? We're a bit tied up showing Bonnie and — I mean our guests around at the moment.'

'Well, I can if you want me to, but you won't want me to,' she says.

'Why not? Who's so important that they can't speak to you?'

'Her.' Polly turns round and points to the top of the slope where a small but very determined figure has appeared on the ridgeline, silhouetted against the sky. 'I told the cheeky little minx to wait in reception but you know what she's like. Thinks she owns the place. Almost did.'

I follow Polly's gaze to the woman making her way down the muddy track in leopard print boots and a black leather mini. My stomach turns somersaults.

Why, why, *why* does she have to turn up now? After all our troubles over the past ten months, I'd hoped we were done with Mawgan Cade once and for all.

4

'What does she want?' I whisper to Polly while the others are distracted by Mitch's wild barks. 'Did you tell her Ben and Lily were here?'

'What do you take me for?' Polly adds in a not-very-whispery whisper that has me sneaking a look at our guests to see if they've heard. Fortunately Cal has distracted them, although I don't think he's noticed Mawgan himself yet. Gulp.

'OK. Sorry but I don't think it can be a coincidence that she's turned up at this precise moment when she hasn't been near the place for months.'

'I haven't breathed a word to a living soul and I've no idea what the little cat wants. She said she had business with you and Cal and when I said you were tied up and she should make an appointment, the cheeky madam plonked herself down in reception and said she'd wait. I had no idea she'd dare start wandering about but I thought I should come and find you myself as I couldn't get you on your mobiles. The nerve of her!'

'Nothing surprises me about Mawgan any more,' I murmur, though I'm amazed at her turning up at Kilhallon at this particular moment. I'm struggling to believe it's a coincidence that our VIPs are here but there is also *no* way that Mawgan knew they were

44

coming. Then again, it *must* just be a horrible coincidence . . . Maybe one of the cafe staff has let it slip that they are here today. I hope not, but I'm going to have to find out. Harry said we'll need to look at security for the event and it doesn't look great that we've made yet another cock-up this early in the process.

Cal glances at me. His jaw drops and he mouths 'what?' as he finally spots Mawgan too.

Mawgan wobbles her way towards us, waving.

Just *what* is going on?

'Can you take Mitch back to the house?' I ask Polly. 'I don't want the day to get any more complicated than it already has.'

Too late. Mitch has seen Mawgan too and lets out a low throaty growl.

'Oh dear,' says Lily. 'Have we upset him?'

Ben takes a large step back from Mitch.

Cal grabs Mitch's collar. 'That's a growl of excitement,' he says, fastening Mitch's lead to his collar.

'Maybe you could take him to the house the back way so he doesn't get too *boisterous*?' I tell Polly in desperation.

With a grim nod, she practically has to drag Mitch over the field away from Mawgan. He doesn't want to let go of the chance to 'welcome' Mawgan but he's also scared of Polly and, in the end, has no choice but to do as he's told.

Cal smiles at Lily and Ben. 'Looks like one of our visitors has taken a wrong turn and got lost. I'll go and help her find her way back to reception. Why don't you let Demi show you the views of the engine house and then go back to the cafe along the coast path for some lunch?'

Lily huddles into her coat. 'Sounds fab.'

'Good idea,' says Ben, shoving his hands into his jeans pockets.

'Is the path safe?' Harry asks.

'It's fine,' I say, aware that Mawgan is only twenty metres away. 'Let's go.'

'Woo hoo! Ben!'

Ben turns round. Mawgan has broken into a trot, almost tripping over in her desperation to reach us. Surely she can't be a fan of Ben?

'Hellooo!' Mawgan shouts, waving wildly as she totters across the muddy grass. There's no chance of us avoiding her. '*Is* it a fan? She seems very enthusiastic,' Lily says as Harry moves discreetly between Mawgan, Ben and Lily.

'I hope not,' says Ben.

'I'll deal with this,' says Harry.

'It's fine. I know exactly who it is,' I cut in. 'Cal will look after her.'

Cal reaches Mawgan at the same time as Ben suddenly breaks into a grin. She is only yards away from him now.

'Mawgan? Mawgan Cade? It *is* you.'

Ben jogs the remaining few steps to meet Mawgan and throws his arms around her. I don't know who's more amazed, Cal, me or Lily. Although I think 'horrified' is probably more accurate for me and Cal.

Ben lets her go. Mawgan's perma-tanned face is even brighter than normal. Her leopard-print pony-skin boots are thick with mud and she's puffing like mad but she's also grinning from ear to ear.

Ben shakes his head and laughs out loud. 'Jesus. What are you doing all the way out here, Mawgs?'

Mawgan gives him a playful slap on the arm. 'I heard you were here and I was passing on my way to a business meeting, so I had to drop in. I couldn't possibly miss the opportunity of seeing my old mate, Ben, now, could I?'

Cal manages to slide me a look of despair before Lily speaks. 'So you're a friend of Ben's? Awesome. Aren't you going to introduce us, Ben?'

'Yeah.'

'What a small world,' I say through gritted teeth.

'It is. Mawgan's a good mate of mine, or used to be until we lost touch.'

Mawgan's ponytail has come undone, but she's grinning from ear to ear.

Ignoring Cal, Harry and me, Mawgan lets go of Ben and gives Lily a dazzling smile. 'Hello, how amazing to meet you,' she says to Lily.

'Her Auntie Georgina used to live next door to us in Penzance. She used to come and visit. Good times, eh, Mawgan?' Ben says.

Mawgan winks. 'The best. Auntie Georgie still lives in Penzance, Ben. She sees your mum every day and says your mum never stops talking about you. I've been following your career, obviously, and I think you should have won an Oscar for *Knife Edge*. You were robbed, not even being nominated.'

'You always liked action movies, Mawgan,' Ben snorts. 'Mawgan always wanted to play the

47

villain: Catwoman, Poison Ivy.' Ben roars with laughter and Mawgan smiles with the closest I've ever seen to genuine happiness. Weirdly, Ben's accent has also changed to pure Cornish, without the transatlantic edge. It suits him a lot better even if Mawgan has inspired it.

'In fact, it was your mum who told Auntie Georgie you were visiting Kilhallon to check it out for your wedding venue.'

'Handfasting venue,' I say. 'And what a coincidence that you were just passing, Mawgan?'

'Yes, isn't it? Though I must say I was very surprised to hear that such huge stars as Ben Trevone and Lily Craig wanted to hold their ceremony here. It's *so* out of the way.'

'That's one reason why we chose it,' Lily says, 'It's easier to keep people away.'

Mawgan throws her a cheesy smile. 'Of course. I only thought it was a bit wild and remote.'

'We love that too. We don't want the glitzy OTT party that everyone expects. Ben and I are homebodies at heart and we wanted to come back to our roots and give back something to the community. We want to be able to say, hand on heart, that it's a thoroughly Cornish wedding. And if we use local people, it will look far more authentic, which is sooo important. Ben and I are known for our authenticity. Aren't we, Ben?'

'What? Yeah. We're totally authentic.'

'So when Isla told us about Kilhallon, we couldn't resist.'

'Ah ha. *Isla* suggested Kilhallon? That makes more sense than you actually choosing this place by yourselves,' Mawgan says.

'You know Isla?' Lily asks.

'We went to school together. Me, Isla and her fiancé, Luke — and Cal of course. I'm surprised he hasn't mentioned me?'

'How could I ever have forgotten,' says Cal. 'And Kilhallon may be wild and remote but it will make a wonderful setting for the ceremony.'

Mawgan laughs. 'If it doesn't rain and blow a howling gale. Don't you remember when that storm almost destroyed Kilhallon house and nearly ruined Isla's engagement party last summer?'

'Oh my God! Did it?' Lily cries.

'It was nothing more than a damaged window, which we've repaired,' Cal says, slightly down-playing the incident where an oak tree smashed through the wall and almost squashed us both.

'And Isla and Luke had a wonderful party,' I say. 'No one would ever have known there had been a storm the night before. I'm sure it won't happen again.'

Ben snorts. 'I hope not, but you know what the weather's like down here. We ought to have a plan in case the weather goes tits up.'

'We're already working on that,' says Cal, causing me to break out in goosebumps of panic. We definitely *don't* have a plan yet.

'Yes, there are a number of options we can explore,' I say. 'But I'm sure the weather will be kind to us.'

Lily seems reassured and Ben is still grinning about meeting up with his old mate again.

'We should all go out for a drink together,

shouldn't we, babe?' he says to Lily.

'Oh yes. And dinner. Our treat.'

Mawgan's eyes gleam with delight. 'That would be fantastic.'

'Bring Mr Cade,' Ben says. 'If there is one.'

Mawgan keeps smiling. I'm amazed her jaw hasn't broken. 'There's no Mr Cade, apart from my dad. Yet.'

'No? Is there anyone else you want to invite?' Lily says, slipping her arm around Ben.

'What about your sister?' Ben asks, 'How is she? Still doing all that arty farty stuff?' Ben asks with a snort.

'Yes.' Mawgan forces a smile. 'She lives with her partner in one of our properties near Truro.'

'So she's shacked up with a bloke while you're still young, free and single, eh? Can't think why, Mawgs.'

Part of me enjoys seeing Mawgan cringe at Ben's awkward questions but I have a horrible feeling about what's coming next.

Mawgan forces a smile. 'Andi's partner is a girl, actually.'

'Andi lives with my cousin, Robyn,' Cal says, cutting in with a smile even more strained than Mawgan's. Even though Mawgan went with Robyn and Andi to see their mother in Australia at Christmas, she is obviously still not comfortable with the idea of her sister living with another woman, and a Penwith too.

Mawgan hates Cal for all kinds of reasons but mainly because Cal's father had an affair with Mawgan's mum. In Mawgan's eyes, that caused the break-up of her parents' marriage and led to

Mrs Cade emigrating to Australia. Then there's the small matter of Cal rejecting Mawgan when they were both young. OK. I get it that Mawgan was devastated by the split and misses her mum, but Cal and I both lost our mothers when we were young. We all have regrets and loss to cope with, but only Mawgan is on a mission to make everyone else's lives a misery. I wonder how much of this story Ben knows . . . He seems in awe of Mawgan.

'Did you say that Andi and Robyn have moved into one of your properties?' he says, sounding well impressed.

Mawgan smirks. 'Yes, Cade Developments is quite a big concern these days as I'm sure Demi and Cal will tell you.' She's obviously far happier to boast about her business empire than talk about her sister's girlfriend.

Ben blows out a breath. 'I always knew you'd get on in life, Mawgs. You never let anyone get one over on you when we were little.'

'And I always knew you'd be a big star,' Mawgan simpers. 'Auntie Georgie used to take us to see him in the local theatre productions during the school holidays,' she tells Lily.

'Oh, I'd have loved to have seen him but he's always been talented. I saw an advert he did for a chocolate bar when he was only around ten. It popped up on a *Before They Were Famous* show and he looked soooo cute. I bet you could tell me so much about him when he was little.'

Mawgan smiles. 'I may know a few snippets.'

Ben groans. 'Don't start that, Mawgan. We both have a few secrets we'd rather keep hidden.'

51

'I'm sure Mawgan is the soul of discretion,' Cal says smoothly.

Mawgan smirks. 'As you've found out, Cal.' She turns back to Ben and Lily. 'We can talk about the old days when we go out for dinner. I can't wait to catch up with all the gossip, though I'm not sure it's my dad's thing to hang out with celebs.'

Lily laughs in delight. 'What a shame, but the five of us can still have a lovely time: I had no idea that you were all so close and you have to come to the wedding, of course. How cool that you know Cal and Demi too! And I'll make sure I bring Louie along next time. This whole wedding thing is going to be just *awesome*.'

5

Two weeks later — second week of March
Cal

'I can't believe that we are going to have to play happy families with Mawgan Cade and Lily and Ben,' Demi tells me in the kitchen at Kilhallon House. It's been over two weeks since Ben and Lily descended on us and she's obviously still fuming about them inviting our arch-enemy to be part of a lunch party. I can't say I blame her but I've other things to lose sleep over.

Demi slaps a piece of dough onto the farmhouse worktop and starts kneading it like it might come to life and attack her at any moment. Puffs of flour fly into the air as she beats it into submission.

She catches me smiling at her. 'What?'

'Nothing. Only that I'm mighty glad I'm not that dough.'

'Well,' she says, crushing her knuckles into the sticky mass, 'I wish it was Mawgan Cade. I can't believe she knows Ben Trevone. And to dare come here to muscle in when she knew they were paying a visit. I wish we could ban her from the wedding.'

'Handfasting . . . '

'Handfasting then. Whatever, I don't want Mawgan sticking her six-inch leopard-skin boots into it.'

53

'I can't dictate to our guests who they can invite — unless that person is a psychopathic nutcase, of course . . . which Mawgan does qualify as.'

'Yes.' Bash. 'She.' Thump. 'Does.' Whack.

Wow, she really *is* giving that dough a working over. It reminds me of my mum. She used to use bread making as therapy when my dad had upset her. Yet at the same time, watching Demi knock seven bells out of that dough is strangely soothing. I never stopped being amazed at how Mum turned a bag of flour, some water and a bit of yeast into light and fluffy loaves. The smell of bread baking makes my mouth water even now. We'd toast it and slather it in butter and homemade raspberry jam from her kitchen garden, or we'd eat blackberry crumble made with berries I'd pick from the hedgerows all around Kilhallon. Me, Luke, Isla . . . it was a happy, simpler time.

We once studied a book at school where someone said the past is another country, or something like it. It feels so true, especially when I think about what happened in Syria with Soraya and Esme. I wonder where she is, or if she still exists at all in this realm. I shake away my thoughts, returning to the present before I turn maudlin.

'Maybe you can arrange for the owl to be a huge eagle that will swoop down and carry off Mawgan again instead of the ring . . . ' I say, trying to lighten the mood for myself as much as Demi.

'Don't mention the bloody owl. Where am I

going to get an owl from?' she asks, pummelling the dough even harder.

'An owl centre?'

She glances up and blows a strand of hair that's escaped her ponytail out of her eyes. 'Ha ha! Then again, it's an idea . . . hmm. There is a birds of prey centre outside St Ives. I could ask them. Why did you have to mention it? I've enough trouble trying to create this 'totally natural and thrown-together-at-the-last-minute' wedding arch and flower decoration. The truth is that Lily only wants it to *look* natural and what she really wants is a fashion shoot recreation of her fantasies! Mind you . . . ' Her voice takes on a mischievous edge. 'Since it was *your* idea to have an owl and you're the one with the DIY skills, I think you should take charge of caring for the wildlife and the arch construction.'

'Thanks a lot.'

'You're welcome.' With a smirk, she goes back to kneading with renewed vigour and complaining about Mawgan and owls. If she glanced up from the tabletop, she'd catch me smiling at her. I love the way she tackles any task with a fierce enthusiasm that's almost comical and yet touching too. I love the way her breasts push together in that old long-sleeved T-shirt. God, I'm shallow but I'm also a man and I'd love to interrupt her bread making now and drag her upstairs to bed.

With that thought, I turn back to my laptop, intending to close the browser, but my eye is drawn to a recent email in my inbox. There among the messages about liability insurance, gas safety checks (yawn) for the cottages and a rogue item asking me if I'd like a much larger erection (I don't think I could improve on the one I have now, *but . . .*) is one that leaps out at me. Its subject line is written in capitals and stops me in my tracks.

PLEASE DON'T GET YOUR
HOPES UP . . .

It comes from someone I rarely hear from nowadays; a good friend who knows that any email from her risks stirring up memories I should have left behind by now. A kind, brave friend who would never send me an email with the word 'hope' in it unless that hope was also preceded by a 'no'.

So to receive an email with the subject line 'Please Don't Get Your Hopes Up' makes my heart rate speed up, my mouth go dry and my hopes soar higher than a gull above the Kilhallon cliffs.

The slap of the dough and the thuds of it being beaten into submission recede when I open the email and read the words from Carolyn, my former boss and a senior manager of the overseas aid charity for whom I used to work.

Hi Cal,
How are you? Still wrestling with rebuild-ing Kilhallon or is it all up and running now? I hope so. I thought you looked well on it when we saw you in London last

autumn, if that's not too patronising. OK. I guess, by now, the title of this email has you gnashing your teeth and scrolling down for the thing you're hoping to hear.

But, Cal, I'm going to preface this nugget of news with the same warning as in the subject line, because I know you too well.

So: *PLEASE* don't get your hopes up. Promise me?

No, I mouth silently. No, I can't promise anything where Esme is concerned.

OK. Now that I've got the warning over with, even though I know it's useless to expect you to heed it, I'll get to the nitty gritty. This is only a glimmer and it may be nothing but as you may have heard, we've been able to move back closer to the town where Soraya was killed and Esme was last seen. The refugee camp is as big as ever with new influxes of people daily from other areas but also some of the people who were here when we pulled out. One of my new colleagues was treating a young guy for shrapnel injuries, and called me to give a second opinion. I thought I recognised the guy and when I spoke to him, I realised it was one of Soraya's extended family, Jaz. You might remember him, because he had a long scar down the side of his face from a shrapnel wound.

He was very grateful and he mentioned you and asked after you. I know you blame *yourself for what happened to Soraya but apparently that's not how her extended family see it. Jaz said they'd been grateful to you for trying to help them. To them Soraya will be considered a martyr and a heroine, which, I know, may not be any comfort to you but . . .*

My stomach turns over. Soraya was a friend of mine, a Syrian nurse who helped me and my colleagues in our work in a refugee camp near the front line. Then I got her involved in smuggling medical supplies and arms to local rebels. As a result of my actions, she ended up in the wrong place at the wrong time and lost her life. I ended up in the hands of insurgents and Soraya's little girl, Esme, vanished in the chaos of the falling town. Sweat breaks out on my back now and I have to clasp my hands together under the table to stop them from shaking. At Christmas, I finally trusted Demi with the story of what happened to me but since then I've tried hard to move on and focus on my life at Kilhallon. I think we both know that I can never move on completely, not until I know what happened to Esme.

I return to Carolyn's email, feeling sick to my stomach with a mixture of guilt, hope and fear.

I took the opportunity to ask if he had seen Esme, and Jaz said no. He also said that her grandparents hadn't seen her since that day and that everyone in the immediate family thought she might have died. But then Jaz *said that he had heard from friends of his parents who knew the family, and he also said that Esme *might* have been taken in by some of their neighbours and they were headed for Turkey and hoping to reach Greece.*

I'm sure you've been scouring social media and online tracing services for her. I've had a quick look but I'm so busy and I haven't spotted her or anyone I recognise on there.

Carolyn is right, I have been scouring the sites in every moment of my spare time but I haven't wanted to let Demi know. She'd only worry about me and it seems selfish to still be focusing on a lost girl when I should have my mind one hundred per cent on the business and on her. But I can't help myself. If there's even a chance of finding Esme, I'll grab it with both hands.

Demi is still kneading the dough into submission and humming along to Radio St Trenyan. I scan the rest of the email.

Cal, I know you will by now be packing your bags to rush to London or even further afield but please, please don't. Let me try to make some further enquiries and I promise I will send any news — good or bad — the moment I get it. IF I ever hear anything, because this could be another false trail and not have a good outcome. There are thousands — millions — of people displaced and there is still ongoing chaos. Finding

Esme could be like finding a needle in a thousand haystacks . . . but I thought you deserved to hear that there is still a glimmer of hope.

I have to go. It's been good to have a few moments to write to you and think of home. I think that when my tour here is over, I might be coming back myself.

Until then, take care,

Love, Carolyn x

It's a minute or so before I can tear my eyes from the email. I let the words sink in before, finally, Demi's voice brings me back into the room.

'Of course, they've left things way too late and I didn't expect them to want everything to be organised locally. I thought they'd bring their own wedding planner and a whole pack of stylists . . .'

'Sorry?'

Demi stares at me. I feel guilty for not listening. This wedding may seem trivial compared to what I've read but it means a lot to her — to Kilhallon — and so it means a lot to me, but I can't summon up the proper level of enthusiasm at the moment.

Demi puts the dough into a bowl, picks up a tea cloth to wipe some of the scraps off her fingers.

'You weren't listening, were you?' She covers the dough with a tea towel. Her hands are sticky with dough and there's a floury speck on the end of her pretty nose. She sighs. 'I don't blame you.

60

I was having a rant.'

I long to scour the email for any scrap I might have missed but I close the lid of the laptop. I push a strand of her chestnut hair out of her eyes and look down into her eyes. She gazes back at me with a mix of exasperation and lust. At least I hope it's lust and not fury that I wasn't listening.

'You have flour on your nose,' I tell her.

'Do I?'

'Yes.'

'I can't do anything until I've cleaned my hands. I'm helpless.'

'Hold on.' I rub the tip of her nose. 'And you, Demi Jones, are never helpless and never will be.'

'Sometimes it suits me to be so.'

'Yeah. Maybe. It's me that's helpless.'

I cradle her chin in my hand like a delicate porcelain cup. She is so fragile yet so strong. Her doughy hands hang by her side. I kiss her, trying to obliterate all thoughts of the email and the memories it stirs in the taste of her mouth. I pull her against me, hoping to crush unhappy memories. Demi deserves better than a man whose mind is on anything but her.

'Whoa. I can barely breathe.'

She breaks the kiss, though her eyes are shining with pleasure.

'Sorry.'

I release her but feel her hands on my bum, pulling me back to her, just not quite so tightly.

Her expression changes to one of concern. 'Everything OK? You didn't seem to want to let me go.'

'Do I need a reason to feel like that?'

Although I promised to share my worries with Demi in future, I'm not going to drop this latest news onto her when it may amount to nothing. She has enough on her plate with running the cafe and planning the wedding and helping to write and produce her cookbook with Eva Spero — not to mention she has had a big change in her own family. It's still early days in her reconciliation with her dad, his partner, her brother and their new baby who arrived at Christmas.

I kiss her again. 'I don't need a reason to keep you close to me.'

Demi lets out a giggle. 'Your bum is all floury.'

Realising what's happened, I twist around and a puff of flour dust flies into the air. I brush the back of my jeans, and find tiny pieces of sticky dough clinging to the denim and my fingers.

'You minx!'

She smirks. 'That'll teach you to be more interested in your laptop than me.'

'Believe me, I'd far rather concentrate on you,' I say. 'But the park accounts won't wait. The accountant read me the riot act about getting the figures in early and the family finances have been in such a mess for so many years that I don't want to let her down again. Polly did her best but we really need to keep a tight rein on the money. We might have to get a bit of help with the admin. Polly has enough to do as it is, managing the bookings and helping with changeovers and guests' needs. We can cope in the low season, but when Easter comes, we'll need more help on the camping side and the cafe.'

'I'm interviewing some seasonal staff for

Demelza's in a few weeks' time. I need to get this wedding organised. I'm supposed to be going to a wedding fair in a couple of weeks but I can't wait for that. We need to get a photographer, florist, cake maker, decorations and a band . . . Some specialists are booked up years ahead and we only have a few months.'

'I know you can do it,' I say to reassure her. She still lacks confidence even though I'm convinced she could be UN Secretary General, England football manager and POTUS if she really wanted to. She'd definitely do a better job than any of them. 'After getting the cafe ready and helping out with the floods, a wedding should be a piece of cake.'

'I think organising a wedding could be worse than both of those put together. Lily has sent over the guest list and that's convinced me we need a professional wedding planner or I'll end up freaking out before the big day.'

'That sounds like a really good idea.'

'In theory but I've already tried over a dozen within the county and into Devon and almost all of them were already booked for those dates. I interviewed one last week but she seemed very inexperienced. She told me she'd helped to organise some friends' weddings but she didn't have a website and only seemed interested in knowing who the couple were. I haven't told anyone that it's Ben and Lily until I'm sure we can trust them to be discreet. I even wondered if this woman had already found out their names. Although I'm not sure how she'd got wind of it.'

'I could suggest a few names . . . '

She rolls her eyes. 'Do they include Mawgan Cade?'

'It's a good bet, although I'm surprised she's told people at this stage, when she obviously wants to keep in with Ben and Lily. Quite a few people know — Polly, Jez, the girls from the cafe and your suppliers will have to know. It'll probably turn out to be the worst-kept secret in Cornwall and these fans have their ways of finding out.'

'Tell me about it.' She sighs. 'There's one more possibility I'm seeing next week so' — she holds up crossed fingers — 'let's hope one of them is suitable or I'll have to look even further afield . . . I can't worry about it too much until after Freya's christening tea on Sunday.'

'That will be a lot less trouble than the wedding. Is there anything else I can do to help?'

'Not yet, thanks. I think I'm ready for that: or at least, Demelza's is. We've closed for the day, which will help, and it's a quiet time of year so I don't think we'll miss out. Robyn and Polly are going to lay out the buffet while we're at the church ready for when we come back and stay to clear up. I've made the quiches and tarts and Rachel's friend has made the cake. I hope it all works out OK but it seemed mad to let Dad and Rachel hire a pub or cafe when Demelza's could put on as good a spread.'

'It'll be even better than anywhere else could do. And I'm here to give a hand any way you want. Happy to put on the apron and Marigolds any time.'

She smiles. 'It's not help with the washing up

I'll need. I don't think I could face the day without you, even though I'm getting to know Dad and Rachel so much better now. I'm relieved that you're coming to the church.'

'Of course I'm coming. I'm not suddenly going to bail out and abandon you.'

She smiles in relief. 'I know you're not into these big formal family occasions, not that it'll be that big or really that formal, but I'll be on show to all our relatives. Some of them haven't forgiven me for 'abandoning my father and choosing to live like a tramp', according to my horrible Auntie Serena.'

'I'll keep her away from you.' I hug her and try to distract her from the ordeal ahead. 'How many are you catering for?'

'I think there'll be about twenty in total, counting us, some friends and relatives on both sides plus my brother, Kyle, of course. Dad and Rachel wanted to time the christening with him being home on leave from the army. I'm excited about seeing him but also nervous because it's been a couple of years since I saw him. We weren't that close at home and while I'm getting used to the idea of being a family again. I'm sure there'll be people there I haven't seen for years and who will be on my case for leaving Dad . . . like Serena.'

Demi mimes a fingers-down-throat action then rolls her eyes. She has my full sympathy where families are concerned but I have to suppress a smile. She manages to look sexy, covered in flour dust and pulling a face. Gently, I pull her down to sit on my lap and she doesn't object. 'Demi, Demi, there is no way in the world that I would miss your little sister's christening or leave you to face the day alone. I will be there, so please stop stressing and try to enjoy it.'

'Hmm,' she says, very unconvinced, and I can hardly blame her. The relationship is still at an early stage although I know she adores the baby and is getting to know Rachel and rebuilding bridges with her father. I can well understand that a formal family occasion would freak her out. There are a few of my relations who were less than impressed with me spending most of my time abroad over the past few years, though I don't care. They have no idea of the full story.

'Rachel and Gary must be pleased you're taking care of the catering.'

She brightens. 'I think so. They've only recently moved back into their cottage in the cove and it's far too small for an event like this.'

'Considering they were flooded out at Christmas, they're very lucky to be back in so soon,' I say, reminding us both of the devastation wreaked on St Trenyan and the surrounding coast by the tidal surge the day before Christmas Eve.

'The damage wasn't quite as bad as expected and their insurance company was one of the ones that paid out quickly, unlike some.' She strokes my arm idly, leaving tiny traces of flour on the brushed cotton of my shirt. 'Thanks for sparing some time to help with the repair work. It meant a lot to them to move out of Rachel's cousin's flat and get back into their own place and start enjoying life with Freya.'

'I didn't mind at all. It's lucky that your dad is an electrician and has so many mates in the trade who could lend a hand.'

'It also helps that he's been off the booze he took to after my mum died. Starting up his own business has been really good for him . . . ' Demi toys with the top button of my shirt, unbuttoning it absent-mindedly but making me shift in my seat. This conversation is going to end with both of us in bed if she stays here much longer. Surely that would a good thing for both of us, not that I need any excuse to take her to bed at any time. 'Even though I've spent more time with them all and things are going well with Dad, I can't help feeling nervous about Sunday.'

'You'll be absolutely fine. It's tough to rebuild relationships with family you thought you'd never see again for one reason or another but Demelza's is fresh territory and you're all making a new start.' I rub my hand along her thigh, enjoying the feel of her shapely bottom in my lap. 'And let's look on the bright side: any social occasion that doesn't include Mawgan Cade has to be a bonus.'

6

Two weeks later
Demi

'Come in, out of this bitterly cold wind. Who'd ever think it was the first day of spring? Oh, let me see the babe. She's turning into such a little poppet. Such a lovely name too. Classic . . . nothing made-up or daft like some have now, and the shawl is beautiful. Reminds me of one my grandma made for me back in the day.'

Rachel glows with pride as Polly coos over Freya Penelope, who is now fast asleep, her little pink face nestled in a lacy bundle of wool. One hand has escaped her wrappings and her tiny fingers are curled around a scrap of shawl as if she knows it's been made just for her and she'll never let it go.

Cal was right. This social occasion doesn't involve Mawgan Cade and it's been way more enjoyable than I expected. So what if the leading lady was a bit of a drama queen when St Trenyan's vicar, affectionately known as Rev Bev, poured water over her head? One of the christening guests told me it's considered lucky if the baby cries at that moment. In that case, Freya should go on to win the lottery several times over.

'I bet you could hear her howls from the harbour,' I whisper to Cal, following the christening party out of the raw March afternoon into the warmth of Demelza's. Despite the cutting wind, Kilhallon seems to have burst into life since Ben and Lily's visit a few weeks ago. The sunnier hedgerows are already dotted with yellow primroses and the copse is studded with little white flowers that Polly told me are wood anemones.

Rachel's sister and cousin did the honours as godmothers while Kyle acted as Freya's godfather. I didn't mind not being asked. I'm not religious and also I think Dad knew that I wouldn't want the spotlight on me in such a public way. I'm far more comfortable handling the venue and catering — and most of all, I'm just so happy to be Freya's big sister.

I watched Kyle taking on the role of godfather in quiet amazement. It's been almost three years and he's shot up: he's a good few inches taller than Dad, and even a bit taller than Cal. Even though he's in a suit, you can tell he's in the army from the way he stands very upright and proud, with his shoulders back. His tawny hair is cropped short and his tanned cheeks are chiselled from all the exercise and drills. I have also never seen his shoes more shiny: when he was young, Mum could never get him out of his battered old Converses or trainers.

We didn't have much time to chat at the church as we were a little late arriving but managed a quick word and a hug while a few photos were taken in the church porch. Now we're back at the cafe, I'm hoping to catch up some more with Kyle.

Cal starts taking people's coats and I head to the kitchens to make sure Polly and Robyn are OK with laying out the buffet. All the staff have had the afternoon off.

Polly practically bundles me out of the kitchen. 'No, Demi, you're not coming in here today.'

'Polly's so right,' Robyn adds, words I never thought I'd hear from her as she's generally not our blunt PA's biggest fan. 'You're going to relax and enjoy the party. You must have so many people to catch up with, especially Kyle. He's quite cute, if he was my thing, that is.'

'Ha ha,' I say. 'Are you sure I can't help out with the tea and coffee? Have the ovens been OK? Because I was worried you'd have trouble with the temperature control. They're so different to the Aga.'

'Demi. Get out of here!' Polly and Robyn chime in unison and Robyn virtually frog-marches me into the cafe area. The truth is that I'd feel far more comfortable in the kitchen or behind the serving counter than making small talk and facing family I haven't spoken to for years. Some of them nodded at me at the church and an auntie on Dad's side gave me a hug but I keep thinking that they're muttering about me.

After all, I *did* walk out on Dad, and for weeks at a time I didn't even tell him I was safe. I must have caused him a lot of worry, even though I felt hurt and ignored by him at the time, while we were both grieving for my mum. I don't think some of my lot can cope with having a relative who was voluntarily homeless for a while.

70

Helped by Cal, Polly and Robyn bring the platters of food into the cafe and start serving glasses of wine and hot drinks. I feel like a spare part, watching other people do my job and not knowing quite what to say to anyone but Freya, except she's asleep in her buggy at the moment so I can't even go and cuddle her.

I take a large gulp of wine and wonder if I dare slip into the kitchens again but spot Rachel make a beeline for me. She's wearing a pretty shift dress and hot pink cardigan that shows off her slim figure. Close up, under her make-up, she also looks tired but that's what you'd expect from someone with the worry of moving home and Freya to deal with. I think she's in her late thirties although her clothes and make-up make her look younger. She's at least ten years younger than my dad and she's known him and me since before I left home.

In fact, Rachel was one of the reasons I walked out. We didn't hit it off immediately but she's been making an effort to be friendly since Christmas. I'm ashamed to say I don't know why I hated her so much, apart from the fact she wasn't my mum. When Dad asked her to move in, I saw it as the final insult and left. Rachel must have taken it personally, but really, the main reason we became estranged was all about my dad and me. The damage had been done long before Rachel even came on the scene. I'm determined not to bring bad memories up today and even if I can't forget how I once felt about her 'taking Mum's place', I'd never dream of spoiling her or Freya's day.

Rachel arrives at my side. 'Demi? This food is fantastic. Thanks so much for doing this. I couldn't have coped with this tribe at the cottage. It's great to have a professional take care of everything.'

'Thanks. I only planned the menu and prepared it; Polly and Robyn have done a lot of the work while we were at the church.'

'This can't be easy,' she adds in a low voice. 'Even though we've been getting to know one another again, this is the first time we've all gone public. I know your dad was nervous about it and I have to be honest, so was I.'

'Really?' I take another gulp of wine.

'I'd be on the wine myself if I wasn't feeding Freya.'

I laugh. 'It's OK. It's not been as bad as I expected. Oh shit. I didn't mean I expected it to be *bad*, only that I didn't know how I'd react to a full-on family reunion. Arghh. I've put my foot in it already.'

She smiles. 'Hey, I'll let you into a secret. A few of your dad's family and mine aren't thrilled with me supposedly stepping into your mum's shoes, moving in with an older man and having a baby with him. Your Auntie Serena's made no secret of the fact she thinks I'm a bit of a slapper.'

'Auntie Serena has always been a nasty piece of work,' I say, sliding at a look at the crow-like woman dressed like she's going to a funeral, sniffing one of my savoury rosemary scones with suspicion. 'She seems jealous of anyone who's happy or successful. Mum couldn't stand her either.'

'We had no choice but to ask her, she was your mum's great auntie.'

'It's fine. It's your — Freya's — day and I'll keep out of Serena's way.' I don't want to have a 'mishap' with a smoothie or a glass of wine, I think, as I have had with Mawgan Cade in the past.

'Come and have your photo taken with Kyle and Freya now we're in the warm. It would be lovely to have a picture of the three of you together.'

Grateful for Rachel's efforts to make me feel comfortable, I join Kyle, Rachel and Dad for a family photo, even though I feel a bit like a cuckoo in the nest. It's definitely a situation I could never have imagined six months ago.

As I see people admiring the place and praising the buffet, I can't help a warm glow of pride myself. I'm glad I suggested holding the christening tea at Demelza's. After we've posed for some photos by the cake that Rachel's cousin made, the sound of corks popping from the servery startles Freya. She throws her tiny arms out and opens her huge blue eyes for a few seconds. Her lips part and everyone holds their breath waiting for her to let out a wail but then she settles back into a snuffly sleep. Rachel puts her in her Moses basket while Cal hands round glasses of Prosecco and Robyn distributes the cake.

'I hope no one minds me doing this but I'd like to propose a toast,' Cal says, holding his glass up. 'To Freya Penelope. Wishing her a long and very happy life!'

Everyone raises their glasses and echoes his words, even Auntie Serena manages to lift her glass of orange juice a few inches.

'And I'd like to congratulate her parents, Gary and Rachel, on producing such a beautiful daughter, and Demi and Kyle on their new sister. Wishing you every happiness,' Cal adds.

People raise their glasses again. My dad steps forward, shuffling nervously. He clears his throat and the room hushes in anticipation. I don't think I've ever seen Dad give a speech and my palms feel damp with nerves at what he might say.

'Thanks for the kind words, Cal. And thank you all for coming to welcome Freya into the world. She knows how to time her entrance: on the day after Boxing Day during the great storm that caused so much heartache and flooded our cottage.

'Now I'm sure there are many on St Trenyan who wouldn't agree with this but every cloud does have a silver lining. If it hadn't been for that flood, we wouldn't be standing here now, enjoying this fantastic spread and the hospitality of Demi and Cal.'

Under my cardigan, my arms break out in goosebumps. Dad's going to say *something* . . . about me — I know he is and I don't know if I can handle it.

7

'Demi will probably hate me drawing attention to her like this and, love,' he looks straight at me, 'it's not easy for me to say it, either, but the ill wind that brought that storm was one of the better things that's happened to me lately. It's no use me pretending that things have been smooth in my family since Penny died . . . '

Rachel's arm slips through Dad's. He pauses and when he goes on his voice is shaky.

'But then I met Rachel and she helped bring back the light into my life.'

There are a few 'ohs' and quiet murmurs of support from my cousins and a family friend. Kyle stands up straighter and his lips are set in a line as if he's trying to suppress any emotion.

A hand rests lightly on the small of my back. Cal knows instinctively that this situation is tough for me, even if I know Dad had to get things off his chest. I don't know what I'd do without Cal sometimes and that realisation makes me feel exposed and raw. Letting down my guard and allowing myself to care about people again has been terrifying at times. It's as if I'm being swept along by a current, unable to stop myself even though I want to.

'As you know, Rachel, Freya and myself were forced out of our cottage by the floods on Christmas Eve,' Dad goes on. 'We were sleeping on the floor of the community hall and due to circumstances, we had nowhere to go. You could say we were homeless. Even though we knew we'd eventually have a place to go, for a few days, we experienced how that felt and it wasn't an experience we'd care to repeat. We thought we'd be spending our Christmas on the floor of that hall.'

Rachel looks down at the floor and back up again, her eyes suspiciously bright.

'Anyway, chance brought us in the way of Demi and Cal and, cutting a very long story short, they put us up here at Kilhallon, as you know. Family life is a shaky business at times, to say the least. We've had more than our share of rocks that we've foundered on. I've not been the best skipper, to use a seafaring phrase, and I've run my own ship onto the rocks in the past and my crew has suffered.'

I see a few gentle sympathetic smiles, but I'm digging my nails in my palm. Cal's hand now rests at my waist. I grip the stem of my glass tightly. The people in front of me swim in and out of focus. My nose itches but I must not cry.

'But we're in sight of the harbour again now,' Dad goes on. 'We're safe and in our home and thanks to the flood, I have all my girls and my son with me for the first time in way too long. I'm thankful for that . . . ' His words are racing by as his nerves get the better of him. I half want his speech to be over too, though I know he had to say these words and I needed to hear them.

He raises his glass and declares, 'To my family. Rachel, Demi, Kyle and Freya. Thank you and good health and happiness to you all.'

He lifts his glass to his lips, takes a sip then puts it on the desk. While everyone is toasting us all, Dad sits down and Rachel kisses him.

'Are you OK?' Cal whispers.

'Hmmghh.' It's all I can manage.

Freya suddenly lets out a loud yawn and everyone laughs.

'She's letting me know what she thinks of my speech,' Dad says. 'Good job I left it there.'

People laugh in relief and normal chatter resumes.

Kyle joins us. 'I'm glad we're all together again, even if it has been a tough journey. Would be good to have a proper catch-up while I'm on leave.'

'How long are you back for?'

'Only this week. Then it's back to Catterick for my unit before we're deployed to Cyprus for six months. I'm a corporal now,' he says, proudly.

'Wow, you've done well. Dad said you'd done two tours of Afghanistan over the past few years. That must have been tough.'

'It wasn't a walk in the park but my mates helped me through.'

I know he's downplaying how horrible it must have been . . . and dangerous. I suppress a shudder. 'I wish I'd known exactly where you were. I'd have called you and written to you.'

'No, you don't. Dad worried about me enough, I didn't need you fretting about me day and night. It's history now and I'm going into a training role soon so I'll at least be in the same country for the foreseeable future.' He pauses. 'I'm sorry I pissed off to the army and abandoned you and Dad. It was a cowardly thing to do but I couldn't handle Mum going and I definitely couldn't handle the way Dad reacted. I know you were cut up by it and you needed me, but I left you. I'm sorry.'

'It's water under the bridge now. We all did what we had to to survive.'

He smiles at me. 'Mum used to say that.'

'What?'

'Water under the bridge. You said it the exact same way.'

'I didn't realise.'

'Shh. Don't go slushy on me. You've been busy too. Look at this place. It's pretty cool. Rachel said you built and got it off the ground yourself.'

I laugh. 'Not with my bare hands. Cal put up the money but he let me have free rein with designing and running it.'

'It's great. Don't you think this . . . ' he says, taking in the room with a glance ' . . . is weird? The Joneses coming together as a family again after everything that happened to us?'

'It's very weird.'

He puts his arm around me and gives me a brief hug, then he's back in Kyle mode. 'Right, I'm starving. D'you think anyone will mind if I have another beer and second helpings of the food? They don't feed me properly in the army.'

'That's not true. I heard you get fed all day long. But yes, help yourself.'

I take a deep breath, happy to have cleared the air a little with Kyle. Cal opens a beer for him and they start talking. Auntie Serena is saying goodbye to my dad at the door after showing her face, so we can all relax now. I sip my wine, and the tension slowly ebbs from my body. I got through today and there's hope ahead. Clouds are clearing over the sea and spring is definitely on its way.

'The view from here's amazing. I've a better chance to appreciate it today. My mind was on other things when we were here for Christmas dinner.' Rachel smiles.

'It was cosy in here at Christmas but I think Demelza's is at its best on a bright day like this,' I say, moving over to the window with her. A few friends and family are enjoying the view too and some have ventured outside though they're wrapped up well against the wind. The swell is up and the Atlantic topped with white caps but the sun is out and the promise of spring is in the air. 'The location is our biggest selling point, even if we're a little out of the way, people will make the effort to come here for the view. The customers love it, even in a storm. Especially in a storm.' I wince. 'Sorry, I didn't mean that storms are a selling point.'

She laughs. 'We both know they're a hazard of living down here. You know that we moved into Porthleven temporarily after we left Kilhallon? Some days the waves were as high as the clock tower. The locals had to time getting in and out of the inn at the edge of the harbour in between the massive breakers. It's a wonder some didn't get swept away and most of them were drenched anyway.'

I shiver. 'How's the work going on your place?'

'Coming on thanks to Gary's mates and help

from Cal. We can't decorate properly downstairs until the plaster's dried out a bit more, but upstairs is fine and we're mostly living up there. It's our own home again and that's what matters. Not that I wasn't grateful to come here and for my cousin's flat, but you know what it's like ... nowhere's as good as your own place. I wouldn't like to be homeless for long.' She giggles and slaps her forehead with her palm. 'Now I've put my foot in it.'

It's almost funny, the way we're dancing round each other, trying not to say the wrong thing. Now that I've got to know Rachel better, seeing her with Dad is becoming more normal and easier to handle. Looking back to when she first came on the scene in Dad's life, she was never particularly horrible to me, but we both used to rub each other up the wrong way. It can't have been easy for her to have a teenager in the house who hated her guts and thought she'd tried to take her mum's place.

'It's way better for us all that I have my own home now.' Heat rises up my neck at the memory of things I said about Rachel to my dad. 'And I love working here and having my own business. I've earned a small sum from the publishers for my cookbook and I'm investing that in the cafe.'

'Your dad told me about your book. That's a great achievement.'

'I haven't finished writing it yet. Although I come up with a lot of the recipes, Eva Spero and her team develop them further and refine them. I don't have time to write every word. The publisher is going to arrange the photography.'

'You should still be proud of what you've done, as your dad says. To be honest, I'll have to go back to work sooner or later. We need the money, especially now we have Freya and the insurance didn't cover all the damage. There have been other costs that we've just had to cover, but I'm not complaining.'

'Will you go back to your old job at Trevarrian Estate?'

Rachel pulls a face. 'I don't think so. I enjoyed working there but I've discussed things with your dad and decided that having Freya could be a new start for us all. I don't mind working hard but I'd like more flexibility so that Gary and I can share the childcare, with my parents' help. Besides, I already felt I was ready to do more than work in the admin office. I'd been doing it a long time.'

I have to admit, the idea of my dad sharing the childcare for a newborn is more than I can process.

'What will you do?'

She looks slightly embarrassed. 'I was thinking of offering my services as a virtual PA to companies. Lots of small businesses can't afford to hire a full-time staff and I have so much experience running the office at the estate. Trevarrian may look like a grand stately home and the owners are charming but they're also totally scatty and eccentric. I ended up doing everything from making sure the roof didn't fall down to organising clay-pigeon shooting and corporate dinners.'

'Sounds like you were very busy.'

'I worked very long hours and the pay wasn't great, though Lord Trevarrian was fun to work for. With a few decent clients, I think I can earn almost as much and spend more time with Freya.' She holds up crossed fingers. 'Trevarrian might let me do some freelance work too but I need other customers. Who knows, it might be a disaster but after seeing how you and Cal have turned Kilhallon around, I feel inspired.'

'Me? An inspiration?'

'Yeah. You made me think I should go for what I want.'

Rachel hugs me briefly but warmly and my throat goes scratchy.

There's a wail from Freya's Moses basket. Freya is very red in the face and clenching her fists. She's also doing what Nana Demelza would have called 'chuntering'. Her face has gone very red and I think she's about to wake up — and make a *lot* of noise.

Rachel winces. 'Oh dear. I think she's filling her nappy.'

I glance down at my savoury scone topped with local ham and piccalilli and find my appetite has gone.

'I'll have to change her. Can I use your customer loo?'

'Course you can. In fact, I'll help you.'

Rachel wrinkles her nose. 'Are you sure you want to do that? Freya's dirty nappy in a confined space isn't the most pleasant prospect.'

'I'll put a peg on my nose and, after all, she is my sister so I'd better get used to helping out when I can.'

'On your head be it,' Rachel replies with a laugh. 'Although I hope it won't come to that.'

'It's fine,' I say, already closing my nostrils. With an idea forming in my mind, I follow Rachel into the toilets, carrying Freya's changing bag.

While I help Rachel, I chat a bit more about the idea for her business.

'Did you say you were in charge of the events at Trevarrian?'

'A few, yes. Lots of corporate shindigs with clay-pigeon shooting, four-wheel-drive 'safaris' round the estates, plus a lot of company dinners and the odd charity ball.'

'Um . . . have you ever organised a wedding?'

Rachel hands me a scented nappy sack. 'Not officially.' She smiles. 'Trevarrian had only just got into the wedding industry when I left but I liaised with the professional wedding planner a couple of times. Why?'

I drop the nappy into our bin.

'I was just wondering if they were difficult to arrange, that's all.'

'Like I say, I've never been solely responsible but from what I could tell from working with the planner and my contact with the brides and their mothers, they can be very scary. Just as scary, if not more so, than a corporate or business event because you're dealing with non-professional people and there is so much emotion involved. The wedding planner told me that you're responsible for delivering someone's dreams or what they think is their dream. It's bloody hard work but can be very rewarding. If you get it right. Woe betide you if you don't but you have to make sure you *do* get it right and be prepared for anything.'

'Um. You think a *lot* can go wrong?'

Rachel cuddles Freya who gnaws at her tiny fist.

'If you ask me, a wedding works on sod's law. Whatever can go wrong will.'

8

So. Everyone's gone — almost. My family, Freya, friends and all the christening guests, even Polly's gone up to one of the cottages to sort out a heating problem for one of the guests.

Cal clears away the rubbish while Robyn and I clingfilm any spare food for later and empty the dishwasher.

'That went well,' Robyn says with a grin. 'I mean, it *really* went well.'

'Way better than I'd expected. I was so worried about it and I don't know why really. Thanks for helping today,' I say.

'It's fine. I enjoyed it, though that crow-like woman kept giving me funny looks. I can't think why.'

'Nor me,' I say, smiling at Robyn's Goth clothes, purple hair and studded nose and imagining Serena's horror.

'Imagine what she'd do if she knew I lived with a girl.'

'Probably have a heart attack. Maybe you should have told her.'

'Hmm.' Robyn leans against the worktop, toeing the floor with her boot. 'She'd definitely pass out if she knew my latest news.

'What's up?'

'Andi and I have got engaged. We're getting married.'

'Wow? Really? That's amazing. Congratulations . . . can I tell Cal?'

'Of course. I didn't mention it earlier because I didn't want to steal your thunder, or Freya's, and also it's a secret.'

'You mean Mawgan doesn't know?'

Cal joins us. 'Mawgan doesn't know what?'

'Andi and Robyn are getting married.'

Cal grins. 'Wow. Big step. When?'

'I don't know. Early next year maybe when we've finished our uni courses. We've no money and we live in one of Mawgan's houses though we do pay some rent. But we thought: why wait? We love each other.'

'Does your dad know yet?' Cal asks. 'Are you worried about what he'll say? I'm sure he'll be pleased for you.'

'It's not my dad's reaction that worries me, it's Mawgan's, and Andi's father. They barely tolerate us living together.'

Cal hugs her. 'I'm sorry they still feel like that. Did your visit to your mum change anything?'

'We haven't really had a proper talk about it. I feel sorry for Mawgan in one way. She's never had a relationship that's lasted more than a couple of months. Mrs Cade's happy with her partner in Australia now and although Mawgan was on best behaviour over Christmas, I could tell she didn't like seeing them together. She just can't seem to stand seeing anyone happy. Andi worries about Mawgan, even though she also hates her sometimes. Mawgan secretly loves her mother but she was so upset and angry when Mrs Cade went to live in Oz. I was amazed when she decided to fly out with us.'

'We wondered how you all got on together.

86

There wasn't a fight, then?'

'No. Mawgan booked into a posh hotel nearby while we stayed with Mrs Cade and her partner. Mawgan travelled business class, of course, so we didn't have to put up with her en route.'

I roll my eyes and Andi blows out a breath. 'Phew, imagine being stuck with her for twenty-six hours? Anyway, it was OK and Mrs Cade was thrilled to have us there, after all this time. But Andi says Mawgan's been acting strangely since we all got back to Cornwall. Even her dad has started seeing a new woman, who's far too nice for him, and seems to be making him slightly more human too. It looks serious to me and I wouldn't be surprised if Mr Cade's girlfriend moves in at some point, so Mawgan won't be First Lady in the house any more. Basically, she's on her own and everyone around her is being happy.'

'She's only herself to blame.' Cal says the thing I'm thinking.

Robyn shrugs. 'Yeah, I know, but I think if we announce our engagement now, Mawgan might flip.'

'You can't hide your happiness away for the sake of someone else,' I say.

'True, but we need time to enjoy it first and make some plans, then we'll sound out Andi's dad and tell my mum and, maybe, my dad. Why does it have to be so difficult? We're not hurting anyone else; we only want to be happy.'

'I don't know. Life and love's compli-cated . . . ' I slide a glance at Cal. 'What else can I say?'

'Nothing. It's been great to share the news with someone. I knew I could trust you both to keep the secret. Thanks.' Robyn grins. 'It's getting late. I ought to get Ruby from your stable, Cal. I don't ride her enough these days so today was the ideal opportunity. I should get home because Andi's coming to Dad's to pick me up and take me back to the flat.'

'Shall I ride back to your dad's with you? It's getting dark and Dexter needs some exercise too. I can't persuade Demi to learn to ride him, no matter how hard I try.'

I put out my tongue and they both laugh. They know I don't like horses and I'm still scared of Dexter, no matter how much Cal insists his horse is 'quiet as a mouse'. I'd rather ride a mouse, that's for sure.

With final hugs and thanks to Robyn for her help, I lock up the cafe while they ride off together. In our darkest days and when I was new to Kilhallon, Robyn was always kind and friendly to me, and Cal loves her dearly. Mawgan has already tried to stop her sister being happy once and I'm glad I played a small part in getting her to at least tolerate her sister's relationship with a Penwith. I can't believe Mawgan would make real trouble now. Then again, who knows? If she's bitter and twisted — and also lonely and hurt by everyone around her being happy — she could do anything. Let's hope I'm wrong.

9

It's Monday, the afternoon after the christening, and I'm sitting in the tiny kitchen of my dad and Rachel's cottage, cuddling Freya. A bottle steriliser and baby paraphernalia take up most of the space on the work surfaces but the newly fitted kitchen units, tiles and cooker gleam. Only the bare plaster walls would tell you that the whole ground floor of the cottage has had to be completely refurbished. Through the kitchen window, the waves lap gently against the slipway opposite. It's almost impossible to believe that the water came so far over the harbour and into the house itself.

Rachel places a cold glass of juice and a plate of biscuits within my reach. 'There you go. Sorry, they're not homemade, like yours.'

I laugh. 'They look delicious, anyway. I'll have one when I've finished holding Freya. The cottage is looking good. I love the new units.'

Rachel sips her juice and looks around with pride. 'Yes, it's such a relief to be back to some kind of normal.'

Freya gurgles and I laugh. 'Thanks for finding time to see me today.'

'No problem and it's lovely to see you again so soon, though I'm gagging to know what this 'mystery proposition' is. Ever since you texted me this morning, I've thought about nothing else. I hope things are OK?'

'They're fine. I just wanted to see you in person. Yesterday when you told me you wanted to start your own business, I had an idea and I wasn't sure whether to mention it. Not because I don't think you can do it, but because I don't want you to feel under pressure.'

She puts down her mug and frowns. 'Under pressure about *what*?'

'About what I'm going to say, because I know you have so much on your plate and it may be too soon or you might feel obliged and I'm babbling on, aren't I?'

Rachel groans. 'Demi, please, just come out with it before I explode with tension.'

'OK. I just wondered if you, er, would like to organise Lily Craig and Ben Trevone's wedding. They're holding it at Kilhallon, although that's top secret for now.'

Slowly, Rachel lowers her glass. Her eyes widen. 'You're having Lily Craig and Ben Trevone at Kilhallon? Oh my God.'

'Yes. I'm finding it hard to believe, myself. Cal's producer friend, Isla, set it up.'

'Wow, that's fantastic but *me*? Organise a wedding for two film stars?'

'Well, I could ask Freya instead if you like.' On cue, Freya snuffles and lets out a tiny cry. 'I think she'd do it, wouldn't you?'

Freya sighs happily but Rachel is still gobsmacked. Eventually she manages to reply to me. 'Does Cal know you've asked me to do it?'

'Um. Not yet, but I know he'll be over the moon to have some professional help.'

'He might not be so thrilled when you tell him

that it's me. And strictly speaking I'm not a professional. It's an amazing offer and I know I said I'd done lots of events, but a big celebrity wedding? You think I could handle it?'

Now I'm panicking slightly that I've put Rachel in a difficult position, but it's too late to back out and I know she could do it. Although, looking at the amount of baby equipment around, I might have *slightly* underestimated the level of stress involved in organising a big wedding and looking after Freya. 'I wouldn't ask if I didn't. It's our first time too.'

'Which is why you should have someone really experienced, even though I'd absolutely kill to do it. I ought to be honest with you.'

'You *do* have lots of experience and I don't think it's a risk. You said yourself you were keen to take on more than an admin role and it sounds to me like you were already doing the events planning at Trevarrian. I hoped the planning would fit in with looking after Freya until the wedding itself and we could all help you on the day. But if it will stress you out and you'd rather not, I totally understand. I maybe haven't factored in Freya quite as much as I should have.'

Freya snuffles and mutters. Rachel bursts out laughing. 'Yes, the Freya Factor is going to be an issue.' She toys with a biscuit as if she doesn't know what to do with it while I kick myself for being so naïve about the work involved with such a young baby.

'Wow. I guess it *will* stress me but it'd also be a fantastic experience. However, if I was even to contemplate doing it, I'd need to talk to your dad and my parents first because they'd need to give me a lot of support with babysitting.'

'I'm sorry. I haven't thought it through.'

'Oh, I'd love to do it. I may regret saying that . . . Look, let me think about it over the next few days and speak to Gary and my mum and dad. If I agree to it, I want to be sure I won't let you down. Is that OK?'

'It's fine. More than fine. Please don't feel you'd let me down if you can't.'

Relief floods through me. I'd lain awake wondering if I should ask her and secretly, it is a bit of a risk for us as well. But it also seems like the best solution around right now. 'I trust you more than any of the wedding planners I've seen,' I say, not mentioning that most are already booked. 'You know us and Kilhallon better than anyone. You have contacts from your job and you won't have to worry about budgets too much. It'll also be a fantastic way to start your business. Imagine the publicity you can get from organising Lily Craig and Ben Trevone's wedding.'

She grimaces. 'I am. Eeek, it sounds so exciting but also *huge*.'

Freya stares at me, wondering . . . I smile at her and blow her a kiss.

'Yeah, I keep thinking the same myself but without someone like you at the helm, someone we can rely on, it definitely *would* be a disaster.'

'Whatever I decide, thanks for the chance.'

Freya gurgles though whether it's a 'yes' or 'no' from her, I'm not sure.

'Cal gave me a chance. Eva and Isla gave us chances too. I was terrified at the time but when someone offers you an opportunity, you have to take it. And after all,' I say, kissing Freya's adorable little nose, 'you are family now, Rachel. I'm sorry for the way we started off.'

'That's in the past.'

'I know but I have to say this. My life is different now, thanks to Kilhallon, but I also have more understanding of what it's like to feel strongly about someone special. I wasn't ready to believe you felt that way about Dad, that you cared about him so much.'

'I love him.' She smiles. 'Hard to believe but I do.'

'I know.'

'And you love Cal very much, don't you?'

There's a sharp tug of emotion when I think of Cal. 'Yes, but don't tell him how much.'

'Because you're scared?'

'Yes, and it's early days, and I don't know what's going to happen.'

'Who does?' She looks around her at the bare walls and freshly painted doors. 'If the floods hadn't damaged our house, we'd never have spent Christmas at Kilhallon with you, and you might never have been reconciled with your dad again, And — whew — I *definitely* wouldn't have been asked to organise a celebrity wedding.'

10

A Tuesday lunchtime was the only time that Lily and Ben could spare for our 'cosy lunch' but it suits me because it's one of the closed days at the cafe. The place Lily chose is called a 'cafe' too, but that label is the only thing it has in common with Demelza's. It specialises in seafood, has a ton of awards and stars and is run by a celebrity chef who I've heard of because he's a friend of Eva Spero. It overlooks a beautiful, if very popular, beach in an upmarket resort, although on a breezy March weekday there are only a handful of people out walking their dogs on the sand.

I slot the battered old Land Rover between a Bentley convertible and a Range Rover with a personalised plate as Harry drives into the car park in the BMW.

Cal turns to me. 'Ready for this?'

'Are you?'

'What do you think?'

'That if I wasn't driving, I'd need several very large glasses of wine.'

'Look on it as research,' he says with a grin. 'And to think you could have been working at a place like this in Brighton instead of serving pasties to pensioners.'

'At this precise moment, I wish I was two hundred miles away.'

We get out and join Mawgan who is hugging

and kissing Lily and Ben.

'How are the wedding plans going? I can't wait to meet Rachel,' Lily says.

'Fine, all in hand.'

I try to sound as if Rachel is the expert wedding planner we had in mind all long, not the slightly terrified one who only confirmed she'd take the job a couple of days ago. She and my dad popped round with Freya early one evening to tell us the good news. Rachel's mum and dad are retired and were only too happy to see more of their granddaughter and Dad has promised to step in when required, so we're on. I almost jumped up and down in relief. There's still plenty of room for things to go wrong but if we all pull together, we'll get there somehow. Not that I'm revealing my 'suck it and see' strategy to Lily, of course . . .

Rachel has already spoken to her by phone and we've arranged for them to meet up next month at Demelza's. To be honest, I'd rather not talk about our plans in front of Mawgan but I can't refuse to answer Lily's questions.

Mawgan smiles. 'Hello,' she says and then to my amazement, and horror, kisses me and Cal on both cheeks as if she's our oldest friends. I'm not a kissy, huggy person though I'm learning posh people do this all the time to people they barely know. But being kissed by Mawgan makes me feel as if I'm about to turn into stone.

Cal is gobsmacked. Mawgan pecked his cheek before he could move and his arms hang limply by his sides. Maybe she really has zapped him.

'Mwah, mwah. Isn't this a-mazing? Who'd

95

have thought we'd all get together like this?'

With gritted teeth, I watch Mawgan simper over Ben and Lily.

Lily puts Louie onto the tarmac of the car park. Mawgan reaches down to stroke him and after a brief mini growl, he lets her briefly touch him.

She laughs. 'He's so sweet. I'm thinking of getting a dog,' she says.

I manage to squash down a gasp as Mawgan loathes dogs and managed to have me sacked last year after an 'incident' with Mitch. However, since she's Ben's NBF, I'm determined to be on my best behaviour and resist the urge to ask if it she's getting a Pit bull.

Louie's definitely had enough 'cuddles' and strains on his leash, sniffing strange scents on the air.

Lily hangs on to Louie who is surprisingly strong for such a little dog. 'How lovely to get everyone together for a proper catch-up,' she says, letting him explore the car park. 'It's a shame Isla couldn't make it but she's shooting in Scotland and Luke's busy with his new business in London. Never mind, the six of us will have a lovely time.'

'Six? Is Harry joining us?' I say as we walk up the steps that lead to the restaurant.

Ben snorts. 'Lily means the five of us and Louie. Harry never eats with us. It's not his thing and he's too busy keeping an eye out for us.'

'Harry's quite shy. He doesn't like to get involved in our social lives,' Lily says, glancing at Harry who is closing the tailgate of the BMW.

'He can take Louie for a crap too,' Ben says.

'Ben!' Lily hits Ben on the arm.

Ben smirks. 'It's true. The dog will need a run. He can't be expected to sit in the restaurant all the time.'

I must admit, Louie is straining on his leash, and I know he'd far rather race about on the flat sands and chase waves than have to behave in a smart eaterie.

'I don't mind taking him for a quick walk now,' I say, realising that I'd far rather be dog walking on the beach than making small talk with Ben and Mawgan. Lily is lovely and she is our VIP but . . .

'Thanks, but I'll let Harry exercise him and bring him back for lunch. If he needs another run,' Lily says, daring Ben to mention anything cruder, 'then I'll take him myself. I don't get anywhere near enough quality time with him and this is a beautiful beach. Harry!' she calls.

Immediately, he jogs over.

'Would you mind very much taking Louie for a walk and when he's had enough, please bring him up to the restaurant?'

'No problem,' says Harry.

Lily lowers her voice. 'Have you got any of those little scented bags for his you-know-whats?'

Harry pats his pocket. 'Always prepared.'

Ben lets out a breath of disgust. 'You don't catch me scooping up dog shit in a scented bag. Imagine if a pap saw that?'

Just in time, I manage not to laugh. 'They'd think you were being a responsible dog owner.'

Lily *does* laugh at him. 'Totally! And hopefully there are no paps around because no one knows we're here.'

'Can we get into the restaurant?' Ben wheedles, then puts his arm around Lily, ignoring Harry. 'You must be frozen, babe.'

'Louie is so cute. What a happy little dog,' I say to Lily as we head for the restaurant.

'Awww. Thank you. I love him to bits. Even more than I love Ben.' She giggles. 'Only joking.'

'Oh, I know exactly what you mean. If there was a fire at Kilhallon, I don't know who I'd save first: Cal or Mitch.'

'I hope we never have to choose.'

We both laugh and Ben stares at us, frowning at our giggles. 'What's so funny?'

'Nothing,' we chorus.

I don't think Mawgan likes Lily and I sharing a giggle, judging by the disgusted expression that flashes over her face, but she manages to recover fast. 'I love the Rockpool,' she says, trying to steer the conversation back to her. 'It's my absolute favourite place to eat in Cornwall. We bring clients here all the time, of course, and we'd come more often if it was closer to St Trenyan. Look, there's Carlos, the maître d'.'

Wreathed in smiles, Carlos greets us at the door and swiftly ushers us into a private alcove overlooking the sweep of beach. While he fusses over Ben and Lily, he makes no sign of recognising Mawgan even when he takes our orders for drinks. Our table — more of a small room — has a fantastic view of the waves thundering up the sand. Newporth is an up-and-coming resort with a lot of expensive flats converted from former hotels and a trendy surf scene. The tide is out and the waves seem miles away on its huge flat beach. The breakers look like wavelets from here, but I know they'll be fierce. If you listen hard, you can hear the dull but constant roar as they pound the beach.

I try to spot Louie and Harry, half wishing I was outside with them on the sand.

Mawgan is talking to Ben and Cal about something to do with their childhood 'games' which seem to involve Mawgan offering to 'watch out for' the younger kids in return for their pocket money. Ben starts boasting about the time he tried to shoot a seagull with a bow and arrow, which Mawgan seems to find hilarious.

Cal is tight-lipped and clearly losing the will to live but is trying to restrain himself for the sake of Lily, me and our business. Running a cafe and holiday resort means welcoming all sorts, with their varied points of view and I've learned to shut my ears to anything that's harmless and not offensive. Cal has a short fuse and struggles far more with that than me. I don't know how long he can last with Mawgan and Ben without saying or doing something he regrets, but he'll have to manage for now.

On the other hand, I'm warming to Lily more and more. She's transfixed by the view over the beach and the big skies. Even the slate-grey clouds on the horizon only add to the dramatic scene. I have to keep reminding myself that I live with this sight every day, but it has a magical effect on many visitors who have to go home to towns and cities, miles from the sea.

She pushes her chair back. 'Look at that view. I think I'm going to take my drink outside until lunch arrives.'

'It's freezing out there, babe,' says Ben, tearing himself away from Mawgan for a moment.

'I'll be fine,' Lily says firmly.

'I'll come outside with you,' I say, relishing the chance to get away from Mawgan, even for a few minutes. Cal will have to fend for himself. This is my chance to talk weddings with Lily without Mawgan listening in and interfering.

After collecting our coats from the maître d' again, we head out on the balcony, which has glass sides so you can take in the full glory of the view. Lily leans on the metal balustrade, shading her eyes against the light reflected off the silvery sand and sea. She pulls her red hair out of her face and takes a big breath of the salty air. 'Oh, this is gorgeous, but I hope Louie isn't too cold. I meant to ask Harry to put his jacket on — oh, I see he has.' She points towards the large man and tiny dog playing on the beach.

Harry hurls a ball for Louie from a flinger and the little French Bulldog races after it.

I smile. 'He looks like he's having a fantastic time.'

'They both do,' she says. 'Harry loves Louie. I wish Ben did but he's allergic to dogs. He only puts up with Louie for my sake. You know, I'm definitely going for a walk on the beach myself later. If I put on Harry's beanie hat and Ben's dark glasses I doubt anyone would even notice me, would they?'

'It's a very quiet time of year. I think you'd be safe.'

'After lunch I will then, and I don't care if someone does see me,' she declares although I think she's trying to convince herself more than me. She sighs. 'Sometimes I wish I wasn't famous. I know I'm incredibly fortunate but I feel as if I've opened a box that I can never close again. Until I'm old and ugly and not famous any more, of course.'

'That won't happen.'

'It will. It always does. I'm not a brilliant actress and I'll never be able to carry off the heavyweight character roles that will keep my career going.'

'Don't say that. I'm sure you could.'

She smiles. 'You're very sweet but I'm only being realistic . . . I turn thirty in a couple of years and there are thousands of gorgeous young actresses all waiting to take my place.' She glances at Ben who's laughing loudly at something Mawgan is saying. 'Ben will be around for much longer. His shelf life will go on for decades if his agent helps him choose wisely, and if he's lucky of course. We both need to be very, *very* lucky in this business and hope the projects we're working on will be hits or we're stuffed, basically.'

If you'd told me I'd feel sorry for a wealthy, famous, beautiful actress, I'd never have believed you, but in Lily's case, I do. I'm glad I'm happy to run my own tiny 'empire', as Cal calls it. I'm thankful to have my friends and, now, my family around me and to have Cal, of course. I don't know what I'd do without Demelza's — or him. I'm glad he's safe with me at Kilhallon and doesn't have to go back to Syria.

Lily's delicate fingers rest on my arm. 'Demi? Are you OK?'

'Fine. Yes. Sorry, I was miles away. When we're on our own later — I mean you, me and Ben — we can confirm a time to meet Rachel to discuss the wedding plans. You did say you could try and fit in a few hours at Kilhallon next week and I think it's really important that you meet Rachel in person. She wants to get a feel for exactly the type of ceremony you want and sort out the finer details. She's got so many ideas but we both need your feedback. It is *your* day. And Ben's, of course.'

'Of course. We'll definitely come over, or at least I will. Ben's got some post-production work to do on his new film. I'll get my assistant, Jade, to double check my schedule but hopefully I can spare a few hours to fly in next week. Oh, look! Louie's in the sea! He normally hates the water . . . '

'He seems to be having a fantastic time chasing the waves,' I say. 'Listen to him barking. He loves the beach, just like Mitch.'

Harry throws the ball along the surf line, making sure the little dog doesn't get drenched. Louie dashes this way and that, yapping at the waves, fetching his ball and teasing Harry with it. Harry shouts at Louie who barks with pure joy.

Lily leans on the balcony. 'I'm not sure who's enjoying it most, Harry or Louie,' she says.

'Both. I love playing on the beach with Mitch.

He adores it and so does Cal.'

'You're lucky. Ben isn't an animal person. I don't think he'll do the owl thing.'

'Maybe you can have the owl land on Harry's arm or your best man's so he can hand over the rings.'

'Oh. Yes, that's an idea . . . yes, I'll ask Ben.'

Ben pops his head around the door and pulls a face. 'Ask Ben what?'

'If lunch is ready yet,' Lily says smoothly. She knows how to manage him though I'm mystified about what she sees in him. Apart from him being a rich, up-and-coming movie star like her, of course.

'The answer is 'yes' and, Lily, your hair looks a right mess in this wind. I don't care at all, but what if a pap spotted us?'

He closes the door. Lily rolls her eyes at him. 'Come on then, let's eat.'

11

There's no point me denying that the food is great. It's beautifully presented with delicious flavours and you can really taste every ingredient. Part of me would like to try out some of the ideas at Demelza's but I'm only an amateur cook and Demelza's is *actually* a cafe not a supercool restaurant.

Yet the food isn't at the foremost of my mind. Mawgan is — and not for the reasons you might think. I've never seen her so subdued or polite — in fact, so relatively 'normal' — and that worries me. If I was being generous, I'd like to think that her visit to her mum in Australia had made her happy and mellowed her. Andi and Robyn said she was surprisingly docile while she was away.

But . . . this is Mawgan and I can't forget how she's relentlessly pursued Cal and tried to wreck his plans and hurt him over the past year.

'How was your visit to your mum in Oz?' Ben asks.

Mawgan pauses, halfway to spearing a peeled prawn. I freeze and even Cal pays attention.

She smiles. 'Sydney was amazing, of course. We had Christmas dinner on a very exclusive luxury yacht in the harbour.'

'Cool. How is your mum? I always liked her. Shame she and your dad split up.' Oh my God, does Ben have any idea he's skating on thin ice?

Mawgan smiles and stabs the prawn. 'She's OK.'

'Still living with that new bloke?'

Cal shoots me a look but I clamp my lips together. We both know that her mum's past affair with Mr Penwith and her new partner are still raw wounds to Mawgan. She could lash out at any moment.

The prawn trembles on the tines of her fork 'They have a fantastic house overlooking Manly beach. I've been thinking of investing in some property there myself. Have you been to Sydney? We watched the New Year fireworks from the best hotel in the Rocks. You've probably been there, Ben?'

'Yeah. A couple of times, and to New Zealand. We did some filming for *Knife Edge* there. Loved it.'

Mawgan pops the prawn whole into her mouth as Ben tells us about his fitness-training regime for *Knife Edge*. Having moved the conversation away from her mum, Mawgan cheers up. She seems far happier sharing more of her childhood stories with Ben. Admittedly, some of them are so Mawgan-ish that I find I'm laughing for the wrong reasons. However, she hasn't made a single dig at Cal or me yet. She's chatted with Cal about Kilhallon and sounded so enthusiastic and complimentary about our 'achievements' — even offering to help with organising the wedding — that anyone would think she was our best friend. It's all a show for Lily and Ben, I'm sure, but for a nanosecond, even I find myself wondering if Mawgan really has turned over a new leaf.

Then I come to my senses.

It was no use hoping that we could discuss the wedding plans privately away from Mawgan because Lily and Ben want to talk about their ideas. That's hardly surprising and their time is precious so I suck it up, making notes and arranging for Lily to meet Rachel at the cafe. Mawgan listens closely, but doesn't offer too many suggestions of her own, which I ought to be grateful for. Finally, we finish our amazing puddings, one of which is a lavender-scented crème brulee that I'd love to try out at Kilhallon in a simpler way. Lily didn't have any dessert, of course, and Mawgan had vowed she 'couldn't possibly fit any more in' but has left her plate cleaner than Mitch's dinner bowl.

As the staff serves coffee and a chamomile tea for Lily, a lean guy with an impressive ginger beard and wearing chef's whites appears at our table. I recognise him as Nathan Trevallion, the head chef and owner of the 'cafe'. He appears regularly in the Cornish lifestyle mags and on regional TV. Mawgan's taste buds seem to revive again.

'How was your meal?' he asks.

'Awesome. I loved the samphire butter on the sea bass, didn't you, Ben?'

'Yeah. Must try it at home,' Ben says.

'I bet you're a brilliant cook,' Mawgan tells Ben, in an awestruck voice.

'We've got a chef, most of the time,' Ben says. 'But I can do a Sunday roast.'

'He's brilliant at roasts, with all the trimmings,

not that I can eat them, but when we have friends round, they love it.'

'Sounds good to me. Everyone should know how to cook a good family roast. Who taught you that? Your mum?' Nathan asks.

Ben snorts. 'No. Our bodyguard, Harry.'

'Harry likes cooking?' I ask.

'Yeah — and baking. He and his partner, Giles, are always at it. They're like Mary Berry and Paul Hollywood,' Ben snorts.

Lily hits him. 'Don't be so horrible. You loved learning how to cook roast beef and a chicken. You weren't laughing when you made that blackberry and apple crumble.' Lily pats her tiny flat tummy. 'Not that I tasted more than a morsel, of course.'

'Well done, mate. Crumbles are a staple pud. What about you?' Nathan addresses me as Ben folds his arms, obviously mortified to have been outed as a crumble expert.

'Well, the whole meal was amazing and I loved the hake curry.'

Nathan smiles at me. 'Did you? It's one of our signature dishes.'

'It was delicious, so tasty. I've tried it with monkfish but not hake. It works really well, doesn't it? The textures and flavours were fantastic.'

'You can use any firm white fish. We decide exactly what goes in it, like the rest of the daily menu, after we've checked out the best quality fish that landed that morning.'

'Totally. I try to use fresh local produce as much as possible,' I say, and then stop when I realise I might sound a bit up myself. A super chef like Nathan won't be interested in the goings on of what is effectively a teashop.

'Demi has her own cafe,' Lily says, before I can change the subject.

'Really? Where's that, then?' Nathan asks, his voice lifting in genuine interest.

I glance at Mawgan, expecting a snigger but she has the face of an angel. On the other hand, I'm squirming. Even though I'm proud of Demelza's, I would never put myself in the same league as the Rockpool Cafe.

'Um. It's based on the coastal path at Kilhallon Park. It's called Demelza's.'

He frowns and then smiles. 'Ah yes, I've heard of it.'

'Really?' I almost drop off my chair in amazement.

'Sure. You must be Demelza herself, then?'

'Yes . . . and this is my partner. My business partner, Cal, who owns Kilhallon.'

'The cafe is all Demi's doing. I claim no credit,' Cal says.

'Good to meet you, mate. You're lucky to have Demi running your place. I've heard good things about her from my friend, Eva. You should have introduced yourself when you came in,' he tells me.

'Oh my God. I can't believe Eva mentioned me to you.'

He laughs. 'Why not? She was talking about your joint canine cookbook when I had lunch with her in London a couple of weeks ago. She's been trying to see if I'm interested in stocking your doggy treats if they go into production. Sounds like a good idea and we have a lot of dog owners using the beach bar and cafe downstairs so I may well be in touch.'

'Wow. Thanks. We find the doggy treats are super popular.'

'I didn't know you did a dog menu! Louie would love it. I think we'll invite dogs to the wedding. Louie could wear a mini tux and your Mitch could wear a bow tie. That would be brilliant!'

Ben's face is a picture and Mawgan's eyes narrow briefly, but Nathan seems intrigued.

'I may give these dog treats a try, then. Hope to see you again soon.'

He turns to the real stars and starts chatting to Ben and Lily. They pose for photos with him and he has a quick word with Mawgan who gushes about the food. Samphire butter wouldn't melt in her mouth today but I'm not fooled. She's up to something, and I'd bet the cafe on it.

When the photos have finished, it's time to leave. Lily calls Harry and arranges to meet him and Louie on the beach. The sun is out and the light has that dazzling brightness of spring. I'm feeling buzzed after Nathan's comments about Eva. I'm realising that it truly is an amazing thing to have a celebrity wedding at Kilhallon. Now that Rachel's on board, my confidence that the event will go well has soared. If only Mawgan wasn't involved, life would be perfect.

We all walk onto the beach, with Louie still full of energy.

Lily crouches down to cuddle Louie. 'Has he

been a good boy? Have you, Louie?'

'He's had a whale of a time,' Harry says. 'I've given him a drink of water.'

'Good. Has he . . . ?'

'Everything's normal,' Harry replies solemnly.

'You little star. Oh, Ben, let's Instagram Louie with the beach behind us and post it on his account.'

'Won't people know where we are from that?' Ben asks anxiously.

'If they can work it out. But we'll be long gone by then. Take his lead off, Ben, and give him to me.'

With a sigh, Ben unclips Louie's lead from its harness. He tries to scoop him up but Louie senses freedom and is obviously having none of it. He wriggles out of Ben's hands and is off up the beach like a greyhound towards the large expanse of rock pools at the far side of the beach.

'Hey! You little sod! Come back.'

'What have you let him run away for, Ben?'

'I didn't know he'd do it! He's so naughty. Harry — fetch him.'

'He'll come back,' Harry says and whistles and calls Louie, but Louie's far too happy exploring a large piece of seaweed.

'Louie!' Lily cries and starts to jog after him but her heeled boots sink into the sand.

'I'll get him,' says Harry, striding over the sand towards Louie, who has found a large rock pool he wants to explore on the far side of the beach. He scampers along the rocks away from us, skirting the edge of the pool, nosing the weed and mussels, obviously having a fine time.

'Louie! Bad boy!' Lily calls as the little dog paddles through the seawater-filled rock crevices. He pays no attention to anyone's calls. Nose down, he clambers over the rocks like a miniature mountain goat. I don't blame him; he probably doesn't get this kind of fun day out too often.

Ben groans as Louie wanders further along the rocks towards the sea. 'Jesus. He'll stink on the way home!'

Ben's probably right and I can't help but want to laugh. 'We could wash him down under the beach shower. He'll come back soon. He must be tired by now, but I don't think he wants to go home yet.'

Ben zips up his jacket. 'No, but some of us do.'

Far from Louie getting tired, ten minutes later he's still paddling in and out of the rock pools with no sign of returning. I'm convinced he's decided to stay in Cornwall forever.

'This is getting ridiculous,' says Ben, standing with his arms folded while Cal, Harry and I try to coax the dog to us with sticks and his ball. Louie ignores us and even Lily when she climbs up the rocks to join us.

'Be careful, babe!' Ben shouts, staying on the beach below with Mawgan. I don't think he wants to get his new pair of custom-made Converses wet.

'Stay back, Lily,' Harry orders. 'I'll get the little chap.'

'I'll help,' says Cal, whose Timberland boots make him one of the few of us dressed for

111

climbing over jagged rocks. Harry makes his way forward, calling the dog. He does sound funny, shouting to a small dog in his cut-glass accent. Mawgan stands by Ben, making concerned noises but basically doing nothing and I suspect secretly enjoying the drama.

My heart is in my mouth. 'Oh God, Lily, would be devastated if anything happened to Louie.'

Cal shakes his head. 'I'll go over to Harry and try and catch him or chase him towards you.'

'Be careful. Warn Harry too.'

'I will but if the dog goes in, it would be madness to jump in after him. The rocks are sharp there and there are dangerous rip currents this side of the beach, not to mention it'll be bloody freezing.'

Cal climbs over the pools to the far end of the rocks to join Harry.

'Is the tide coming in?' Lily asks, now balanced precariously on a rock next to me in her heeled boots. 'Because some of those waves over there look very big. I don't want Louie being frightened.'

'It is but Louie's well back,' I say, although I've been a bit worried about some of the breakers for a few minutes now. Louie has wandered to the very end of the rocks and the tide is coming in fast. It's not so much him being scared by the surf that worries me as him being washed away. We need to catch him soon.

'We'll get him,' I call to Lily and pick my way towards Cal. I'm in low-heeled boots myself but they're not the best things for clambering over seaweed-covered rocks.

'Oh, please keep him safe! Those waves could easily wash him off and he's only tiny.' There's desperation in Lily's voice as we watch Cal and Harry try to coax Louie towards them.

Spray seems to be breaking over their heads now and they must be getting soaked. They're shouting to Louie who is standing on top of a high rock as if he's king of the castle. I think he's bitten off more than he can chew. He's wet through and trembling and lets out a pathetic yap.

'Oh my God, he's stuck!' Lily's voice reaches me over the roar of the surf slamming into the rocks. A few people are now watching us from the cliff above the beach and the restaurant balcony. So much for being discreet, but we have to get Louie fast.

Slithering and sliding, I manage to get within a few yards of Cal and Harry who are trying to coax Louie down from his perch while holding on to the rocks as the waves break over them.

'Come on, old boy,' Harry calls, holding out his arms.

'You've had your fun, now let's have you back,' Cal adds. His hair is wet and there's an edge of real anxiety in his voice.

'Louie!' Harry shouts, holding out his arms.

Louie shivers on the rock, lets out a bark and then launches himself at Harry. Harry's knees buckle and he seems to have Louie safely in his arms but then a wave hits him and he totters. Louie barks furiously, Harry shouts something and then a massive surge of surf engulfs him and the dog. Lily screams. Seconds later there's only boiling foam where dog and man had been standing.

12

Lily screams again. 'Louie. Noooo!'

I stumble but recover as she knocks my arm and starts to scramble over the rocks towards Cal and the crashing waves.

'Wait!' I shout, but Lily is wading through the rock pools, almost lost in spray as the breakers smash against the rocks. Cal is yelling too, scanning the sea at his feet while trying to avoid the waves. Oh God, please don't let him go in too. I remember when Mitch went in an angry sea last summer, Cal went in too and was drunk and we all almost drowned. I shiver at the memory. I was terrified for Cal and Mitch, and it was summer then. This sea is even angrier and far colder.

'Call 999,' I shout to Ben and Mawgan, standing on the beach. 'Get the RNLI out.'

They pull out their phones but I'm afraid that by the time the rescue boat arrives, it will be way too late.

'I think I can see them,' Cal warns, 'Lily, keep back!'

But Lily either can't hear him or is too blinded by panic to listen as she slithers over the rocks to reach him. I follow her, getting myself soaked in a rock pool in the process. 'I can't lose them. I can't. I c-c-c can't. Someone do *something*,' she sobs, teetering on the edge of the rocks.

Cal takes her arm. 'No. It'd be crazy for

115

anyone else to go in. We have to let the RNLI do their job.'

'Where are they? Where?'

'I saw Harry and Louie a second ago bobbing around that big rock. And the lifeboat station is over on the far side of the beach. They'll be here soon.' Cal sounds frantic and I definitely can't see the lifeboat launching yet.

Luckily I can see Ben on his phone and a few people gathering next to him. But even if the RNLI launch right this instant it will be a few more minutes before they get here. Harry and the dog could have drowned by then. It takes moments in this freezing water.

'Look!' I shout and point to a large jagged rock a few yards ahead of us. Harry is swimming towards it but keeps being beaten back by the surf. 'It's Harry, and Louie too. I'm sure I spotted him.'

'Where?' Cal shouts and Lily wails.

Harry has disappeared again and I wonder if I imagined my glimpse of Louie.

'Why isn't anyone going to help them? Why not?' Lily shouts to Cal.

Cal wavers. Lily grabs his arm and screams at him and then he starts to take off his jacket.

'No. No, Cal!' My shout makes him hesitate. 'You can't go in there. It will only make things worse.'

'There's Louie!' Lily screams and without warning takes a flying leap from the rocks into the angry sea.

I might throw up. There are now three of them in the water and Cal is taking off his boots too

116

despite my protests. I scramble forward, ignoring the sharp rocks and the slimy wet pools until I can grab him. 'Don't go in, Cal, *please*,' I beg.

'I need to do *something*.' He sounds completely desperate.

'Look. The lifeboat's on its way!' I point to the station across the other side of the beach where the orange inshore boat is now clearly visible on the slipway. 'They're coming. Please don't go in and make it even worse.'

Cal holds his head and shouts 'Shittttttt!' but I'm so relieved because he realises I'm right. My relief lasts a second because I've spotted Lily bobbing up in the surf and flailing her arms. There's no sign of Harry or Louie and I start to fear the worst.

'I'll stay here to try and keep sight of them,' Cal says.

'Be careful.'

'I think I see Harry — and look, there's Louie!' he shouts.

Louie has somehow scrambled up the cliff at the edge of the beach and is shivering on a tiny ledge. Harry's head pops up a few yards away, making for Lily who's being tossed around by the waves. There's a high-pitched whine as the lifeboat zooms towards us across the bay. Please, please let them get here in time. *Please.*

Cal points across the water at the spot where Lily can just about be seen, guiding the lifeboat towards her. She's like a little ragdoll, picked up by the swell and dropped again, and she's very quiet. Harry comes into view. There's red on his face — he's cut himself — but he's somehow struggled free of the currents and has almost reached Lily. The lifeboat is closer now and Cal shouts: 'There, over there,' holding his arm straight to mark the spot.

Fighting the churning surf, Harry reaches Lily and pulls her onto her back and starts to kick for the shore. The lifeboat nears them but Harry is already dragging Lily though the surf. Ben wades into the water but is almost knocked over by another large wave. Mawgan seems to have gone in at the edge of the sea too but I'm way more concerned about Louie again now.

'I'm going down to the beach to help,' Cal tells me.

'I'll keep an eye on Louie to make sure he stays put.'

'OK, but be careful and don't do anything stupid,' Cal warns before clambering back over the rocks towards the beach.

I make my way back towards Louie's perch by keeping close to the overhanging cliffs at the very edge of the rocks. The cliffs are crumbly and there are danger signs up warning of rock falls but Louie is terrified and I daren't leave him. The spray of the largest waves spatters my hair so I press closer to the cliff and edge, as close as I dare get to the wet and shivering Louie. I'm not sure he can hear me but I call him, gently, coaxing him. He creeps along the narrow ledge towards me and then, to my huge relief, jumps down onto a lower, broader ledge. Like a tiny mountain goat, he makes his way under the cliff overhang towards me.

As soon as he's within reach, I scoop him up

and tuck him inside my coat.

'You've scared us to death, boy,' I say, soothing him and rubbing his soaked fur through my coat. He licks my hand. 'At least you'll live to fight another day.'

On the beach, Cal is helping Harry carry Lily out of the surf. A drenched Ben is lying on the sand, with Mawgan kneeling over him, appearing to give him the kiss of life. Is he in a bad way too after a wave knocked him over? It's Lily who concerns me most. Fortunately the RNLI have leapt out of their boat and are now taking over from Cal. Two paramedics are running down the sand towards everyone. Realising I'm shivering as much as little Louie, I make my way back over the rocks to the beach.

13

Over an hour later, I'm finally allowed into Lily's hospital room where she's still in a gown but sitting on the edge of the bed, her legs dangling. Though pale and shaken, she's fine after a thorough checkup by the doctors at the nearest large hospital. Harry has already been discharged and is on the phone to some of Lily and Ben's people. Ben sits by Lily's bed, holding her hand, with a neat dressing on his tanned forehead.

'How's Louie?' she demands the second she spots me.

I give her an encouraging smile. 'Fine. A local vet checked him over and he's now having a rest with Cal in the Land Rover. Cal's fed him too. He had to have a pouch from the shop, not his special food. I hope that was OK?'

'Of course it was. I'm sooo thankful he's alive. Thank you so much for saving him. I don't know what I'd do if I lost him.'

'Well, I didn't save him really. He scrambled out himself in the end,' I say, embarrassed. 'How are you and Ben and Harry?'

'Harry's calling his boyfriend, Giles,' Ben says, scrolling through his phone, obviously having recovered very quickly from his 'ordeal' of being knocked over by a wave and 'cared for' by Mawgan.

'We don't *know* they're actually partners, Ben,' Lily cuts in.

Ben snorts. 'Don't be naïve, babe. They've lived together all the time he's been working for us and they're not brothers or cousins, that's for sure. They share a cottage near us in the Cotswolds and Giles has a gay pride sticker in his car.'

'I don't think it's right for us to discuss Harry's personal life.' Lily lowers her voice even though there's no one around to hear. 'Harry's had a tragic past. We ought to do a film about it. His father was an earl and when he was little they lived in a huge stately home in Gloucester-shire. But his dad lost a fortune in a mining venture in Argentina and then he was killed in a helicopter accident.'

'That's awful,' I say, not missing the fact that Lily is discussing Harry's personal problems in detail after trying to protect his privacy. Not that I mind hearing more of Harry's story, of course.

'Harry's brother, Piers, inherited the title and a load of debts so he sold what he could and went to work for an investment bank. Harry's technically an Honourable.'

Lily giggles but Ben snorts. 'He'd kill you if you mentioned that to his face. He'd die of embarrassment.'

'What's an Honourable?' I ask, not being an expert on aristocratic titles, surprisingly enough.

'It means the younger son of an earl or viscount. I had to do lots of research into the peerage for one of my roles,' Lily says, glaring at Ben and daring him to interrupt her. 'Harry's mum still lives in the dower house but she has to rent it off the tech company who own the big

121

mansion now. Harry joined the paras and was a major until he was injured in an explosion in Afghanistan so he left to work in a close protection company. We met Harry's brother and his mum at a party near where we live and they told us about Harry and that's how he started doing our security. He's amazing, really. I don't know what we'd do without him. Like today.'

Ben scrolls through his phone. 'He did actually fall in, babe. That's not exactly heroic and he did put you in danger. Why did you jump in after that bloody dog?'

'Don't start that again, Ben. Louie means everything to me.'

He glances up at her. 'Everything?'

'Not everything. You *all* mean a lot to me. Louie, you and Harry. I couldn't let him and Louie drown even though I know it was stupid now.' Lily reaches for his hand to reassure him.

'Harry and Louie were fine. What if I'd lost you? What would people have said? You put everyone in danger and God knows what might have happened if Mawgan hadn't dragged me out after I was knocked against that rock by the waves. *She* saved my life, no thanks to Saint Louie the mutt.'

Lily snatches her hand out of his. 'Sometimes I hate you, Ben Trevone!'

'Yeah, but what were you thinking of? Leaping in after a dog.'

'A dog *and* a human. Don't forget that Harry fell in while he was trying to help Louie. I was out of my mind with worry and I reacted instinctively.' She lies back on the bed and curls up, facing away from him. 'And I don't want to hear any more about it. I just want to go home.'

Hmm, I think, now is possibly not the best time to talk about their wedding. I also feel like pushing Ben back into a rock pool, and Mawgan with him. 'Um. I think I'd better give you some time on your own. I'm going to see how Louie is.'

Tears shining in her eyes, Lily turns back to me again. 'Oh, thank you for taking care of him. Do you mind waiting with him until we can collect him? I think they'll discharge me soon and our people are on their way, but I want him to be with someone he knows until then.'

Lily is still very pale. She's lucky to be alive and, possibly, I think the shock of her ordeal is starting to truly hit home. I smile. 'No problem. Louie is a sweetheart and I know Cal will love to have him for as long as possible.'

Well, a little white lie never hurt anyone, according to my Nana Demelza, so she'd be proud of me now. When I get back to the Land Rover, Cal is sitting in the driver's seat checking his phone but puts it away as soon as he spots me. Through the passenger window I see Louie nestled in a scruffy tartan rug on the passenger seat, with one corner pulled over his little body. My heart goes out to him and to Cal, who must have tucked him in.

Cal gets out. 'How's Lily?' he asks.

'Badly shaken up but more worried about her dog. How's he doing?'

'He's had another little stroll round the car park.' Cal pulls a face and points to a small plastic bag on the passenger seat. 'He seems none the worse for his swim but he's knackered now and having a kip. I don't blame him. What a day.'

'You're telling me.'

'How are the other humans?'

'Lily's waiting to be discharged. Ben's minor cut on the head has been stitched and Harry's fine and when I left I heard him in the corridor, on the phone to his boyfriend, Giles.'

'I thought that looking after Ben and Lily would have taken all his time up. They're like a pair of kids.'

I laugh. 'Harry and Giles live in a cottage near to Ben and Lily in the Cotswolds when Harry's not on the road with them. He has a tragic past, according to Lily.'

'Join the club,' says Cal, pulling me towards him and hugging me. 'For once it wasn't us in the water. I'm glad they're OK and happy to have you in one piece even if you are a little wet.'

He raises his eyebrows and I shake my head at his very naughty innuendo. It does remind me though that I'm still damp and starting to shiver in the cold evening air. Grimacing, I look down at my damp jeans, which are shrink wrapped to my thighs and in danger of cutting off my blood supply.

'You're soaked,' Cal murmurs.

'I've been too busy to do anything about it. You're still wet too.'

'I declined an offer of a gown from one of the nurses,' he says and pulls a face. 'I think their other patients needed them more.'

'Funny. The nurses didn't offer me one.'

'Maybe the prospect of you getting naked in front of them wasn't quite so appealing.' He gives me a wicked grin.

'You think they're interested in you when they have the chance of getting their hands on Ben Trevone?'

'It was worth a try . . . but you are wet and you have goosebumps on your goosebumps.' He nods at the thin top underneath my coat which clings to my breasts, showing my nipples.

'Even my knickers are wet after sitting in my soggy jeans for a couple of hours and the shops are all shut now, so I can't even buy last season's beachwear and a pair of Crocs,' I say, starting to shiver. 'Never mind. We'll warm up in the Land Rover on the way home.'

'We would if the heater wasn't shagged. I keep meaning to get it fixed. Hmm.' Cal rubs his face thoughtfully. 'Polly asked me to take some of her stuff to the charity shop in St Trenyan last week and I still haven't done it. It's better than nothing.'

Quietly, so as not to wake Louie, he opens the rear doors and points to a charity bag. I do hope the air ambulance charity shop won't mind us borrowing a few pieces.

I pull out a pair of leggings with holes in them. 'I think they might be relieved. Have you seen some of this stuff? It's only fit for the recycling skip.'

'It's dry and will keep us warm on the way home though,' he says. 'So hop in.'

We can't help making a bit of noise while we

125

take off our clothes and rummage through the bags but Louie dozes on in his makeshift doggy bed, knackered after his adventure.

'Tell you what,' he says, eyeing me up as I strip to my knickers. 'Let's forget getting dressed at all.'

'It's one way of keeping warm but what if Louie wakes up?'

'Good point, but I'm definitely going to have you as soon as we get home.'

We're not gonna make it that far, I think, drinking in the smooth tanned skin and muscled abs like a woman dying of thirst. Cal's down to his boxers and delves in the bag for a pair of ancient trousers. 'Jeez, I think these were my dad's.'

With a grimace, he pulls a pair of well-worn navy suit trousers over his calves and thighs. They're two sizes too big round the waist and a few inches too short in the leg. They look like they're about to fall down so he ties them up with a pink dressing gown cord. I giggle as he puts on a tatty olive sweatshirt with a fading logo on the front.

'Penwith Scything Festival 1998,' he says. 'I think it must have been Polly's partner's. Who does any scything these days?'

'No one I know. I think you look very stylish.' I grab a piece of clothing before I die of cold. 'Oh God, look at this.' I hold up a striped silky dress with a pie-crust collar, shoulder pads and ribbon at the neck. 'This was Polly's 'posh frock' when she was a teenager. She had it for Princess Diana's wedding street party in St Trenyan. She told me she couldn't bear to part with it until now but 'seeing as Prince William worked for the air ambulance' she didn't think HRH would mind, if she happened to be looking down.'

Cal shakes his head in disbelief but I'm desperate now and there's no way I'm squeezing back into those jeans, it would be like trying to put toothpaste back into the tube. I also grab a hoodie with a broken zip and pull that on over the top.

'Wow. I don't think I can keep my hands off you but I think you need these to complete your ensemble.'

Cal hands me a pair of fisherman's socks with holes in the toes.

'Oh, sexy.' I pull them on, grateful to have cosy feet again. 'I love your hipster trousers by the way. Very on trend.'

Cal glances down at his bare ankles poking out of the trousers. 'I think we need another fashion shoot.'

'Our wet boots will have to do because I'm not driving home in fluffy slippers and broken flip-flops.'

He kisses me over the open bag of clothes, which perfumes the air with a slightly musty scent. Louie is forgotten as we enjoy a wonderful warm snog surrounded by the contents of Polly's wardrobe.

'Why drive home yet at all? That lot will be ages.'

'You know, I think you're right.' My resolve melts, not that I have any resolve where Cal's concerned these days. We collapse in a heap on the floor of the Land Rover, with a pile of random garments for a bed. Cal tugs at the ribbon, pulling it loose and opening a modest 'V' in the dress. I slip my hands inside his trousers, which isn't hard considering they're much too big.

'I love you,' Cal whispers. 'Even looking like a crazy woman who went nuts in the charity shop.'

'Me too,' I whisper, warming up rapidly. 'Even smelling of mothballs.'

'Mmm.' Instead of diving on me, he hesitates and touches his forehead to mine. 'There's something I want to tell you.'

'Go on, then.'

Sharp yaps startle us and the Land Rover shakes as someone thumps the side.

'Louie! Louie! Have you missed me?'

We spring apart and I scramble to my knees.

Cal groans and hisses at me. 'It's Lily.'

'I know,' I mouth. 'We'd better get out.'

'Hello. Anyone in there? Oh, I hope they haven't locked Louie in their car on his own!'

'I'm sure they wouldn't do that. They must be inside.' Harry's voice is distinctive.

'Should we break the window?' Ben asks.

'No, no, please don't do that. We're coming,' I call.

'Sadly, we're not,' Cal whispers but turns the handle on the rear door. Lily, Ben and Harry appear at the rear, with several new faces behind them, all of whom frown at us in total horror like they've come across two rough sleepers dossing down in a skip.

Cal lets go of me. 'Sod it,' he mouths.

'Louie!'

'Yap, yap, yap!' Louie scrambles over the back of the passenger seat, lands on a pair of pink jeans and then launches himself at Lily.

She cuddles him and her eyes widen as she spots us sitting in the van.

'Hello. We were trying to get out of our wet clothes and thought we'd use these old ones.'

'The shops were shut,' Cal says helpfully.

'Who exactly are these people?' asks a short woman with jet black hair caught up in a bun like a doughnut.

'They're the people arranging the wedding. Jade, this is Cal and Demi. They saved Louie.' She kisses him again and his eyes close in pleasure, which is more than I can say. A pale young guy with a man bun, a ginger wisp of beard and wearing a mismatched tweed suit glares at us down his long nose. Somehow, I don't think he's had to resort to the charity shop. That suit looks deliberate.

'Jade's my publicist and Addison is our agent,' Lily says, then titters. 'I love the outfits.'

'Recycled chic,' I mumble and scramble out of the car. My face must be the same colour as the lobster Cal had for lunch. He climbs down beside me and looks less like a hipster and more like a hobbit in the rolled-up trousers and braces. All he needs are hairy feet and pointy ears.

'And *you* are the people in charge of organising Ben and Lily's wedding?' Addison asks, as if he's found a slug in his quinoa salad.

Mawgan pushes her way to the front of the

group. 'Oh, I'm sure it'll be a memorable occasion with Demi in charge,' she says in a voice that doesn't match her eyes. 'Demi's appearances at events always are,' she says, referencing the times when I 'accidentally' dropped food on her, ripped her dress and when Mitch took a liking to her. Oh shit, she must have told them about my past mishaps. Her butter-wouldn't-melt act is slipping fast.

'It'll be fun,' says Lily firmly, although I think even her breezy confidence in us is wavering judging by the doubt in her eyes. Perhaps it's only her delayed shock, but I've a horrible feeling that Jade and Addison have a lot of influence over her.

'If there's anything I can do to help, you know where I am,' Mawgan pipes up. 'As a successful entrepreneur, I'm skilled at managing multiple projects and I'd be delighted to help my old friend Ben, and you too, Lily. It's so exciting to be involved.'

My heart sinks as Mawgan reels off her LinkedIn profile.

Lily gives a weary sigh. 'We're going to our hotel to recover this evening but Jade will be in touch to confirm the time of my meet-up with you and Rachel at Kilhallon.'

'Of course. I'm so glad you're all OK,' I say.

'Thanks to Mawgan,' Ben adds.

'Oh, I didn't do anything. Just happy to be in the right place at the right time,' she simpers.

'Thank God everything turned out OK. Otherwise, today could have been a disaster for brand Ben and Lily,' Addison says coldly.

Because he and Jade would have lost their cash cows, I think.

'Well, fortunately, they're both alive, and Harry too,' Cal says sharply. 'Which I presume is what you mean?'

Addison flings a withering glare at Cal, but Jade smiles. 'Nothing matters but the welfare of Ben and Lily. She pats her bun and tucks a wayward strand back into it. 'And now we know everyone is safe and well, we can manage the situation to our advantage. In the end, the publicity will keep Ben and Lily on the front pages for days. Weeks if we can handle it properly. Interest in them was flagging slightly and this will do the trick nicely. Come on, my darlings,' she drapes her arms around Ben and Lily, 'let's get you two safely tucked up in the hotel while I arrange some interviews. If we're quick we might catch the later editions tomorrow.'

'Anyone would think they planned it,' I say to Cal on the way home.

'I don't think even Jade and Addison would go as far as to arrange a near fatal drowning,' he says while steering the Land Rover off the main road and into the high moorland lane that leads to Kilhallon. 'Though I wouldn't put it past them. They're parasites. I can't stand people like that.'

'They should get on well with Mawgan,' I say. 'But why did they have to catch us looking like this?' I tug the edges of my tatty hoodie together to try and keep warm in the unheated Land Rover.

131

Cal's bare ankles are a pale blotch in the foot well as he pushes the clutch down. 'It wasn't the best way to make an impression with Ben and Lily's team. I have a feeling they'll be all over us now and interfering with the wedding. If there still is a wedding,' he says grimly.

'Do you think things are that bad? Will they try to cancel and have it somewhere else?'

'I don't know and I'm not sure if I care. I like Lily. Ben's a tool, but Louie's OK.'

'I thought you refused to be seen with a toy dog like Louie.'

'I've decided that Louie's cool. I hadn't realised the dog had such a spirit of adventure. Apart from Harry and Lily, I don't care much about the rest of them, though. Isla was trying to do us a favour by encouraging them to have their wedding here but now I'm wondering if they'll be more trouble than they're worth. Whatever we try to dress it up as, Kilhallon is a glamping site not a luxury wedding destination. I don't like us trying to be something we're not.'

'We can still put on a great show if we all pull together. I know we can. With Rachel's input we'll find some amazing suppliers to help us create their dream day. Lily was definite about not wanting bling and OTT glamour . . . But there is *no* way on the planet that I will allow Mawgan Cade to help plan this wedding.'

'Hmm. I'm not sure if the Gruesome Twosome will agree with Lily and if Mawgan sticks her oar in with Ben, we may have no choice. We'll see.'

We rattle over the cattle grid into Kilhallon

land. The new sign is still smart but there are a few splodges of mud on it from the recent downpours. It needs a clean and polish. Can we handle this wedding?

'Thanks for the vote of confidence,' I mutter.

Cal slows the car. 'I'm sorry. I ought to be more positive and supportive about it but I'm not in the right frame of mind. I need some dry clothes. My own dry clothes plus a hot meal and a very warm bed.'

He stops the car outside reception. 'And most of all I need you . . . ' His gaze lingers on my retro ensemble. 'And not only in the obvious way.'

Hairs prickle on the back of my neck, partly through lust but also because I'm unsure that I'll like what he has to say. 'I think you were going tell me something until Lily interrupted us?'

He sighs. 'Yes. I was. I will. Come into the house and I'll confess all.'

14

Cal

Demi stands by the kitchen table, still wearing her charity shop outfit. There's something about her that stirs feelings deep within me and not only in a physical way. She's unselfconscious and warm. Despite her recent experiences, her capacity for caring for people — friends, strangers, even a lost soul like me — always amazes me.

She bites her lip nervously. I must have worried her. 'Is it about Esme?' she asks.

'Yes. She's been seen. *Possibly* been seen.'

'Oh my God, that's fantastic news. Where is she?' Her face falls. 'She's OK, right? Oh, tell me she's not hurt.'

'She's OK. *If* it's her. It's not one hundred per cent certain. Carolyn's contacts have located a young girl with the same name who's about the right age in a refugee camp. The girl's not entirely sure of when her birthday is because she's traumatised, and she doesn't appear to have any relatives or friends with her who can confirm her identity. They need to find the girl again in the camp and ask if it's OK to get a photo of her so we can make a positive identification.'

'I really hope it's her.'

'Me too.' Demi throws her arms around me

and for a few seconds, I lose myself in the comfort of her body.

'I've been looking for her online for months. Some families contact the international Red Cross and Red Crescent all the time when they've lost touch with loved ones who're making their way through Europe. The organisations try to help but it's almost impossible to track people when they're on the move or not registered in the country they're staying in. Then there's the language barrier, of course. My charity's overwhelmed because the crisis is getting worse all the time. They have so many other things to deal with. I guess that I could wait until they locate this girl and email the photo but . . .'

'You want to go to see Carolyn anyway?'

'Yes.'

'You have to go, Cal. You won't rest unless you do.' Her voice is fierce.

'I'm not sure how I can help but I feel I need to speak to her in person and, if possible, talk to the people in the camp.'

'When do you want to go?'

'Soon.'

She bites her lip and I wonder what's coming. 'Eva emailed me last week and said we need to set up a meeting to discuss *Dog's Dinner*. We could go to London together if it fits in and I could visit the publisher while you go to the charity office. If you want me to come with you, that is.'

'Of course I do.' Even as I say the words, I'm not sure I *do* want Demi to be around me because I'm worried about holding it together if there's bad news, and I don't want her to see me in that state. 'Of course, I want you with me,' I say again, reminding myself that *she* probably needs to come with me.

Going to London could well turn out to be a completely futile gesture but I feel so bloody helpless here. If there's the remotest chance that this 'sighting' is of Esme then I want to make sure that every effort is made to find her. With the best will in the world, my ex-colleagues can't cope with helping the people in front of them, let alone one lost and possibly dead little girl.

'Even if this girl turns out not to be Esme, I need to hear the latest evidence about Esme in person instead of fourth or fifth hand. I'd like to set up a video conference with some of the people and aid workers in the camp. If I can talk to people out there directly, I might pick up a clue as to where she is.'

Despite the warmth of the Aga, I can't help but shiver and hope Demi hasn't noticed.

'I understand, and if you think it will help Esme and yourself, then you should go.'

I smile. 'But first, I think we should get out of these clothes.'

'You're so predictable, Cal Penwith.'

'I thought I was the opposite. Come here.' I press her against me, probably a little too firmly but by now I know she won't break and I need to lose myself in her. We both smell of the damp and clothes that have been in a plastic bag for a little bit too long but I don't care. While I'm kissing her, my fingers fumble with the ribbon of her dress, teasing it undone, ready to finish what I started in the back of the car. She sighs as I trail kisses on her exposed throat. Then she lets out a gasp of pleasure and shock as I lift her onto the kitchen table.

'You look so innocent in this dress,' I say, sliding the hem higher up her thighs. 'No one would know what you're really like.'

'Thank the Lord you're back. I was — oh!'

'Polly!'

Demi's eyes widen. She smooths down her dress hastily and half slithers, half falls off the table.

'Sorry. I can see I've interrupted something but I saw the car and had to know why you're home so late. No one answered their phones but I can see you're fine. I'll go to my bed.'

'No, wait. Polly.'

'I'm sorry, Polly. I meant to answer your text but it's been a crazy day,' Demi says, her cheeks flushed with embarrassment.

'I can imagine.' She frowns at me. 'Why are you wearing your dad's trousers?'

'Um . . .'

She stares at Demi. 'And what on this earth are you doing in my Princess Diana dress?'

15

Demi

'Well, so much for this wedding being a discreet affair. The cat's out of the bag now.' Polly spreads her newspaper across the tables in Demelza's Cafe the morning after our dramatic lunch date with Ben and Lily. She brought the paper down to the cafe as soon as it arrived.

'Look at this!' Polly pokes her finger at a story occupying most of page three. It's accompanied by two photos so clear, they must have been taken close up or on a long lens. One of them is of Mawgan appearing to snog Ben and one of the RNLI helping Lily out of the sea. 'What a load of piffle. This wasn't what you and Cal told me last night.'

Polly puts on her glasses, which otherwise dangle from a cord around her neck as she's so fed up with losing them. She reads the article out loud, while Nina and Shamia pretend to be very busy behind the counter while trying not to snort.

'*There was drama at Newporth beach yesterday when movie stars Ben Trevone and Lily Craig and a third man, believed to be their bodyguard, had to be rescued from the water by friends and the emergency services.*

'*The actors, who became engaged last October, were lunching at the exclusive Rockpool Cafe and had ventured onto the beach to exercise Ms*

Craig's dog, Louie. The dog ran onto rocks at the edge of the beach and the bodyguard and Ms Craig appear to have entered the water to save him but ended up almost drowning.

''It was surreal' said an onlooker, walking his own dog nearby.

'Hmmph, I wonder who this onlooker was? Needed to go to Specsavers by the sound of it.'

Polly carries on reading.

''Some bloke fell in the sea with one of them little dogs and then Lily Craig leapt in after him and her dog,' the man commented.

'I saw them in struggling in the water and the bloke got to Lily. Big bloke, I think he's their bodyguard. Ben Trevone dived in the surf without a thought for himself but the waves beat him back and a woman was giving him CPR. I think she saved his life. Someone else got the dog.'

Polly glances up at me over her glasses. 'Not the sharpest tool in the box, is he, this 'onlooker'? Your account of the whole thing was different.'

'We were a bit busy trying to stop people from drowning,' I say.

'Quite right too. Listen to this: While the couple's bodyguard and a local man helped Lily to safety, Ben had been swamped by a wave and was in difficulty in the surf where reports say he'd knocked his head on a rock. The woman, who reportedly was part of the lunch party, bravely entered the water and pulled him out before administering first aid.

'Ben's heroic rescuer is local businesswoman

Mawgan Cade, who runs a property development and management company. Ms Cade, thirty-two, had apparently recently been on a first-aid course with some of her office staff. However, when questioned about her life-saving skills, the shy heroine was reluctant to take any credit.

''I didn't think about my own safety,' Ms Cade said. 'Anyone would have done the same seeing a friend in danger. I'm glad I was able to pull Ben to safety and that Lily and everyone else is OK.'

'Ben Trevone was quoted as saying that Ms Cade deserved a bravery award but while praising the efforts of Ms Cade, the bodyguard and other members of the party, emergency services said it was fortunate there was not a tragic outcome and that no one should enter the sea in dangerous conditions.

'Well, have you ever heard such rubbish? Mawgan Cade the shy and reluctant heroine? That's not what it sounded like to me. Did she save Ben?'

'Apparently Ben did trip over a rock in the surf and she did drag him out of the way of the waves but the paper has obviously made up the story they want.'

Polly snorts. 'I bet you a pound to a penny this 'onlooker' works for her or had been paid by her.'

I agree with Polly but I don't want to get into a bad-mouthing session about Mawgan with the staff watching. None of them likes Mawgan but I'm not sure it's professional to start slagging her off, no matter how much I want to.

'Can I have the paper, please?'

Polly pushes it towards me. 'Course you can. There's no mention of you and Cal in there.'

'That's fine by me, and we didn't do anything. If Mawgan wants to take the credit, then let her,' I say calmly, while fuming inwardly. Mawgan was in the right place at the right time and she did help Ben but it's obvious she's engineered the situation so that it looks like she saved the day. She must be trying to worm her way into Lily and Ben's world even more closely. It must be for financial gain or to piss us off or for the publicity — or all three.

'Thanks for bringing the paper. We're opening shortly so I'll have to get back to work but we can have a natter about it all later at the farmhouse. Come round for a bite to eat if you're not going to Zumba,' I tell Polly.

'Thanks, but it's my belly dancing night,' Polly says. 'Much more fun than Zumba and the instructor is gorgeous,' Polly says.

'You have a male belly dancing instructor?'

'He — she — was. She's transgender and absolutely fabulous. You should come along. There's all ages, from twenty to ninety, and some men too. It's not just a bunch of middle-aged women shaking their booties like Beyoncé, you know.'

'Thanks,' I say, with multiple images of belly dancing pensioners seared on my brain. 'I'll think about it.'

After Polly leaves, the cafe is busy with walkers and surfers making the most of some early spring sun and surf. It's two p.m. before I have a moment to scan my tablet for more news of the drama. I find a video clip on a local news website. After witnessing Ben and Lily's argument at the hospital, I was slightly worried the wedding would be off so I'm relieved to see them all smiles in the video.

In the clip, they're so tightly entwined you'd think they'd been sewn together. They appeared at the hospital entrance to flash-bulbs lighting up the night sky and giving a statement thanking the medical staff, the emergency services and 'their friends and family' involved in their rescue.

The reporter wraps up the video by saying that the couple had already made a large donation to the RNLI and air ambulance. It ends by them being whisked away by Harry in their BMW, with Lily smiling through the half-open rear window, waving one of Louie's paws. It could all be a show for the cameras, of course. I've no idea what to believe any more.

I'm also still thinking of Cal's news about Esme. I'm glad he shared the news with me so I can support him. I hope these reports turn out to be true. Ever since he told me what happened to him in Syria, I've thought about the little girl too. When I see Freya, I think how lucky she is to be safe. I can't imagine her or any of us having to live through a nightmare like Esme and her family have had to.

Back at home, Cal puts a steaming bowl of homemade lentil curry in front of me, and a plate of Peshwari naan. It's awesome to have someone cook for me at the end of a busy day in the cafe kitchen. I'm also ready for a break. By the time we got to bed last night, it was almost midnight. Even after Cal and I finally finished what we'd started in the kitchen, I still couldn't sleep for a while. I lay awake, listening to Cal breathing softly.

He joins me at the table and clinks my bottle of cider. Mitch brushes against my legs, hoping for some scraps.

'Busy day?' Cal asks.

'Yes, the nice weather brought out the walkers and the book club met again in the afternoon. Mind you, we almost had to separate two women. They were screaming at each other over a novel about kidnapped children. How can people come to blows over a book?'

Cal stops with a chunk of naan halfway to his mouth. 'Beats me. I thought book clubs were meant to be gentle affairs with Earl Grey and cake.'

'Not this time. We had to bring out extra brownies to shut them up. I also arranged for Rachel to come over for a council of war before we meet with Lily and Ben again.' I hesitate but know we need to discuss what Cal told me last night on the way home about possible sightings of Esme. 'How was your day? Any more news from Carolyn?'

'Not yet but I've suggested I should go to London and she's going to get back to me. She didn't specifically tell me not to go. By the way, this morning I had a call from a tabloid asking me if we're holding the wedding for Lily Craig and Ben Trevone. I didn't tell them anything after Jade warned us not to make any comments.'

'Shit. I've had a couple of unknown missed calls on my phone. I thought they were spam calls but they could be from newspapers, though I don't know how they got my personal mobile number.'

'Does Mawgan have it?' Cal asks.

'Yes . . . yes she does, she's had it for a while.'

'Then you have your answer.'

'Shit.'

'The publicity will be good for Kilhallon,' he says, stroking Mitch's ears.

'Yes, but we wanted to manage the situation. We wanted to keep the event quiet until far closer to the day.'

'I don't think that was ever going to happen.' He manages a crooked, sexy smile but I can see he's distracted. The wedding plans of pampered celebrities aren't high on his list of priorities at the moment, even if they are important to Kilhallon. I understand that. 'Well, at least Ben and Lily are the centre of attention and their 'people' will love that.'

'We will have to promote the park, though. Sooner or later we're going to have to raise our profile to keep the bookings rolling in. When *Dog's Dinner* comes out, I'll have to do media interviews with Eva Spero too.'

'I know, and you'll be very good at it. But I'll be happy if I never have to appear in the press again. I just want to get on with my life, run Kilhallon and find Esme if I can. Beyond that, these days, all I want is a quiet life with you here at Kilhallon.' Cal reaches for my hand. Spending a quiet life together at Kilhallon sounds idyllic but I know it will never happen.

'I didn't want to say anything about Carolyn's email at first in case it turns out to be a false hope,' he says softly. 'You have enough to worry about.'

I lean over the table and kiss him, guessing that what he really means is that he was terrified of being disappointed and hurting himself.

16

A few days later Cal bursts into the cafe brandishing a newspaper. 'Jesus, have you seen this?'

My heart sinks. 'What? Is this about Ben and Lily again? Or Mawgan?'

'If only. *Look.*' He throws the paper onto the table and spreads open the pages. The headline leaps out at me despite a brown patch over part of the lettering.

CRAPPY EVER AFTER?
Lily Craig 'losing sleep' over nightmare wedding venue

For a few seconds I don't get what he's so worked up about: a few grainy pictures of sheds and a muddy field . . . then, my stomach clenches hard.

'Oh. My. God. Is that . . . *Kilhallon*?'

'I wish it wasn't but, sadly, yes. Polly almost had a heart attack when she saw it this morning. That stain is where she spilled her tea over it.'

I groan and steel myself to take a closer look at pictures, even though they make me want to throw up.

Judging by the weather, the photos must have been taken yesterday. The dark skies, gloom and constant rain we had would make a tropical paradise seem miserable but in these pictures,

Kilhallon looks like a prison camp. No one would believe that we're now officially into 'British Summer Time'.

'They really have done a hatchet job on us. I can't believe we didn't notice them taking the shots.' I wince as I take in the full horror of the shoot which promises more 'exclusive pictures of the 'boutique wedding venue'' online.

'Public footpaths cross the land and anyone with a camera could have shot these at any time. We can't take people's cameras away and stop them taking pictures on public land.'

'I wish we had. This is crap. I hope Lily isn't losing sleep over the wedding. Oh sh — ' Forcing myself to focus on the whole-page story again, I peer at the pictures. There's Polly lugging a bag of empties to the dustbins behind the farm-house. There are the newly pitched yurts marooned in a sea of mud before Cal had constructed the decking around them. Seagulls peck at the lids of the trade bins behind the cafe. One picture features a wet and scowling Cal carrying in some new sanitary bins to the ladies' wash block. And, oh no, to top it all there's a large picture of Mitch cocking his leg up against one of the log seats in the glamping glade where Lily and Ben will hold their ceremony. I could swear the pictures have been put through a dark filter too.

'This is so unfair. They chose the one angle of Demelza's that's not lovely and customers don't even see the refuse area.'

'There are some even worse ones in the online version.' Cal drops his phone on top of the paper but I can't face looking at more yet.

'All Kilhallon needs is barbed wire and an armed guard to look like a maximum security facility,' Cal says, and he's right. It doesn't matter that none of these eyesores will be visible to guests at the wedding and everything will be ready. The copy is short but agonising. Words jump out at me from the feature: 'rubbish', 'sea of mud', 'basic facilities' and 'stray dogs wandering around'.

'Stray? Mitch is not a stray! And we'll have posh bogs brought in and an event tepee. There'll be gorgeous decorations and lighting and beautiful flowers. It might even be sunny!'

I sweep the newspaper away, close to tears. I have no idea how we can counter terrible publicity like this.

Cal tries to hug me. 'It's bad, I grant you, but people will forget it eventually.'

'No, they won't. Oh shit, I bet we've already had people cancelling their holidays and no one else is going to want to book here now either. I bet Jade and Addison have already persuaded Ben and Lily to cancel. I'm sure Mawgan is behind this.'

'Maybe she is but maybe she isn't. There are tons of people in the press who wouldn't give a toss about running a story like this. They probably sent a pap down for this very reason.'

'We'll have to respond, of course,' I say, shaking with shock and frustration. 'I'll call Lily now and talk to her about it.'

Cal's phone rings. He glances down at the screen and winces.

'You don't have to. This is her on the phone now. Do you want to take it or wait until we've had time to think about how to respond?' He holds up his phone, which buzzes angrily.

I take a deep breath. 'Best get this over with. I hope I'm an even better actor than Ben.'

'Wouldn't be hard,' says Cal and hands me the phone.

★ ★ ★

Soothing Lily turns out to be the least of my worries. By early afternoon, we've had a string of anxious people phoning to cancel their bookings at the cottages and yurts. We managed to reassure some that the photos painted a very unfair picture and that Kilhallon is still a lovely place to stay, though others still cancelled.

A few people wanted us to confirm that Lily and Ben were getting married here but we had to fudge that as the official line from Lily's publicist is that 'we don't disclose details of our guests' plans'. As well as the tabloid piece, the local press are all over us now too, demanding to know the full story. It's difficult to be polite when we want to maintain a positive relationship with them while keeping our plans under wraps. Polly and Cal are finding the whole thing even more of a strain than me. Cal hates pretending to be something he's not — even though he keeps his own secrets — and Polly is just . . . Polly.

It's with enormous relief that I open the door to Rachel late in the afternoon. She'd left a message on my phone not long after we saw the newspaper, offering to come over. It's after hours and I've had a busy day dealing with an unwelcome hygiene inspection and the press, but I'm so grateful to see her that I could cry. After my phone call to Lily, soothing a very anxious bride, I may have slightly lied and said that Rachel had already presented me with an 'amayzing' plan for the wedding and that everything was in hand.

I wander around the cafe, trying to soothe a tired and grizzling Freya, while Rachel sets up her laptop in the cafe. Freya has hold of the knuckle of my little finger between her cherubic lips and is nuzzling it like a suckerfish with her eyes tight shut. At least she's happy now.

Finally Freya falls asleep and is laid in her travel cot very, very carefully. Rachel is understandably anxious at the negative publicity but is trying to put on a brave face.

'OK. I've been thinking and decided that it's time to roll out Operation Wedding Rescue,' Rachel says in a low voice. 'There are two parts to this plan. One, we need to rebuild confidence in Kilhallon to counter those nasty photos in the newspaper. It's not a great situation but I had to deal with something similar a few years ago when there was a food poisoning outbreak after one of the Trevarrian Estate charity dinners.'

My confidence plunges. A food scare is my worst nightmare and the one thing guaranteed to have people avoiding Demelza's for the next hundred years. Thank God we passed the hygiene inspection with five stars again.

'Now, I suggest we hold a wedding fair here as soon as possible, dress the cafe for a wedding breakfast and set up some demonstrations of what Kilhallon can offer. It would mean sacrificing one of your Sunday opening days — but a Sunday afternoon is the best time to hold the event. The clocks have gone forward now and people feel spring is properly here. Even though their weddings may be over a year or even two away they'll be in the mood for firming up their plans.'

'I'm happy to blank off a Sunday afternoon but where are we going to find wedding suppliers to join in at such short notice?'

'Kilhallon's USP is that it's quirky and unusual. You're never going to get those couples who are dead set on a traditional formal wedding in a big hotel or stately home. That's fine for the people who want that kind of ceremony and reception but Kilhallon can't and shouldn't try to compete. So I suggest we concentrate on smaller, more unusual wedding suppliers.'

Rachel's idea gives me a flicker of hope. 'The event tepee people are handling the fixtures and fittings for the interior. It's included in the hire cost though I'm hoping people will be able to be outside for the ceremony and it's a handfasting, back-to-nature theme anyway. I researched it and it's an old pagan tradition but Lily and Ben don't want a pagan or any other kind of religious ceremony. They definitely want their hands bound using ribbon from each of them. And Lily wants an owl to deliver the ring.'

Rachel pulls a face. 'An *owl*? Okayyyy.'

151

'Well, you did say you could get quirky suppliers. Don't worry, Cal's sorted the feathered suppliers. He phoned a birds of prey centre and they have a falconer called Holly and a tawny owl called Boris who's experienced in ring delivery so I booked them both.'

Rachel raises her eyebrows. '*Boris* the owl?'

'After Boris Johnson. Apparently, Holly's mum fancies BoJo and this owl has a spiky tuft of feathers on his head.

Rachel pulls a face. 'Eww. Some people need professional help. At least we don't have to worry about owls if Cal's got it covered. Are you doing all the catering yourselves?'

'Not all; Demelza's can't handle that many people for an entire day.'

'I agree. Do you have any caterers in mind?'

'I've spoken to a few but . . . have we left it too late? Lily and Ben messaged about it and then dropped this on us but they're obviously used to having stuff done no matter how late in the day.'

Freya lets out an unexpected burp in her sleep and we both laugh. 'Hmm. It is very late but I'll get on to it straight away. A few people spring to mind who have supplied catering for the estate's events. I'll see if they're available. Maybe not the ones who caused the food poisoning though.' She pulls a face and then smiles. 'Don't worry, I'll find a great caterer. What other ideas did you have?' she asks me.

'I thought of holding the main wedding 'breakfast' in the tepee with afternoon teas and evening cocktails and canapés at Demelza's, so we only need to worry about one meal. Lily's

152

mulling over a few options for the menu and is going to get back to me. I think she'd love it if guests could pop in and out of here for cream teas and cocktails in the evening.'

'That sounds perfect . . . in fact, I had an idea about the cafe too: have you thought of putting a temporary awning over the outside seating area so that guests can make the most of those lovely views, whatever the weather?'

'No. Being honest, I'd thought of using the regular cafe umbrellas, although I must admit, they're already weather worn.'

'If Lily and Ben are paying, we could get a fabulous canvas awning fixed from the cafe over the seating area and hire in tables and chairs and other decorations in keeping with Lily's theme.'

'Hmm. Lily wanted it to look like they'd done everything at the last minute.'

Rachel snorts with laughter. 'That's her fantasy. Reality takes months of planning. We'll choose a quirky awning and decor and have the florist make up some natural floral displays. Have you got a florist in mind?'

'Not yet.' I feel very hopeless but running Demelza's and developing the recipes for my book has taken up all my time, not to mention the huge dent to my confidence that the press photos created.

Rachel makes another note in her book. 'I'll look into the florist and the cost of hiring versus investing in an awning. Maybe you could use it for future events?'

'Do you think the tepee company might do that?' I ask.

'They might. Have you thought about hiring the tepee for the wedding fair too? The suppliers are going to need shelter.'

Rachel reeling off these lists makes me feel I'm being grilled on a TV politics show. 'Arghh, there's so much to think about.'

She puts her notebook down with a sigh. 'I know. I've spent ages making lists but we'll only have to do it for the first time once!' She brightens up. 'After we've done one wedding, the next one won't seem so scary to us.'

We need to get through this one first without a disaster, I think, but I put on my positive face. 'It's OK. I'd rather we've thought of every scenario than get caught out.'

I make a note on my tablet to ask the tepee people if they can supply a marquee at such short notice. Hopefully, as it's very early in the year, they might. 'If I offer refreshments from the cafe during the fair, I might make up the cash I'd lose from closing the cafe to the general public,' I say.

Rachel laughs. 'Bear in mind that lots of people don't come to the wedding fair because they're getting married. Lots of people just want a free cup of tea or Buck's Fizz or to live out their fairy-tale fantasy. We held one at Trevallian and the wedding planner told me lots of stories.'

'They really do that?' I say, neglecting to mention I crashed a few events of this nature when I was 'between sofas'. A free cup of tea and a sausage roll for Mitch were very welcome at times.

'Yes, but even though some visitors may not

want to plan a wedding immediately, they're all potential customers for the cafe, and for holidays and events, so it's worth offering a free cuppa to the first few or a free coffee with a slice of cake.'

I scribble 'free tea' on my notepad. 'This all sounds great but how do we get a wedding fair organised at such short notice?' I ask.

'While I was doing my research, I found out there was a fair scheduled for a golf club near St Trenyan but they've had a fire and have had to cancel. I know a couple of the businesses who were due to attend so I thought we could ask some if they want to come along to Kilhallon's fair at a reduced rate. They still get the exposure and save money. Do you know anyone?'

'One or two people I suppose. There's Tamsin who owns the spa in St Trenyan. She was going to offer pop-up and mobile services for our guests over the summer. Robyn could bring her jewellery along. She wants to set up in business after her course finishes. There's her friends from the Cornish folk band too who played at our launch last summer. They were really quite good.'

Rachel scribbles in her notebook. 'Ask them to come then. Get the band to play during the wedding fair.'

'OK. I'll have to get Cal on board to showcase the events tepee and set up the glamping glade — I hope it's not raining. Maybe he could set up a small exhibition inside one of the yurts, with lanterns and decorations. Even if it *does* rain, that would still work. It is April. It could be horrible.' I grimace. 'Whatever happens, we need to get moving. It has to take place the weekend before Easter week — by then we'll be too busy with guests and the campsite opens.'

'We could pick the same date as the cancelled golf club fair?' Rachel suggests.

'Yes . . . that would work, I think, but it's less than three weeks away.'

'We have to go for it,' Rachel says grimly. 'I'll email all the suppliers tonight. You get your contacts on board, and Cal. Can you contact the local press too? You could do it as a 'this is what Kilhallon is really like' story. They'll all want to come in case they can get any snippets about Lily and Ben. You don't think either of them would come, do you?'

I shake my head. 'No. No way. Even if Lily agreed, the Gruesome Twosome — that's their agent and publicist — would never go for it. But you'd better meet her. I'll arrange that.'

Rachel grimaces. 'Oh. Even I'm feeling nervous now. Does she know I'm a novice at this?'

'Um. I thought it was better not to mention that.'

Rachel swallows hard. 'Good idea.'

A few minutes later, I lift Freya out of her travel cot and glance at the window. Outside, the sun is still bright in the sky. It really is spring.

Freya opens her eyes and, oh my God, makes a beeline for the 'V' in my top. 'I think she's hungry.'

Rachel laughs. 'She's rooting. I'd better feed her. Then we can get going on the rest of the plan. There's no time to lose.'

Freya lets out a loud wail. Rachel winces then we both laugh. 'OK. OK. Freya comes first. We know that, little one.'

While Rachel settles down to feed Freya, I pour Rachel a drink and make myself a hot chocolate. I'm so glad she's on board because even though I'd made my own plans, there was so much I hadn't thought about. Like the electrics for the lighting and sound and other services required out of doors. Cal might have covered this already but he hasn't mentioned it so I'd better get it sorted. Rachel said that my dad had suggested he handle the electrics but hadn't liked to ask me or put me under any pressure. That makes me feel a bit guilty and I resolve to take it up with him myself. It means we're going to have to work together more, even though Cal will be in charge of the basic services to the site.

Rachel sips her presse while feeding Freya. We have nursing mums in the cafe sometimes and a mum-and-baby group meet here every couple of weeks so I'm used to little ones but it's still strange to see my own little sister in my cafe. Strange but wonderful. It gives me a little tingle of pleasure.

'Are you sure you can handle all the planning alongside looking after Freya? It's not too much pressure, is it?' I ask Rachel, realising again how much work a small baby is.

'I might regret it at some point. I probably will, but I won't know if I don't try. Gary's already taken over some of the duties after he comes in from work and my mum came round to take care of her last week so I could do some research and pop out to see some potential suppliers. I must admit I'm even more knackered than usual but organising a celebrity wedding is way too good an opportunity to miss. I'm sure it'll be all right on the day, as long as we prepare properly.'

My nod and smile hide my real feelings. Yes, so far everything at Kilhallon and Demelza's has been all right on the day. Even Cal and me. Yet the pleasant tingle of happiness at seeing Freya in 'my' place soon fades. The wedding fair is just weeks away. Surely it's impossible to organise an event like that at such short notice, no matter what Rachel says?

I also realise I'm going to have to get some temporary staff at the cafe earlier in the season than I thought or we'll never manage. Even with a great plan, and Rachel's help, I have a horrible feeling I might have bitten off more than I can chew this time.

17

Soon it's time for Rachel to leave and get Freya ready for her bath and bedtime. While I cuddle her, Rachel packs away her laptop and notepad. I gently rub Freya's back. She's drowsy and very content after her feed. She reminds me of a baby koala, curled over my shoulder. She's impossibly cute but I still can't believe she's my sister. I definitely can't see the resemblance that Polly constantly points out — usually when Freya is either wailing or filling her nappy.

'I'd no idea how complicated and stressful weddings could be until I ended up in the middle of one,' I say. 'I've no idea why anyone wants to go through that kind of drama.'

Rachel smiles at me and I feel ever so slightly patronised. 'Really? Have you never thought about having your own wedding?'

'*Me?* Never.'

Freya grumbles slightly at the shock of my exclamation.

'What about Cal?' Rachel asks.

'He's never thought about getting married either. Not to me, anyway,' I say quietly.

'Oh, I see.' Rachel grimaces. 'Sore point?'

'It's fine. I'm cool. He went out with Isla for a while before he met me. She's the film producer who persuaded Lily and Ben to hold their wedding here. He's over her now. He *says* he's over her . . . '

'But you're not convinced that Cal is really over his ex?'

'I don't think 'convinced' is the right word. I'm only being honest. It was the flooding that finally pushed me to move in with Cal. A homeless family needed my cottage over Christmas and . . . I finally realised it was the right thing to do.'

This is only partly true. It was also down to Cal's decision to be reconciled with his half-brother, Kit Bannen, and the way he had finally shared his experiences in Syria with me. Until then I wasn't sure I could ever live with such a troubled, turbulent guy.

Kit is Cal's half-brother who lives in London. Cal didn't even know that Kit existed until he turned up at Kilhallon in the autumn. Kit didn't tell us who he was until the whole story came out at the Harbour Lights Festival and caused a huge bust-up between him and Cal — and me too.

Cal's father had strings of affairs while he was married to Cal's mum. They included Kit's mother who was down here on holiday when she was a young woman. Kit was the result of a holiday 'romance', but Mr Penwith refused to acknowledge him publicly as his son. A sort of peace has descended since Kit returned from his home in London to help with the floods rescue. Kit realised he'd been jealous and vindictive towards Cal and he's keen to make it up to him. We've heard from him a couple of times since then and slowly, I think, they're both learning to accept and trust each other, though it's still early days.

'Demi?' Rachel's hand is on my arm. I hadn't realised that I must have been miles away. 'Tell me if I'm being nosy but it sounds like you needed a big push to move in with Cal?'

I hesitate because Rachel doesn't know the full story. 'I needed to trust him and I needed to give up my independence. It's not easy learning to rely on someone when you've been hurt and let down. Oh shit. I didn't mean you and Dad let me down.'

'It's OK. Your dad *did* let you down. He knows that.'

'Neither of us was blameless but we were both so . . . lost after Mum died . . . I'm sorry I was vile to you.'

She shrugs. 'Yeah, well. I wasn't the nicest person either, I'm sure. I didn't really relish the role of wicked stepmother and I knew you hated me barging into your life and taking your mum's place. I can't say I blamed you and I probably wasn't the most sensitive person in the way I handled things back then.'

My face colours but I can't deny that Rachel is right. She said some harsh things to me, even though I probably deserved some of them at the time.

'We were all right and all wrong in our own ways. Let's forget it. Now I want to concentrate on the wedding because I definitely need all the help I can get.'

Freya lets out another burp and we both laugh out loud. 'That's what Freya thinks of us all, and the wedding too.'

We fasten Freya into her car seat. 'She's right. It's all a bit mad. I mean, owls flying around with rings? Handfasting? Colour-coordinated flower arches? How did we get here?' I ask, pulling a face that makes Freya smile at me. Either that or it could be wind again.

'Every wedding eventually turns the sanest, most reasonable person stark staring mad. Which is why me and your dad have never got round to it, I suppose.'

'Yet.'

Rachel looks thoughtful. 'Yes. Hmm. I must admit that organising this wedding has focused my mind. Maybe it's time we did think about tying the knot ourselves, but I have to get this one over with first!'

I laugh. 'Well one thing's for sure. There's no way Cal and I will be doing it. Hell will freeze over first.'

'What won't I be doing?' Cal emerges from behind the counter. He must have come through the staff door but neither of us heard him. He could have been there for five seconds — or five minutes for all I know, and my stomach flips when I realise he might have heard some or most of my conversation with Rachel.

Rachel glances at me. 'We were talking about weddings.'

Cal grimaces. 'Then I might walk straight back out again. I've already had enough of weddings, and especially this one.'

'So much drama, and we're not even the ones tying the knot, eh?'

He laughs. 'Exactly. If someone else's wedding can be this much trouble, imagine the trauma if it was your own!'

162

Rachel is quiet, watching us.

I think Cal's joking but you never know. Weddings were never going to be his thing and he has a lot on his mind but I hope he can rustle up *some* enthusiasm. Then again, if he heard what I said to Rachel . . . *Ouch*. I didn't quite mean that hell would freeze over before I'd agree to marry anyone. Rachel pushed me, she was teasing me and after seeing what's involved in the whole wedding bandwagon, I don't think I'd want that hassle, and the fuss and the public show . . .

Shit.

'Rachel's given us some fantastic ideas on how to rescue Kilhallon's image and for organising the wedding. It's going to be amazing.' God, now I can't even convince myself.

Cal tickles Freya's tummy, and she smiles and makes a gurgling sound of pleasure that is definitely not wind. If he heard me, he's hiding it well. He can't have. 'I'm really grateful you're helping us, Rachel — and Freya too.'

As if she recognises her name, which she must do now, Freya reaches for Cal's thumb and grasps it in her doll-sized fist.

'She's strong,' he says. Cal glances at me. 'Like her big sister.'

'I'll open the door,' Rachel says.

I carry Freya out to the car. Gulls circle and cry high above us and the smaller birds twitter like mad from the hedgerows and stone walls next to the cafe. Spring is definitely here, which focuses my mind on next month's big event even more.

After we've waved off Rachel and Freya, Cal follows me into the cafe. He was smiley enough as we said goodbye and said he'd get on to the list of jobs that Rachel and I have drawn up for the wedding fair, but there's a tension in the air. A chill that goes beyond the cool spring evening. Maybe he did hear what I said about never settling down but, even if he did, why would he care? If there's one thing I know, it's that hearts, flowers and hand-fastings are not for me and Cal. We've known each other less than a year and been living together for less than three months. I said we'd take each day at a time and that's working for us. Which is fine. It's absolutely *fine*.

'It's OK. I can lock up without you.'

'I know you can but I'll still help.'

I know when it's pointless to argue with Cal. Most of the time it's pointless to argue with Cal. He checks the doors to the terrace and waits in the cafe until I've turned off the lights and power. I lock the door behind me and we walk back to the farmhouse, chatting about setting up the yurts in time for the Easter season.

The sun is still bright but under the clear skies, any heat is rapidly escaping and I think we might even have a frost tonight, even here on the coast. Cal goes off to the storage barn to collect some wood for the fire, leaving me to walk into the farmhouse alone. He seemed normal enough, whatever normal is for Cal. I don't think he even heard what I said to Rachel when he walked into the cafe . . . so why do I get the distinct feeling I've hurt him in some way? And that he's holding something back?

18

Cal

On the early train to London with Demi, I pretend to answer my emails, update the bookings calendar, order some spares for the sit-on mower, but all I really have on my mind is two girls.

One is sitting next to me now, working on the edits to her cookbook. She's intent on the screen, frowning.

I glance out of the window at the trees coming into leaf, and the late March sunshine sparkling on the waves as we skirt the coast at Dawlish. They had to rebuild this section of the line a few years ago in floods similar to those which devastated St Trenyan. It's good to see it open again and the village getting back on its feet. I wish I could be as optimistic about my personal life.

The coastline only holds my attention for a few seconds before Demi's words from last week in the cafe ring out in my mind.

'Well one thing's for sure. There's no way Cal and I will be doing it. Hell will freeze over first.'

No one ever overheard anything good about themselves, my mother would have told me. But those phrases 'no way' and 'hell will freeze over first' are seared on my mind. I steal a glance at her, tapping away on her keyboard and sticking out her tongue in concentration. Even with a lot of help from the publisher, she's found this book a big challenge.

Obviously, she finds me even more of one.

At least I know where I stand with Demi. Can't say I blame her.

She's young — only twenty-two — whereas I'm ten years older and I'm carrying more baggage than the Paddington to Penzance on a Bank Holiday. I know she'd have plenty of offers and, anyway, lots of people don't even bother getting married these days.

My first shot at it never even got off the ground. I never even had the chance to ask Isla. Which turned out to be a good thing . . .

We arrive at Paddington at lunchtime and Demi walks to her publishers' office while I get the tube to our charity office. I've arranged to meet her at a pub next to the station before our train home to Cornwall later this evening.

We part with a kiss and she plunges down the street, carrying a laptop bag, looking for all the world as if she belongs on these streets. My breath catches: she's come so far from the girl I met at a cafe, desperate and hungry. Watching her blossom over the past year has been one of the highlights of my life: she's grown alongside Kilhallon. I don't kid myself that I had a hand in any of that other than providing the occasional opportunity. After emerging from the tube, I take a turn down a side street and to the small suite of offices that are part of a larger block.

A buzz at the door lets me into the reception area, which serves as a storeroom too by the look of it. There's chaos as usual with the small team, their equipment and some supplies crammed into every available space. The bustle lifts me. Carolyn texted me first thing to say they were arranging a video call with the actual aid worker who'd spoken to the man who'd seen Esme. I can't believe that in a few hours I might have a photo and detailed news of her.

Carolyn's assistant meets me at the door and tells me to go upstairs to Carolyn's 'cupboard' at the top of the building. Before I even reach her door, halfway up the final flight, she appears on the landing and I know. She doesn't have to say anything.

One look at Carolyn's face: at the grimace of sympathy and I know it's bad news. I'm wading through the sea, fighting against the current and backwash from the waves. My chest tightens and I can't breathe.

'I'm sorry,' she says, and meets me on the landing. 'It wasn't Esme. My colleague called. He could have waited for the video conference but he wanted to let us know as soon as possible. I'm sorry you came all this way for nothing. We all thought — hoped — it was her. The girl looked like her and she was the right age and her story of fleeing from the same area sounded too much like a coincidence. But this girl isn't Esme. A family member contacted one of our aid workers and confirmed who she really is and the little girl has already spoken to them on Skype.'

'I'm glad for her,' I say, although my skin crawls with disappointment and I want to scream. 'I'm happy one family has found some

167

relief from this fucking awful mess.'

Carolyn holds her door open wide. 'You're a good guy, Cal, even if you don't believe it.'

'Yeah. Whatever you say, boss.'

'I'm not your boss now but come inside anyway and I'll give you the same advice I'd give one of the staff, whether you want it or not.'

Half an hour later, Carolyn pours me a second mug of tea and sits in a well-worn easy chair next to mine. It's the chair of doom: the one where she delivers bad news and gives comfort to the staff. We used to joke about it, I even used it myself to hand out tea and sympathy to junior members of staff a couple of times.

'OK?' she says, holding out a pack of biscuits.

'Chocolate Hobnobs. Wow.'

'I rate this as a chocolate Hobnob moment.'

'Like a three-hankie weepie?'

'Most people round here would rather have biscuits than a Kleenex, even one of those with the balm, and you're not a crier.'

Not in public, I think. 'I'm with them.' I take a biscuit and dunk it in my tea, not because I want one but because I want Carolyn to think she's helping. Though I suspect she knows she isn't. We play this game with the people we love and care for, don't we? We maintain the lie that we're OK, because our pain is only doubled when it's shared, not halved. I'll play the game again when I face Demi later.

I bet she gets a better class of biscuit at her fancy publishers.

Carolyn leans forward in her seat. 'Will you be OK? Or is that a stupid question?'

'Yes and yes, but that's not your fault. It's mine.'

'We've been through this. You were offered counselling. Maybe you should consider it again.'

'I have all the comfort I need at Kilhallon. I'll get over it. It was stupid to have built up my hopes. You did warn me several times this could end in tears — and biscuits.'

'Kilhallon was doing you good — is still doing you good — and this isn't the end, you know. There's still a chance she's alive and well, though I ought not to say that. The tracing sites are probably our best hope.'

'I know all that . . . You know there's a cat in hell's chance of her being found OK. She could be stuck in a detention centre anywhere in Europe. Or taken by traffickers . . . If she got out of the city in the first place.' Or much worse, I think and shudder.

'All of the scenarios you mention are possible. However, we don't have any evidence for them yet. We'll keep on looking and doing what we can to find her. I'm sorry we can't spare the time or resources to do more.'

'I should be sparing the time.'

She sighs. 'No. You shouldn't. You should be living your own life.' She pauses. 'Cal. I hate to say this, but I have to. Are you sure this quest is about Esme and not about you?'

'What do you mean?'

'How much of this pursuit is about your own guilt after leaving her and Soraya? A guilt, I stress, that you don't need to carry around with you.'

169

There are times when people say things to you that you just can't answer.

I dump my mug on the table. 'I'm going home.'

'Cal. Wait. Don't go off like this.'

'Like *what*? Like I'm an idiot. Like I've lost her — them — all over again? Like I should dance out of here with a cheery smile on my face?'

Carolyn calmly looks at me and waits.

I groan. 'I'm sorry. I shouldn't have said it. Not to you.'

'No. You should. Rant and shout all you like. Cry and throw things. I've seen a whole lot worse.'

'Shit. I keep saying the wrong things to people.'

'You always said the wrong things to people, way before you were captured. It's your nature to say the wrong things and to piss people off, whether you love them or hate them. But you say them for the right reasons, usually — because you're passionate about what you believe to be right. Because you feel deeply about the people and things you love. It may not make you easy to work or live with but that's the way you are. Now, sit down. Don't go yet. Give yourself more time.'

'Because time heals?' I ask, feeling cold with despair as the disappointment starts to sink in.

'No, but it gives us chance to kid ourselves we're OK. It gives us the breathing space. Rant at me but don't take this disappointment and rage home to Demi. I know I said there's still

170

hope, but part of me thinks it would be better if you let it go. I feel bad enough for even allowing you to hope, but I'd feel even worse if I'd kept the news from you.'

'Never be afraid to give me hope.'

She gets up and hugs me. Only briefly because Carolyn, for all her compassion, is not a huggy person, even to her friends or family. I don't think she dares get that close to anyone these days.

She lets me go and I blow out a breath. 'A hug. Wow. You must be worried about me.'

She smiles. 'Nope, I needed one myself. It's no hardship that it's you.'

I laugh. 'Even looking like death warmed up.'

'I won't flatter you any more. Now, finish that bloody awful tea, have a moan and then piss off back to Cornwall for this celebrity wedding.'

'Jesus. That. I can't . . .'

'You can. It's your livelihood and it's Demi's, and the people who work with you. You owe it to them to make that place work because I sure as hell won't have you back working for me.'

'Thanks for nothing, boss.'

She thrusts the biscuit packet at me. 'Shut up and have another Hobnob. It's an order.'

★ ★ ★

'Hi, how was it? Is she found? I texted you but I didn't get a reply and I thought you might be busy with Carolyn or speaking to Esme on the phone . . .'

'It wasn't her, unfortunately.'

171

Demi's smile fades. Her disappointment revives mine and it saws at me like a knife. She's joined me in a pub near the station. At five-thirty p.m., there's standing room only and we're hemmed in on every side by tourists and workers laughing and celebrating the end of the working day. Even if I wanted to shout and scream, I couldn't do it here and that's probably a good thing for both of us.

'Oh no, Cal. Is there no news?'

'Not of her specifically but one of Carolyn's staff said that she's heard that Esme's uncle was spotted in a camp in Northern Greece. But the girl that the staff member thought was her turned out not to be related at all and the uncle has vanished. He's probably moved on now.'

'I'm really sorry. I don't know what to say.'

'There's nothing more to say. Let me get you a drink then I want to hear all about your day with your publisher.'

'My good news about the book doesn't seem important compared to your bad news.'

'Don't ever let me hear you say that again,' I say, more fiercely than I mean, judging by her flinch. I attempt to do my brooding scowl though it's the very last thing I feel like doing. 'That's an order from the Hot Vampire,' I say, joking about the nickname she had for me when we first met. She rolls her eyes then breaks into a smile. 'Look, there's a stool and a table free up the corner. Grab it while I get the drinks.'

A while later, I'm back at the table. The crowds have thinned slightly and I find a seat next to Demi's.

'So. How was the glamorous world of publishing?' I ask, aware that every word sounds like I'm being sarcastic though I really don't mean to be. I want, desperately want, to be engaged in her answers and her breathy excitement, for her sake and mine.

'They showed us the cover and some of the initial photography. Oh. My. God. You should see it — I can't believe how beautiful it is! I can't believe my name will be on the cover and, oh shit, I almost actually cried. I had to pretend I was going to sneeze because the tears were in my eyes. I've got the images on my tablet. Do you want to see them now or when we're on the train?'

'Now. I can't wait until then.'

'OK. You won't believe it.'

Demi shows me the cover of her book and the photos of some of the recipes and dogs that the publisher has shot. I want to cry too, because they're lovely photos but mostly because she is so happy and excited. No matter how low I felt when I walked into this pub, seeing her ready to pop with joy is almost more than I can take. I don't know what I'd have done if I'd been coming to this pub on my own after the disappointment earlier: if I'd been travelling home to Kilhallon on my own.

'What do you think?' she says.

'I think they're brilliant. You're brilliant.' I lean over and kiss her, tasting wine on her lips and feeling the excitement in her body.

'I didn't do that much and I feel like a bit of a fraud. I provided some of the dog's recipes and most of the human ones but Eva did a lot of the introductions and the publisher has commissioned all the photos and the design. I need to get some pictures of Mitch done next but the photographer's coming to Cornwall to do those. I also thought of asking Lily if she'd mind Louie being in the book. Eva and the editor went wild when I mentioned it and I almost wished I hadn't in case it doesn't come off. They want me to get Lily to write a foreword. I need to get that sorted before the wedding fair because our deadline's approaching. Now, what do you think about . . . '

Demi carries on chatting, sipping her wine and flicking through photos and generally bubbling over like a glass of champagne. For myself, celebration is the last thing on my mind but being here with her is the ultimate comfort. She looks stunning too, those skinny jeans show her impossibly pert bum to perfection, the heeled boots make her legs seem even longer and her chestnut hair is piled in a messy-sexy way on top of her head and makes me want to drag her straight off to bed. I need to get her home to Kilhallon and lose myself in her right now, but it's time to get our train and I'm not sure First Great Western will approve of me doing that on the six thirty-nine to Penzance.

It's dark and drizzly when I wake up, just as our train pulls into Penzance station. My whole left side is numb where Demi has been asleep on my shoulder. The train manager's voice is telling us to collect all our belongings. It's fortunate we've reached the end of the line, or I might have dozed my way off the end of Cornwall and into the Atlantic, taking Demi with me. I shake her gently awake.

'We're home,' I say and the words give me a small lift, like the first sip of whisky when the heat hits the back of your throat and warms your stomach. Kilhallon soothes me, Demi too. With my rucksack on my back and a bag with a gift for Polly, we make our way to the car park. Sheets of fine rain are blown across the tarmac like grey veils. The orange lights reflect in puddles. Strange to think that in a few hours it will be dawn again.

I know why I couldn't speak when Carolyn first accused me of pursuing Esme to purge my guilt. It was one of those times when you can't answer because you're too angry with someone for daring to say what you know in your heart to be true. Because they've spoken the doubt that's been gnawing at a raw corner of you.

'Cal . . . '

Demi speaks to me when we reach the Land Rover. Despite the rain, she throws her arms around me. 'I'm sorry. Really, really sorry for what happened to you today. It's shit. It's totally shit and you must be shattered.'

It is, indeed, shit. But being held by Demi isn't shit. It's the best thing, by far, in my life. I'm lucky to be here to enjoy what I have. Bloody lucky.

'I should have known it might end in disappointment. I shouldn't have raised my hopes. Carolyn did warn me at the very start not to be too optimistic. She said it was a slim chance.'

'You couldn't help it. Don't lose hope. Not yet,' she says. I touch my face to hers.

'I think I have to.'

She whispers something I can't hear. I have her. I'm here. It's time to leave everything that happened behind me and move on. The rain chases itself across the car park. Demi's hair is plastered to her face. I taste the rain on my lips: cold fresh water, maybe not so clean but at least I know I'm alive.

'Let's go home,' she says.

I climb into the car and watch Penzance roll by in an orange haze as she drives us home. It's time to let go of the past and be grateful for what I have: Demi, Polly, Robyn, Kilhallon, my friends — even Mawgan Cade, God help me, isn't actually out to bomb my home and kill me. It's time to get on with the rest of my life, however silly and trivial that seems right now — and if a barking mad celebrity wedding is my salvation then bring it on.

19

Demi

After Cal's bitter disappointment in London last week I thought he'd find it hard to summon up any enthusiasm for the wedding fair next Sunday but he's surprised me by throwing himself into the whole thing with enthusiasm. He arranged a meeting with my dad to discuss the electrics and has met with a mate of Dad's who does the sound and lighting for music festivals. Cal drew up some designs for the archway and has promised to liaise with the florist that Rachel has booked for the wedding and invited to the fair.

The arrival of April seems to have put everyone in the wedding mood. I've made some mini scones and I'm trying to come up with a sophisticated way of putting the jam and cream on them and possibly a tiny strawberry. I want to perfect them so I can show them to Lily when she flies in — literally — after the wedding fair. Ben has a shoot so he might not be able to make it but Lily has recently finished a one-off US TV drama and can spare a couple of hours before she has to do some promotion for a film.

Just as I'm trying to pipe a tiny rosette of clotted cream onto the scone, which is spread with Polly's homemade jam, the reception bell rings. I wait for Cal to answer it because he's working in his study. Polly's gone to the dentist.

'Cal!' I call, balancing the scone lid on the cream rosette.

The bell rings again. Abandoning the scone I grab a tea towel to wipe my hands and scoot along to Cal's office. 'Cal, can you see who's in reception? I'm baking.' His office is empty and the bell dings again so I resign myself to greeting the visitor. With my 'Welcome to Kilhallon' smile firmly in place, I open the door to reception.

A tall man, with tawny hair curling into his collar, smiles at me from the other side of the reception counter. For a moment or two, I'm speechless, hardly able to believe my eyes.

'Kit! What are you doing here?'

The last person I expected to rock up today was Kit Bannen. My first thought is that I wonder how Cal will react when he finds his half-brother on the doorstep. Cal didn't even know Kit existed until just before Christmas and after a disastrous start, their relationship is still on fragile ground.

'What do you think? I've come to read the electricity meter,' he says, then points to the rucksack next to him on the tiles. 'I'm supposed to be staying here.'

'You . . . But . . . I didn't even know you'd booked in here . . . and . . . *are* we expecting you?'

He smiles. 'Yes and no. I booked online a couple of days ago but I wanted it to be a surprise so a mate made the reservation in her name and with her credit card. I wasn't sure I'd be welcome but now I'm slightly regretting the subterfuge. I hope Cal won't be too angry. Or you.'

'No. No, I don't think so. You should have phoned us, though. It um . . . might be a shock to him.'

'Sorry. I realise that, but I only decided to come a few days ago. Is he in? If so, I'd rather get the meeting over with and see if he'll let me stay or chuck me out again.'

'You know he won't throw you out. He told me you've spoken to him a couple of times since Christmas.'

'Yes, I phoned twice in the new year to see how the village was doing and if I could do anything else to help. He said no, but it was a reasonably polite no, not a 'piss off, you git' kind of no.'

'That's probably major progress with Cal.'

'Hmm. We didn't exactly get off on the right note but I'm trying to put that behind me.' He pushes a lock of hair out of his eyes. His hair has grown since Christmas and he looks more like a laid-back surf dude than ever. I know he's neither laid-back or a surfer: he's as edgy and unpredictable as Cal beneath the surface charm. While it's good to see him and even though he seemed to have turned over a new leaf at Christmas, part of me is still wary of his motives in being at Kilhallon.

'All of us are trying to put things behind us,' I say. Cal's tried to put a brave face on things but I caught him staring out of the window most of the way home from London, as if he might find Esme out in the darkness. Cal thought I was asleep but I saw the pain in his eyes and I've seen him scrolling through social media since he's been back, hoping to find out about her. I worry about him but there's nothing more I can do.

'I have a lot of bridges to build here. Make that the Severn, the Forth and the Humber combined, in fact. Has Cal mentioned me much?'

I neglect to say that I don't think Kit will ever quite gain Cal's trust but it's good if he wants to try.

'Not really, sorry, although that might be a good thing and he does refer to you as Kit now, rather than Bannen.'

'That's a giant leap forward.'

'Yes. You wouldn't expect him to talk about you. Cal doesn't talk about his feelings any more than he can possibly help it. So, why are you here?'

'Two reasons actually. One is that I need to get the final edits to my novel out of the way and Kilhallon is a peaceful place to do it. The second reason relates to the floods. One of the features editors I know was talking about the devastation the tidal surge caused and I mentioned I had links to the area and had been involved in a very small way.'

I smile. Cal told me that he'd found Kit some really shitty jobs to do when they were helping to clear people's homes out before Christmas.

'Anyway, I persuaded the editor to commission me to do a feature on how people are coping after the floods. Show the place getting back on its feet and highlight some of the ongoing problems. That sort of thing.'

'There's been a lot of rebuilding but some are still not back in their houses because of the insurers not paying out. I'm not sure some will ever go back. My dad and Rachel moved in a little while ago but they were lucky.'

'Cal mentioned they'd stayed here and that the baby had arrived. Congratulations. It's going well with your family, is it? There didn't seem much chance of a reconciliation at the Harbour Lights Festival.'

'There wasn't, but things have changed. I've met up with my brother, Kyle, while he was on leave from the army. Dad and I are slowly getting to know one another again and Rachel and I get on much better than I ever thought we could, and Freya is so gorgeous. She smiles at me now and I even change her nappies.'

'That's beyond the call of duty.' He smiles. 'I'm glad things are going well for you. Genuinely. I don't expect Cal to welcome me with open arms but if he sees I'm here to try and do some good, he might be slightly more welcoming.'

'You'll find out soon enough,' I say, feeling he still deserves tormenting after what he put us through last year. 'Look, he's coming over the yard.'

Kit mouths 'shit', but then stands up a little straighter in readiness for his encounter with Cal. 'I'll brace myself.'

A couple of months ago, Cal had Kit up against a wall. His bitterness towards Cal's father — their father — spilled out into some serious rage and vindictiveness. I'm pretty sure Cal's still

181

very wary, even though they buried the hatchet when Kit returned to help out in the floods. My stomach flutters because even I'm a little nervous of the reaction. I wish Kit had warned us he was coming but it's too late. I believe his story that he was as wary of coming back as Cal may be of seeing him here.

Cal strides towards us. He's in a T-shirt because the spring sun has some strength in it today and he's obviously been working on something. He pushes open the door and hesitates momentarily.

Kit flashes him a brief smile. 'Hello, Cal.'

Cal looks him up and down. The hairs on the back of my neck prickle. Should I take cover behind the counter or stay and act as referee if needed.

'What are you doing here?' he asks.

'Hoping to stay for a few weeks.'

Cal frowns. 'At Kilhallon?'

'Yes, if you'll have me. I'm not here to cause trouble, I promise. I'm hoping to do some good.'

Cal folds his arms, his expression stern. 'You do some good?'

'It may be hard to believe but on this occasion, yes. I've persuaded an editor of one of the broadsheets to run a feature on how the village is managing after the tidal surge.'

'Managing?' Cal snorts. 'Considering what some people have been through, and the lack of real help from outside the area, they've done a bloody amazing job. There's still a lot more to do though. Some people feel they've been abandoned by the powers that be and don't get me started on the insurance companies.'

'That's exactly why I'm here. Demi already highlighted some of the problems,' Kit replies calmly.

'She's right. The flood left many with massive problems that still haven't been tackled but we don't want to be portrayed as an abandoned dump. The most important thing is showing the public that the town is open for business while letting people know we still need help.'

Kit nods in agreement. 'I can see the dilemma but I hope you'll trust me to reflect things as they really are.'

Cal hesitates before a small smile touches his lips briefly. 'I'll make sure of it.'

'We've a cottage vacant for a couple of weeks,' I say, neglecting to mention that Kit has already secretly booked in. I'm relieved that Cal's angrier about the floods than with Kit turning up. Clever Kit: he must have known that Cal would never pass up the chance to have a rant and help the villagers at the same time.

'That's lucky,' says Cal, and I don't *think* he's being sarcastic.

'I'm also hoping to work on my edits too while I have some peace and quiet,' says Kit. 'Maybe we can get together for a beer or two? And it would be great if you could suggest some local people I could speak to,' Kit says. 'When you're not too busy.'

'I'm always busy,' Cal says with a grunt. 'But yeah. I can spare a time for a beer and a few words if it helps the community. I can't stay and chat now though. I'm in the middle of fixing the mower. I'm sure Demi will sort you out.'

Actually, I was baking, I think, and planning a wedding menu . . . but Cal is gone.

Kit watches him stride away over the car park then turns to me with a raised eyebrow. He sighs. 'That went well.'

I laugh. '*Well*? I half-expected him to chuck you out. Come on, I'll get the keys to Enys Cottage so you can settle in before he changes his mind.'

★ ★ ★

Later in the farmhouse, I'm curled up on the sofa with the laptop, working on some final tweaks to the text in *Dog's Dinner*. We've added doggy popcorn and some new flavours of muffins as well as recipes for dog walkers. Cal sits in the armchair, a book in his lap, but he's not reading it. He holds his whisky glass and stares into the fire. He doesn't know I'm watching him; I'm not sure he knows I'm even in the same room. It's half a minute before he takes a sip from his glass and catches me looking at him.

'I'm not much company tonight, am I?'

'I'm supposed to be working. I have to do this copy-edit thing and send it back tomorrow.'

He smiles. 'Copy-edit? Sounds important.'

'It's hard work. It's my last chance to change anything in the text of the recipe book. Eva's reading it through too, and the publisher, of course, but it's so scary thinking it might be read by thousands of people. If I've got anything wrong . . . I'd hate someone's dog to be ill.'

'Haven't all the recipes been checked by a vet and nutritionist?'

'Yes, but . . . ' I put my laptop down. 'I'm not worried about that but this is another big step for me and Demelza's. Everything's happening so fast, sometimes I feel as if I've been swept up by a whirlwind and dumped in a strange place.'

'I've lived here all my life and I often feel that I've been picked up and dropped here.'

Cal looks thoughtful but his statement doesn't make me feel better. I've had doubts that he's truly happy back home and running Kilhallon ever since I first came here. Initially, I thought his heart lay with Isla, but lately, I've wondered if he's as committed to staying here as he makes out. If he wants to leave, there's nothing I can do about it . . . my stomach flips. I'd get over it, I'd carry on — I told myself over and over not to tangle up my hopes and dreams and future with his.

'I'm glad I know what happened to you in Syria,' I say, switching the focus to Cal.

'A problem shared is a problem that can make two people unhappy rather than one,' he says with a bitter edge to his voice. 'Part of me wishes I'd never laid the burden on you.'

'It's not a burden.'

He smiles very briefly, then kisses me. 'Forget it for now. Let's talk about something important. I've booked Boris the owl although the falconer says he's been out of sorts lately and she might have to substitute him with a female eagle owl. Believe it or not, she's called Theresa.'

'You're making that up!'

'Cross my heart,' he says, making a sign over his chest.

'Really? Eww. That's creepy. An eagle owl called Theresa? That sounds a bit dodgy. Ben won't like an even bigger, scarier bird than Boris landing on him.'

Cal smiles and then winks.

'You *were* making it up. You ratbag.' I jump from my seat and grab a cushion and start hitting him. He fends me off but in seconds we're both on the sofa, me on top of him. The cushions are abandoned and we're snogging, and Boris and the wedding and the whole world can go away.

20

The next day I'm in Demelza's, relishing the chance to have a 'normal day's work' that focuses on the cafe and customers without any wedding drama or any dark thoughts. Cal talked to me about business last night, about how busy bookings were looking for Easter and how long we needed to close for the wedding.

Many of the plans are now in place. We've decided to shut the whole resort and cafe from the Wednesday evening until the Monday. It will cost Lily and Ben a lot of money but that doesn't seem to be a problem. Harry has sent us a dossier outlining the security plan and called to discuss it. Addison and Jade are, of course, never off the phone or email, checking that everything is 'progressing'.

Business is steady, but not spectacular on this grey and cool morning which has given me a chance to sift through some of the applications for seasonal staff and arrange some interviews. We're definitely going to need a few pairs of extra hands with all our events and the summer season coming up.

Jugs of candy-coloured tulips on every table lift the mood in the cafe, which is filled with comforting aromas that seem to have lured ramblers and regulars inside. There's even a hardy group of dog walkers out on the terrace, swaddled in coats and fleece hats, cradling hot chocolates to warm their hands. The canine customers, two Labradors and a lively young Puggle, are enjoying some of my new savoury doggy popcorn.

I'm taking a moment to deal with some admin during the early afternoon lull when Kit walks into the cafe.

'Am I too late for lunch? I needed to finish a chapter of my editing.'

'You're always late, but I'm sure we can find you some scraps.'

He smiles. 'I guess that's all I deserve. Humble pie.'

'I can do slightly better than that.'

Although I'm still not one hundred per cent sure of Kit, as my Nana Demelza would have said, I'm going to give him the benefit of the doubt for now.

I grab a coffee and a cheese scone for my lunch and sit down next to him while he tucks into a jacket potato topped with vegetable chilli and local cheese.

'This is bloody good,' he says, re-loading his fork with the chilli. Strands of cheese stick to the tines.

'It was a new recipe for spring. We'll probably keep it on until Easter when the weather warms up.'

'It's going well, then?'

'The crappy photos in the papers didn't help us but the regulars took no notice and a few people came out of curiosity to see if it was as bad as it looked. We've been lucky to have the boost of the photo shoot, the filming and now this celebrity wedding.'

'Crappy photos? Big wedding?' he says after swallowing a mouthful of chilli. 'You've lost me.'

'You must know about the wedding the newspapers have been speculating about? That's why Kilhallon ended up in a tabloid. They sent a pap down here and took some photos that showed the place in a terrible light.'

He blows out a breath. 'I may be a journalist but I've been totally caught up in the editing and launch plans for my book. When I do read the papers it's for the environmental and political features relevant to it. Sorry, I'm not up to speed with the celebrity gossip.'

'You *must* have heard of Lily Craig and Ben Trevone?'

He frowns then blows out a breath. 'Ah. Those two. Yes, I have heard of them. He made that crappy action film, didn't he? I seem to recall her being OK in that period drama that won an award?'

'Yes. Lily had a lot of praise for Isla's costume drama that won a big award. Ben's *Ocean Furries* animation was nominated for an Oscar too. He was the sea otter.'

'A sea otter? I'll take your word for it. What have they got to do with you?'

'They're getting married at Kilhallon. Although that's meant to be a secret but all the newspapers know about it anyway. Their people don't want to announce it officially.'

'Thereby guaranteeing complete obsession with every last detail and continuous press coverage for months? Bloody hell though. Kilhallon — I mean, it's nice for us ordinary mortals but for Hollywood movie stars?'

'We can scrub up,' I shoot back, annoyed that Kit's voicing exactly the same thoughts that I've been having. 'You're right and I'm worried about it too. They say they want a low-key, authentic wedding-slash-handfasting thing. They want the event to seem as if we've thrown it together at the last minute, which is exactly what was going to happen until Rachel helped us out.'

'Christ.'

'Cal said that. But I hadn't thought about the mystery adding to the publicity value. That's not my worry. Kilhallon had some bad PR in the daily rag a few weeks ago. They sent a pap on a horrible wet day and posted a load of pictures of our bins, Mitch weeing up a log and Cal looking pissed off next to the toilets.'

'Cal looked pissed off? I can't believe that.'

'Don't be sarcastic.'

'It's my job.' He grins. 'Bastard journos. They're all evil.' God, sometimes he is so like Cal, I could kill him. They must have inherited the same gene for being infuriating and sarcastic.

'I'm amazed you didn't see it. The ones who wrote the lies about Kilhallon are awful and now I wished I hadn't asked another one to help,' I throw back at him. I don't want to sound tetchy bit I can't help reminding Kit that he was willing to make Cal's life a misery by writing a story about Cal's experiences in Syria — or what Kit thought Cal had been up to in Syria. As it happened, Kit didn't know the full facts at the time.

Kit gives an apologetic smile. 'I know. I was joking.' He sighs. 'And I'm sorry for being a git. My sense of humour doesn't always translate as funny. I rarely read the rag and I didn't catch the online gossip because I've been trying to keep offline while I finish my edits. Sadly, there's not much I can do about restoring the image of Kilhallon, however much I want to help.'

'Actually, there *is* a way you could do me, Cal and Kilhallon a big favour.'

He frowns. 'Yes?'

'How would you like to help out at the wedding fair on Sunday?'

'Me? At a wedding fair . . . ' He screws up his face. 'Do I have a choice?'

'No. Call it rehab.'

He sighs. 'You two are really going to make me suffer for this, aren't you?'

'Believe me, the wedding fair will be nothing compared to when Polly sees you.'

He groans. 'Polly. I feel bad about not being open with her. She was so nice to me and I do genuinely like her. Salt of the earth as they say, they broke the mould etcetera, and I deceived her . . . Oh shit, how can I face her now?'

'Wearing full body armour?'

He winces.

'Fortunately for you, Polly only knows that you and Cal are half-brothers but not the full details. Cal sat her down in the New Year with a large glass of his best whisky and broke the news. Apparently she was speechless for a full minute when she heard and burst into tears but she said she knew that Cal's father, Mr Penwith, was a 'philanderer', which isn't a compliment. Once she was over the initial blow, she said it made sense. If she knew everything that had gone on between you and Cal and Mawgan, she'd *never* forgive you.'

He swallows hard. 'I don't blame her. I've struggled to forgive myself. I was bitter and twisted and I did the one thing a journalist — a decent one, not a hack — should never do: prejudged the situation and come up with the story I wanted instead of what was really there. But I'm only human and when I got here I could tell Cal loathed me at first sight. I guessed you and he were in a relationship, and having heard about your backstory, I decided he'd taken advantage of you when you were vulnerable.'

'Cal never took advantage of me and I've never been vulnerable.' I lower my voice, aware that Shamia is watching us closely. 'And we weren't, technically, in a relationship back then, though we are now. You probably know I've moved into Kilhallon House.'

'Ah. I had sort of guessed when I saw your old cottage had been refurbished. I'm genuinely happy for you.' His eyes plead with me to believe him. I do. This *is* a different Kit to the guy who turned up last year. He's dropped the façade, I think . . . unless he's showing a new façade.

'Cal's a very lucky man . . . but when I rocked up here last autumn, spoiling for a fight myself, Cal came across as difficult, arrogant, bloody minded and always right.'

'That's an accurate assessment, but it still gave you no right to try and make him even

192

unhappier. Has he told you what happened to him in Syria? What *really* happened to him?'

'He's told me his side of the story. It was crap for him, a tragic outcome. No wonder he's found it hard to readjust. Maybe he'll open up more when we talk about the feature I'm writing on the floods.'

I hesitate before I reply. 'Maybe. Sometimes, I think it's better if some people don't know everything.'

'Perhaps, but if he talked more, I might be able to help,' says Kit.

'That's up to him. Concentrate on the wedding fair and the feature for now.'

'The feature I can do. The wedding fair is what scares me. Please don't say I have to arrange flowers or sashay down the catwalk in a bridal gown?'

'Don't panic. Both of those jobs are way out of your league.' I pat his arm. 'I'll find you something a lot easier to do than that.'

21

The Wedding Fair

Primroses still dot the sunny banks and the birds are singing their hearts out as Tamsin and I 'plant' a trail of shepherd's hooks hung with jars either side of the matting that leads into the event tepee on the morning of the wedding fair. Now April is well underway, the bluebells are just coming out, adding their pretty buds to the white of the wild garlic in the copse.

Mitch scampers around, sniffing at the myriad strange scents and generally distracting people from their work. I'm in secondhand Hunters and Tamsin's in Joules wellies because the newly mown grass still glistens with dew. The wind blew a front across the peninsular last night and the morning's as fresh and bright as Polly's whites fluttering in the breeze behind the farmhouse. There's a fresh scent in the air: wet grass, sea breeze sharpened by the early chill. It's full-on spring and Kilhallon has never looked more beautiful.

I check out the sky: a washed-out blue the same colour as Cal's best shirt. 'Polly's right about the weather,' I say to Tamsin.

'I know . . . wow, would you check *that* out?' Tamsin points at Kit who's helping Cal fix the willow wedding arch in the glade in the middle of the glamping field, under the watchful eye of

Hazel Tremain, the florist who's also taken a stall at the fair.

'Now, *how* hot do those boys look?' she adds.

Cal and Kit are both stripped to T-shirts. Cal is the darker of the two and his muscular biceps and forearms are tanned year-round from his outdoor lifestyle. Kit is fairer but slightly taller. His arms are paler and he may not be as buff, but he's lean and strong from his running and gym habit.

'How did I not notice they were brothers?' Tamsin asks, pushing her shepherd's hook firmly into the damp turf. Not that the 'boys' would notice us ogling them, they're too busy fixing the arch in place.

'I didn't notice but now I know, the likeness is obvious, from their features to the way they stand. And they're both sarcastic and spiky when they want to be, which is most of the time.'

'And secretive?'

'Cal's improving. I don't know Kit well enough yet but I'm willing to give him the benefit of the doubt. He has a lot to prove, especially with Cal.' Tamsin knows that there's been trouble between Cal and Kit but not the finer details. She thinks their rift only relates to the affair between Cal's father and Kit's mum. She knows nothing about Cal's experiences in Syria and I won't be sharing, however much we get on. That story is between Cal, Kit and me.

'Kit must want to try and make up for what he did or he wouldn't be here. The two of them look as if they're getting on fine this morning. Maybe they've already kissed and made up.'

Tamsin makes me laugh out loud. 'Who knows? By the end of the century, maybe.'

Kit's on his knees, hammering in a stake to secure the arch to the turf, with Cal standing over him, hands on hips. Then he stands up and Hazel comes over to them and nods approvingly. Cal and Kit exchange glances and they both laugh.

'They seem to be getting on,' Tamsin says again.

'OK. Maybe it will only take fifty years for Cal to trust him completely.'

'Does Kit have a partner?' Tamsin asks as I hang a jar from my crook. We need to fill the jars with fresh flowers once the crooks are all safely in place.

'He's never mentioned one.'

Her face falls. 'Is he gay?'

'Not as far as I know.' I don't tell her I thought he might be interested in me last year, although I'm beginning to think his interest was only to get at Cal.

'And he definitely wasn't interested in Mawgan? Because if he was, I'd consider him to have crap taste and judgement and I won't even bother with him.'

'No. That was a business arrangement on his part and hers.'

'What a shame she's coming to the wedding.'

'Tell me about it.' I stand back from the crook aisle and take in the tepee.

'What do you think about the tepee?' I ask Tamsin. Even on hire for the day, it was a big investment so I hope it pays off. It's actually two giant tepees joined together with twin turrets to make it look like a canvas castle complete with pennants flying. One side has been left open as it's a fine day.

'It's fabulous. Much nicer than setting up in a windowless function room.'

'Even if we don't get many prospective customers, the photos will look great and the suppliers won't have to be rained on or blown away. The last thing we want is another disaster today. Some of the local and regional papers are coming along, not to mention the wedding bloggers. If they're hoping for Lily and Ben, they'll be disappointed — Lily's too busy so she's coming next week when things have quietened down.'

'Do you think there's any chance Lily would let me do her make-up?'

'Sorry, hon, but I already know she wants to bring her own hair and make-up stylist. I know this isn't as exciting but would you come and do my make-up on the morning of the wedding? I'd like to look my best.'

'Of course I will. I'd love to be around anyway and see what's going on.'

Tamsin adjusts the jar on the final crook at the entrance to the tepee. 'We can put the flowers in the jars now and then I ought to start getting my stall ready.'

'Do you need a hand setting it up?'

'Thanks, but I've got it down to a fine art now and my sister's coming along later to give me a hand when the visitors arrive. I wonder if Kit fancies trying out one of my groom's pre-wedding facial and massages?'

Kit stretches his back after moving the wedding arch over to the log 'altar' in the glade. The arch is stunning, the twigs are intertwined with roses and peonies in a palette of soft white, pastels and blushes.

'You could ask him. He's really not as scary as I thought.'

'I'd like to find out for myself. Hmm. A good shave, some sexy stubble and an eyebrow trim would do wonders for him, not to mention a scrub and regular moisturise. And if I could get him on my treatment table for a massage . . . '

'I thought you were supposed to be strictly professional with your clients.'

'I am. Always.' She draws a halo over her head.

'Look. He and Cal and have finished the arch. What about if I introduce you and we grab a quick drink together before you set up your stall.'

With a gleam in her eye, Tamsin beams. 'That would be awesome. I'll offer him a freebie.'

★   ★   ★

Our drink and chat with Cal and Kit didn't last more than ten minutes, although judging by the way Kit was laughing at Tamsin's cheeky banter, he might come round to the idea of a facial and massage after all. Although I don't imagine lying down and relaxing with a scented candle is on his or any of our minds today because there's so much to do.

Robyn and Andi were up until midnight last night setting out the cafe as it might appear for a wedding tea. The tables have already been laid with vintage china we salvaged from the farmhouse last year, complete with some new paper tablecloths. We're offering a limited but cute afternoon-tea style menu for the refreshments but have a table showcasing some of the menu ideas we can offer.

Kit and Cal are now busy unfolding stripy deckchairs hired in from a local supplier. Added to the log 'pews' with their pretty retro cushions, the site is starting to look more like a wedding glade and less like Glastonbury after the loos have been towed away.

And one by one, the suppliers have started to roll in to Kilhallon, marshalled by Rachel, who's left Freya with her mum. Dad's busy double-checking the power and lighting to the tepee. As well as Hazel the florist, we have two very different bridal-wear suppliers, a grooms-wear hire company, photographers, a videographer, a stationery designer and a vintage wedding bus which is parked next to the cafe. Robyn and Andi arrive late morning to set up Robyn's jewellery design stall. Tamsin's pop-up spa is ready and her sister has joined her to offer mini-makeovers to prospective bridges and their guests.

There's even a company that offers neon signs in the initials of the bride and groom, as well as providing event lighting. Rachel and I take a look at them when we rendezvous in the tepee for a five-minute powwow.

'Lily and Ben would love those signs,' I say.

'I thought we could get their names made to match the Hollywood sign and so when they come into the tepee for the evening party, they get a huge surprise,' says Rachel. 'It was your dad's idea. He came across them when he was wiring a design company's HQ in Plymouth. They had the signs in their reception but this company do temporary ones for events and weddings.'

'Are they expensive?'

'Does it matter?' Rachel asks.

'No, because their PA is dealing with it, but I think we ought to get her approval. Lily says we can do what we want but Addison and Jade keep emailing me. I suppose I'm not surprised.'

Rachel wrinkles her nose. 'I've spoken to them a few times. Jade is seriously scary but we have to deal with them. Has she said any more about when we can officially announce that the wedding's being held here?'

'Not today. I don't know. Originally, Lily and Ben said we could publicise it in advance but I think Jade has persuaded them to change their minds. It doesn't make feel very confident that they won't let us say anything, although I can see why for security reasons.'

We turn away from the neon signs and wander past the stalls towards the florists' display. 'I think it's the worst-kept secret in Cornwall. It's one reason I had so many acceptances from the suppliers, even though I couldn't confirm or deny the rumours. People love being associated with a celebrity wedding.'

'Even after the newspaper pictures?' I ask.

'Even after that. Look' — she flashes me a reassuring smile — 'nothing's going to go wrong today. I'm sure we'll have lots of visitors, even if they're only curious to see if Kilhallon really is that terrible.'

'Shit.'

She gives me a quick hug. 'But it's *not* going to be terrible. It's going to be brilliant and you'll have loads of bookings after this. What you need to do is think how many weddings you can cope with and at what time of year.'

'We've discussed that. We're keeping July and August purely for holidays and we're only going to accept a few a year. The income is welcome and important but we're a holiday resort first and foremost and I don't think I could cope with this stress every weekend. Hey — Mitch! Get your nose out of there!'

Mitch turns his head, debating whether he dare carry on sniffing the florist's stall.

I whistle at him and, reluctantly, he trots back to me. He's submitted to a smart neckerchief that looks like a bow-tie on a tux. He'll put in a brief appearance but for most of the day will be running free with some canine companions and Nina at the animal shelter she helps to run with her mum. She's offered to look after him because with all the strange people, smells and tempting treats around, he's sure to get over-excited.

'Not long to go now,' Rachel says, checking her watch. 'Some people are bound to be early so we'd better have someone on the gates of Kilhallon in advance.'

On a decked area in the corner of the tepee, the student folk band is setting up its instruments. They're going to play quirky cover versions of traditional folk songs and wedding staples.

'I hired two of Robyn's mates to man the gates,' she continues, 'when they've finished helping the band set up.'

'I had no idea there was so much to do. This is even more stressful than the launch,' I say, already feeling as if I've run a marathon.

'It's a good rehearsal for the real thing though my feet are killing me already,' Rachel says. 'Which is one reason I suggested it for both of us! How's the cafe set up?'

'OK. We're nearly ready. Thank goodness we got most of it in place last night. I haven't had a second this morning but I have to whizz down there as soon as people start arriving.'

'What time do you start serving the teas?'

'We open at two-thirty to give people time to look around the tepee before they start thinking about a cuppa, but I need to go now. Are you sure you'll be OK to run things up here?'

'Of course. It's a good job my mum could have Freya because I couldn't possibly have managed this without her help. It seems strange to leave her but I won't always be able to take her to meetings and events if I'm going to start my business, even part time. Even though I know she's safe and happy with her nan, I can't help the anxiety that niggles in my mind.'

'It must be so hard to leave her. She's gorgeous.'

'Most of the time.' With a smile that turns into a grimace, Rachel slips off her shoes and wriggles her toes. 'These look smart but I've learned my lesson. Comfy old shoes next time I do anything like this.'

We wait at the entrance to the tent and on the stroke of two, our first customers begin to arrive, ushered from the car park to the glade by a line of bunting and box trees with ribbon created by our event florists and decor specialists. Considering the event was organised at short notice, we have a healthy amount of visitors, some of whom are actually interested in getting married rather than a free cup of tea.

Hastily, Rachel puts her shoes back on and goes into professional mode. 'I managed to get a quick mention feature on Radio St Trenyan though I did find myself dodging a question from Greg Stennack about Lily and Ben,' she says in between greeting visitors with a smile.

'You know, I think we should just pretend that we might have a celebrity wedding every year. They don't seem to care whether the rumours are true or not. They only want some juicy gossip to share.'

'As long as people come and nothing disastrous happens and they go home with the right impression, we'll be OK,' she says with a smile.

With a nod, I head for the cafe. After recent events, the chances of all of those things coming together seems a bit slim, but all I can do is cross my fingers and get on with my part of the job.

But within ten minutes of the fair opening, I realise that's a forlorn hope.

22

'Come on, love. When are you going to give an official announcement that Lily and Ben are holding their wedding at Kilhallon?'

'As far as I know, they're not holding a *wedding* anywhere.' The smug reporter from the *South Western Bugle* thrusts his mobile phone almost up my nose. My words are strictly true, because it's a handfasting.

He snorts. 'Oh, come on, Demi. Everyone knows they're getting married down here and you were seen with them at the Rockpool. It's the worst-kept secret in the county.'

'How do you feel about those terrible photos that appeared in the *Daily News*?' a woman from the *St Trenyan Mercury* asks.

'Look around you today,' I say, then have to clear my throat because I'm so nervous. 'You can see for yourself that Kilhallon would make a wonderful wedding venue for any couple looking for a special place to hold their ceremony and reception.'

'So the wedding *is* here!' Mr Smugface pipes up.

'When is it?'

'Has Lily chosen a dress yet?'

'How much has it cost?'

'Why have they chosen Kilhallon? You have to admit it's not Hollywood.'

Arghh. The press are like a pack of seagulls

dive-bombing me with questions. I've never been in a situation like this and I feel like throwing up. It's as bad as facing down Mawgan. Fortunately, Rachel steps in before I blurt out anything that really could ruin Kilhallon's reputation.

'When — and if — there's an announcement about a wedding, it will come from Ben and Lily and until then, we ask to you respect their privacy,' she says politely but firmly. 'Thanks for your interest in Kilhallon and for coming along. Now, please have a look around the fair and if you have any questions about the venue itself, Demi, Cal and I will be happy to answer them. We've made our statement about Lily and Ben and that's all we are prepared to say for now.'

'That's a 'yes' then,' says Mr Smugface with a snort. 'You'd have denied it if they weren't. They'd better be getting married here after this or you're going to look pretty stupid.'

This guy is really getting to me. 'Don't you want a look around the wedding fair?' I ask him sweetly, but with murder in my heart. 'Or would you prefer to visit the cafe for a cup of tea and a scone?'

'Nah. I need to get this video uploaded to our website and social media pages. But thanks for the offer.' With a delighted grin, he walks off, clicking away on his phone as I realise he was videoing the interview with us. It takes all of my customer-service skills to avoid telling him to shove his phone where the sun doesn't shine. Luckily, since I 'accidentally' threw a smoothie over Mawgan Cade a year ago, I've learnt a few more coping strategies, but even they're wearing thin.

'Lily and Ben will have to make an official announcement soon. We can't go on like this. It's driving me mad,' I tell Rachel.

'They're enough to drive you up the wall but the mystery is great for business.'

'I don't like having to lie and fend them off all the time. Imagine what they'd do if they knew Lily was going to be here after Easter. I guess they'll be watching us like hawks from now on.'

Rachel shrugs. 'Whatever you say to them, the papers will print what they want.'

'I know. I expect the big tabloids will probably make it up anyway.'

A couple approach us, and to my relief actually want to talk about the possibility of having their silver wedding anniversary party at Kilhallon next summer rather than gossip about our celebrities. After a quick chat about the food that Demelza's can provide, I leave them with Rachel and run down to the cafe to see Nina. I've already left her alone for too long.

However, apart from having to fend off the reporters, the day seems to be going really well. It's still fine and dry and we've had a healthy number of visitors considering the short notice. The suppliers all seem to have people looking at their stalls. The folk band has started playing their quirky versions of wedding favourites, which adds to the atmosphere. I wouldn't say I start to relax, but my confidence is back and I believe that we can pull today off without any major disasters.

The sight of people sitting outside the cafe makes me smile. There's a mixture of the visitors to the wedding fair and casual customers who've wandered in off the coastal path out of curiosity. I hope we've got enough food . . . maybe we should break out the cakes and scones from the freezer . . .

As I reach the cafe, I spot Nina's mum with a few of their rescue dogs and Mitch. He barks joyfully when he sees me and although I'm busy, I can't help going over for a quick word and a belly rub.

'Is he being good?'

'Having a great time. We took the dogs to the beach earlier.'

She lets him run to me and he drops at my feet, snuffling happily before rolling over onto his back for a belly rub.

'He looks happy. Thanks for having him.'

'No problem. He's fun to look after.'

Mitch scampers along the path.

'Mitch!'

Instead of coming back, he darts into the gorse, on the trail of new and unfamiliar scents. I shout to him sternly but he's hell bent on running towards the camping area and wedding fair.

'Mitch! Not now!'

'I'll get him,' Nina's mum says.

'Thanks, but I'd better go after him. He might listen to me. I'll be back in a minute.'

At least, I hope to be back in a minute as I set off towards the wedding fair with Mitch at full tilt ahead of me. I need to get hold of him quickly because not everyone likes dogs and the last thing I want is him running amok in the tepee. I don't fancy the chances of the flower arrangements with an over-excited Mitch on the loose.

Too late. Mitch is heading straight for the yurts. Heads turn and people stare at me. Some clutch their kids closer, obviously afraid there's a wild runaway hound on the loose.

'Excuse me. He must have scented a rabbit,' I say, and run over to get Mitch under control. But he breaks free and hares back towards the yurts.

I run after him. It's not the dignified 'everything-under-control' image we want to portray, chasing an out-of-control animal through our wedding area. Especially not one hell bent on rooting out a fluffy bunny in front of the happy couples. If people weren't paying attention to his barking before, they are now. Mitch stops by a yurt and barks. Then he starts digging at the entrance. Dirt flies up in the air.

'Mitch. What the heck are you playing at? There are no rabbits in that tent. Stop it!'

As I make a grab for his leash, Mitch barks and dances around. His neckerchief is black with dirt, like his muzzle, and he's going mad. He starts scratching at the door of the yurt and suddenly worms his way under the open flap. I try to grab Mitch's lead but he growls softly and digs his claws in. He ignores me. Nothing new about that but a growl isn't his style unless he's warning me of danger, or letting me know that Mawgan's in the vicinity.

Mitch can go a bit off piste but he's not a bad dog and there must be a good reason for his behaviour. I crawl into the yurt and my breath catches in my throat. Mitch lies at the entrance, his head on his paws. A few feet away, curled up on the furry throws, is a little boy. He can't be more than three or four and despite the barking and Mitch's attempts to tear down the yurt, he's fast asleep.

Moments after I spot him, I hear voices I recognise and some I don't. Cal's voice and Kit's too, then a woman crying and a man saying: 'Is it him? Keegan?'

'Oh my God. Is he OK?'

'He's fine. He's in here. He must have crawled in and fallen asleep.'

I open the flap and a woman in tears pushes her way in. 'Keegan!'

His mother flies at him and scoops him up and hugs him so tightly. 'Too tight, Mummy.' The sight of his mum in floods of tears, squeezing him, and his dad muttering, 'What if he'd fallen over a cliff', is bound to upset him. In fact, Keegan was fine until he saw the adults around him freaking out.

'Want tent!' he screams as his mum carries him away. 'Wanttttt tenntttt. My tent!'

I follow them out of the tent and Cal walks over to me. His face has gone as pale as my pastry. 'His mother thought someone had taken him or he'd fallen over a cliff. They've been looking for him for twenty minutes apparently and Rachel put a call out in the tepee. We'd just organised a search party to see if we could find him before we called the police.'

'You look as white as a sheet.'

209

'That's all we needed, a lost kid.' He tries to make a joke of it but I can see he's shaken up. 'Remind me never to have one of my own.'

'You don't mean that. You love kids.'

'Some of them. Some of the time. Shit. I'll leave you to soothe the parents. I've had enough of all that. I'll be in the tepee if you need me.' He rubs Mitch's ears. 'Thanks, boy. There's an extra-large chew in this for you later and maybe a bit of steak.'

Mitch answers by glancing up momentarily before returning to inspect his privates.

'Are you sure you're OK?' I ask Cal.

'Why wouldn't I be?' he snaps. 'Have to go, I was talking to a couple about a party when this kicked off.'

'Wait, Cal.' He's already walking quickly away from me, and away from the yurts into the woods. I could take offence at him snapping at me but he was genuinely rattled.

After taking the parents and little boy into the cafe and seeing them settled with a cup of tea and a squash for Keegan, I try to leave to see where Cal is but I'm needed by half a dozen people wanting to know about holding events here and where the toilets are and do we do outside catering? Finally I notice the clock and Shamia pulling anxious faces at me from behind a pair of sixty-something dog owners who want to know if we can cater for a wedding between a miniature Schnauzer and a Chihuahua.

I'm still slightly worried about Cal but the yurt has given me an idea for entertaining the kids at weddings. I know that we'll have at least a dozen children under twelve at the wedding and some teenagers. I think we could have two yurts dedicated to them. With DVDs, books and toys for the younger ones and a chill-out tent with games consoles for the older ones. We could even hire a nanny if Lily and Ben agree.

Soon, it's time to shut up shop but the cafe is half full and there's no way I can slip away to see what's wrong with Cal, *if* there's anything wrong with him at all. His face was so pale and I swear his hands shook.

He surely didn't mean what he said about not having kids — he was great with the evacuees we had at the flooding and he never needs an excuse to act like a big kid. Despite throwing himself into the wedding fair and saying his mind is here at Kilhallon, there's a lot I don't know about him and may never know.

23

Maundy Thursday

For a week now, the cafe has been filled with the spicy aromas of hot cross buns, Cornish saffron cake and chocolate cupcakes. Cal reckoned you could smell it from a hundred yards away. Hard to believe that it was last Easter, a year ago, when I first came to Kilhallon. Even harder to believe that Demelza's has now been open six months and that the cafe and resort are about to enter their first full season. From now until the end of September, we're going to be open from Tuesday to Sunday and we've taken on an extra chef and two more waiting staff to help.

'Remind me that I never want to see another chocolate egg, bunny or Easter nest,' I say to Nina and Shamia as we clear up the cafe after a busy 'Maundy Thursday', as Polly calls it. She's tried to explain about it being the day when the Queen gives her small change away to pensioners but all I know is that it's Good Friday tomorrow and the cafe has been jam-packed with over-excited kids. We invited the children who stayed over at Christmas after the floods as an Easter treat and they've had a whale of a time decorating cupcakes, along with some of our younger cottage and yurt guests.

Melted chocolate, Rice Krispies and corn-flakes spatter the paper cloths covering the tables at one end of the cafe. I pick a squashed fluffy chick off the floor and get down on my knees to rescue a chocolate bunny that's rolled under the radiator and is melting onto the tiles.

The kids and their families spent a couple of hours making Easter nests and biscuits as part of a fundraising tea for the Flood Appeal. Lots of locals turned up to support it, along with the usual walkers and guests. Eva donated some of her cookbooks and Tamsin offered a spa voucher for the raffle. It was great to see everyone having a good time but the noise level under the rafters was deafening.

Apart from a few meetings in London, Kit has stayed on at Kilhallon, working on his articles and a new book idea. He arranged for a freelance photographer to take pictures of some of the families affected. They've given him the positive side of the story: St Trenyan rebuilding and gearing up for a new season and the downside: some homes and businesses still not habitable because of insurance claims and other problems. He's also interviewed Cal in his role as vice-chair of the Floods Committee, managing a hardship fund and supporting people as they try to rebuild their lives. While most of the businesses have managed to re-open, some of the residents are still in short-term accommodation and are battling with their insurers.

A celebrity wedding seems trivial in comparison but we need to make Kilhallon a success to be able to employ local people and bring in visitors to the area. The wedding fair was hard work, both to set up and dismantle, but I'm glad we did it. At least we have all got more confidence that we can pull off the real thing now.

On the day itself, we took two deposits for weddings, one for this autumn and one for next spring, plus enquiries for several more. The suppliers were happy. It all seems a lifetime away because Easter is one of the busiest times of year for Kilhallon and Demelza's. Much to our relief, Lily was delighted with the pictures we sent of the venue and has been talking to Hazel about the flowers and styling for the wedding. So things, for the moment, seem to be progressing in the right direction.

It's been a long but fun day at the cafe but I'm glad to slide into bed this evening. Cal walks into the bedroom, towelling his hair after a shower, another towel tightly knotted around his waist. I'm already under the duvet, in prime position to enjoy the spectacle. I'll never take it for granted and my body responds to the sight of his toned arms and stomach with the most delicious feelings.

He drops the towel on a chair and stands by the bed. 'You know this is a special occasion, don't you?'

It's special enough for me with him so close. Tiny droplets of water glisten in the springy hair that dusts his chest. 'Special? Why?'

He raises his eyebrows as if he's surprised I don't know what he means. Of course, I do, but I'm not going to let on that I've been thinking about our 'anniversary' all day and wondering how I ever got this lucky.

'It's been a year to the day since I first saw you at Sheila's Beach Hut,' he says.

'Oh God, has it? That's exactly a year since I lost my job. Not my finest hour.'

'And it's been a year since I set foot in Cornwall after my little holiday in Syria. It wasn't my finest hour either: I should have stuck up for you with Mawgan but I walked off. I was too wrapped up with my own problems.'

'You had a lot on your mind. I know that now, but at the time I did think you were another hipster only interested in himself and his surfboard.'

'I've never owned a surfboard. I've never been any good at surfing.' He sits on the edge of the bed, naked. 'Now look at us.'

'Look at you.'

'Hmm. You have that effect on me.' His kiss is warm, gentle but confident. Fresh from the shower, he smells great and his skin is still damp and glowing under my fingertips. I still haven't got used to falling asleep and waking up next to that lean and gorgeous body, and the sometimes confusing puzzle that's Cal, with all his quirks and problems.

He climbs into bed and lies beside me. He pushes my hair off my face. 'How's your first year been? Any regrets about accepting the job?'

'Too many to list, but I'm still here. How are you, Cal?'

'I'm fine.'

'Are you? Really fine?'

He frowns. 'Why do you ask?'

His overreaction with the missing boy at the wedding fair is on the tip of my tongue but

215

something in Cal's tone makes me wary of mentioning it.

'Nothing.' I smile.

'I'm OK. The past, you might say, is all behind me,' he murmurs, laying his hands on my bottom and pressing me against him. He kisses me and stifles any more dangerous talk. We're both lost in each other but later, when he thinks I'm asleep, I hear him get out of bed. I sneak a look at him, staring out of the window at the starry night. I know he's not here at Kilhallon but thousands of miles away and I can't do a thing about it. Long after he's climbed back in beside me and has finally fallen asleep, I make up my mind that I have to try to help, even if Cal wouldn't approve of the idea. I must try.

★   ★   ★

On Easter Monday, Kit walks into the cafe as we're closing after a hectic bank holiday. I make him a coffee myself and sit down with him while the staff clear up wearily around us.

He sips his espresso thoughtfully. 'Wow. Allowed in after closing time again. That must be a good sign I've been accepted.'

'Don't bank on it. The last time you were allowed in after closing, Mitch and I fell down a hole,' I say, reminding him of the night we were hanging Christmas decorations when Mitch ran off into the fog.

He winces. 'I worried that I'd left the door open when we went to fetch the holly. That it was my fault.'

'No. I think I left the door open. It doesn't matter now, everything turned out OK.'

'No thanks to me.'

I smile. 'Forget it. Even Cal is getting over it. He uses your first name now and said you were doing a decent job with the article.'

'Wow. High praise.'

I cradle my mug, wondering if I dare share the idea that's been swirling around my head for a few weeks now. 'There's something else you could help with, though, if you did want to do more, although it's probably a much harder job than your flooding feature . . . ' I say, hoping I'm doing the right thing. Then I suddenly worry that Kit will think I'm going to suggest he asks Tamsin out on a date. She still has hopes in that direction.

Kit sips his coffee before asking, warily. 'What would that be?'

I dive straight in with my request. 'Help me track down Esme.'

Slowly he lowers his cup and replaces it in the saucer.

'Hmm. That *is* a hard job. Impossible even . . . ' He pauses and I wish the words were still unsaid. 'However, I could make a few calls and send some emails,' he goes on. 'I do know some colleagues who have contacts out there but I can't see how I can do much more than Cal and his colleagues. Trawling the people-tracing agencies is their best bet.'

'I know but I wanted to try. I won't tell Cal I've asked you.'

'Best not. The likelihood is it'll turn out to be

pointless anyway but I'll do some digging and if I have the slightest lead on Esme or her family, I'll be in touch with you right away. You realise she's probably not even alive?'

I feel sick when he says the words out loud but he's only echoing Cal. 'Yes, I'm prepared for that, which is why I'd rather not tell him I've even asked you to help. He's had enough disappointment for one year and I don't think he could take any more right now. He said he just wanted a quiet life from now on.'

'A *quiet* life? Cal?' Kit huffs in disbelief. 'Things must be dire. When I get back to London, I'll see what I can do, and I'll let you know, even if I turn up bad news.'

24

'Oooo, it really is as cute and pretty as I remember!' Lily says, beaming at us from the open door of the BMW. It's the Monday after the Easter holiday week and the first day that the cafe has been closed for eleven days straight. I've worked right through to make the most of the holidays and I'm hoping I don't keel over with exhaustion. Although judging by the look of Lily, she may flake out first.

Harry helps her down onto the cafe parking area like she's a grand lady descending from a carriage. Despite her breezy manner and smile, I'm a bit shocked. She's even thinner than she was and her eyes are puffy and dark as if she hasn't slept for days.

'I'm sorry Ben couldn't make it, He had some ADR work to do for his latest film.'

'Oh, I see. I think,' I say, though I've no idea what she means.

She laughs. 'It means he has to re-record some of his lines from the film. Sometimes the dialogue isn't clear the first time or they make last-minute script changes before the movie comes out. I'll probably have to do some myself soon.'

'Hi, Harry. How are you?'

'Very well, thank you.'

'Rachel's on her way. Can I get you both a drink and something to eat?' I ask.

'A chamomile tea, please, and do you have any of those rice cakes with the dark chocolate on them? I know I shouldn't but I feel like pigging out and Ben's not here to see me.'

'Surely he doesn't mind you eating?' I'm shocked.

'No, of course not. I'm not under Ben's thumb.'

'You need to keep your strength up,' Harry says before turning to me. 'Do you have any figgy 'obbin today?'

'Sorry, no, but I've made some sample canapés and there are some triple chocolate brownies and a citrus cake. How does that sound?'

He rubs his hands together. 'Would it be awfully rude of me to try one of each?'

'No. I'd love to know what you think of them. Lily says you like baking and cooking?'

'Gosh, no. It's Giles who's the baker. I'm more of a main course man.'

'We'll have to swap some recipes. I'll get your drinks and cakes.'

There's still no Rachel by the time I've served Lily and Harry so I make an excuse about the lack of mobile signal and head outside to phone her. It's not like her to let me down and we really can't afford any more disasters after the last two meetings. I let out a huge sigh of relief as her car rolls into the cafe car park and hurry to meet her. Immediately I spot Freya in the passenger seat and she's screaming fit to burst.

'Sorry! I had to bring Freya. My mum's gone down with a bug and there was no one else to have her at this short notice . . . and guess what happened on the way here even though I only changed her before I set out. Shh. Shh. Darling. I'll sort you out in a minute.'

'Do you want me to ask Cal to have her?' I say as Freya lets the whole of Cornwall know how she feels about being stuck in the car in a dirty nappy.

'Would he mind? I can't take her in to meet the celebrity couple in this state.' Rachel wrinkles her nose.

'I'll call him if I can get a signal. Let me take her into the customer loo and clean her up while you go in and talk to Lily. Ben couldn't come,' I call loudly, while freeing Freya from the seat belt. 'Which isn't a bad thing,' I whisper to Freya who momentarily stops howling.

Rachel grabs her tablet and Freya's changing kit.

'Let's go round to the staff entrance,' I say over the sound of Freya's wails. 'And I'll sort her out while you speak to Lily. I'll message Cal over WhatsApp if I can't speak to him.'

'This is beyond the call of duty,' Rachel says.

'Well, she is my sister.'

Cal jogs over within a few minutes as I'm walking Freya around the cafe, trying to distract her with a toy.

'Good timing,' I say.

He grins. 'I came as soon as I could.'

'I bet.'

'You're lucky I was working on the campsite wash block. I get all the best jobs. I need to wash my hands and then I'll take Princess Freya,' he says, smiling at her.

She lets out an even louder howl.

He winces. 'I must be losing my touch. I also think I should have brought the ear defenders I was using while I was trimming the bushes behind the toilets.'

After he's washed his hands in the customer loo, I hand Freya over and take a few deep, calming breaths before I face Lily. As I walk in, I can see that Rachel has everything in hand. Harry sits in the corner, flicking through a food supplement in one of the lifestyle magazines.

'Right, sorry, I was tied up. What can I get everyone?'

While I gather a plate of the mini scones that I'd like to serve at the wedding celebration tea, I pop my head around the door of the loo. At least Freya calmed down once she was out of her seat and lying on the changing mat. Her eyes are huge, taking in all the new sights and the mobile we hung from the ceiling above the flip-down changing mat.

Cal flips the lid of the nappy bin and drops a heavily scented purple bag inside.

I can't help but giggle.

'I ought to get a picture of this for the blog.'

'Very funny but I've seen worse than this, you know.' He turns back to Freya. 'But not much.'

She gurgles at him and reaches for the mobile, before treating Cal to a cute smile. 'How are you, little Miss Grumpy Pants?' he says, tickling her tummy.

'Not Miss Grumpy Pants any more by the look of it. Rachel's mum has a bug so Rachel had to bring her to this meeting. She's gorgeous but we need to concentrate so would you mind looking after her for an hour?'

'Me?' Cal addresses Freya. 'Would you mind, Freya? Would you?'

He picks her up and she smiles again and blows a bubble of approval. Cal holds her against his shoulder as her mouth widens at having a new view of the world.

'See, she likes me,' he says. 'Don't you, Freya?'

'You are so smug sometimes, Cal Penwith.'

He grins. 'You're only jealous. I'll take her up to the farmhouse. Polly will be in ecstasy when she sees her.'

I leave him struggling to get a pair of tiny tights on a pair of wriggling little legs. It's funny but I've never been a baby person, and never imagined Cal as one either, but then I realise how attached he was to Esme and how much he enjoyed working with the children in the camp. I wonder if he ever thought about having a family one day with Isla. I wonder if he still does? I can't imagine being responsible for a Freya. Not yet anyway. One day?

Wow. That's way too big and scary to think about. Gathering up my tray, I head into the cafe where Rachel has managed to make Lily smile.

'Can we announce that your ceremony is being held here?'

'Yes. Addison and Jade are dealing with all that. We've sold the rights exclusively to *Grapevine!* We're happy to split the fee fifty-fifty between our charity and yours. Do you have one in mind?'

'I need to discuss it with Cal.'

Lily goes to use our bathroom. I hope she won't mind it not being luxurious. Rachel lets out a sigh of relief. 'Is Freya OK? I heard her crying and had to tell Lily about her. Then things went quiet.'

'She was fine once she was changed.'

'Are you sure Cal didn't mind looking after her?' Rachel asks.

'He used to work with kids, though I don't think he changed many nappies. He's taken her to see Polly. You may never get her back now.'

'Thanks. I appreciate it.'

'How's it going with Lily, do you think? She seems OK about the arrangements?' I ask.

'She seems happy to leave it all to us. She said that Addison and Jade can be 'very forceful' but it's her and Ben's decision to hold the wedding here. Oh, hello, Lily.'

Lily walks in. Her face is even paler than before.

'Are you OK?' I ask her.

Lily waggles a hand. 'I feel a bit icky to be honest.'

'Can I get you a glass of water?'

'Yes, please . . . that might be a good idea.'

Harry is over to our table like a shot, crouching by her side. 'Do you want me to call a doctor?' he says, looking into her face the way Mitch does when I have homemade dog treats in my pocket.

Lily smiles and pats his hand. 'I'm OK. Really.'

'You can't be too careful. Is it something you ate? A bug?'

Oh no, I think, while I fill a glass from a fresh bottle of Cornish spring water, please don't say Lily's got food poisoning from Demelza's even though she's only had a nibble of a Cornish Yarg canapé and that was barely half an hour ago.

'Harry. I'm *fine*. Stop fussing. I've had a few late nights and there's possibly a bug going about. There always is.'

'Shall I take you home, then?' he asks.

I hand Lily a glass of water and the rest of the bottle. And she mouths a thank-you.

'I think we've covered everything. I can email everything else and we can Skype you to save time.' Rachel smiles at her. 'Harry's right. You should go home and rest. Everything's being taken care of here.'

'OK. It might do me good. Harry's going to drive me back tonight and Louie misses me so much. Ben will be back later too. It's not often we have time together in our cottage like a normal couple.'

'Will Louie be attending the ceremony?' I ask her while Harry holds up her coat.

'Oh of course!' She brightens up. 'I've found him the cutest little tux to wear.'

'I thought he might like to have his own cushion in the front row of the log pews,' I say.

Lily smiles. With her huge furry coat, she looks tinier than ever but I do really like her. I wish she'd found someone nicer than Ben to marry but we can't always help who we fall in love with, I suppose.

'That sounds perfect,' she says, kissing me and Rachel goodbye. 'Thanks so much for organising this. I'm totally confident it's going to be a-mazing, even if Addison and Jade think it will all be a disaster.'

Rachel and I share glances and I know we're both thinking the same thing at the same time: *well, thanks for sharing that confidence-booster, Lily.*

She walks outside and stops by the car.

'Oh, there's something else I ought to tell you,' she says. 'Though I'm pretty cross with Ben for doing this without asking me. I mean, I shouldn't mind really and I do have two of my own friends and Ben doesn't have any sisters or female cousins . . . and Ben says she *is* practically family *but* . . . '

I brace myself for what news is coming next as Lily sighs.

'He's asked Mawgan to be a bridesmaid — and she's agreed.'

25

Five weeks later — late May

'Gather ye rosebuds while ye may.'

I turn away from the rose bush outside the back door of Kilhallon House to find Polly smiling at me. This is a very good sign because she's not done much smiling since she heard about Mawgan being a bridesmaid after Lily's visit last month. It took quite a while to pick Polly off the ceiling when she found out and to convince Cal that I wasn't winding him up. I should have known that Mawgan would find some way of putting herself at the centre of the wedding and the lives of Ben and Lily . . . but over the past month, with time racing by, Mawgan has been the least of our worries.

'Is that a line from the Bible?' I ask.

Polly rolls her eyes. 'Course it isn't. It's a poem. Can't remember the bloke's name. Something about time flying and taking your chances while you can.'

I let go of the rose. 'Right.'

Polly joins me and lifts the soft bud of the rose. 'Cal's mother loved that rose bush. I'm glad it's still thriving.'

'It smells beautiful.'

'Yes . . .'

Polly drops the rose head. 'Well, I can't stand here sniffing flowers. I've work to do. You know that guest who wears the sequinned skirt and those ridiculous hairy boot things? The one whose husband looks like *him* — I flat refuse to say his name out loud.' Polly shudders.

'Um. I think so . . . ' The image of our guest in her Uggs and her Donald Trump lookalike partner makes me want to giggle.

Polly huffs in disgust. 'Well. Right pair, *they* are. They're complaining they can't get all the Freeview channels in Poldark Cottage and they asked me why they can't have another TV in the bedroom, like they're used to in their 'main home'. I mean, I ask you, who comes all this way to the seaside to watch the bloody telly? And what do they want to watch it in bed for?'

With another huge huff and without waiting for an answer, Polly bustles off, and I reluctantly turn away from the rose and hurry back down the yard towards the cafe. I'd only come up to the farmhouse to change my polo shirt after a toddler decided to use it as target practice for his ice cream. Polly caught me during the only five minutes I've had to myself since I rolled out of bed this morning. It's been non-stop for us since Easter. May has flown by and the weather has been largely kind, luring out the early campers to our new site. Thankfully, bookings have recovered for our yurts and cottages, which are now almost full until September, so Cal's hard work in the resort is paying off. With Nina promoted to deputy manager and some more seasonal staff to lend a hand in the cafe and resort, we're just about coping with the extra workload.

The air is filled with birdsong, the scent of cut

grass and the hum of Cal's mower. Our visitors have shed their fleeces and boots and wander around the site in shorts and T-shirts. The new ice-cream freezer at the cafe does a roaring trade for humans and canine guests. Cal is always tanned and sometimes smiling, and Polly loves queening it over the seasonal staff and has grown into her job on reception without scaring off too many guests.

We've all been working our socks off to give our guests a wonderful holiday and by and large, our reviews are good and our reputation as a boutique holiday resort is slowly but surely building.

Rachel has clocked up many hours in between nappy changing and feeding and fortunately Freya has settled into a good sleep routine and she's been able to keep on top of the wedding plans. So we're all ready for the suppliers to roll in on Thursday.

After another busy day at the cafe, I flop down on the sofa at Kilhallon House with a huge sigh. My feet are killing me and I need ten minutes before I take Mitch out for his evening walk. I close my eyes and try to ignore the cold, wet nose poking my side.

'Demi? Demi?'

'Ow. Mitch, can you please get your nose out of there?'

'Now, that's an offer I can't refuse.'

Cal comes into focus, standing over me, holding a huge padded brown envelope. He's in shorts and a T-shirt, a grin on his sunburned face.

I push myself up the sofa and Mitch yips hopefully. Cal holds out the package.

'A courier delivered this to reception while you were asleep.'

'Me asleep? I was only resting my eyes.' I blink. 'Are you sure it's for me? I'm not expecting anything.'

'Well, it's addressed to you and Polly had to sign for it.'

Cal hands over the envelope.

I tear at the sealed edge. 'I've no idea who it's from — oh, wait. Oh. Oh my God.'

'What?'

'Look. I can't believe it.' Carefully I slide the sheets of paper out of the huge padded envelope. 'These are the page proofs for my cookbook. You can see all the text and pictures just as they'll appear in the finished book. It's real now. Isn't it amazing?'

'They look fantastic. You should be proud.'

'I feel I haven't done anything. The home economist and publisher commissioned a photographer. I only provided the recipes and jotted some ideas for the editorial. Lily wrote a foreword — look at this photo of her with Louie, and here's Eva with Betty. Betty looks *so* cute and . . . oh, it's me. Me with Mitch.' I hold out the pages. 'Cal, I can't believe it.'

Cal glances at the pages and smiles. 'Believe it. This deserves champagne.'

'It's a work night.'

'Go on. You earned it.'

While I leaf through the page proofs, still unable to believe what I'm seeing, Cal disappears into the kitchen and returns with a bottle and glasses. He hands me a glass and squeezes next to me on the sofa.

'I'm not one for a lot of words, or rather I'm not one for the *right* words, but I am so very proud of you.' He clinks glasses with me and my eyes fill up, but I don't want to drip champagne onto the page proofs so I pull myself together.

'Woof!'

'See. Even Mitch is impressed,' Cal says.

'No. He wants his walk.'

Mitch lays his jowls on the page, leaving a big slobbery jaw print right on top of a photo of Betty the pug.

'Oh, Mitch!'

Cal puts down his glass. 'I'll take him out. You enjoy your book.'

'We'll both take him,' I say, reluctantly setting the proofs aside. 'But I might sleep with those pages tonight.'

'As long as that's the only thing that comes between us, I can live with that.'

We grab Mitch's lead from the porch. 'Things seem to be going so well for us, don't they? After all our problems last year and at Christmas, business is great and I'm even beginning to think we really can pull off this wedding.'

Cal smiles. 'It certainly seems that way. Come on, let's get out. Then I think we should take the rest of the champagne to bed after dinner and have an early night.'

When we get back to the house, I indulge myself with another look at the pages while Cal heats up the remains of last night's coq au vin for our dinner, with garlicky potatoes too, judging by the smell drifting in from the kitchen. By now I know the words off by heart and the champagne is working its magic on me. There are manic days ahead but this has to be one of the most satisfying moments I've ever had in my life. I can't stop smiling. I think about helping Cal but allow myself one more minute to read the pages again. Maybe I really will sleep with them by the bed in case I wake up in the night and want to stroke them.

Sometime later, I glance up and sniff the air. The smell has changed. Not garlic but burning. Seconds later the smoke alarm starts screeching and Mitch barks.

'Cal!' I'm off the sofa like a jackrabbit and dashing into the kitchen. A grey haze fills the kitchen and the alarm is beeping like crazy. Mitch goes wild, barking and dashing to the kitchen door. Coughing, I grab the oven mitts and rescue the blackened remains of the spuds and casserole from the Aga.

I throw open the back door and run outside, eyes streaming.

Cal stands in the middle of the yard, with his back to me, his phone clamped to his ear.

'Cal!'

At my shout, he turns and looks at me, his mouth opens in horror when he sees the smoke coming from the door. He mutters into the phone and then runs towards me.

'Oh Jesus, I forgot about the dinner! Do we need the fire brigade?'

'No. I was just in time. The dinner is ruined

and the smoke alarm is screeching but no fire.'

He closes his eyes and groans. 'I'm sorry. Christ.'

I wipe my eyes with a tissue. 'What happened? Who was that on the phone? They're not cancelling the wedding, are they?'

'No. No. It was Kit . . . he called about Esme. He thinks there's a very good chance she's been found.'

★ ★ ★

After we've opened all the windows and doors of the farmhouse to let out the smoke, Cal takes me into the sitting room. He paces around the room. His face is pale under the tan.

'I can't believe it. I want to believe she's OK but I daren't let myself. And I don't quite understand why Kit was calling me?'

'I asked him to search for her. I thought it was a long shot but that he might still have some contacts who might be able to help. I didn't say anything to you because I didn't want to get your hopes up and I never thought it would come to anything. I hope that's OK. What did he say?'

'I'm glad you asked him. I'm not angry but I'm . . . I don't know what to feel or think. I almost wish he hadn't called in case it's not true. But his contact is ninety-nine per cent certain it's her. It must be. He's forwarding a photo. Any time now' — he stares at his phone — 'I'll know for sure.'

I grab his arm. 'Cal. I can't believe it. I thought I was interfering.'

He looks at me. 'Thank you. Thank you for interfering.'

His phone pings. He glances at the screen and swallows hard. 'That's an email from Kit with a file.'

'Open it.'

He looks at me, agonised. 'What if it isn't her?'

'You'll only know if you look.'

'Yes . . . ' he says, holding the phone down by his side. 'But I have to do this on my own. Do you understand?'

I let him go and stand aside. 'Do what you have to but remember I'm here whatever happens.'

He nods and walks silently out of the room. His footsteps echo on the boards and there's a creak as his study door opens and a soft click as it shuts. I lie back on the sofa and as if he senses the tension, Mitch jumps on top of me. I hug him, burying my face in his fur. All I can do is wait for Cal to come back and hope that it's good news.

26

It's been twenty minutes since Cal closed the door to his study and there hasn't been a word from him or even a sound from his study. I can't stand the tension any more and as I'm about to barge in on him, Cal walks into the sitting room.

My heart almost leaps out of my chest and I spring up from the sofa. He holds his tablet down by his side. His face is pale. 'It's her,' he says.

'You're sure?'

'I've seen the photo. She's grown, she's thinner, but it's her. There's a photo of her grandfather on the email too, with her.'

'Cal. That's amazing. It's fantastic news.' I launch myself on him and finally he hugs me back. I kiss him and he holds me tightly and finally there's a smile on his face. 'I was so worried when you didn't come out of the study. I thought it wasn't her or you'd heard bad news.'

'She's safe. She's alive . . . I'm sorry I didn't come in to tell you. I wasn't sure how I'd react, whether it was good news or bad, and then I kept having to check the photo against an old one of mine. I knew immediately but I couldn't accept it after all this time searching. Then I called Kit and Carolyn.'

'How did Kit find her? Did she turn up on the Red Cross or Facebook sites?'

'No. Kit made enquiries among his colleagues

who cover human-interest stories in the Middle East. One of the journalists had been doing some features on families escaping Syria and moving into Europe. She did some digging and spread the word about Esme's family: names, ages, etc.' Cal drags his fingers through his hair, still looking totally shell-shocked.

'A few days ago, the journalist heard from a man in a camp in Northern Greece who thought he'd met Esme and her family while he was on the road. He'd definitely heard her name and even spoken to some of her relatives. She seemed the right age and the family circumstances matched.'

'So she's with her family? That's a hundred times better than her being alone.'

'If she'd been alone, I doubt she could have survived.' He hugs himself as if he's cold. 'Kit's journalist friend actually spoke to Esme and her family and they remembered me. My God, Esme remembered *me*.'

'Why wouldn't she? You were good friends.'

'I — I don't know . . . You know Kit didn't want to pass on the news until he was absolutely sure but this evening his colleague emailed the photo to him. He wondered all day what to do but then said he realised he had to risk disappointing me.'

He holds out the tablet. 'Would you like to see her? I've got some old photos of her and Soraya of my own. I wanted to compare them with this new picture, to make sure because I don't trust my memory any more. I haven't been able to look at these or show them to anyone until now.

Demi . . . you need to understand that I've been trying to forget it all and put the past behind me.'

'I know that. I even understand the way you feel. When I left home, I thought I could run away from my family and the past, but it was impossible. I tried to lock the bad memories away and live on my own with Mitch as if they didn't exist but it didn't help me. Maybe the breathing space helped me for a little while but the guilt and the grief didn't go away. In the end, my family and the memories found me. I'm glad they did and I'm glad you found Esme.'

We sit next to each other on the sofa. Cal lifts the cover of the iPad and taps on the photo in the email. A little girl stares back at me through wide, dark eyes. My heart jumps into my mouth. You don't have to know Esme's story to see what she's been through. Her lost gaze says everything, despite her smile.

'She's so young.'

'She's nine now. She's grown so much, but she's thinner.'

'She's smiling.'

Cal smiles briefly too. 'I guess she was relieved to have something to smile about but Kit's colleague says she's attending the camp school a few mornings a week. She loved school until everything fell apart out there. I remember her showing me a picture she'd drawn of her with her mum and grandparents.'

'What made you become close with that family in particular?'

'I don't know. Maybe it was Soraya's bravery

that stood out for me, or Esme's. Soraya could have left the city months before when her hospital was destroyed but she wanted to stay and help her people. We were very grateful for an extra pair of skilled hands. You know, Esme told me she wanted to be a nurse like her mother? Even after witnessing the horrors that she did, she still wanted to be like her mum.' Cal stares at the photo, silent for a few moments, as if he's been transported back to the war zone.

I slip my arm around him and lay my head on his shoulder as the tablet wavers between his hands. He runs his finger over Esme's face.

'And now she's asked to see me. Her family are being moved on to another camp in a couple of days, though no one's told them which yet.'

'So soon?'

'Yes. I can't go, of course. I haven't told Kit's colleague yet but I can't take off out there, not with the wedding.'

I don't know what to say. The thought of losing Cal now, at one of Kilhallon's biggest moments, makes me go cold. Yet the thought of keeping him away from someone and something that means so much to him is unthinkable. I can't do it to him, or Esme, no matter how much I want and need him.

'Cal. You *have* to go while you know where they are. You might lose touch again if you wait.'

Immediately he shakes his head. 'No,' he says firmly. 'I can't leave you, not with this wedding to orchestrate.'

'There will be lots of weddings, but this could be your only chance to meet Esme. You've waited so long and she's asked for you after all this time and searching. How can you let her down now?'

He rubs his hand over his face. 'A dozen reasons. You need me, the business needs me . . .'

'That's only two reasons.'

He puts his head in his hands and then lifts it. 'What if she hates me for her mother's death? What if her family blame me?'

'They wouldn't have asked for you if they did. You have to face them and talk to them. You'll never be happy at Kilhallon unless you do. We'll manage here somehow. Can you get a flight tomorrow?'

He shakes his head. 'I guess so. Hell, I don't know. I haven't even thought of how to get out there.'

'I'll get on the airline sites now while you set up the meeting with Kit's friend and Esme's family.'

'If you're sure . . . but I'll be back in time for the wedding. I'll fly out first thing tomorrow and I'll be back on Saturday.'

'I'll do my best to find a flight. Cal, you realise that you're going to have to tell Polly and Robyn where you're going and why? You don't have to share all the details but they're going to want to know why you've left Kilhallon before the wedding.'

He groans. 'Shit. I never thought of that.'

'You'll have to trust them with some of the story because I'm not lying for you. It's too big a secret.'

'You're right. OK, I'll speak to Polly and I

239

need a lift off Robyn tomorrow so I'll talk to her on the way to the station. You'll be too busy here, Demi. Thank you for this. I don't know what to say.'

'You don't need to say anything. Just go.'

27

Wednesday — early morning
Three days before the wedding

At six a.m. the next morning, Cal wolfs down a bacon butty while scrolling through his phone.

I cradle my mug. 'OK. You're checked in on the three p.m. flight from Bristol to Athens and the last one home on Friday night. You can get the very early train here on Saturday morning but it only gives you a couple of days in Greece. Is it long enough?'

'It will have to be. I'm hiring a car at the airport to drive north to the camp.' Cal gulps down the dregs of his coffee. 'You won't be on your own here. Kit's driving down to help tomorrow. He's finished his edits and he has a few days free. He was going to have a break but he said he's happy to come here to help us.'

'Kit's coming here?'

'You don't look too happy about it. I can tell him to keep away if you like.'

'No. We need all the help we can get, I'm only amazed that you said yes to him staying here while you're away.'

'Yeah. Well. Maybe he isn't too bad, and helping out a celebrity wedding will all be part of his rehab.' He smiles.

'You mean he'll hate it.'

'Exactly, and I think he's OK. Any trouble,

kick him out but I don't think there will be.' His phone beeps and he grimaces. 'That's Robyn. She's outside. I can't miss my train and she's already freaking out that we'll be late.'

He gathers me to him and kisses me. Not a long enough kiss but a warm and delicious one to remember. 'Thanks for making me feel it's OK to go. I'll be back before you know it, I promise.' He smiles. 'And I swear I'm not doing this to get out of the wedding preparations.'

'Yeah. I believe you.'

Picking up his overnight bag, he gives me a final brush on my lips and he's on his way. I follow him as far as the door, not wanting to make a slushy fuss in front of Robyn or our holiday guests who are packing up and leaving today as we prepare for the wedding guests. We'll be rushed off our feet checking everyone out and supervising the freelance cleaners who come to do the changeovers but I'd rather be busy than dwell on losing Cal, even for a few days.

He's off to Greece, I remind myself: it's a holiday destination not a war zone and nothing will happen to him. Then again, he's a stranger going into a camp . . . But I'm more worried about his emotional safety than what might happen to him physically. What if Esme's family *do* blame him for what happens or prevent her from seeing him? I can't think why or they wouldn't have asked him to go but I can't help thinking that so much could go wrong. His parting words tumble through my mind. *'I'll be back before you know it, I promise.'* They sound familiar.

242

Through the window of her car, Robyn shouts and points at her wrist. 'Cal. Come *on*.'

He climbs in, the engine revs and the tyres spin as Robyn shoots off the car park, as if she's in a rally. They're gone now so I return to the kitchen and my untouched bacon sandwich, remembering where I've heard Cal's final words before.

Of course, it was Robyn who told me what Cal said when he left for Syria on the aid mission that ended with him being taken prisoner.

'I'll be back before you know it, I promise.' Robyn told me he also said the same words to Isla and he never returned to her. A shiver runs down my spine.

I laugh at myself. It's not only Robyn and Isla who have a taste for drama round here. Cal will be back on Saturday as planned and we can finally get on with Lily and Ben's happy ending.

28

Thursday — early morning
Two days before the wedding

'Woof! Woof!'

Thursday morning starts with a hairy muzzle in my face and throbbing eardrums. Though it's a good job Mitch has woken me because I must have slept through the alarm clock — or maybe I forgot to set it at all. I crawled into bed last night after staying up late.

After Cal left for Greece, I spent the day fending off questions about the details of the wedding and reassuring our Demelza's regulars that we'll be open next Tuesday as usual. While we cleaned the kitchens, Cal texted me to say he was about to board his flight to Athens. Even though I'm busy, I keep wondering how he's getting on and if he'll find Esme and her family in time — and how they and he will react to each other.

Mitch sleeps in the kitchen now but he got into our room in the night and I was too knackered to take him downstairs. Besides, Cal isn't here and I wanted the company. As I come round and sit up, he jumps off the bed and runs to the window, claws clattering on the floorboards. He rests his paws on the window ledge of the sash and woofs again. Between the barks, other sounds reach my ears: engines rumbling, voices shouting and reversing warnings beeping.

'OK. I know you want me to see something.'

Parting the curtains reveals a scene of chaos. In the car park, a lorry loaded with portaloos vies for space with several other vans and a truck. Knowing I should have been up an hour ago, I close the curtains again. My stomach turns over and my skin prickles. I recognise the feeling: the same mix of excitement and sheer terror I had on the opening day of Demelza's.

'It's started, boy,' I whisper to Mitch as if we're hosting a wake not a wedding, but I know I'm only anxious for everything to go well. I pull on my jeans, drag a T-shirt over my head and pluck a hoodie from the same place I dropped it last night. There'll be no time for toast now, even if I felt like eating breakfast. The wedding contractors will need guiding to the glamping field. Some have travelled quite a way and been up since before dawn so I bet everyone's going to be gagging for a cup of tea. Luckily, Demelza's has that covered.

I need to give Mitch a run but it's not safe for him to be out among the vehicles so I leave him in the kitchen and hurry into the car park. Polly is already in the thick of it, clutching a clipboard to her chest and directing the portaloo lorry down the track to the glamping area. At least it's a dry and calm morning, but the clouds are low and lumpy ... and there's something else, a sharp and not-very-pleasant 'tang' on the air that reminds me of when Cal cleans out his horse's stables.

245

'Morning,' Polly says, before ticking an item off her list.

'Really sorry I overslept, Polly. I meant to be up to help you.'

'Everything's under control,' she says. 'The posh loos are here and the power generator people are already setting up in the field. Your dad phoned and said he'd be over as soon as the tepee people arrive.'

'The loos don't smell very fresh. They're meant to be the most luxurious ones Rachel could find. I hope they won't stay like that.'

'That's a farm smell. It was here before the loos arrived.' Polly sniffs the air extravagantly. 'Hmm. I'd say it was getting stronger.'

I inhale deeply and immediately want to gag. 'Oh, shit.'

'Exactly,' says Polly. 'It's coming from Gwennap's farm over the hill.'

'Eww. I know the farmers have to fertilise the fields but I thought Mr Gwennap had done his earlier this spring and he knew the wedding was coming up.'

'He certainly did. Cal went up there a couple of weeks ago and he didn't mention any plans to muck spread.'

I allow myself to breathe in again and wish I hadn't. Once you're tuned into that pong, you can't un-smell it. I may be a country girl but it's beyond acceptable and our wedding guests certainly won't be impressed.

'I hope it goes away. Lily will be here tomorrow afternoon, and — arghh — with Addison and Jade too.'

Polly sighs. 'I'll try to find out what's happened but there's nothing we can do about it now, my bird. I'll check the weather forecast. We'll just have to carry on as normal and hope the wind changes.'

She gives my arm a squeeze. Hoping the wind changes sounds like something out of *Mary Poppins* and I've never felt less like bloody Mary Poppins in my life, although I wish I could wiggle my nose and everything at Kilhallon would be instantly perfect for the wedding.

'I'll take Mitch out for a quick run then I have to get down to the cafe. We're laying on early refreshments for the wedding contractors. Hopefully it will keep them sweet, which is more than I can say for the famous Kilhallon fresh air.'

By lunchtime, a massive wedding machine has rolled into Kilhallon, taking over every inch of space on the main car park and down at Demelza's too. Cal has designated one of the smaller fields for parking. The tepee people, posh loos, power-generator hire, light and sound people have all arrived along with my dad and his mates with their electrician's vans. Tomorrow, the florist and event stylists will rock up, followed by even more people who will be arriving on the morning of the wedding itself.

Our mobile catering stand from the Harbour Lights has been set up near the glamping field/wedding glade with one of the new staff serving refreshments to all the people setting up. The official event caterers arrive later today. Rachel and I recommended a local company from St Trenyan whose premises were damaged by the floods and we're delighted that Lily agreed to use them.

By late afternoon, the canvas structure of the tepee is up. It's bigger and even more stunning than the one we hired for the wedding fair, with a service section at the rear where the caterers will have their field kitchen. My dad has helped the loo-hire and generator people connect up the facilities to the campsite electricity supply. Early this evening, a funky cocktail bar for the tepee arrives. In the meantime, the finishing touches are being made to the flooring in the tent and matting walkways have been laid from the car parks to the marquee.

Even as the sun starts to set, a few workers stay on to slot the final boards of a stage in place. My dad's up a stepladder fixing a problem with the fairy lights round one of the tent poles. Kit passes some tools up to him. Rachel left after lunch to collect Freya from her nan's, but she'll be back tomorrow. She looked tired and I wonder if she feels she's bitten off more than she can chew, but she said she was fine. Having seen all the work involved, I now know that we couldn't have done this wedding without her. Even with the support of my dad and her parents, she's worked a miracle to fit in the organisation around caring for Freya.

Polly joins me in the centre of the tent and for a few seconds, we're frozen to the spot, both unable to believe this is Kilhallon. Now that most people have left for the night, our voices sound loud in the cavernous space: literally, it's a big blank canvas, which is ready to be decorated tomorrow morning.

Her eyes widen. 'It's like one of them music festivals. We only need the mud and people smoking funny stuff now.'

'I hope we don't get either,' I say, hating to sound more Polly-ish than even Polly.

'They'll doubtless be bringing some arty types with them. You know what they're like in London,' Polly says darkly. I'm thinking we have plenty of alternative 'arty' types on our own doorstep and that I know quite a few. I wonder what the guests will make of Kilhallon. Ben and Lily's close friends and family are from the South West but there are people from all over the country descending and even a few from America.

'If you need any help, Kit's ready to lend a hand.'

'Hmm,' says Polly. 'I wasn't very happy with him turning up and dropping the bombshell about being Cal's brother. I can see it upset Cal and you but he's made himself useful during the floods and again now so I suppose I might forgive him.'

'I genuinely think he wants to help. Even Cal seems to tolerate him now and he did help him find Esme.' I feel sorry for Kit, having to endure Polly's withering looks. She's really made him suffer for not being open with any of us when he first turned up. Thank God she doesn't know the full extent of his previous behaviour: trying to hurt us and getting involved with Mawgan Cade. But that's another story.

'That's another thing that'll end in tears.

Fancy swanning off to Greece when he had a job to do here. Sometimes he needs his head examining.'

'It's not ideal but I didn't have the heart to stop him. In fact, I didn't want to stop him. He needs to find out that Esme's all right and speak to her and her family in person.'

Polly tuts. 'Hmm. I fear for the little girl and I suppose you're right. Cal will never rest until he sees her again. Have you heard from him yet?'

'A text came through in the middle of the night but I'm not sure when he actually sent it. He was on his way to the camp where Esme and her family were reported to be. He's hoping they haven't been moved on yet.'

She shakes her head. 'I'm as worried about him as you are. What will he be like if he can't find her?'

'He's promised this is the last time. He'll put it all behind him after this,' I say, trying to believe it myself.

'Tosh. Cal never forgets anything. Anyway, we've other things to worry about. That Addison and Jade and Lily will be here tomorrow.' She glances at the pennants on the marquee, which are still limp and sad as if they're as depressed about the whole thing as us. 'We need that blow Greg Stennack promised us.'

By eight o'clock, the contractors and suppliers have left for the evening. I've returned from the cafe.

Kit arrives, with Mitch on a lead.

'Thanks for offering to take him out. Has he behaved?'

'He's been fine. I let him off the lead on the moor and he even came back when I called him.' Kit ruffles Mitch's ears. 'You were a good boy, weren't you?'

Mitch's grumble of pleasure raises a smile. He's learning to trust Kit now too. 'Great. One less thing to worry about,' I reply.

'Have you heard from Cal yet?'

'A quick word in a text. He's on his way to the camp now. He's hoping Esme's family haven't had to move on before he gets there.'

'I hope so too. He'd be devastated if he got so close and then missed them.'

'Yes . . .'

'So you're still worried about him?' Kit asks.

'It's the fear of the unknown. If he misses them it would be awful. But if he does see them, who knows what their reaction will be. It could finish him if it all goes wrong.'

'He's a big boy, he knows the risk he's taking.'

I nod, grateful for Kit's efforts but not in the least bit reassured — so God knows how Cal must be feeling.

29

Friday morning
The day before the wedding

It's Friday morning, and Lily and her entourage arrive later this afternoon. If I hadn't been so busy yesterday I don't think I'd have got any sleep but I was so tired that when I finally got to bed, I fell into a deep sleep. Fortunately, the alarm wakes me even before Mitch. It's six o'clock and for a few minutes I think about climbing out of the window and running away.

In the kitchen, I blink away sleep and fill the kettle in the hope that a caffeine injection will bring me round. The water hasn't even boiled when Polly bursts through the back door with the newspaper. It's the *Daily News* again and my skin turns instantly icy.

'They've done it again. Read this.' She slaps the open newspaper on the table in front of me. The headline swims in front of my eyes.

WEDDING SMELLS FOR BEN AND LILY
Celebrity couple kick up a stink at whiffy wedding venue
    There was a right old ding-dong at the country wedding venue where Lily Craig and Ben Trevone are due to get married when a local farmer dumped a load of stinky muck on the fields next to the reception location.

The foul pong, which could be smelled for 'miles' around, has put Saturday's reception plans into doubt. The stench is so rank that sources close to the couple worried that the celebrations will have to be moved to an alternative venue.

A close family friend commented: 'It would be awful if the wedding had to be called off now. Lily's assistant has been looking at other places because the stench is intolerable.'

Rumours are rife but the manager of the Seagull Spa, a luxury hotel in St Trenyan, refused to comment when asked if it had been contacted with a view to hosting the wedding if the couple do decide to move it.

'The Seagull Spa? Doesn't Mawgan own that place?' Polly asks.

'I don't know. Possibly. Probably, she owns half of St Trenyan.'

'I bet she's 'the friend of the family' too,' says Polly.

I groan. 'Beam me up, somebody, please. I can't handle this. Not with Cal away.'

Polly puts her arm around me. 'Yes, you can. They won't cancel now. Everything's gone too far and that's only the paper stirring things up. Oh and by the way, I phoned Gwennap's but his daughter answered. The old boy is in hospital recovering from a hip operation and his daughter apologised for the muck spreading but said she had no idea the contractors were planning to do it. She says her dad must have ordered it to go ahead while he was out of action.'

I sigh. 'Never mind. It's too late to unspread it now.'

The phone in the house starts ringing. I glance at Polly. Then my mobile starts buzzing so hard it almost jumps off the table.

'That'll be The Gruesome Twosome,' Polly says. 'Don't answer it.'

'I have to. It's not fair on Lily to ignore it.'

'Let me make you a cuppa and get you a bite to eat before you face them. And as for the nasty niff, all we can do is hope the wind changes.'

Before I can work up the nerve to call Addison and Jade back, the pair of them descend on the farmhouse like a pair of vampire bats. Addison actually has one of those Japanese-style face-masks over his nose and mouth and Jade is muffled in a scarf.

'Give me strength,' Polly mutters, insisting on facing them with me for moral support, even though I've tried to persuade her she's far too busy. 'It's Hannibal Lecter and the Bride of Dracula. What are they like?'

'Please be tactful,' I say but it's too late, as Addison and Jade stride towards us, clutching their protective masks to their faces. 'It's not that bloody bad,' I mutter.

'This is unacceptable,' Jade says, muffled by her scarf.

'It's a health hazard,' Addison squeaks.

'It's a normal country smell,' Polly declares.

'I know it's not pleasant but we've been assured it's only temporary and it's definitely not hazardous. Does Lily know?'

254

'We've kept it from her for now. She doesn't need any more distractions or stress, but Ben's not happy. Not happy at all.'

'He's a Cornish lad. He should be used to it,' Polly says unhelpfully.

Addison lowers his mask for a second. 'This isn't good press. It's terrible.'

'I appreciate your concerns but it's much better than yesterday and the wind's changing. It'll all be blown away by tomorrow,' I say.

'It's the country,' says Polly. 'You have to put up with a few stinks, or you've no business being here.'

'But this is a wedding venue and Ben and Lily are a *very* special bride and groom,' says Addison in a peculiar twang, obviously because he's trying to keep his nostrils tightly shut. Maybe we've got used to the odour by now.

'Really, it's so much better than it was.'

'The gales overnight will blow it away, you wait and see,' says Polly.

'Gales?' Jade says with a gasp.

'A fresh breeze is forecast,' I say firmly.

'Greg Stennack said we're in for a right old blow,' Polly rattles on, obviously relishing winding up the townies.

'Who's Greg Stennack?' Jade demands.

'Local DJ. Not known for his correct weather forecasting but Polly's right: the Met Office is predicting a fresh offshore wind and that'll blow the smell away. They've also forecast a lovely, sunny, warm day for the wedding. There's absolutely nothing to worry about. Everything's under control.'

255

'Hmm. I sincerely hope so. If this wedding turns out to be the disaster that we always thought it would be, we'll know who to blame.'

'Everything's in order. You should see our preparations. The tepee is stunning and the flowers and stylists are arriving today.' I'm getting desperate now.

'I think we should leave, Jade. We need to do some fire-fighting with the press and reassure *Grapevine!* that the site will be ready and sanitary.'

Polly's red in the face with fury. 'There's nothing insanitary about Kilhallon.'

'We'll see. We'll be back tomorrow afternoon with Lily and her party but I'll be checking in with you at *very regular* intervals to see how everything's going.'

'We must leave, Jade. I've got an interview with a fashion magazine set up for Lily and I want to sit in on it to make sure she's on message.' Addison practically drags Jade away, coughing and spluttering dramatically as he goes.

Polly bristles. 'Silly buggers. He's a right delicate flower and she needs a slap. There's nothing unclean about Kilhallon.'

I ought to laugh. Polly's right and I feel like telling both of them where to shove their updates. But I also feel as if a great big wave is bearing down on me and is going to wash me right over the cliff. I worry about high winds that could blow away the tepees and awning. Or no wind and a tremendous stink instead. I think of my part-time wedding planner and my full-time novice wedding organisers. Of Mawgan Cade being at the heart of everything and of Cal thousands of miles away and unable to help.

But Polly's right. For now, all we can do is carry on and hope the wind changes.

★ ★ ★

By lunchtime, Kilhallon has been invaded once again. I've spent the morning laying the inside tables at Demelza's with cloths and vintage china and pretty jam jars filled with local flowers that echo Lily's boho theme. Jez and I have prepared the cakes and scones in advance today, but tomorrow it will be all hands to the pump. Shamia and our two new staff will all be in to help. Nina's in charge here tomorrow as I know I'll be needed to help Rachel — and hopefully Cal when he returns tomorrow morning. Focusing on the place I know and love best has soothed my frayed nerves but I need to pop up to the marquee to see how Rachel's getting on supervising the decor and caterers.

As I walk from the cafe, I zip up my hoodie. It's a fine day but cool and I glance up at the pennants on the tepee. They're no longer limp but fluttering. I sniff the air, realising that I hadn't noticed the smell because it's almost gone. So, Greg Stennack was right after all . . .

Almost skipping with relief, I hurry towards the tepee. Smart matting leads into the tent, flanked by the flowers in jars hung from shepherd's hooks. It makes a simple, natural yet beautiful entrance to the tent. I step inside the tepee.

Wow.

In the cafe, my nose was full of the aromas of warm scones and chocolate cupcakes. On my way here, the fresh sea air was a wonderful relief. Now, different scents fill my nostrils. Sweet, rich fragrances and, oh, the *colours*.

The sight in front of me brings tears to my eyes. It looks so wonderful. Hazel the florist and a team of three assistants are putting the finishing touches to their decorations. The poles are entwined with floral garlands in blush pinks and soft blues. The linen company has been and covered the tables with pretty cloths. There are stunning flower centrepieces on the tables and a beautiful arrangement on the top table where Lily, Ben and the bridal party will sit.

'I recognise the cornflowers but what are the other flowers?' I ask, breathing in the gorgeous scents and admiring the pale creams, baby pinks and pastel blues.

'Nigella and peonies — some of the flowers are locally grown,' says Hazel, tucking into a takeout coffee and pasty I brought up from the cafe. 'Thanks for the drinks. Sometimes we don't even get offered a glass of water while we're working.'

'It's fine. I'm glad you could make it. The place looks incredible and the scents are beautiful. I can't believe it's Kilhallon.'

'A pleasure.'

Rachel arrives with her mum pushing Freya in the buggy. 'Mum's brought Freya to see what all the excitement is about,' she says, pointing to her mother who has lifted Freya out of her buggy to look at the bunting. 'My dad's gone to see if he can help Gary with anything. It means I can get on with organising too. Are you pleased with how it's all coming along?'

'Pleased? I'm amazed.'

Rachel's face lights up. 'It's always incredible to see a space transformed like this. Organising this wedding has been a challenge, but it'll all be fine in the end. The caterers will start laying the tables when the florists have finished and we'll be ready for tomorrow. Have you seen the bridal glade yet?'

'No. I've been too busy at the cafe.'

'Come and take a look, then. Where's Cal by the way? I haven't seen him around . . . I didn't like to ask.'

I take a deep breath. 'He's gone to Greece. It's complicated.'

Rachel's face falls. 'Oh God, Demi. Is everything OK between you?'

'It's fine. He had urgent business out there.' I cross my fingers. 'He's flying back this evening so he should be back in the morning for the wedding. Can I tell you more about the circumstances after the wedding's over?'

She smiles. 'Course you can.'

'Thanks, and please don't worry about us. Let's take a look at the glade.'

With me pushing Freya, we walk down to the glade. The florists have already set up the willow bridal arch that has transformed the glamping glade into a country-style bridal bower exactly, I hope, as Lily envisaged it.

'Mum's taking Freya home so Gary can get on

259

with the electrics and I can greet the bridal party with you. They'll be here around six o'clock, right?'

Lily and the bridal party have taken over the cottages. Lily's staying in Poldark while her bridesmaids, Harry and family members occupy the other cottages. Some of their guests are already in the yurts.

'Ben's booked into a smart hotel a few miles away with his best man, Addison and Jade. I'm so glad they're not staying with us. I don't need any more hassle.'

'What about Mawgan?' Rachel asks.

'She's making her own way here but I heard she's sending a chauffeur to Penzance for Ben's parents and his auntie.'

'I'm looking forward to meeting your famous film producer Isla too. Is she coming down from London?'

'You will do. She and her fiancé, Luke, are staying with Robyn's father. They're old friends.' I wonder what Isla will say when she finds out Cal has dashed off to Greece. He left her to work in Syria and it was the start of the end of their relationship. I know the circumstances are different this time but I can't help comparing them.

After Rachel's gone home, I head back to the cafe. The contractors have finished installing a cream awning over the terrace. It looks like a giant sail and is stunning. Once the contractors have set up the furniture, it'll create a spectacular chill-out space for guests to enjoy afternoon teas and evening drinks overlooking the ocean and Kilhallon Cove.

The contractor smiles at me as I admire the awning. 'Could be blowy up here for your wedding,' he says.

'It'll be fine. People can wrap up or come inside,' I say, aware I sound as breezy as the weather. I'm so relieved that the bad odour has blown away and Kilhallon is starting to emerge as the wild and beautiful venue we know and love. Cal will be gobsmacked when he gets home tomorrow. While I panicked when I heard he was going away, there's a big satisfaction in knowing that with everyone's help, I might manage to pull off this wedding without him. I smile: I can use this to tease him for months, years . . . when he comes home.

My phone beeps with a text. It could be Cal telling me he's found Esme and he's coming home, but it's not. It's a message from Polly, short and sweet.

They're here.

The furry moths beat their wings in my stomach again. No matter how amazing I think Kilhallon looks, it's Lily's opinion that counts. Pasting a big smile on my face, I hurry up to reception to meet her.

Lily is her usual self, smiley and twittery, although maybe a little quieter than 'normal'. Jade makes up for ten people, moaning about the narrow lanes around the resort and *how dare a farmer move his cows at that time of day and who on earth uses an actual bus down here, why don't they get a car, for God's sake?* I've shut my brain to her deluge of crap, but Polly stalks murderously behind the reception desk, jingling her keys and trying to turn Jade to stone with a look.

'Will you show Harry his cottage, please?' I ask Polly, desperate to get her out of the way of Jade.

Trying to blot out Jade's stream of whinges, I show Lily into her cottage. My stomach swirls with nerves. We've done our very best to make them look perfect but, at the end of day, they are only holiday cottages and Lily — and Jade — are used to the best hotels in the world.

Admittedly, the cottages have some extra touches: fresh flowers from Hazel, a fridge stocked with organic nibbles and breakfast packs plus bottles of champagne that would pay for a slap-up meal for Cal and me — and the staff — at the poshest restaurant in St Trenyan. Jade provided the list of 'requirements'.

Jade zones in on the kitchen as soon as we walk in and is popping the cork on a bottle of Krug.

'Hmm. Krug . . . ' she says, rubbing her finger around the top of a wine flute. 'Champagne, Lily? It could do with being slightly more chilled but it'll do.'

'I'd rather have a cup of chamomile tea,' Lily says, perching on the armchair in the sitting room. 'This is such a sweet little cottage. Did you say that tin miners lived here?'

I smile. 'Only the mine captain and officials could afford this cottage.'

Jade flops onto the sofa with a thud and slurps her champagne. 'Lily's family and bridesmaids

262

arrive later. I'll keep her company until then.'

'Really, Jade, I'll be fine on my own.'

Jade waves a hand. 'No, I couldn't possibly leave you here on your own on the evening before your wedding. You might need something.'

'If I do, there are plenty of people around to help. Mum and Dad and Thea and Fen. And Harry, of course. He's only in the next-door cottage so I'll be fine. Besides, you must have so much to do.'

Jade hiccups and giggles, which believe me is sooo not like her. 'Oh, excuse me. The bubbles went up my nose. No, nothing more important than you.'

'I'd really like some time to myself. I've been rushing all over the place for weeks. It feels as if I haven't had a moment to stop and think.'

Jade snorts and hiccups again. I know it's naughty of me, but she reminds me of a pig with a bun. 'Time to think? What do you need that for? Tomorrow, you, my love, are going to marry Ben Trevone and create the most bankable couple in entertainment. You should be celebrating, not thinking.'

'If you are staying over, Jade, can you let me know because I'm sure you won't want to drive if you have any more champagne, will you?'

'Demi's right. You mustn't stay here drinking if you're going to drive back to your hotel.'

'Unless you're going to sleep on the couch?' I say. 'Our accommodation is full to bursting, although there's always the floor of the cafe.'

Lily giggles and I see a fleeting glimpse of why

she is such a star. When she smiles with real happiness she lights up the room like the sun bursting through a cloud. 'We can't have that. Why don't you go home, Jade, and leave me to have some chill-out time? I'm sure I'll be seeing *plenty* of you and everyone else tomorrow.'

There's a steeliness in Lily's tone that surprises me. Jade opens her mouth then closes it again. She dumps her glass on the coffee table, sloshing at least twenty quid's worth of champagne on the table.

'If you really feel like that,' she says sniffily, 'then I'll leave you to it. I'll go back to the hotel to see how Ben is but if you want *anything*, if you're worried about the slightest little thing, then you know where I am.'

Lily jumps up and hugs her, while mouthing a 'thank you' at me over Jade's shoulders.

On her way out of the cottage, out of Lily's sight, Jade shoots me what Polly would call 'a death look'. I'd be stone if she had her way.

'*Nothing* had better go wrong tomorrow,' she says in a tone of doom. 'And if it does, young lady, I'll hold you personally responsible.'

30

Friday afternoon — a refugee camp
north of Athens
Cal

Sweat trickles down my spine. Even through my sunglasses, the light bouncing off the sea of white canvas tents blinds me. I've been here and done this so many times before, but nothing has prepared me for seeing such a tented city again.

I have to shade my eyes. Dust rises and swirls around my feet as we walk towards the school in the camp. We pause at 'reception' — a gazebo with an old table — and the aid worker who's showed me into the camp stops to speak into her phone. She brought me here after I'd met Esme's family and I'm still reeling from that, from their generosity and welcome to me, from the way they haven't judged me, from their kindness.

Beyond the gazebo, through the open flap, I catch a glimpse of the inside of the tent. It looks like a school and sounds like a school. There are paintings and charts on the walls, the backs of heads, a teacher crouched down on the floor, talking to a group of kids. The children are painting, dipping brushes in and out of jars clouded with pigment. Some are hunched over their paintings, tongues out in concentration. Others are making broad brush strokes on the paper, laughing and chatting.

It's a school, just a different kind of school, one with canvas walls and plastic patio tables for desks and students who never wanted or planned to be here.

The young woman clicks off her mobile. 'The kids have art therapy once a week,' she says. 'It's one way of helping them to release the stress and trauma but you must know about that from your work.' She pauses. 'Would you like to join the class now?'

'Can I?'

She smiles briefly. 'Of course. I wouldn't have asked otherwise.' Barely older than Demi, she sounds weary and looks even wearier, but by the time we walk into the classroom, she has a broad smile on her face. The kids turn round and some grin at us; others go immediately back to their art. One head, a little girl's, is intent on her painting, carefully adding some fine detail. She doesn't see me but I know her.

I stop. My throat dries. My heart seems to seize up. I don't think I've ever felt more fear in my life: more terror of the unknown. Every instinct tells me to run away and I don't know why I should be afraid of this young girl — or perhaps I do know.

It's too late. The teacher has spotted us and walks over. She puts her hand on Esme's shoulder.

'Esme. There's someone here that you might know. It's Cal.'

Esme puts down her brush and somehow I make my leaden feet move towards the desk. It's her. Light brown, almost blonde hair pulled back into a ponytail, dark brown eyes and a pink sweatshirt with a picture of a bear on it.

'You remember Cal?' the teacher says.

Esme nods, slowly, up and down.

'Hello, Esme,' I say.

She looks at me without any malice, any shock: just as if we had gone back eighteen months to the day before I lost her and her mother. As if nothing had ever happened.

'Hello, Cal,' she says in English.

The teacher smiles. 'Esme's been painting. She's worked very hard on her picture today, haven't you?' She asks the question in English and in Arabic.

I look at the three figures on the paper. A girl, a woman and a man, hand in hand, with broken buildings all around and the sun shining in the sky.

'Who is it?' My voice cracks with the heat and the dust.

'You. You and me and mummy.'

'Your painting has really come on. I love the detail in the dresses and I can almost feel the heat of the sun,' her teacher says. 'Can't you, Cal?'

I can't speak. My throat is numb, my chest feels as if it's cracking open. I shouldn't have come in here, in front of the children. I should have waited, been better prepared, even though I've been waiting too long already. And no matter how hard I try, how much I swore to myself that I would not do this, I can't stop the tears running down my cheeks like a river, falling into the dust.

The teacher stands silently by my side, the

kids grow quiet and a small warm hand slips into mine. 'Why are you crying?' Esme asks me in Arabic and then again in English. 'Don't cry. Not any more. You found me.'

31

Friday evening — Kilhallon
Demi

My evening walk with Mitch takes me from Kilhallon Cove to the farmhouse — I needed some quiet time to myself after my run-in with Jade. She must have trained at the same school of scariness as Mawgan. On my way back, there are still streaks of coral pink across the sky. It's strange to think the sun is still there somewhere, lighting up someone else's day. Mine will start again all too soon and it'll finally be Lily's wedding day.

I wonder how she feels. How Ben feels. How *I'd* feel if I was making a 'forever' commitment to Cal. Mitch keeps close to me this evening, nose to the ground, scenting the traces left by new people and dogs. My wellies sink softly into the dewy evening grass as I walk across the glamping field, now dominated by the tepee, its creamy canvas sides tinged a soft rose hue by the sunset.

Lamps glow from the cottages and lanterns flicker outside the yurts. A campfire has been lit in the communal area and a group of guests are laughing and chatting. Glasses clink and someone strums softly on a guitar. There's a lump in my throat at the sight and sound of it all. How far we've come since last Easter, Mitch and me and Cal, and all our friends and family. I reach the car parking area by the farmhouse where the mobile signal is more reliable and hope my phone will beep with a message from Cal, but there's nothing.

The farmhouse seems very big and quiet without Cal. Mitch settles in the sitting room and I go into the study to check the answer phone for messages. There are a couple about forward bookings, which I make a note to reply to, and one from a newspaper, which I delete. I sit in Cal's battered leather swivel chair and decide to grab my chance for an early night because I need to be up super early tomorrow and full of energy to last well into the early hours. I'm about to get up from the desk when I spot a letter on Cal's desk. He's never been great at admin but I'm not sure he would have intended me to see this. He must have left it when he rushed off to catch his plane: it's dated on that day. It's a letter from his solicitor but it's the document attached to it that makes me grow cold.

LAST WILL AND TESTAMENT
This Last Will and Testament is made by me, Calvin Ross Penwith

I HEREBY REVOKE all former Wills and codicils made by me and declare this to be my Last Will ('My Will')

My hands are shaking. I know I shouldn't read it but I can't help myself. I suppose I shouldn't be that surprised that Cal's made a will, but why would he do it now? He hasn't gone anywhere dangerous, unless he's planning to in the near future . . .

There's a section about executors — Robyn and his solicitor and then a short list of 'legacies' which amount to cash gifts for Robyn and Polly. After that there's a hefty donation to the charity Cal worked for plus a generous sum for the St Trenyan Community Fund. It's too late to stop reading now, even though I feel guilty about prying into such a personal document.

I come to a section called 'Property' and one relating to 'Other Assets'.

'No. No, he can't do that.'

Even as I blurt out the words, I drop the will like hot coals.

No. I *must* have made a mistake. I force myself to pick the letter up again and read the rest of it. Then I scan it again — and again — but it *is* true. Cal has left Kilhallon House, all the cottages, the resort — and Demelza's — to me in the event of his death.

'No. No, I don't want them. I don't want any of it.'

I'm muttering aloud in an empty room and I glance around guiltily. There's no one to hear. My stomach somersaults.

'I just want Cal.'

I hate the thought that Cal might not be around one day or that he even thinks he might not be around. Why would he make a will now unless he planned on going back to his aid work? It's not as if he's in any danger here at Kilhallon, or in Greece, so the only reason to update his will was if he was heading to somewhere dangerous.

Helping Esme and her family was bound to have a big impact on him. He never wanted to leave them in the first place; if he hadn't been captured, he'd still be in Syria now, taking risks. Why would he stay with one person when his real love and passion is with many people?

I throw the will away. It lands on the threadbare rug that Cal refuses to get rid of, despite Polly saying it's moth-eaten. That rug is part of Kilhallon now. So am I, I'm part of Kilhallon now . . . But without Cal, the place would mean nothing to me. I could never carry on without him on my own.

My heart almost jumps out when the phone extension on the desk rings out.

'Hello, Kilhallon Park?'

'Demi? Thank God I've got hold of you.'

'Cal!' I burst out laughing in relief at hearing his voice after my silly, gloomy thoughts.

'Why are you laughing?'

I turn my back on the will. 'Nothing. I was only thinking about you and the phone rang out.'

There's a pause his end which could be a delay. 'Are you in the study?'

'Yes. I was checking the answer phone messages before I went to bed. Have you met Esme?'

There's a long pause while I hold my breath. 'Yes, I have.'

'And? How was she? How are you?'

'She's OK. She's more than OK. I — I'll tell you more when I get back.' I can barely hear him with the faintness of the signal and the tooting of horns and engine noise but I can sense his relief and happiness.

'Where are you? Outside the airport?'

'I wish. I haven't even got there yet. I'm in a taxi en route but the traffic in Athens is hell and I don't know if I'll make my flight. I'll try everything, I swear, but there's a chance I might miss the wedding if I can't get on a plane tonight.'

After the day I've had and finding the solicitor's letter, tears are so close but I don't want Cal to know. 'Oh . . . I hope you can make it.'

'I know. I'll do everything I can. Hold on . . .' Horns blast and I hear shouts down the line then Cal asking the taxi driver if there's any other route to the airport. He comes back to me. 'We're going to try a detour but it'll be tight even if we can find a way through the jams. I'm sorry, Demi. Are you all right? Is everything going to plan?'

'Yes, I'm OK and everything's going to plan.' Sort of. 'Kit, Polly and the staff have been fantastic.'

'I knew you could manage without me,' he says loudly.

'I didn't mean that. Cal, I hope you can make it. I want you to be here, I need you . . . Cal? Can you hear me? *Cal*? Are you there? Cal!'

The call has dropped out again. In the gathering gloom, I wait by the phone in case he tries to ring me back, unable to move, until the dusk turns to darkness and I can hardly see the words in front of me at all.

32

Early Saturday morning — Kilhallon

I always love this time of day at Demelza's, when the cafe is open, waiting for its first customers. When everything is clean and bright and perfect, and we're all still full of morning enthusiasm and energy.

The tables, inside and out, are all laid out for teas and champagne cocktails. Glasses sparkle in the sunlight streaming through the windows. Fresh Cornish flowers, arranged in vintage glasses, act as centrepieces to each table and fill the air with scent. Greg Stennack's *Saturday Breakfast Show* is playing as we do our final prep for the day, telling us excitedly that 'Cornwall's wedding of the year' is taking place at Kilhallon Park and that his invitation must have been lost in the post.

I got up super early to walk Mitch before dropping him off at the animal shelter, where Nina's mum will take care of him for the day. He didn't seem to mind and I'll be much happier knowing he's playing with his canine friends than getting into trouble here. On my way down to the cafe, I made a detour around the wedding site. The caterers were already onsite and the florists and decor stylists were making final checks on the tepee and wedding glade.

Everything would be perfect if I'd only heard

from Cal but there's been nothing since his call dropped out. I lay awake waiting for a call, I checked WhatsApp and my emails in the night but there was nothing and I've no idea if he caught his flight or not. I'm sure he was focused on getting on board, rather than calling me. His meeting with Esme sounded hopeful and positive but not something he would — or could — talk about on the phone in a taxi.

I try to focus on the day ahead. The ceremony is scheduled for three p.m., which seems ages away but also frighteningly close. Tamsin will be here later this morning to do my nails and make-up, though God knows when I'll find the time. I thought I ought to make myself look decent. I've even splashed out on a slinky new blue dress from a boutique in Truro. Everything has come together against all the odds. Kilhallon looks amazing and we're good to go.

The cafe phone rings and Shamia pops her head around the staff door. 'It's for you, Demi.'

'Who is it? Cal?'

'No. It's that Jade woman. She sounds hysterical.'

'Jade? She's probably broken a fingernail or something. I'm coming.'

Ready to hear a rant from Jade about the flowers not being the right shade of blush or being told that the fridge needs restocking with Krug, I pick up the receiver then immediately hold it away from me. A long high-pitched wail assaults my eardrums.

'What's the matter? Is everything OK?'

'No, it is not OK,' Jade shrieks. 'I knew I

should never have left the silly little cow! I begged her to have this wedding in London or at least somewhere half-civilised. I knew something would go wrong at the arse end of nowhere!'

Resisting the urge to say some very rude words to Jade, I speak slowly as if Jade is a toddler. 'Lily seemed fine when we left her last night. Is she all right?'

'All right? Don't be stupid! She's probably fallen off a cliff or jumped into the sea.'

I grip the phone, feeling sick and also pissed off at being called 'stupid' by a woman for whom the word 'stupid' was clearly invented. 'Oh God, what's happened?'

'What's happened? She's gone missing, that's what's happened, and it's all your bloody fault.'

33

Nina shakes her head in disbelief when I pass on the news of Lily's vanishing act to the staff.

'It can't possibly be your fault. How does that Jade woman work that out?'

'I don't know but she sounded hysterical and if Lily really has disappeared, it's serious. Apparently she wasn't in bed when one of her bridesmaids went up first thing this morning with a Buck's Fizz. Her bed had been slept in and Louie was gone too, so if you ask me, she's probably only taken him for a long walk.'

Nina rolls her eyes. 'Why's Jade freaking out, then?'

'She and the bridesmaids have all tried to call Lily but had no answer.'

'The signal's so bad on the cliffs, that doesn't mean anything.'

'Lily was due for a hair, manicure and make-up session. The ceremony doesn't start until three but by the time they've all finished getting ready and had a load of photos taken with the wedding party time will fly by. The hair stylist is already waiting at the cottage.'

'Have they actually tried looking for her?' Nina asks.

'Jade's on her way over to Kilhallon but Harry's looking for her now. Jade blames him for letting her 'slip the net', as she puts it.'

Nina wrinkles her nose in disgust. 'Anyone

would think Lily was on a community service order, not getting married.'

'Exactly . . . I guess she's gone for a walk and it's taken longer than she thought. Or Louie's gone AWOL. I hope not, remember what happened to Mitch in the autumn?' I picture little Louie vanishing down an old tin-mining shaft and shudder. Then I picture Lily doing the same . . . I tell myself to get a grip: this is a fine bright morning, not a thick fog on a dark night.

'I think I'd better join the search party and try to find her before Jade arrives. Ben doesn't know. Apparently Jade and Addison don't want to freak him out. That's all we need. A wedding but no bride. I'll go down to the cove and see if I can spot her.'

I don't even have time to take off my apron before a small figure appears at the cafe door, peering through the glass. It's Lily with Louie on a long lead so I rush to the door and pull it open.

'Lily!'

'Hello.' Her face is bare of make-up and she's in an oversized waxed jacket that must be a man's it looks so big. The jacket is damp yet there's been no rain. Louie hangs back, pauses and lifts up one paw. He's not sure whether he wants to cross the threshold of this strange place.

'It's OK, Louie. You'll be safe here. We both will.' She scoops him up, kisses him and comes inside.

'Are you OK?' I ask.

She frowns. 'I'm fine. Why wouldn't I be?'

'No reason.'

Still cuddling Louie, she looks around her.

279

'Wow, the cafe looks so beautiful. The sail over the terrace is cute too. I checked it out before I came inside.'

'Glad you like it.' I smile at her, still wondering how to play the situation. 'Have you been for a morning walk?'

'Yes. A long one. I walked and walked and walked over the fields on top of the moors and then through the bracken down to the sea. It was very tall and very wet so I had to carry Louie inside my coat. Then we went past the tin mines up to the lighthouse and beyond that. I'm sure I could see Land's End and some low islands on the horizon — or maybe I imagined those.'

'You didn't imagine them. They're the Scilly Isles. You can see them on a clear day like this, but not until you get beyond the lighthouse and that's well over two miles away. You've probably done at least five miles.'

'Wow, I didn't really notice until I was on my way back, though my feet hurt a little now.' She holds up a foot, showing a pair of dark navy wellies. 'I found these in the porch of my cottage and they're a little bit big for me.'

'Didn't you tell anyone where you were headed?'

'No . . . I didn't want to disturb anyone. I left before they woke up and didn't plan to be out quite so long, but it's a gorgeous morning and I kept stopping to look at the view. Louie paddled in some of the rock pools and once I almost took off my wellies to go in the sea myself but it was a bit cold.'

'The water would be chilly this early in the

year but it is very pretty down there on a day like this. Our guests love Kilhallon Cove so I can see why you wanted to stay down there.'

'The sea's like glass, so still and tranquil and there was hardly anybody about, except for a few people with dogs and a jogger. Once I reached the lighthouse on the headland beyond the cove, I sat on top of the rocky outcrop and tried to spot the islands. I couldn't decide if they were a mirage in the morning haze or real . . . ' Her voice tails off then she snaps back to reality. 'It was so hard to tear myself away but Louie was getting cold. He was tired by the time we got back, even though I carried him some of the way, so I called in here. He needs a break and a drink.'

I think we all know who really needs the break but I go along with it. 'Let me take your coat and fetch you both a drink. Here. Come and sit by the radiators. We've got the heating on to warm the place through even though it's fine now. Shall I call someone for you to let them know you're OK?'

'Have people been looking for me, then?' She sounds surprised although I get the feeling that she's only acting surprised. She *must* know that everyone's been wondering what happened to her.

'Well, Harry and Jade and Addison were — slightly concerned.'

Lily looks down at her boots. 'Were they? I haven't had a signal.'

'We have Wi-Fi on site so we can email them. Shall I?'

She grabs my arm. 'Not yet. Please?'

Her eyes plead with me and there's a desperate edge to her voice. 'Of course, I won't call anyone. You don't have to if you don't want to. Are you *sure* you're OK?'

'Hmm.' She nods and rubs Louie's muzzle. 'But Louie's exhausted, aren't you, poor baby.'

'I'll fetch Mitch's bed for Louie and get him some water and breakfast. I've some doggy muffins prepared for the wedding and he can have one if you say it's OK. Can I get you a cup of chamomile and something to eat?'

'I don't think I could manage anything but the tea.'

'I think you should try. You need to after such a long walk.'

I stroke Louie's silky coat. He yips happily as he recognises my scent. 'Morning, Louie.'

'You're so busy. I don't want to put you to the trouble . . . '

'It's no trouble. You're the bride and it's your wedding morning.' I feel so sorry for Lily. She looks like she hasn't slept for a week. While we settle Louie with his breakfast, Nina prepares Lily's chamomile tea and a thick slice of granary toast drizzled with creamy honey.

'Here's your tea and some toast. This is local bread with organic flour and the honey's from a few miles away. It'll make you feel better.'

Lily smiles. 'Toast and honey. Not had that for ages; not since I was at home. I try to avoid carbs but I supposed it is my wedding day and I do need the energy to face the world.'

She nibbles at the toast and sips her tea. I have

a hundred and one things to do but I can't leave. I don't want to; I never thought I'd feel deeply sorry for a rich, pampered actress, but I do. I'm also worried about her and I don't want to scare her even more. Sooner or later though Harry ought to know that she's here with us. I don't really care about the Gruesome Twosome and I don't blame Lily for wanting to get away from those parasites or the whole wedding machine. I know one thing. If I ever get married, I don't want the whole big bandwagon, even a Kilhallon-style bandwagon. I'd just run away and do it ... not that I can ever see it happening.

Once he's fed and watered, Louie happily plays with a rope toy of Mitch's. He looks even tinier than ever, swamped by Mitch's dog bed. At least he's happy now, but there's still Lily to sort out. Despite saying she couldn't eat she's demolished the toast and has said yes to another cup of tea and a bowl of fresh strawberries with Cornish yoghurt. Her cheeks look a little pinker but I'm still worried.

As she tucks into her strawberries, I take a seat beside her. 'Have you been comfortable in Poldark Cottage?' I ask, concerned about her pale face and dark eyes and keen to bring her back to something like normality — reality — for a moment.

'Oh yes. Thank you. I couldn't seem to settle, even with Louie in bed with me. I kept pacing about.'

'It must be weird without Ben next to you.'

'Oh, I'm used to that. We actually don't spend

that many nights together with our work and it won't change after today.'

'I hadn't thought of that . . . I miss Cal now. At first it was strange sharing the bed with someone else, because I'd been so used to sleeping on my own in all kinds of places. Now, I don't like being without him.'

'Is he not here, then? I haven't seen him about and I was wondering what had happened to him.' Lily pops a strawberry into her mouth. 'These are yummy, by the way.'

I smile. 'Cal's been away for a few days but he'll be back later in time for your wedding. I'm hoping he'll be back . . . '

Lily frowns. 'Is everything OK?'

'Yes, it's fine. It's just that he had to go away urgently for a few days.'

She pats my arm and her mouth turns down. 'Poor you.'

'Oh, it's not what it sounds like. I mean, it's nothing bad. He went to Greece to try and find a little girl called Esme. Cal worked in a refugee camp in Syria until last year and he's been trying to trace Esme and her family since then. On Wednesday, he found out that she might be in a camp in Greece so he went to see if he could find her.'

'I bet that was a shock, when you must have wanted him here with you, with all of our wedding crap going on.'

'Yeah. It was a shock and I did really want him to stay but . . . '

'Why did you let him go, then? I don't think I would have.'

'Let Ben go?'

'No, let Cal go.' She smiles. 'Obviously it would have been weird if Ben had wanted to go away when we were getting married.'

'Yes.'

'So why did you let Cal leave, at the time when you needed him most and you're not totally sure he'll be back?'

'Because . . . because he needed to see Esme while he had the chance. Because he offered to stay here but I knew that in his heart what he really wanted was to see her and talk to her. He has unfinished business with her, and the family were going to be moved from the camp so he daren't wait until after the wedding.'

Lily blows out a breath. 'Wow. You must love him a lot.'

'I suppose . . . I mean . . . yes, I guess I must.' Suddenly I realise that the conversation has turned from her to me, but if it makes her feel better to listen to me, then it's fine, I think. I glance around me but Nina and the other staff are all busy behind the counter or in the kitchen area. No one's listening. Funny how it's often easier to talk to a relative stranger about your fears than someone you actually know.

Lily sighs. 'You're both very lucky to have each other.'

'I hope so.'

'But you're worried he might stay there?'

'No. Not in Greece, but sometimes, often, I wonder if Kilhallon is enough for him.'

'So he's torn between two loves: you and his work and that girl and helping people like her?'

My stomach feels achingly empty and goosebumps prickle my skin. Lily has said out loud the things that have nagged at me for a long time. First with Isla and now with Cal's work. Will I ever be enough for him? And why did I ever let myself start to worry about that? When did I bind up my future so closely with his?

She scrapes out the remaining yoghurt with a spoon.

I change the subject. 'Shouldn't you be getting ready for the wedding?'

'There's plenty of time. The cafe looks adorable. I can't believe all of this is for me. The work and the people everywhere — all for me and Ben.'

'You must be used to a lot of fuss and people around you?'

'Yes. We are, and it gets too overwhelming at times. Which is why I slipped out first thing this morning. I just needed some time and space to myself. I had a good feeling about Kilhallon and Demelza's as soon as I stepped into the cafe. It's the kind of place, with the big skies and the sea, that makes me feel as if my problems are very small. Do you know what I mean?'

'Yes, I know exactly what you mean.'

'I could escape down here and not have to go back to real life . . . not that I know what my real life is sometimes. I — we, me and Ben — live in a weird world. I never know what's real, we're always creating a fantasy and the people around us are reinforcing that.'

Louie trots over from his basket, putting his paws on her knees. She picks him up and hugs him. 'At least Louie is real but he can't travel all over the world with me. Not always.'

Nina catches my eye and mimes a 'you've got a phone call' sign. It has to be Jade or Addison demanding to know if we've seen Lily and I can't ignore them or lie forever. I've already kept Lily here too long. They're bound to freak out and Harry will probably be genuinely worried . . .

'Lily? Thank God I found you.'

Just as I'm thinking of begging Lily to call him, Harry bursts into the cafe. I know it's him by the physique and voice but he looks different somehow. His buzz cut has grown into a short choppy cut that's even darker than Cal's and it suits him. He's wearing charcoal jeans and a grey long-sleeved T-shirt that shows off his broad shoulders and six-pack. If I didn't know better, I'd have said he was the movie star, not Ben.

He kneels at Lily's feet. 'Lily, Lily, *why* did you go off like that? Ben would have been so worried if he'd known you'd disappeared. Jade and Addison have been hitting the roof.' Nina holds up the phone in despair but I shake my head. There's no way I'm speaking to the Gruesome Twosome now.

'But Ben *doesn't* know,' says Lily firmly. 'And I don't want to be rude, but I don't *care* what Jade and Addison think. It's my wedding day and my life. I can do what I like and no one — not even you, Harry — can stop me.'

Stunned into silence, Harry stays on his knees.

'I'm fine. I'm sorry you were worried but I needed to get away and have some time to myself. Totally to myself.'

287

'I didn't know where you'd gone. I thought . . . I thought . . . '

'Louie and I had a long walk and, since then, Demi's been looking after us.'

Lily reaches out and rests her fingers on his shoulder while Harry gazes up at her as adoringly as Louie, though he reminds me more of Mitch: a great, shaggy, faithful hound who'd do anything for me. I haven't met Giles but he must be a very special man to have Harry.

When he speaks again, his voice is soft and gentle. 'I know that. It's your life, Lils. I only wanted you to know that I — we — care about you. More than you can ever know.'

'I do know you care and I'm sorry for causing so much trouble.' She stands up and so does Harry, towering over her by a foot at least. 'I'm ready now. Thank you for the breakfast,' she declares to me and everyone in the cafe. She heaves a big sigh. 'Come on, you'd better do your duty and escort me back to the cottage. Let's do this.'

34

We can hear Jade's voice from the garden gate of the cottage. The front door is open and she has her back to us ranting at some unfortunate person but the moment she catches sight of Lily, she rushes out and squeezes her until Lily almost gasps for air.

'You silly girl! We thought you'd fallen off a cliff!'

'I didn't,' says Harry.

'You, shut up! Call yourself a bodyguard? Lily could have been kidnapped or fallen down one of those holes. Yes,' she says to me, 'I heard that you were almost killed last autumn. Your PA told me!'

Thanks, Polly, I think but Jade has moved on. 'Why didn't you call? Why didn't you ask me, or even Harry, to come with you if you were that desperate for some fresh air?'

'I should have phoned you, I know, but there was no signal. I wanted to be alone for a while.'

Jade takes Lily's arm and her voice is smooth as butter. 'Yes, but you're not Greta Garbo, now are you, darling?'

'It's Lily's life and she's fine,' Harry says.

Jade rounds on him, her eyes flashing fury. 'You are paid to make sure that she's safe, not to have an opinion. After this fiasco and the sea incident, you'll be lucky if we keep you on. I'd hire someone else if it wasn't Lily's wedding morning, but you can pack your bags after today.'

'Leave Harry alone! I decide who works for me and that goes for you too, Jade,' Lily snaps back with a passion I haven't seen before. 'Now, I'm going to have a nice relaxing bath and then I'm going to get ready for *my* wedding in *my* own time and neither you nor anyone else is going to spoil today. And you do not *ever* speak to me like that again. Is that *clear*?'

Leaving Jade gulping like a stranded fish on the beach, Lily stomps upstairs. Harry rushes to the foot of the steps but Jade clamps her fingers on his arm. 'Leave her alone. This is your doing. She would never have turned on me like that if you hadn't let her escape. She's had far too much time to think.'

Harry glares down at her as if she were a cockroach. 'Escape? What kind of a word is that? You're spouting absolute bollocks, Jade, and you know it. If anyone's upset her, it's you and Wonderboy Addison, you grasping pair of leeches.'

Jade's eyes widen. 'Right. That's it. You can get out of this dump right now. I'll look after Lily from now on.'

Harry folds his arms and his huge biceps bulge. 'I'm not leaving until I know Lily's in safe hands and I consider yours to be about as safe as Lady Macbeth's. You and Addison are complete parasites. I'll be outside the cottage, briefing the security team, and I won't be letting Lily out of my sight for the rest of the day.'

I wouldn't say that Harry flounces off, because

I don't think it's possible, but he strides out of the door and shuts it very firmly. Jade is left in his wake, like a stranded goldfish.

'Can I do anything to help?' I ask, standing well clear in case she decides to lash out.

'Actually, you can. You can sort out the fact that Lily's hairstylist is going ballistic because Lily's not even had a bath yet, and the fact that her friends are getting pissed on the free Krug and it's not even ten a.m. and you can find out where that cunning minx Mawgan Cade has got to. *And* you can find someone who can get all three bridesmaids looking like they belong at a celebrity wedding, not a circus. I'm going to my car to do some mindfulness and centre myself but I tell you this, if Lily Craig so much as crosses the threshold of this cottage before it's time for the ceremony, I'll blacken the name of this shitty little hole from here to Timbuktu.'

With that, she storms off, slamming the door of the cottage so hard the frame shakes.

It's probably a good job Cal isn't here because I don't think he'd have been much help with what's happened. He might have thrown Jade out himself. I don't give a toss about Jade's threats; I'm more worried about Lily and Harry and the way Jade treats them. She and Mawgan would make a wonderful pair. No, forget it: the world doesn't deserve that kind of drama.

There's silence for a few seconds while I regain my breath. Then, from the kitchen, a girl with a large bag emerges. 'Is it safe to come out?'

'Yes. I think so.'

She lets out a long breath. 'Thank God for

that. I'm Carmel, Lily's hairstylist. Contrary to what Jade said, I wasn't going ballistic, I was only taking cover from Jade. There's also plenty of time to get Lily ready, I'm well prepared for glitches like this. All brides are twitchy on their wedding morning and Lily's always late anyway.'

'Really?' I'm not so sure there is plenty of time, despite what Carmel claims, but she does know Lily a lot better than I do.

'It'll be fine in the end, I'm sure, although I think Harry's been given his marching orders for real this time.'

'Has she sacked him before, then?'

Carmel laughs. 'Jade's sacked everyone at some point but I've never heard Harry go for the jugular before. There's no going back from that, though I don't blame him. If I didn't love Lily to bits, for all her foibles, I'd have quit too. Jade is a grade-A bitch and a parasite, as Harry says. Addison isn't quite so bad but he's pathetic and under Jade's thumb.'

'Poor Lily, though I was relieved to see her stand up to Jade.'

'Me too,' Carmel replies. 'But there is something I haven't told Jade or Lily that could be another issue. Jade would have totally lost it if I had.'

My heart sinks. 'Oh, no. What now?'

'Don't panic. It's not the *complete* end of the world but Lily's make-up artist isn't going to make it. She's gone down with food poisoning from the hotel they stayed in. Her assistant's gone down with it too. They texted me while Jade was ranting.'

'No make-up people? Can you do it?'

'Sort of. I'm trained and I can manage Lily as well as her hair but I'll need help with the bridesmaids. God knows how we're going to get someone decent up here at this short notice, even if they know its Lily Craig's wedding.'

My brain makes the leap and I sigh in relief. 'That's one thing I can help you with.'

Carmel stares at me. 'Are you a trained beautician?'

'No, but I know a woman who is. My friend Tamsin's coming over to do mine and Polly's make-up but I'm sure she could switch to the bridal party. I'll call her.'

'Do you think she'll mind?'

Finally I find something to smile about amid the chaos. 'Oh, I think she can cope.'

Five minutes later, I break the news to Tamsin.

'What? Who? Me? Are you joking? Really? I'd love to!'

I can't stop smiling. 'The downside is that you have to make Mawgan look like a fairy princess.'

Tamsin grins wickedly. 'That's not a downside. I've been waiting to get my hands on those eyebrows since we were in primary school.'

★　★　★

Phew. What a relief. Cal has made his train to Penzance after all. I get a delayed message while I'm walking back to Poldark Cottage. That's a huge load off my mind. It's late morning now and the cosy sitting room is crammed with people. The bridal party and their entourage

293

occupy every inch of space so that I can barely open the door. Lily's parents can't stop beaming even though Jade is barking orders at just about anyone. The bridesmaids — including a gleeful Mawgan — are giggling and sipping champagne from mini bottles through silver straws.

Standing behind them, armed with her toolkit of brushes and a jaw-breaking grin, is Tamsin. Lily's make-up artist has created a look for Lily and her bridesmaids, which Tamsin has, amazingly, even adapted to suit Mawgan.

Stripped of her Tango tan, Mawgan now has a natural pale golden glow. Her dewy foundation is enhanced with a creamy blusher and subtle eye shadow that brings out the colour of her eyes. Tamsin has somehow managed to work a miracle on her over-plucked eyebrows too. The slinky column dress in a cornflower-blue shows off her figure, enhanced by a fresh flower in her hair and a beautiful posy of Cornish flowers in dusky rose, pale peaches and creams. She looks sophisticated yet natural; chic yet innocent.

It's weird. Seriously weird . . . and very disturbing. And somehow, a tiny part of me feels a teeny bit sorry for Mawgan who has been de-Mawganned. It's almost cruel, like pulling the claws of a sabre-toothed tiger.

'Wow. You all look stunning.'

The photographer shouts over the giggling. 'You look a-mazing! Now, be careful, ladies. We want you to stay perfect for the pictures.'

Mawgan smirks and throws a small and satisfied smile at me and seems about to say something but we're all cut off by a collective gasp from bridesmaids and entourage.

Lily descends the narrow stairs into the room with her dressmaker holding up the train.

Jade starts hyperventilating at the sight of her biggest asset. 'Oh my God. You look breathtaking, darling.'

For once I agree with Jade. Lily doesn't look like a mere mortal. She's a goddess. Her pale gold dress is simple but beautifully cut, with long fitted sleeves, an embroidered bodice and a nipped-in waist that shows off her tiny figure to perfection. Her hair is loose and crimped into soft flowing waves, all set off by a circlet of Cornish flowers in bud. She looks like a medieval princess from a painting.

The silence is broken and everyone bursts into applause.

'You look amazing,' I tell her when I can eventually get a word, almost afraid to get too close to her.

'Thank you.'

'Ben's very lucky.'

Jade looms next to my shoulder. 'So is Lily,' she cuts in. 'They're both very lucky to have each other. They're the perfect couple, aren't you, Lily?'

'Yes, I'm very lucky,' Lily echoes.

'Is there anything else you need? Anything at all? I'm going down to the ceremony area to double-check everything's on schedule but if you need me — for anything at all — please call me.'

'Oh, don't worry. We will,' says Jade.

Lily flashes me a smile. 'I'm fine. I trust you and Kilhallon.'

Lily winces as Jade takes her elbow. 'Lily, darling, the photographer wants to take some shots in the cottage garden.'

'See you at the glade,' I murmur but Jade has already swept Lily away into the giggling chaos of the bridal party.

★ ★ ★

After checking with Rachel that everything's running smoothly at last, I dash up to the house to change but not before trying to get hold of Cal for a quick word on his progress. His mobile goes straight to voicemail but I don't leave a message because I don't think it will help. It's no use me panicking or getting upset; I'm going to have to keep my focus on today and hope he turns up at some point, but I can't help feeling disappointed.

'Still no word from him? I bet his train's delayed or cancelled. I heard they had a signal failure at Tiverton Parkway.'

With this helpful statement, Polly enters the kitchen and dumps a handbag on the table. She's wearing a coral shift dress and a little black cardigan with a matching fascinator in her freshly styled hair. Her make-up knocks years off her but she's still the Polly I know and love, so I can't be too cross with her for her less-than-positive news about the trains.

'He might still make it, you know. I'm sure he's doing everything he can.'

'He made the train. I got a delayed message while I was walking back up here but I'm not sure how the journey's going.'

'Fingers crossed.'

I force a smile. 'Wow, you look lovely. That dress suits you and the make-up's great.'

She glances down at her outfit. 'Tamsin's a miracle worker. I don't look too 'done', do I?'

'No, you look fantastic.' I hug her.

'Didn't want to let Kilhallon down and you never know where the photos might end up. Can't have Mawgan Cade or anyone round here saying I looked like a bag of rags.'

'You look stunning.'

'Hmm. Your turn now, madam. Tamsin's on her way up here after finishing Lily's lot. Come on, get a move on.'

'I don't think I have time for much pampering. We're running late.'

'Yes, you do. Sit down. Oh look, here's Tamsin.'

She taps her watch and I realise it's half past one. In ninety minutes the ceremony starts. Polly makes me a cold drink while Tamsin sets to work on my nails. She's doing a super quick-dry nude varnish that will dry while she does my makeup.

My phone beeps.

'That could be Cal!'

'Don't you dare touch that phone until your nails are dry,' Tamsin orders.

'Wait.' Polly turns on my phone and shows me the screen.

'It *is* Cal. He says the train's running an hour late but he's still hoping to make it as long as there aren't any more hold ups . . . but he still has to make it from Penzance to Kilhallon. What if there are no taxis? It's Saturday and they'll be so busy with holidaymakers.'

'Keep still, hon!' Tamsin orders.

Polly holds a drink with a straw to my mouth. 'If he makes it home, he makes it home. If not, then there's nothing we can do and anyway, we've done the hard bit already. It won't make a scrap of difference to the wedding now if Cal's here or not.'

But it will make a difference to *me*. I'm desperate to hear every detail of what happened with Esme, and see for myself how Cal feels. I won't rest until I see him with my own eyes so I can judge.

'How did he sound when you last spoke to him?' Polly asks me, while Tamsin applies a final topcoat in swift, expert strokes.

'OK. He's seen her but his battery was dying and he'd forgotten his charger. I don't really know. I hope he's not worse for it.'

'Nothing you can do now, my bird. Nothing any of us can do.'

'Can you please keep still and shut up for *one* minute?' Tamsin pleads. 'I need to finish your face and if you hadn't noticed, we've got a wedding to go to in less than an hour.'

35

After all the drama of this morning, I can hardly believe I'm finally ready. With half an hour to go to the start of the ceremony, my windswept hair is tamed with a crystal clip, I'm wearing the new blue dress I fell in love with and had to buy, despite the price. My make-up has even made me look like an actual wedding guest, rather than, according to Polly, 'a scarecrow who's spent the morning being dragged through a hedge backwards'. Polly has gone to help Rachel who's at the wedding glade, ready to greet and usher the close family to their seats and make sure everything looks perfect. Tamsin has re-joined the bridal party for any last minute touch-ups. Picking up my bag, I make my way downstairs and hear someone walk into the kitchen.

I hurry down. 'Cal!'

'No, it's me.'

Isla meets me in the kitchen. She's elegant in a pale-green vintage silk tea dress and her cheeks are glowing softly. I don't think I've ever seen her look more beautiful and I try to hide my disappointment.

'The door was unlocked so we walked in. I wanted to thank you for the amazing job you and Cal have done for the wedding. We've had a look round and I wouldn't recognise the place from when Cal first came home.'

'We should thank you for persuading Lily and Ben to have their ceremony here.'

'I did wonder if I'd handed you all a poisoned chalice. Lily and Ben can be hard to pin down at times and I heard you had some ups and downs along the way. It's Jade and Addison who are the real tough nuts. Have they been a terrible pain in the arse?'

I don't know how to reply to this but my face must give my feelings away.

'Hmm. I thought as much. You deserve a medal for dealing with them but on balance, I'd hoped that the wedding would be a good thing for Kilhallon.'

'It has been. The publicity's been great . . . on the whole. We've had tons of bookings and attention. Thanks.'

'Hmm. Kind of you to be so tactful. I wonder if Cal feels as grateful.'

'I'm sure he would if he was here.'

She raises her eyebrows. 'Last minute glitches to fix?'

'Not at Kilhallon. He's been to Greece to find Esme.'

'Esme? Oh . . . I . . . I hope everything's OK between you?' I could kick myself. I remind myself that Isla knows nothing of Cal's experiences in Syria and that he trusted me with the full story. It's too late now. I must tell her something.

'It is. Esme's a young girl. He met her in Syria and he's gone out to Greece to meet up with her in a refugee camp. You know Cal . . . when he needs to do something, there's no stopping him.'

She frowns. 'Cal? I — I think so. Yes, he does what he wants, no matter who it affects . . . but to go so far away *now*? That must have been a nightmare for you.'

Damn it, I wish I hadn't even told Isla this much about Cal but how can I lie to her when Polly and Tamsin know he's gone away and where. It's too late to keep the truth hidden, even if no one but Cal and I will ever know the whole truth. 'We've managed with Polly, Kit and Rachel and all our friends. We've coped and it was important to Cal that he went to see Esme. He did offer to stay but I didn't want to hold him back or make him stay here when his heart was somewhere else.'

Isla stares at me.

'You know him better than me, Demi. You're more in tune with Cal than I ever was.'

'I wouldn't say that. I don't think I'll ever know him totally.'

'If we knew someone totally, it would be a boring life.' She smiles. 'I'll wait for Cal to tell me more about this little girl, if and when he wants to. I'm only now getting over the shock of finding out that Kit is his half-brother. I knew Cal's father was a rogue but not that he'd actually fathered another son.'

'How did you find out?'

'Robyn told me earlier this year and I was as gobsmacked as she was. When I met Kit at the shoot last autumn, I'd no inkling so I can't imagine how Cal reacted when he found out. I keep racking my brains to see if I noticed a resemblance between them but I can't say I did.'

301

'Once you know, you can tell.'

'I'll have to go and say hello later. It must have been a hell of a shock for Cal.'

'You could say that, but they're both slowly getting used to it. He's been writing a feature about the floods and working on his book so he stayed on to help us.'

'There's so much I've missed while I've been away.' She puts her hand on the back of the chair to steady herself.

'Are you OK?'

She sits down quite heavily and is very pale. 'Yes. Could I have a glass of water, please? I feel wobbly.'

Wow. I never thought the news about Esme and Cal would have such an effect. While I fill a glass I spot the clock. Twenty-five minutes to the ceremony. No Cal yet and I don't think there will be. He must have been delayed further. It was a long shot to even think he'd make it. He knew he wouldn't and so did I, deep down. Never mind, we'll manage but it would have been so good to have him here.

'Thanks.' Isla takes some sips from the glass of water and a few calming breaths.

'Are you OK? I hate to leave you but I ought to go to the ceremony. I can't leave Rachel to handle everything and Lily might need me. Shall I find Luke?'

'He should be here any minute. He stopped over in the yard to chat to Polly . . . and I'm fine, honestly.' She gives me a weak smile. 'I may as well tell you. I'm pregnant.'

'Wow . . . that's amazing. Congratulations.'

302

'I came to share the news with you and Cal while we had a few moments' quiet but I can tell him later when he gets here.'

'If he gets here. His train was running late.'

'He will. Eventually. Demi, he would never let you down.'

But he let you down and went away, I think. He put his love for people in general before his love for you and you were the love of his life. I don't expect any special treatment, an ordinary being like me, not against the rest of the world.

'You're perfect for him, you know.'

'What?'

'You and Cal. You should hold on to what you have here, with every ounce of strength.'

My skin tingles with discomfort at Isla's words, but I laugh them off. 'We're doing our best, though it might finish us both off to keep Kilhallon running.'

'I didn't mean Kilhallon, though you've done an amazing job to make it a success.' Isla reaches for my hand and rests hers on it. 'I meant you and Cal. You should never let each other go. You can handle his moods, you brought him back from the dead — or at least, you brought him back to life.'

'Yeah.' I laugh again but Isla takes my hand.

'I'm sorry if I'm embarrassing you. Maybe my hormones are making me slushy but I wanted to say it while we're on our own. You and Cal are a far better match than Cal and I would ever have been.'

'We've only been together for a year, and even then, we've only just moved in together.'

'Doesn't matter. What does matter is that you'll never find each other again if you fall apart now. You let him go to Greece. I'm not sure I would have been so understanding about him leaving just at this moment.'

I smile, remembering how jealous I once was of Isla, and how I would have killed to be in her place. Maybe she's right and maybe she's only being over emotional, I don't know, but my stomach is swirling and my throat is swelling.

'Thank you for being so nice but I'm not thinking beyond the next hour for now. I can't wait to see Cal. That's all I want now.'

She smiles and let's go of my hand. 'I know.'

'*Isla?*'

Luke appears at the door, a worried frown on his face. Despite the anxious expression, he's looking well. He's tanned, he's put some weight on and it suits him. He taps his watch face. 'We're going to be late. Are you OK?'

'Isla isn't feeling very well,' I say.

His face falls and he rushes to her side. 'No? Poor love. Feeling sick again?'

Isla kisses him. 'I was but it's passed now. Demi's helped me. I'll be fine in a few minutes. Don't fuss.'

My phone beeps but it's only a text from Rachel, asking me to join her and the wedding celebrant in the wedding glade. The falconer has already arrived and has Boris the owl ready to deliver the rings.

I pick up my bag. 'Sorry, I have to go now. You're welcome to stay here as long as you like and I'll see you at the ceremony.'

'Thanks for looking after her,' says Luke, sitting down next to Isla and taking her hand.

'I'll be OK in a moment. Thanks.'

'A pleasure. Come and find me if you need any more help.'

★ ★ ★

Grabbing my phone, I leave Kilhallon House and make my way to the wedding glade, knowing this is one of the last moments of quiet I'll have today. I pull my wrap around my shoulders. There's a decent breeze but nothing to blow the tepee over.

The parking area is crammed with vans and trucks while guests' cars roll in down the track to the makeshift car park. Women in elegant dresses hold on to their hats as they pick their way down the track to the wedding glade. There are men in designer suits, open neck shirts and pointy shoes; little girls in their new dresses and boys in bow ties, their hair stiff with gel. As I walk, I try to spot the arty, actor types from the local friends and relations. I imagine Lily and Ben getting nearer to the moment when they're going to 'tie the knot', if not legally, then for all intents and purposes.

But mostly I think of Cal because despite what Isla's said, I know she came to tell *him* her news, not me. She must have been as disappointed as I was that Cal was away, though she seems happy enough with Luke and he's definitely crazy about her.

I don't know how Cal will react when he hears

305

Isla is pregnant. Will he be happy for her or think of what might have been, if only for a moment? Will he wonder 'what if': what if Isla's baby had been their child? Or will he be too wrapped up in the life of a different child, Esme?

I've known him just over a year. She's known him his whole life and no matter what she told me about us being perfect for each other, I don't think either of us know him completely. Or if we ever will.

I push those thoughts aside. Kilhallon's big day has come and I need to focus on this moment for now.

Wow.

From the top of the slope, the whole wedding glade is spread out below me. The tepee is a canvas fairy castle, its twin turrets topped by pennants fluttering in the breeze. Guests are taking their places in stripy deckchairs in candy colours. Flowers in jars hang from the shepherd's hooks and mark the path down the grassy 'aisle' that leads to the willow arch.

OK. It doesn't quite look as if the guys have 'rocked up and constructed it out of a few twigs' but it is natural and beautiful. It's a stunning focal point for the glade, which is filled with soft spring colours and fresh scents. The log 'altar' is adorned with flowers and fairy lights. I'm sure Lily and Ben are going to love it. Cal is definitely going to be amazed when he turns up, *if* he turns up.

Polly spots me and joins me at the rear of the glade where a row of chairs has been reserved for 'staff'. Rachel is still with the bridal party and my dad's double-checking the PA system is ready for the celebrant. Isla and Luke arrive and take their places near the front of the glade next to an actor I recognise from *Game of Thrones*, who met a very nasty end. Polly almost fainted when she spotted him because apparently he'd been in *Downton* a few times too.

There's a buzz of excited conversation and expectation. People clutch their pashminas or check their fascinators are pinned on. Most are wearing sunglasses. The folk band are playing some traditional Cornish love songs as the final guests find their seats. Dotted around the edge of the guests on each side are security guards wearing dark glasses. In the tepee and at Demelza's, I picture Nina and the team waiting for the guests to swarm in, starving and thirsty after the ceremony, and Lily and Ben starting their first dance as a married couple — well, a handfasted couple.

'I never thought this day would come after all the cock-ups, but we did it,' Polly says to me. 'I think we should give ourselves a pat on the back and a large G&T once this ceremony's over.' She pauses then clicks her tongue against her teeth. 'Oh, he's turned up, then, has he?'

'Did you think Ben would chicken out?' I whisper to Polly, secretly relieved because I thought the same myself.

'I wouldn't have bet my house on it, that's for sure.'

Polly raises her eyebrows as Ben and his best man, an actor friend, take their places in front of the willow arch. Jade scuttles around the side of the glade to bag her reserved seat in the front row next to Lily's parents. Addison is already in place next to Isla and Luke. Harry is standing at the edge of the copse, cupping his hand in front of his mouth as if he's talking to the other security guards.

Above us a low buzz whirrs and we look up to see a small drone hovering above the glade.

'I hate them drone things. Should be banned,' Polly grumbles.

'It's taking pictures,' I say. 'Kilhallon will look good.'

'I don't care. They're a damn nuisance.'

Polly purses her lips but returns her attention to the celebrant, a lean, tall man in a corduroy jacket and jeans, whose charcoal hair is tied back in a ponytail. 'I know him, the vicar. It's that Neil Polgreen from the Reiki Healing Centre in St Trenyan, him that always smells of patchouli. I went to school with him. He took me to a folk concert in Par but I lost touch with him when we left. He's worn well, I'll say that for him, and he's still got a good head of hair.'

'I didn't recognise his name and I'd no idea he was a humanist celebrant, but I know his place. I slept in his shop doorway once, but Mitch didn't like the smell.'

Polly clutches my arm excitedly. 'Oh, here we go.'

The music has stopped and the celebrant lifts his hand for quiet. Everyone gets to their feet and turns round to watch the bridal party: Lily and her bridesmaids, walking carefully down the slope from the cottages to the glade.

'My God. Is that who I think it is?'

'Yes. Amazing, isn't it?'

'I'd never have believed it if I hadn't seen it with my own eyes. It's scary.' No names have been mentioned but we've both homed in on Mawgan, walking behind Lily, clutching her candy-coloured posy, a serene smile on her face.

'Innocent as a new-born babe, I don't think.'

Polly lets out a snort, and someone glares at us. The bridal party draw nearer. I have a lump in my throat at the sight of Lily. Of all the people who might not turn up this afternoon, I'd have bet Kilhallon on it being Lily, but she's obviously far more enthusiastic about marrying Ben than she seems. She's smiling and looks happy enough.

There are audible gasps as she reaches our line of deckchairs and enters the top of the 'aisle', murmurs of 'wow' and a few people sniffling into hankies.

'Lily looks gorgeous. She's not a real human. No wonder she's a star,' I whisper as Lily wafts past, her dress rustling in the breeze.

'Yes, she's a very beautiful girl. Still can't think for the life of me what she's marrying him for, but each to their own.'

Mawgan spots us and smirks. I nod politely and smile, even though it hurts me. She looks around as if she's trying to spot Cal but has to concentrate on not tripping over her dress. Far be it for me to ruin Lily's day but I can't help thinking that it would be fun if Mawgan did end up flat on her bum on the grass.

Polly nudges me. 'I've just heard something from my Zumba mate, Karen. Did I tell you she's married to Mr Gwennap's brother?'

'Er. No.'

'Well, you know that I found out that Mr Gwennap was away when his fields were spread? Apparently, his hip replacement was paid for by 'a generous member of the local community' who arranged for him to have it done privately. The old boy was taken aback but he needed the op and he wasn't going to say no, was he? Karen said she'd promised not to reveal the name of the 'well-wisher' but she dropped enough hints for me to guess.'

Polly nods at Mawgan. 'Besides, who round here has the cash to offer to pay for someone's op and arrange for a load of slurry to be dumped on someone's land?'

We both fix our eyes on Mawgan, looking sweet and innocent in her bridesmaid's dress. Butter wouldn't melt in her mouth. The drone hovers in the sky above Mawgan's head, as if she'd specially arranged for it to do a close-up.

Polly purses her lips then says in a loud voice, 'Muck never sticks in some places, does it?' She whispers again. 'Of course I can't prove it and if the contractors were paid cash by a third party, we can't get evidence. Whoa!'

In the nick of time, Polly stops her fascinator from sailing off in the breeze and out over the Atlantic. 'Oh well. It's an ill wind, eh? I'd rather be holding on to my hat all day than holding on to my nose.'

Polly makes me smile, but I want to be smiling

at her with Cal by my side. Is he driving up the road to Kilhallon even now? Is he trudging wearily down the track or sitting in a station cafe? I can't wait to hear how his reunion with Esme went. I try to refocus. Lily hands her bouquet to her bridesmaid and joins Ben under the willow arch. They face each other and hold hands. Every eye in the glade is on them as the celebrant smiles and in his strong Cornish accent, says:

'A very warm welcome, everyone, to the joining together of Lily and Ben on this beautiful afternoon.'

At that moment, a hand closes around mine and a familiar voice whispers in my ear, 'Sorry I'm a bit late.'

'Cal!'

People stare at me but I couldn't help myself. I want to laugh and burst into tears all at the same time. Ignoring everyone, Cal kisses me. I close my eyes and everything and everyone around me vanishes for those few brief moments. I want to dance down the aisle and shout but I can't even squeak because the celebrant is talking about the joining together of Lily and Ben and something about nature's ways . . . and I've no idea what else because all I can see, hear, smell and touch is Cal.

'Sorry,' he mouths and squeezes my hand.

'You made it,' I mouth back, fizzing with relief.

Polly leans forward and glares at us, but mostly at Cal.

He smiles and shrugs. His shirt is rumpled, his

boots are dusty. He looks tired, but the tension etched on his face has gone. Whatever happened between him and Esme in Greece, it doesn't seem to have made things worse.

The celebrant must have told us to sit down because everyone's back in their seats and the folk band is playing a quirky version of one of Ben and Lily's favourite songs. While they're playing and some people are clapping and singing along, Cal takes his chance.

'I'm sorry I didn't call you. Phone problems, no signal and then I didn't dare call in case you were here at the ceremony and most of all I didn't want to raise your hopes that I'd be back in time. When I saw the queue at the taxi rank, I had my doubts. I should have called and booked ahead but the past few days have been crazy and I haven't exactly been thinking clearly.'

'It doesn't matter now. What about Esme? How is she?'

He breaks into a smile. 'I'll tell you more later but she's alive, she's well, and she's with a loving family who are helping her deal with losing her mum. There's hope of a better life. They want to apply for asylum in Germany. Esme's auntie is there and she's offered to adopt her if they can get asylum.'

'I'm so glad. It must have been terrible to leave her.'

'Yes . . . but not what you think. It wasn't like I thought — Ow! Jesus, Polly, that really hurt!'

Cal rubs his side where Polly has poked him hard in the ribs. She puts her finger to her lips and gives him the evils.

'Later,' he whispers to me, still wincing, 'I promise I'll tell you everything, as soon as this is over.'

36

'Strangest wedding I've ever been to,' Polly whispers as a hush falls over the glade while the celebrant invites Lily and Ben to make their vows to each other. I don't care how strange or weird it is. All I know is that my whole body has heaved a massive sigh of relief. The wedding's actually happening and Cal's home and not in despair. His fingers brush mine, making my skin tingle deliciously, as we listen to the celebrant talking. Ben is reading out his vows about how amazing Lily is and how kind and gorgeous, but I'm trying not to giggle.

'What's up?' Cal whispers as I clamp my hand to my mouth.

'That's his brave hero voice,' I say. 'It's exactly the voice he used for the sea otter in *Ocean Furries*.'

Cal smiles. 'You're a very bad girl.'

I bite my lip as the celebrant invites Lily to speak. Unfortunately, he drops the microphone and everyone lets out a collective wince as the feedback unleashes a piercing shriek of sound. Then there's laughter as Ben rescues the microphone and hands it to Lily. We all wait as she composes herself. And we wait some more. She seems to be taking a few deep breaths to calm herself but there's an air of tension creeping in.

Seconds pass and the only sound is the drone

hovering over the altar, waiting, and the cawing of crows in the trees.

'Oh dear,' Polly whispers.

'Shh.'

'From the first moment I met Ben, at the read-through for *Desperate Poets*, I knew I'd found my best friend.'

You can almost feel the sighs of relief as Lily finally speaks.

'I have to say that our first meeting wasn't an auspicious one. Ben had only just finished shooting a thriller and he had a terrible buzz cut and a bad attitude,' Lily says.

Everyone laughs again. 'Despite that beginning, we seem to have got together and here we are now. About to be joined together forever.'

Awws of delight echo around the glade. A few people applaud. Louie, sitting on Addison's lap, lets out a yip.

'And so . . . '

Lily's words are drowned out by a baby screaming. A little boy pipes up with, 'Can we go in the tent yet?'

Everyone laughs and then hush falls again as we wait for Lily to carry on. The baby is hurried off in her buggy and the little boy is quiet again.

'And so . . . ' Lily begins again, still holding hands with Ben.

'She is an actress — it's probably for dramatic effect,' Polly chirps up.

It's hard to see Lily's face from the back. Butterflies stir in my stomach. What if . . . ?

'And so,' she says in a loud voice that makes us all jump. 'I can't think of anyone else that I'd

315

rather spend the rest of my life with.'

'Phew. Thank goodness for that,' I whisper to Cal. 'I'm amazed they made it this far.'

'Hmm. Slightly tense moment.'

The celebrant starts talking again about the birds and the bees and nature and the stars and then addresses us all.

'Dear friends, Ben and Lily will now seal their eternal love by exchanging rings.'

Polly snorts. 'Eternity's a long time.'

'Shh!' hisses a woman next to her.

Cal stifles a laugh.

'So, now, we invite a very special guest, Boris, to deliver the rings to Lily and Ben.'

There's an air of confusion, a few mutter 'who the hell is Boris?' with people glancing at each other in puzzlement. Knowing what's coming, I smile.

Cal squeezes my hand. 'This should be fun.'

Everyone turns round to see the falconer with a beautiful tawny owl perched on her glove. There are gasps of amazement as she releases Boris and he flies swiftly down the aisle, his golden feathers flashing past, a tiny pouch dangling from his talons. Ben is wearing a leather glove and holds his arm straight out and rigid. From here, I can see he's cringing as he braces himself for the landing. The drone whizzes up and hovers above the altar.

Boris flies straight past Ben's glove and up into the copse.

After a few seconds' confusion, everyone laughs.

'Ah. Boris has decided to keep us waiting a

while longer,' says the celebrant.

Jenni, the falconer, jogs down the aisle and whispers something to Ben, Lily and the celebrant.

'Boris can be a bit unpredictable, apparently, but his owner assures us he'll come down soon,' says the celebrant.

'Does that bird really have the rings in his pouch?' Polly asks me.

'Yes. The falconer tried to persuade Lily to put her substitute rings in the bag, in case this happened, but Lily wouldn't hear of it. She thought it was cheating to use fake rings.'

Polly rolls her eyes.

'I'm sure Boris will come down soon,' Cal says, though I can feel him shaking with the effort of trying not to laugh himself.

'If he's anything like his namesake, he'll change his mind when it suits him,' says Polly.

Ten minutes later, the falconer is still trying to lure Boris down from his perch. The guests are all talking among themselves and the kids have started to chase each other about in the aisle. The falconer is desperately trying to tempt Boris with his favourite snack: raw rabbit chunks. Some of the kids have now wandered closer to watch the entertainment.

Cal blows out a breath. 'Boris isn't going to budge, is he?'

'I don't know, but I need to do something.'

Rachel joins the falconer to talk to her. Jade is on her feet and pacing up and down and glaring at Rachel, as if it's her fault. Ben and Lily are talking to each other. Lily seems to be in tears.

People are staring at them.

'Shit. This isn't what we want. I have to go and see what I can do.'

I've no idea what help I can be but when I reach the bridal party, I can see Lily's in tears and Ben is furious. He rips off the glove and throws it on the ground. 'I knew this was a barking mad idea. That owl isn't coming down any time soon. Why didn't you let it have the falconer's rings?'

'Boris is a wild creature,' Lily says reasonably, 'and I wanted him to have the real rings. I wanted this whole thing to be authentic and natural and not fake, unlike the rest of my life!'

Ben glares at her. 'Fake? What are you trying to say, Lily?'

Jade leaps up and grabs Lily's hand. 'Now, darling, calm down. We don't need that bloody owl. We can use some other rings until we get them back. Here, I'm sure someone's got one to spare.' She catches sight of me. 'You. Find two rings so we can get on with the ceremony *now*.'

Rachel jogs over. 'I've got the spare rings from the falconer. They were her grandparents' and she keeps them for this very purpose. They're not ideal but they'll do for now so we can carry on and enjoy the most important part of the ceremony.' She puts her arm around Lily. 'How does that sound?'

Ben folds his arms. 'Fine by me. Lily?'

Lily stares at him and then slowly looks around at all of us ranged in a circle around her. Me, Ben, Rachel, Jade, Addison and the falconer. She turns away and looks up into the trees where Boris sits on a branch, watching us all.

'I'm sorry.'

'It's not your fault. It's that damned stupid bird!'

'Shut up, Jade!'

Lily's shriek makes us jump and the buzz of conversation stops.

'You're stressed and upset. I can believe it after all the cock-ups but everything's going to be fine. Come on, take the rings and let's get on with this.' Jade tries to take Lily's arm but Lily pushes her away.

'I can't do this. I know you'll all hate me and I'm very, very sorry, Ben, but you know it wouldn't be real. You know that, Jade knows it and even Boris knows it. That's why he flew into the tree.'

'No, he didn't. It was the drone, that fucking drone!' Jade shrieks.

Neil, the celebrant, steps between her and Lily. 'Please, madam, this is a solemn occasion.'

'No, it's not. It's a farce. A bloody farce. Letting my biggest clients have this wacky shambles of a wedding in this godforsaken corner is a farce. Now, Lily, come to your senses and marry Ben.'

Jade makes a grab for Lily who backs away just as Harry bursts out of the copse and into our group. 'Get your hands off her,' he thunders.

Jade lets go of Lily and rounds on Harry. '*What* did you say?'

Everyone stares at us. My pulse races. Ben's mouth is open. Neil and Rachel are frozen, their expressions horrified.

'I said, keep away from Lily. If she doesn't want to marry Ben, that's her decision. Everyone knows you've badgered and harassed and bullied them into this.'

Jade expands like a puffer fish, spitting venom. 'How dare you! How dare you poke your nose in, you interfering pleb!'

'How *dare* I? Because I love Lily. Truly love her with all my heart and soul. I'm sorry, Ben, but I know you don't. Not in the way this amazing, wonderful woman deserves to be loved. And if you, Jade, or anyone else tries to stand in my way, you'd better watch out.'

Lily stares at him. Her face has turned as pale as her dress as Harry faces down Jade. She seems genuinely shocked at his words.

'Don't you talk to my daughter like that, you bitch!' Lily's mum weighs in, followed by her father. Then Ben's parents muscle through and start shouting at Lily's lot.

'Will you all calm down! This isn't helping anyone,' Cal orders, but everyone ignores him.

'Wait!' The falconer hurries up to us, with Boris on her arm and the rings in her other outstretched hand. 'I've got him down and the rings. Everything's going to be all right. You can carry on with the ceremony!'

'Carry on?' Ben snaps. 'This whole thing has turned into a joke. You've made us a laughing stock, Lily.'

Lily stares at the rings and at Ben. 'I'm sorry I've humiliated you in public but it was better that I ended things now.'

Ben snorts in contempt.

'You can't do this to us!' Jade wails and takes a step towards Lily again but Harry moves between them like a huge granite wall.

'I told you to leave her alone, Jade. I meant it.'

Jade shoots him a poisonous look but stays where she is.

'Lily, I can't keep it hidden any longer. This business with the rings was a sign. A sign that I should tell you how I really feel. How you know I really feel.'

'Oh for fuck's sake!' Ben sneers.

Bewildered, Lily looks from Harry to each face around her. Then she takes Harry's large hand in hers and glances up at him. 'No one knows how I really feel, Harry. How could they, because I don't know *myself*.'

With a sad smile, she turns away and walks off towards the copse.

'Wait, Lily! Come back!' her mum shouts.

'Lily!' Harry calls and starts to follow her.

I grab his arm. 'Stop. Let her go!' I say. 'Leave her for now. Everyone leave her be, please.'

'I *can't* leave her. I need to go to her,' says Harry.

'In a little while, mate.' Cal is here now, his hand on Harry's arm. 'Give her some space. That's what she needs more than anything.'

'I'm outta here before I vomit,' says Ben to his best man. 'Come on, mate.'

'Wait, Ben!' Jade screeches. 'We can smooth things over.'

Ben snorts and turns on his heel with his best man in tow.

Jade gives Addison a push. 'Don't just stand there, you wimp. Get after him and sort things out.'

But Addison is frozen to the spot, watching hopelessly as Ben and his celebrity mate thump off. There's weeping and wailing behind me from the mothers and ranting from Jade who's being unsuccessfully soothed by Addison. Lily's brides-maids are talking to each other frantically, debating what to do. The guests at the back of the glade are straining to hear what's happening while some have already got their phones out, tweeting and texting the gossip to the world. Rachel holds her hands up in sheer amazement and Ben and his best man stride off out of view. The *Grapevine!* photographer follows them, snapping away.

Louie has started yapping, furiously. He leaps out of Lily's mum's arms and dashes towards Harry.

Rachel joins me and Cal while Jade and Addison argue with the two feuding families. 'Oh hell. Of all the problems I'd anticipated, I never expected *this*. I'd better let the caterers and suppliers know what's happened,' she says. 'And try and think of what to do next.'

'I'll find Lily in a few minutes,' I say. 'Can you try and calm the parents down and persuade them to let her have some time alone?'

Rachel eyes the rowing families with horror. 'I'll do my best.'

'Maybe leave it a few minutes to let them simmer down,' says Cal.

Rachel nods. 'Good idea. I'll see to the caterers first.'

She hurries off to the tepee. Cal hugs me. 'Oh my God, has there ever been a bigger wedding disaster in the history of wedding disasters?'

'It's not our fault,' Cal says. 'For once in our lives, it's not our fault or Kilhallon's . . . but it's definitely going to make headlines, that's for sure. I bet Mawgan's dancing for joy.'

'She's been very quiet so far. In fact, where is she?'

We both scan the bridesmaids' seats. Lily's so-called mates are both on their phones but there's no sign of Mawgan. Anyone would think she'd melted away.

'Jesus, I knew she was up to something,' says Cal.

Harry's sitting on a log, cradling Louie who licks his face. Everyone else has forgotten him.

I close my eyes and take a deep breath. 'I'll try to find Lily and speak to Harry. He looks completely lost, although Louie's obviously decided who he wants Lily to be with.'

'I'll try to find Ben,' Cal says.

Polly arrives and plants her hands on her hips. 'Well, that was a turn-up for the books. I thought you said that Harry had a boyfriend? Well, it's probably for the best. I never took to that Ben. Now, what I want to know is, who's going to eat all that food?'

323

37

I didn't need the text from Nina to tell me where Lily might have gone. I tried Poldark Cottage first but could tell by the ranting coming from inside that Jade had got there first and hadn't got hold of Lily. I'm honestly on the verge of getting that woman escorted from Kilhallon land. However, I could hear Lily's mum and dad blaming Jade for pressurising Lily as I slunk away.

Holding up the hem of my dress, I run down to Demelza's. To my enormous relief, Lily's sitting on a stool in the staff kitchen, still in her wedding dress, sipping from a bottle of water. Nina shrugs in despair behind her back and then leaves us.

Her first words are: 'Where's Louie? I wish I'd brought him with me but I wasn't thinking straight.'

'Relax. Harry's got him.'

She heaves a huge sigh. 'Thank God for that. I'm so sorry to have brought all this trouble to your door but Demelza's was the only place I thought I'd be safe. I know I don't deserve to be safe because I've hurt Ben and my parents so much — and embarrassed my family and friends.'

'You did what you had to. You couldn't go through with it if it felt so wrong. That would have been hurting Ben even more.'

'I hope he'll be OK. I think he knew how I felt. I knew how he felt and he didn't want to do this either.'

'Then why did you? Did Jade and Addison bully you into it?'

'Yes. No. *No*, that's a cop-out. Jade *did* pressure us both, it's true. Almost as soon as we started seeing each other, she sensed the opportunity for us to become a fairy-tale couple. She knew we'd be in the media even more as a couple, rather than on our own. I liked Ben, he's fun sometimes and he's gorgeous and . . . he liked me and we had some great times but I'm not sure it was ever love. Actually, I know it wasn't. I know what love is and I don't feel it for Ben.'

'Do you feel it for Harry?'

'Yes. Yes, I probably do, but I've been hiding the fact so long, from everyone around me and from him and myself, that I'm not sure. I feel exhausted with the whole business of the wedding and trying to convince myself it was what I wanted. I should have ended this long ago and never left it until the last minute. It was humiliating for Ben. I need to see him but I can't face him. Will you see how he is? Will you let me know?'

'Cal's gone to find him. Can I let your parents know you're OK?'

'In a minute. Let me have some time first then I'll face them.'

'And Harry?' I ask.

'I'd like to see him first. He's not gay, you know. Giles is gay but he's Harry's best friend, not his partner. They served in Afghanistan together and Giles was given a medical discharge because he has PTSD. Harry invited him to flat share and because there have never been any girlfriends around, people just assumed. People assume a lot when they have no idea what's going on under the surface. They have no idea about the real problems. It suited me to let Ben and Jade think Harry was gay. It threw them off the scent. It was easier for me so they couldn't guess he'd fallen in love with me — and that I love him too.'

'Lily!'

The back door of the cafe bursts open and Harry rushes in, carrying Louie.

Nina throws up her hands in despair. 'Sorry, I couldn't keep him out!'

Louie leaps out of Harry's arms and onto Lily who manages to catch him. He barks joyfully and starts licking her to death. Harry stands back, unsure of what to do.

'Lily? Will you ever forgive me for what I've just done?'

'What's there to forgive? I'm the one who threw the bombshell into the wedding.'

'And I'm so glad you did but I shouldn't have blurted out how I felt in front of everyone, but you *must* have guessed' — he kneels at her feet — 'how I still feel about you now.'

Lily holds the wriggling Louie away from her face. 'I had my suspicions but I was in denial and overwhelmed by dealing with my feelings — or lack of them — for Ben. Poor Ben, but I had to be honest with him for everyone's sakes.'

'You're not angry with me, then? When you ran away I thought I'd blown it with you.'

Lily pats his head, just as if he's a big shaggy version of Louie. 'I could never be angry with you, but I'm not sure I'm ready to start another relationship right now. I want to talk to you, properly, but I need to get away and have some time to myself first.'

'I understand. I can be patient. I've waited so long already.' Harry stands up. 'Whatever you want, I'll do as you ask.'

Lily turns to me. 'Is there any way we can get out of here unnoticed?'

'Over the moor?' Harry cuts in. 'I can have one of the guys bring his car to the end of that track by Gwennap's farm. There's an old bridleway that leads into his yard that we can reach via the coastal path and through the heather.'

'That's right,' I say. 'I walk Mitch up there sometimes.'

'I checked out the whole area before the wedding,' says Harry. 'But you'd attract less attention if you got out of this dress. I'm sorry.' He turns to me. 'Is there anything you can lend her?'

'I've a spare uniform in the locker in case someone has an accident. Will that do?'

'Great,' says Harry. 'We need to go now before someone finds you. It's only a matter of time.'

In the staffroom, Lily strips off her wedding dress and hands it to me. 'Here, find a good home for this.'

'I can't do that. It's yours and it must have cost thousands.'

'I don't want to be reminded of today. Auction it for charity if you don't want it yourself. It'll be worth ten times more now.'

'Thanks.'

She pulls on chef's whites and a Demelza's apron and tucks her hair under one of Jez's spare chef's caps. Then she borrows some cleanser and washes the make-up from her face. You could almost imagine she was an ordinary mortal.

'The shoes will have to stay,' she says, pointing to her satin ballet pumps 'but I don't think anyone will notice.'

'You'll never get over the moor in those. Here, borrow these. They'll be a bit too big but they're better than your pumps.'

I pull off my flats and hand them to her.

'Thank you, Demi. For the wonderful wedding, even though it never happened. For being kind and for making Demelza's a place I felt safe for a little while at least. And for making me realise that I didn't love Ben enough to spend the rest of my life with him and that it was cruel to even think I did. And for making me realise I should go all out for what I know is my dream, whatever the cost.'

'But I never meant to do all that . . . ' I protest.

Harry speaks into his radio and then turns to us. 'Lily. We need to leave. The car's waiting.'

Lily hugs me. 'I know, but don't feel bad. It's wrong of me to run away like this but I can't face everyone yet. I promise I'll phone my parents once we're away from Kilhallon and I'll speak to Ben if he'll let me. Please tell me how he is.'

'I'll try, but I daren't let on I helped you.'

'No, I wouldn't put you in that position. Can you and the staff pretend you haven't seen me? I'll be eternally grateful,' she asks.

'I'm sure they can. Good luck.'

Harry checks outside the back door and they slip out. 'Keep walking as far as the engine house,' he says. 'Then take the right turn by the signpost. I'll be nearby.'

And they're gone. There are a few wedding guests with children on the cafe terrace at the front. One of the new staff is serving them afternoon tea as they gossip about the wedding that never was. I close the door. The rest of the staff stare at me, waiting for an explanation. Jez throws a cloth on the counter top. 'Will someone please tell us what the hell is going on?'

38

Cal

I know I promised Demi I'd find Ben Trevone but I'm pretty sure he'll have legged it by now. The way he took off out of that wedding glade, he's bound to have got the hell away from Kilhallon and I don't blame him. I don't like the guy myself — he's a tosser and definitely doesn't deserve Lily Craig. However, being jilted by your fiancée at the altar is going to sting, especially when it looks like she might end up with a guy you thought was your friend — or in Ben's case, his employee.

I've sort of been in Ben's position myself with Isla. Luckily for me, I never actually made it to the altar with her, but I know how it feels when the woman you love, or thought you loved, decides she wants to be with someone else.

Now I know that's a good thing or I'd never have found Demi and I've come to believe I'd never have been the man I am if I had married Isla. Maybe I'd have always been restless and unfulfilled and wondering what else there was in the world: Demi has made me see that I have to carry on fighting for what I believe in.

I hope she's managed to find Lily and look after her.

Most of the guests have stayed down in the glade, consoling themselves with the champagne that Rachel's arranged for the caterers to serve. A few have wandered back to their cars but most have decided to hang around for the free booze and epic gossip.

But wait . . . that *is* a turn-up, as Polly would say. Trevone *is* still here, or at least his car is. I recognise his BMW SUV parked outside the rear of the farmhouse, next to a Merc limo which belongs to the Cades. Demi told me that Mawgan had arranged for Ben's parents to travel here in style with her.

I approach Kilhallon House and hear voices in the kitchen. I stop outside. I recognise them: Ben's transatlantic Cornish twang and Mawgan Cade's voice, though I can only catch snatches of the words. What the hell are they doing in Kilhallon House?

The back door is open a few inches. Ben and Mawgan are talking in the kitchen.

Or rather Mawgan's talking. Ben's not saying much. I peer around the crack in the door and listen in.

'Ben. This must have come as such a shock. How could Lily be so cruel? You must be devastated.' Mawgan of course. What did I expect?

'I'm OK.'

'You need someone who appreciates you. Lily's out of her mind.'

Ben grunts. 'Yeah, maybe. Then again she's done me a favour. I wish it hadn't been in front of all those people but I don't regret it.'

'You're so brave, Ben . . . Do you really mean that you didn't want to marry Lily?'

'Yes and no. Shit, Mawgan, I don't know but the more I think about it, the more I feel as if she handed me my life back. I'm free to do what I want now. You're a free agent, Mawgs. You must understand what I'm trying to say?'

'Yes. I do. I understand exactly what you mean. Oh, Ben, I knew from the first moment I saw you at Kilhallon that we were meant to be together.'

Before I even have time to think: Jesus, did I really hear Mawgan make a move on Ben minutes after he's been jilted at the altar, there's a strangled cry, the harsh scrape of a chair and an almighty crash.

'Get off me!'

I shove the door open. There's a chair on the floor surrounded by smashed crockery. Ben is backed against the scullery door, with Mawgan snogging him for all she's worth. His hands are in the air and then on her arms.

'This is what you really want,' she purrs.

Ben takes a gulp of air. 'Mawgs. No, you've got the wrong idea. I like you as a friend. We've had a laugh and I'm grateful for the sympathy but I don't want *this*.'

'What the hell's going on here?'

Mawgan turns round. Ben's shoulders slump in relief. Taking his chance, he slips past Mawgan.

Her eyes shoot daggers. 'What are you doing here?'

'It is my house, if you hadn't noticed.'

'Do you mind? You've interrupted a private moment.'

'No, you haven't,' says Ben, edging away. His face is white and he holds up his hands in naked terror as Mawgan, a foot shorter than him, faces up to him. So this is the big brave star of *Knife Edge*, is it? I don't know who I feel most sorry for, him or her. Then again, they both deserve each other.

'I think there's been a misunderstanding, Mawgs. I don't want anyone. I . . . '

Mawgan is about to do one of two things. Leap on me or Ben and rip us both to pieces — or cry. Frankly, I could handle the first far more easily.

'I bet you're laughing at me, aren't you?' she says, but I'm not sure which of us she means.

'I don't think today's been very funny,' I say.

Ben takes a step forward. Bold move. Ouch. 'Mawgan, wait . . . I still want us to be mates. Just not . . . anything else.'

She narrows her eyes. Ben will be toast if he actually tries to touch her.

'I thought . . . you led me on. You made me think that I was special. You asked me to be bridesmaid and you took me out for champagne and told me not to tell Lily. You told me I could come to Hollywood any time.'

'Yeah, as a friend. You never thought that I'd actually be interested in you that way, did you? I mean, you're an attractive girl when you want to be, but you're no Lily, are you? And I'm Ben Trevone . . . and well, you do the maths.' He shrugs.

'Friends? Attractive?' Mawgan advances. 'I could have ruined you. I could have told Lily what you'd done. I could have invited a pap along or told the papers but I didn't because . . . because.'

She had her eye on the main prize, I think.

Ben shrinks up against the dresser. 'Shit, I didn't mean to upset you, Mawgs. It was only a bit of a laugh. You must see that.'

'Do you see me *laughing*?' Mawgan says in a hiss. 'You led me on. You're a spineless creep and, what's more, you couldn't act your way out of a paper bag.'

Mawgan takes another step forward. Ben works his way behind me. 'There's no need for violence!' he bleats.

Jesus. I shake my head in disbelief at his callousness. 'I rarely find myself agreeing with a Cade, but you really are a bit of a prat, aren't you, mate?'

'I don't need your help. I can fight my own battles.' Mawgan snatches her bag off the table and marches up to Ben, standing right in his face. 'You have no idea what I can do. No idea.'

'She's right,' I say. Ben's face blanches. 'You'd better wait in the sitting room.' Ben doesn't need any more excuses and scuttles through the door, leaving me alone with Mawgan.

'Get out of my way,' she says.

'I will but first I have something to say.'

She laughs but her eyes are bright. 'What? You want to laugh at me, do you? I know you and Demi will spend the rest of the day sneering and laughing at my expense and I didn't need you to defend me from Ben.'

'I would say that you don't often cause hilarity

in either of our lives, Mawgan, but on the rare occasion you do it's entirely your own fault. I walked in here feeling sorry for Ben, and at one point, I even had sympathy with you, but now I think you deserve everything you get.'

Mawgan sniggers. 'Piss off, Cal.'

'Fine, but before you go, you need to know that your mother is here.'

Mawgan's mouth drops open then she spits out the words. 'You're lying. You're saying that to get me away from this pathetic piece of work.'

'No. Robyn's been looking for you. Your mum's on her way to Kilhallon. Andi picked her up from Newquay over an hour ago and they were heading straight here. She'd have been here earlier but her flight to Heathrow was delayed.'

'My mother's on her way *here*? Why?'

'She was coming over for Andi and Robyn's engagement party and wanted to see you being a bridesmaid. She thought she'd surprise you both.'

Mawgan visibly deflates in front of my eyes. 'What do you mean? Andi and Robyn's *engagement*? I don't understand. They haven't said anything to me.' Her voice rises in a shriek. 'They can't get married. Everyone's getting married except me. I won't have it!'

My heart bleeds. Mawgan has brought all of this on herself. 'Before you see her, tell me one thing. Did you pay the drone operator to buzz Boris when he delivered the rings?'

Mawgan stares at me. 'Yes. Yes, I did but . . . ' She collapses onto a kitchen chair, totally gobsmacked. 'I can't believe she'd fly all this way to see me,' she says quietly.

'I'm here, darling.'

A tall, tanned woman with bobbed hair stands in the doorway. Mawgan stares at her mother as if an alien has just walked into the kitchen.

'Hello, Cal,' Mrs Cade says before turning her attention to Mawgan who has her hands over her mouth in disbelief.

'Mum, I didn't know you were coming.' Mawgan stands up as her mother approaches her.

'I wanted it to be a surprise,' Mrs Cade says in her Aussie accent. 'I only told Andi when I landed. I wanted to see you be a bridesmaid and to celebrate the girls' engagement. After you came and visited me at Christmas and we had such a happy time, I thought I'd come back and spend some more time with you girls. Now, I hear there's been a problem with this wedding.' Mrs Cade looks Mawgan right in the eyes. 'I hope it hasn't anything to do with you? You promised me you'd changed your ways at Christmas, Mawgan. I did hope you meant it.'

Mawgan shakes her head and wheedles. 'Trouble? No. No. It's nothing to do with me. Why would it be?'

'Hmm. We'll see about that, because if I find you've been spiteful and causing trouble again, I can get straight back on that plane and go home.' Her mother walks forward. 'Now. Aren't you going to give me a proper hug?'

Mawgan shoots me a look, half loathing and half agony. She can't bear to show emotion or weakness but it's too late. It's obvious she adores her mother and they embrace each other.

'Darling. It's so wonderful to see you. You look gorgeous, sweetheart. I was so worried that I wouldn't make it on time to see you today . . . '

Mawgan gulps back a sob. She's reverted to a little girl and it's just weird. I don't feel I can handle any more drama today.

'I'll leave you to it,' I mutter, grateful to slink past them and out of the kitchen.

In the sitting room, Ben stands in front of the fireplace with a crystal tumbler of amber liquid in his hand.

'Hope you don't mind. I helped myself,' he says, nodding to the decanter and tray on the dresser. 'Not a bad malt.'

'It was one of my dad's,' I say, wincing at the level in the bottle.

'He had good taste. Sorry to invade your place, Cal, and for that scene with Mawgan. I needed some space away from people. Jade and Addison mostly, but I never expected Mawgs to go for me like that.'

'Where's your best man?' I say, still furious with him.

'Arranging an emergency exfil ASAP.' He grins. 'If you know what I mean by the military jargon.'

I do because I've been on the receiving end of an emergency 'exfil' myself but in slightly more dangerous circumstances. I somehow don't think Ben has any idea of what it's like to be rescued by Special Forces before you're executed by insurgents. Then again, perhaps the experience might do him good . . .

'Have you seen that little shit, Harry, by the way, or has Lily sent him packing by now?'

'I don't know what his or her plans are,' I say, wondering if Demi has tracked either of them down. 'And I hope you don't mind me saying it, but you don't exactly seem heartbroken by what's happened.'

He knocks back my whisky like it's lemonade. 'That's because I'm not. OK. I'm pissed off about her doing it in public but in the end, it's for the best. I like Lily. She hot and she's fun and I guess I was in love with her. I still *do* love her, but more as a friend. I never wanted to get married to her but my agent and publicist said it would be great for both of us. They said we could get divorced in a couple of years. I told them I didn't want to do that to Lily.' He finishes his drink.

'But you were going to?'

'Yeah. No. I . . . Lily is braver than me. She's a much better person and she deserves someone better. But Harry? Jesus.'

He's right about that. So right and it's all I can do to restrain myself from not chucking him out of my house.

'What do you want us to do with all the food, the band? The guests are being fed in the tepee now but there's the evening party too.'

'Carry on, if anyone wants to stay. I can't handle that now. I bet everyone feels sorry for me. Poor Lily, she'll come off worst in all of this. Jade and Addison will stick with me, if I ask them to. I'm worth more than Lily at the moment.' His phone rings. 'I have to take this. It's my best man.'

He mutters a few words into the phone then

338

says, 'There's a car waiting for me outside. I'm going to get legless somewhere no one can find me. I'll deal with this when I'm ready but that could be a while. All I want now is to get the fuck away from all of it.'

He swills the final dregs of my whisky, tosses it back and dumps the glass on the mantelpiece.

'You must know what I mean. Haven't you ever wanted to pack up and leave all the shit behind? Screw everything and everybody and take off, look after number one? Do what *you* want and to hell with the consequences?'

'Yes. Yes, I have.' I've done it. Gone off and said screw the consequences. Done what I wanted and what I thought was right for me, and sod everyone else, like Isla and my father. I took those arms when I should have said 'no', I let Soraya get involved . . .

Ben sighs. 'Well, thanks for organising the wedding — and to Demi too. I never thought you'd be able to put on a show like this but hats off to you. It's all paid for so I'd get pissed with your mates and enjoy the party at our expense if I were you.'

'Thanks,' I manage through gritted teeth. 'What about your mum and dad? What shall I tell them?'

'I'll call them once I'm safely away from here. See you around, maybe?' he adds.

'Yeah. See you.'

And he's gone. And I don't feel one iota of sympathy for him, or pity other than for the fact he's a total jerk and there's no cure for that. I've no doubt that those leeches Jade and Addison will paint him as the injured party although any publicity will probably be lapped up by Lily too. As for Harry, I don't envy the bloke living in that cauldron of publicity. There's a lot to be said for the quiet life . . . if I can only find it.

Wincing at my depleted whisky bottle, I walk into the wrecked kitchen. Mawgan and her mother have left the house and I suck in a huge breath of Kilhallon air, trying to take in all the events of the past few hours and days. I pick up the chair and gather the broken crockery in a piece of newspaper — including one of Demi's favourite breakfast bowls and an Il Divo mug she bought Polly for Christmas. It can be replaced.

'Cal!'

Demi's voice cuts through the quiet and the window. I spot her hobbling across the yard in her slinky dress that shows off every gorgeous curve. Her hair has escaped from its clip and is flying wantonly in the wind.

We meet in the porch and she flings her arms around me. 'What is it?' she says, 'What is it about Kilhallon that attracts so much drama?'

Her cheeks are pink from running and she's wearing the safety shoes she uses at work. My breath catches in my throat. She looks gobsmackingly sexy and funny and I hardly know what to do with myself.

Or maybe I know exactly what to do.

'I have no idea but it seems to have something to do with a certain person whose name begins with a D and ends in an I. Let's call Rachel and try to sort out the mess down at the wedding glade and then, I want to talk to you.'

39

Demi

After we've called Rachel and made sure that the remaining guests know that the party's still going ahead — without the bride and groom — Cal pulls back a chair from the table. I've tried to focus on our discussion with Rachel until now, but my pulse stirs when I see the serious look on his face.

'Sit down, I want to talk to you now we finally have five minutes' peace.'

I take a seat and a much-needed deep breath. 'Is this to do with what happened in Greece?'

Cal sits next to me. 'Yes, and other things, relating to Lily and Ben and what happened today. They're linked in a weird mixed-up way so bear with me.' He takes a breath before going on. 'I finally found out how Esme escaped from her mother's house. One of the neighbours' daughters found her with Soraya's body just before I arrived and virtually dragged her away while hell was breaking loose around them.'

Nothing I can do but listen, knowing how hard this must be for him.

'In the time I spent with her mother and searching for Esme, the girls managed to get a lift out of town. It's thanks to the neighbours that she stayed relatively safe, and a few weeks later they were able to reunite her with her grandparents and cousins. Eventually, they made it through Turkey, survived the sea crossing to the Greek islands and have been living in various camps while they make a claim for asylum in Germany.'

'Do you think they'll get it?' I ask as he hesitates.

'It's not guaranteed but she has an auntie and uncle already in Frankfurt and as she has no parents now, we're hoping she and her grandparents will be allowed to live with them soon. The miracle is that she survived and she's found her family. After what happened to her mother, and what might have happened to her if she'd been making that journey alone, it's the best outcome, by a million miles, that I could have wished for.'

I squeeze his hand. 'I'm so glad. I'm relieved that you found her and you're here.'

'Her family were so generous to me. I told them everything and they don't blame me. Her cousins said she would have wanted me to help in the way I did. I can never be so forgiving to myself, but I'm going to try very hard to take their advice.'

'What was their advice?'

'They told me to let go of Esme and Soraya, of my guilt — of everything that happened. When you lose someone — like my mum and dad and Soraya — you live with more fear but more determination to do the things you want to do. I was trying to right a wrong I could never put right. Esme's family have reminded me I can't turn the clock back or work miracles.

'I'll never forget Soraya and I'll keep in touch with Esme and her family and do what I can to help them.' He stands up, as if he can't bear to be in one place any longer, despite what he's saying.

'It would be wrong for me to say that everything's fine and OK now I've come to terms with what happened. I — none of us — can ignore what's happening to people like Esme and her family, but I also want to do as they told me: to come back home and live my life with you at Kilhallon.'

'You told them about me?' I ask, amazed he had time to mention us.

'Of course I did. They wanted to hear what I was doing; how I'd escaped and what had happened since. Esme wanted to know about you, what you looked like and what you liked doing. I said you liked cooking and baking and that you had a dog. I showed her a photo of me and you with Mitch.'

'Oh, Cal . . . I have a confession to make too. I found your will in the study. You left me Kilhallon! I don't want it, I only wanted you home and it scared me.' I grow cold even now when I remember finding it, but Cal laughs.

'Why are you scared? We all have to go sometime.'

'Don't joke. It's not funny.'

'Why are you so upset that I've left you this place? Is it because you'd find it a burden? I can leave it to Mitch instead if you want. Come here.' He holds me and strokes my hair.

'No. Stop it. I thought . . . I thought that it

meant you were planning to leave here and work in the Middle East and put yourself in danger again. I thought you might never come back.'

'I've been there and done that and I don't fancy doing it again. I always intended to come back but I needed to sort out my affairs. I've never done it before because I wasn't ready to face up to it after I came home from Syria and I had no idea who I even wanted to leave a worthless wreck like Kilhallon to. Now we've made the place into what it is, I am ready. Call it a sign that I'm moving on and can face it now, call it a grown-up thing to do. Life's precarious: I didn't want to leave the place in limbo. I wanted to make sure Kilhallon and the things I care about were left to the people I care about.'

'But why me? I don't deserve to have all this, even if I could ever imagine looking after the place without you.'

He rests his hands on my waist. 'Who else should have it but you? Besides, I need to make a will anyway, as things are going to change between us.'

'What do you mean, 'things are going to change between us?' I don't want things to change.'

Cal's smile slips. He drops his hands from my waist. 'Don't you?'

'No. I like things how they are unless — if you're not going away, what do you mean? Do you want me to move out of the farmhouse? Do you think things aren't working between us?'

He groans and shoves his hands through his hair. 'Demi, you have completely the wrong end of the stick.'

'Then why should things change? I don't want any more change. I've had enough change over the past year. I don't think I can cope with any more. Losing my job, finding another, meeting you, Mawgan causing trouble, starting the cafe, losing Mitch, meeting Dad again, the floods and Freya, the book and moving in here. I feel as if I can hardly catch my breath. Please. There's only so much I can take. Just for a while, can't we have a few boring months of nothing happening?'

He takes a step back. Rubs his hand over his mouth in the way he does when he's worried and stressed. Have I said something so wrong? Damn.

'Can you genuinely not take any more excitement or change?' he says quietly. 'In that case, I won't pressure you. I won't do what I was about to.'

'For God's sake, what were you about to do?' I raise my voice in frustration.

'Well, I . . . I don't know whether to say it now. But . . . Ben said to feed the guests who are left and enjoy the party.'

I'm ready to rip out my own hair in frustration and tension. 'Yes, and Lily said the same. So what's that got to do with your mysterious plans?'

'So, shall we?' Cal asks. 'Have the party anyway. I think the guests are already being fed. Rachel's told the caterers to go ahead because everyone was starving.'

'From the sound of things, the party's going on whether we want it to or not. It feels strange without an actual ceremony and bride and groom.'

'Yes. It does.' He looks thoughtful. Unsure. 'What a waste.'

'As Robyn and Andi are engaged, they might enjoy a free wedding.'

Cal frowns. 'Robyn and Andi?'

'And Isla and Luke were going to get married sometime. They might want to stand in for Lily and Ben? If Isla feels up to it, of course. Oh . . .'

'If Isla feels up to it. What do you mean?' His brow creases in sudden concern.

'I should have let Isla tell you herself but it's too late now. She's pregnant. She came to the house before the wedding that wasn't and wanted to see you.'

Cal does a double take. '*Pregnant?* Isla?' I can see he's shocked and doesn't seem to know what to say. The news is bound to be a body blow to him. He must be thinking that he and Isla could have had children one day; that their baby might have been his.

'She wanted you to know first but she felt a bit shaky and had to confess. It's a shock to you, I know.' I braced myself for his reaction; he's even more shocked than I expected — or hoped.

'A shock? No, I'm happy for Isla and for Luke.'

'*Really?*'

He frowns. Wow, he *is* serious. 'Why wouldn't I be?'

'I . . . I don't know. There's so much history between you.'

'And that's all it is. *History*. I'm happy she's

346

happy. Isla will be a fantastic mum but I'm not interested in the past any more. I'm only interested in now and the future.' He holds both of my hands. My senses tingle, my knees feel ever so slightly weak; yes, it really does happen. He's about to say something — momentous and scary.

'Oh, Cal, tell me what you have to say. Put me out of my misery.'

'OK. I'm not going to ask Robyn and Andi or Isla and Luke to take over this wedding — that's not a wedding — thing because I want you and me to.'

'Oh.'

The world stops. Did I hear what I thought I heard? Or has this whole surreal mad day finally tipped me over the edge into a parallel universe?

'I realise that you said you'd never dream of marrying anyone. Even if Neil joining us today won't be legal or binding I want to do it anyway. I want to tell all these people — strangers, friends and family — that I want to be with you at Kilhallon until we're old and grey and turn to dust.'

My legs are wobbly. I can't believe I'm hearing this, but it's a good kind of shock. The kind I want to hear more about.

'I heard you tell Rachel that hell would freeze over before you made that kind of commitment so I'm probably about to crash and burn here but if there's one thing that the past year has taught me, it's that life is precious and fragile and if you want to do something, truly want to do something, then you have to go for it and not wait for the tide to turn or the wind to change,' Cal rushes on, babbling uncharacteristically. 'So, I said I'd never be perfect, and life with me might be a bumpy ride and I know you're young and could have your pick of men, but here you go.'

Finally he shuts up. His expression is agonised.

'Wait a minute. Can I just check . . . this *is* you proposing to me?'

He smiles. 'Yeah. I guess so. I know you'd have plenty of offers and let's face it, lots of people don't even bother getting married these days, but try me out. We can arrange a civil ceremony after today, *if* you want to. I'm as ready as I'll ever be but I can see you might need time to be convinced.'

'Unlike Lily I don't need to convince myself and I didn't mean that thing about hell freezing over. OK, I *did* mean it but I was only saying it because . . . because . . . '

'What?'

'Because I thought hell would freeze over before *you'd* want to make a commitment like that. After all you've been through I was protecting myself. I'd never thought of getting married, but I do know that I never want to think about leaving Kilhallon or you. I can't imagine it, even though it's only been just over a year since I met you.'

He holds my arms, rubbing my skin gently. 'You're shaking. Are you cold?'

'No. I'm not cold, but I don't know what to say.'

'Say 'yes', and let's enjoy the party. Do the thing. Let's not waste the band, and the flowers and that bloody willow arch. Let's watch Polly's jaw drop through the floor and make Neil's day worthwhile. There's no point wasting him, is there, since he's been cheated out of his special moment. Where is he? I need to find him fast if we're going ahead.'

'I think he's with Polly . . . ' I laugh, because part of me is soaring somewhere above Kilhallon, and the other half wants to burst out laughing. I don't need Cal to ask me to marry him to complete my life — far from it — but I can't deny how happy it makes me feel. Float-up-to-the-sky happy.

'So. It's a 'yes', then?' He peers nervously into my eyes.

'Yes. I must be out of mind but yes. Let's do it.'

In the next moment, we're one person. We kiss each other softly and he holds my face between his hands. His stubble rasps my skin and I'm aware he's still wearing the clothes he travelled in overnight. Nothing has changed. He's still scruffy, unpredictable Cal; still with a lot of baggage and ready to flare up if someone gets to him. And I'm still me, ready to jump in with both feet whether I'm wanted or not. Still only twenty-two and agreeing to take on this place and Cal in all his moods.

It's a big risk but I know I'd never have things any other way.

'I've made some bad decisions in my life, and done some selfish things in the name of what I thought was 'right' for other people, but was probably right for me,' he says, his eyes shining. 'I won't stop making the wrong decision, I'll probably get it wrong, and keep on getting it wrong but being with you is the right decision, and I know I'll never regret it. If you can live with that, then I'll be happy.'

'I can live with it.'

A huge smile spreads over his face and we kiss each other like there will never be another tomorrow.

'Come on, then. We've a wedding to sort out. Second time lucky, eh?'

40

With me still in my safety shoes and Cal in his scruffy travel gear, we almost run down to the wedding glade. I feel as if I've been reincarnated as a glass of champagne, ready to bubble over at any moment.

Some people are walking past us, still stunned by the disappearance of the bride and groom, but judging by the noise at the tepee, most are inside tucking into the canapés and cocktail reception. Obviously, Lily and Ben's immediate families have gone although her bridesmaids are still around.

Neil, the celebrant, has a pint in his hand and is chatting to Polly at a table outside the tepee. I can't wait to tell Dad and Rachel our plans, but first we need to make sure Neil's happy to 'marry' us instead of Lily and Ben.

We stop a few yards away from them and Cal takes my hand. 'Ready?' he whispers.

I take a deep breath. 'No, but let's do it anyway.'

The news has barely left our lips before Polly's glass goes flying off the table, soaking Neil in expensive fizz. '*What*? You two? Tying the knot? Oh God, I'm sorry, Neil!'

She grabs a napkin and starts dabbing at Neil's trousers while firing questions at us like a machine gun. 'Getting married? Now? Today? Can you? Is it legal? Why now?'

Cal picks her champagne glass off the grass. 'Yes to the first three and no, it's not legally binding, and now because we both want to. We're going to do the legal bit as soon as we can arrange it.'

Polly stares at us, breathing heavily. 'I'm gobsmacked. Can you do that?' She turns to Neil who's staring at the unfortunate stain spreading over his trousers. 'Can they, Neil?'

'I've never been contracted to marry one couple and ended up doing another but I don't see why not. It's not a civil ceremony anyway, as Cal says, although most guests who attend events like this never actually realise that.' He glances from one of us to the other. 'However, as long as you're both sure and sincere about the contract you're entering into, and you've thought about it long and hard, I don't see why not.'

'We are,' says Cal.

'I'm sure,' I say, deciding to ignore the 'long and hard' thought part.

'Are you?' Polly asks.

'I know what I'm doing.'

Neil smiles. 'Then, why not? I felt like a fraud anyway, turning up and not actually conducting the ceremony, so I'm up for it.'

'Well. Well . . . ' Polly switches her gaze from Cal to me, and back again. He slips his arm around my back. It feels right, warm and right and as if it's been there forever and should stay there forever.

'You two. I'd be the first to admit I thought it was a bad idea him ever bringing you here to Kilhallon. I thought you'd get ideas and he'd get ideas of a different sort and that you'd both end up hurt. And until recently, I still felt the same way.'

Cal laughs. 'At least you're honest.'

'I try to be though I've held my tongue more than a few times.' She fixes me with a hard look. 'Are you sure you know what you're taking on, Demi?'

'Of course I do!' Cal protests.

Polly snorts. 'Not you. *Demi*. Is she sure?'

'As sure as I've been about anything.'

Polly shakes her head and sticks her hands on her hips. 'Well, my bird, you've stuck with him and Kilhallon and all of us this long, through some of the worst times, and you've toughed it out so you may as well enjoy the best times.' Her eyes glisten and her voice cracks. 'I suppose you deserve each other. You're definitely due some happiness, the pair of you.'

She hugs me until I can barely breathe and want to cry, and then she hugs Cal who pats her back warmly as a tear falls down her cheek. 'Your mum and dad would be happy for you. I know your mum would, especially.'

'She'd think I had the best of the bargain,' says Cal.

'Oh, I'd say that was a fair assessment.' Polly gives a big sniff. 'So, we'd better get this show on the road, if it's OK with you, Neil?'

'We need time to let everyone know at the cafe and in the tepee to see who wants to stay on. It'll be weird that some aren't our guests but it's been a very weird day so what's new?' I say.

Polly smiles. 'Neil and I will speak to the

353

caterers and band and let them know they'll be required for the rest of the day. I know some were hoping to pack up and go after the meal but they can stay on now.'

'How long do you need before we can go ahead with the ceremony?' Neil asks.

'We need to break the news to a few close friends and family first and then can you make an announcement? Everyone who wants to stay for our moment and the party is very welcome. So what about we go ahead at around seven p.m. when there's still sunlight in the glade?'

'Sounds perfect. Demi?'

With the state of excitement that I'm in, I'd probably say yes to anything. 'Yes, yes . . . seven o' clock. Where's Tamsin? I need to tell her too.'

Polly rolls her eyes. 'Search me. I haven't seen her for a while.'

'Kit, then?' I ask.

'Haven't seen a lot of him, either. Oh, wait, isn't that them?' Polly shades her eyes and points towards the edge of the glade.

Kit and Tamsin are sitting on a rug under a tree with a bottle of wine, laughing and chatting.

'I don't want to disturb them,' I say.

Cal grins. 'Then don't. They'll know about our news soon enough. Come on, let's find your dad and Rachel.'

★   ★   ★

'Congratulations, love.' Dad hugs me and shakes Cal's hand. 'And to you, Cal. This is a surprise.'

'I wish Kyle could be here,' I say to Dad.

Secretly, I wish my mum could be here too, but I don't want to upset Rachel or spoil today by mentioning it. Maybe she is watching me. With that hopeful thought, I enjoy the excited chatter around me.

'Yes, I know, but it wasn't planned, was it? Maybe we can sort out something later when he's home on leave again.'

Rachel hugs me too. 'Wow. That's another twist to the story that I didn't see coming.'

'Neither did we. At least Demi didn't. I had slightly more of an idea that it might happen. I hoped it would happen,' Cal says with a smile for me. 'But probably not today. Now, I think it's the perfect moment. Why wait? Life's too short.'

'Too right. Congratulations again.'

'You don't seem as shocked as I thought you'd be,' I say.

My dad laughs. 'We're not shocked. Surprised that it's today, though it makes good sense. Save you money too — and me.'

'Gary!' Rachel hits him playfully on the arm, but I laugh.

'We wouldn't have expected you to pay for it anyway.'

'I know you wouldn't have expected it but I'd have wanted to make a contribution.'

Rachel smiles. 'I'd do as the bride and groom have told us: enjoy the party. When else will we get to drink vintage champagne and all of this?'

Dad nods. 'True.'

'Why would we be shocked? You were with Cal when we first found you again. You both invited us into your home and you've both been together ever since, through thick and thin from what Polly's told us. Since we all got together again, you and Cal have been a couple and we can see how much he means to you and vice versa. The fact that you two want to be together is the least surprising thing about the whole day.'

My dad gives me another brief hug and shakes Cal's hand.

'I wish Freya could be here,' I say.

'Oh she has to be! How about I phone my parents and ask them to bring her down here?' says Rachel.

'I'd love that! Will it disrupt her routine too much?'

'Routine? What routine?' Rachel laughs. 'I think she can cope just for today. It's not every day you see your big sister get married, even if she won't remember the details.'

*　*　*

We find Isla and Luke enjoying drinks in the evening sun on the cafe terrace. I'd suggested that Cal could break the news on his own but he insists on us doing it together. I'm almost getting used to saying it now, after telling Polly and my family. Almost. It's that split second after we say the words 'We've got some good news. We're getting married' and before they react that's the most nerve-wracking.

Isla has more colour than she did earlier and is sipping tea from a china cup on the outside terrace. There are a couple of other people at the far end of the tables but it's about as private a location as we're going to get today.

We take each other's hands, without really thinking about it, as we walk up to them. They both smile.

'Cal. Hello. I'm happy to see you home safe.' Cal kisses Isla on the cheek.

Luke shakes his hand warmly. 'Hello, mate. Happy you made it home in time.'

I'm relieved to see Cal on good terms with Luke again, even though Luke did some shitty things to all of us under pressure from the Cades. Maybe Cal has forgiven his friend, even if he can't forget.

'Are you feeling better?' Cal asks Isla.

'Yes, better than earlier . . . ' She glances at me. 'Has Demi told you my news?'

'Yes. I hear congratulations are in order.' He bends down and hugs her warmly and with love — the love of an old friend.

'How many weeks are you?' he asks.

'Thirteen.'

'Mornings are the worst,' says Luke and grimaces.

'For both of us,' says Isla, with a smile. 'Luke's used to holding my hair out of my eyes while I throw up. I'm sorry about the disaster with the wedding. I had no idea that Ben and Lily wouldn't go through with it at the last minute. They're capricious, they're a law unto them-selves sometimes, but I genuinely thought they were in love.'

'I think they *were* in love,' I say.

'Once,' Cal adds. 'But not enough to make a lifelong commitment. Not even enough for a temporary commitment in Lily's case. I've spoken to Ben and he's pretty chilled about it.' Cal shakes his head. 'He said he was cowardly not to have put a stop to the whole bandwagon sooner and I agree with him.'

'Even if the split is the best thing for Lily and Ben, I'm still sorry that you two have had to deal with yet more unscripted drama and trouble,' Isla says.

Cal shrugs. 'The publicity won't be bad for Kilhallon and we still have one hell of a party to enjoy.'

'Still, it's a shame that all your hard work is going to waste and the guests have turned up for nothing. You can have a wedding without all the trappings but not without the happy couple.'

Cal and I exchange a look, each waiting for the other to speak, but he knows and I know that it has to be him to break this news to Isla and to Luke. I feel no triumph or gloating. I just feel happy. Deeply and quietly happy that for one moment, right now, life is completely perfect.

Cal rests his arm on my waist and pulls me closer. 'Actually, the party can still go ahead because Demi and I have come up with a cunning plan . . . '

★ ★ ★

'Only the staff at the cafe to tell, now,' I say after we've shared our news with Isla and Luke. 'If telling people we're getting married is this exhausting, I'm not sure I'll have the energy for the actual event.' I'm joking but it is almost six p.m. now and the sun is starting to mellow. The light is softer and I can tell there's going to be an amazing sunset from the cafe.

'As long as you make sure you save plenty of energy for the *really* important part later,' says Cal, before stopping me on the path to the cafe and giving me a long and glorious kiss in full view of the guests on the cafe terrace.

We walk into the cafe. Jez has his eyes closed, listening to music on his phone. The girls are chatting over a cup of tea. As soon as we walk in, Nina jumps up.

'What's happening? How's Ben? Has he gone mad? Should we carry on doing cocktails?'

'Ben's going to lie low for a while. He seemed OK,' Cal says.

'And yes we're still going ahead as planned with the party — apart from one slight change.'

'What now?'

Jez pulls his headphones out and folds his arms.

'There has been a change of bride and groom.'

'What?' Nina cries.

Shamia holds up her hands. 'Who?'

'Um. Us. Me and Cal.'

'You and Cal . . . what?'

'We're taking over from Ben and Lily. We're getting married — well, joined together. Handfasted.'

Jez shakes his head in disbelief but smiles. Nina and Shamia do their best goldfish impressions while the other staff look at each other in confusion. Then they all burst into applause and we're engulfed in hugs and kisses and questions until my ears ring and my head spins.

'Nice one, mate,' says Jez, slapping Cal on the back.

Nina laughs and hugs me. 'About time.'

'You two are dark horses!' Shamia says, almost dancing in delight.

'And so,' Cal says as we finally make our escape from the congratulations at Demelza's, 'all we have to do now is make an announcement to the guests. Are you ready? Because there really is no going back from this and I don't want Boris flying off and ruining the moment again.'

I laugh. 'I think we'd better leave Boris out of this one.'

41

The sun is slowly sinking as we stand at the top of the wedding glade, waiting for our cue from Neil. Cal's hand tightens in mine. I'm still wearing my new blue dress, but I swapped my shoes for a pair of glittery flats. Tamsin retouched my make-up and I'm carrying the posy of Cornish flowers that was meant for Lily. Hazel made up a corsage that she and Tamsin fixed in my hair. As for Cal, he scrubbed up OK too. He's in a crisp white shirt and his black jeans, with a casual jacket with a corsage to match mine.

'Calvin and Demelza, would you like to join me for the ceremony?' Neil says in a booming voice. I can almost feel Cal's laughter at Neil's solemn announcement of our full names and I'm sure I'm going to get the giggles. Although it's not legal, this is meant to be a serious commitment and it feels like it, but I'm bubbling over with a silly, dream-like happiness that I can't keep a lid on.

'Are you ready?' Cal whispers.

'Oh, go on then.' I glance over my shoulder. 'Come on, boy.'

Mitch jumps to his paws and wags his tail. I'm sure he thinks he's going for a walk so I hope he won't be disappointed when he has to sit quietly with Nina while Cal and I do our stuff.

There are lots of 'aws' and I'm aware of phone

screens glowing as we walk down the 'aisle' to the altar, but I'm sure most of them are for Mitch, who looks dapper in his tux scarf, as arranged by Lily.

A surprising number of Lily and Ben's guests have stayed on to see us tie the knot, and they're all smiling at me. It's almost too much. Too much attention. Too much happiness. Too much emotion. If I dare to think for a second about the people who are missing, of my mum, I'll never make it through the ceremony.

Cal draws me closer. 'Look.'

'Oh. Oh wow. Is that Sheila? And the Reverend Beverley — and Max with some of the flood families? How did they get here?'

'Polly called them. They didn't need asking twice.'

And now we reach the front rows where Polly, Rachel and her parents, my dad and Robyn and Andi are sitting, with Freya, quiet as a mouse, in her buggy. She's not asleep, though. I can see her tiny hand grasping at the air as if she's trying to reach for the twinkly lights strung over the wedding bower. It's still bright outside, of course, but the fairy lights have been lit. On the other side, Tamsin, Isla and Luke smile at us.

'Where's Kit?' I ask.

'Here.'

Kit steps out from behind the shadows of the willow arch.

'I'm the best man,' he says. I glance from Cal to Kit in astonishment. 'Or rather a slightly better man than any of us expected.' He pats his pocket. 'I've got the rings.'

'What rings?' I ask.

Cal winks. 'Don't get too excited.'

Too late for that, I think.

'Are you *ready*?' Neil says in a low, ever-so-slightly-annoyed voice.

Cal takes my hand and we share one final glance. He smiles and in one voice we both say, 'We are.'

'So, dear friends, we gather together — again — on this glorious Cornish evening to celebrate the joining of Calvin and Demelza.'

★   ★   ★

Fairy lights twinkle in the trees and the sound of drums and singing hum from the tepee, which glows like a giant lantern as twilight falls on Kilhallon. Many of the guests from both weddings are still partying inside. 'We answered the pleas for a first dance despite our protests and stayed a while to party with our friends and family. Now we've slipped outside into the dusk. Moths buzz in the shafts of light from the tepee and the air smells of wedding flowers and dewy grass and fresh spring leaves.

'Shall we go down to the cafe and say our goodnights?' Cal asks, standing beside me, looking down on the fairy-tale grotto in front of us.

'Goodnights? It's not even fully dark yet.'

His voice is low. 'Yes, but the Hot Vampire can't wait to get you back to his lair.'

'Is that a threat or a promise?'

Cal's hand rests lightly on my bottom, curving

around my cheek through the slinky dress. 'Both,' he says and then kisses me. Goosebumps pop out on my bare arms but it isn't the chill evening air that makes me shiver.

Hand in hand, we pick our way through the twilight down to the cafe, which is glimmering against the evening sky, lit by strings of lanterns. The sky in the far west is still painted in orange, rose and lilac though the sun has long gone. A handful of guests, friends and strangers, are sipping cocktails in the chill-out zone and a few couples are dancing on the terrace to the strains of the distant band.

Tamsin rests her face on Kit's shoulder and he leans forward, his eyes closed. Neil has his arms around Polly's waist, chatting to her as they sway to the music. She's laughing at something he says and then I hear her exclaim, 'No, go on with you,' before laughing at him again. Isla and Luke are at a table near the door to the cafe. Luke is draping a wrap around Isla's shoulders while one of our staff brings her a cup of tea. They've worked so hard today, my amazing team. I feel a lump rise to my throat when I think of all I owe them, and our friends.

There are nods and smiles as we join the dancers and hold each other, moving slowly as the music drifts across the terrace. Behind the low chatter and the distant music, I can hear the crash of the waves breaking on the rocks below the cafe.

'So, Demelza, how does it feel to be a handfasted woman?'

'I didn't think it'd feel any different to being a

non-handfasted one. But I do feel different.'

'In what way?'

'Weird. As if I'm in another universe. As if all of this from the moment you walked into that cafe was a surreal dream and I'm going to wake up in that shop doorway and find none of it ever happened.'

'I think you'll find that was the plot of *Dallas*,' he says. 'And you are different. We've both got the rings to prove it.'

He holds up his left hand, which features a silver skull-and-cross-bones with ruby red eyes that glint in the glow of the fairy lights.

The giggles erupt again, like they did when we were presented with the rings on a cushion by Kit. Then tears when I saw my ring.

I twirl the gold band around. 'I can't believe you found my mum's wedding ring.'

'I asked your dad if there was anything 'old' you might like to have today and your dad went to fetch it from the cottage when he collected Freya. He said you kept it in your room at home but left it behind when you walked out.'

'It broke my heart to leave it but I knew I couldn't keep it safe when I was moving about. It was always slightly too big for me and anyone could have taken it and that would have finished me off.'

'We can get it made smaller or you can have a brand new one. I was worried you might be upset.'

'No, I want this one. You should keep yours too. Where did you get it?'

'From Robyn, of course. It's one of her best

sellers on her online jewellery store.'

He laughs and our friends look at us.

'So, what now?' I ask him.

'I guess we carry on as we are, trying to make a success of Kilhallon and the cafe. Things can surely only get better for us, after all the blood, sweat and tears of the past year. I hope so . . . And I've been thinking about Esme too. If you agree, we'll do all we can to help her and children like her, here on our own doorstep and far away. I want to support her in the future as much as I can, if her family are happy with that.'

'I want to help too. We could hold fundraising events at the cafe for a start. It seems a trivial thing to do set against all the terrible things going on around us. We're protected in our bubble here. It's hardly as if baking can save the world. But we can try.'

Cal kisses me. 'My mother used to say that anything done with love and kindness can make a small difference. This life is, as they say, a bittersweet symphony. Bitterness is in ready supply, so we need to create and spread as much of the sweet as we can to get us through. Which leads me on to you.' He raises his eyebrows. 'It's been a very long day, and I think it's time we went to bed.'

I feign a yawn, even though sleep is the last thing on my mind and my whole body pops and fizzes with anticipation. 'Can you stay awake?' I tease.

'I might manage to. After all, it sort of is our wedding night and maybe one day soon we'll have a real wedding night and who knows, perhaps a little family of our own.'

I gasp. 'Wow. I love Freya but I'm not *quite* ready for one of my own. *Yet.*'

Cal pulls me closer. 'You can have all the time you want,' he says softly. 'But the sooner we start practising, the better.' The final sliver of sun slips below the horizon. As we stand under the cafe awning, everything I ever wanted — and will ever want — is reflected in his eyes.

Acknowledgements

Sometimes writing a book turns out to be almost as much of a journey for the author as the characters. When I started the series, I'd no idea where it would lead me. I have to thank Elley Westbrook and Elaine Lawson of the charity, People in Motion, for giving me insight into the possible journey of Esme and her family. I genuinely could not have written this novel without their advice. Hazel Shaw, event florist extraordinaire, *Poldark* superfan and creative director of Eden Blooms has also been an invaluable source of advice, not only on flowers but on the planning of a wedding in general.

I've been lucky enough to have not one, but three fantastic Avon editors helping me in the production of this book at various stages. So I want to thank Eloise Wood, Natasha Harding and Rachel Faulkner-Willcocks for all their expert help across the whole Cornish Cafe series. It's been a privilege and a pleasure to work with them and the entire Avon team, including Helen Huthwaite, Helena Sheffield, Louis Patel, Phoebe Morgan and Joanne Gledhill.

My agent, Broo Doherty, has been an inspiration and support for over ten years now and we're still going strong. Thank you, dear Broo.

I also couldn't have got where I have or stayed the course this long without my author friends Nell Dixon and Liz Hanbury, and my best mate,

Janice Hume, who also happens to be a fantastic bookseller.

My family have been my rock, sharing in my triumphs and disasters, so much love goes to my parents, to Charles and to The Youths, Charlotte and James.

Finally, this book is dedicated to my husband, John. We celebrated thirty years of marriage in April and he's still in the acknowledgements. I think that's a pretty good achievement. In the words of Steve Ovett, ILY xx

Recipes

You'll notice there are cocktails mentioned in this book. Here are a couple of our favourites, which should be suitable for consolation as well as celebration.

Pousse Rapière (a.k.a. The Rapier's Thrust)

This is possibly our household's favourite cocktail. It was first made for us by two friends, Duncan and Claire. They got it from their friends in France. I like to think it's called a Rapier's Thrust because this cocktail delivers a real *coup de grace* — you'll probably only need one, although you'll definitely want more.

Ingredients

1 × 25 ml measure of Armagnac
1 × 25 ml measure of orange syrup — You must use orange syrup for this, not juice or squash. You need the concentrated sweetness of the syrup. You used to only be able to get it from French supermarkets in those funny 'tin' bottles but you can now get it from most coffee shops and some supermarkets — Monin make it, for example. We buy ours from Caffè Nero.
Chilled sparkling white wine — Prosecco, Cava, sparkling burgundy are fine. If you're a movie star, use the best possible champagne, darling.

1. Pour the orange syrup in a flute glass and add the Armagnac.
2. Top up with the sparkling wine. *Salut*!

Sea Breeze

Alcohol is not a healthy option but the healthi*est* cocktail surely has to be the Sea Breeze. It's got to be one of your five a day, for sure. Leaving out the vodka, of course, and replacing it with ginger beer, makes it a refreshing non-alcoholic cooler.

Ingredients
1 × 25ml measure vodka
50ml cranberry juice
50ml grapefruit juice
lime wedge
ice cubes

Mix the vodka and juices together in a tumbler, add ice and the lime wedge. Enjoy.

Lemon Pots

I know Lily said she wanted clean eating and healthy, yummy treats at the wedding but Demi had slightly different ideas. This treat is yummy but definitely not healthy. The recipe was given to me by the author Veronica Henry and is the quickest, easiest pud ever. You don't need much of it so serve in small pots or ramekin dishes with the prettiest biccies you can find.

Ingredients
juice and grated rind of 3 lemons
1 pint/600ml carton of single or whipping cream

150g caster sugar

To serve — posh biscuits (Bonne Maman langues de chat or continental-style biscuits from Aldi or Lidl. Waitrose also do some very pretty lavender-flavoured heart-shaped shortbread if you're feeling flush)

a few raspberries or blueberries if you want to be healthy

1. Add the sugar, lemon rind and cream to a saucepan and cook over a low heat until at simmering point. Keep stirring for a few minutes until it starts to thicken.
2. Take the pan off the heat and allow to cool slightly.
3. Stir the lemon juice into the lukewarm cream and sugar mixture.
4. Pour the lemon cream into the pots and leave it to set in the fridge for a couple of hours or overnight if you can.
5. Serve with the biscuits and a few berries if desired.

Cheat's Lime & Mascarpone Cheesecakes

Another simple recipe that's a favourite with the family of a friend of mine. Thanks to Caroline for sharing her version of the recipe. You can make the cheesecake in one loose-bottomed metal tin but it looks and tastes great in around six individual ramekin dishes.

Ingredients
2 × 250g tubs of mascarpone cheese
200g ginger biscuits

50g butter
40g icing sugar
2 limes — juice and grated zest
dark chocolate or a Cadbury Flake

1. Crush the ginger biscuits and melt the butter and stir together.
2. Press the buttery biscuit mixture into the bottom of your ramekin dishes and chill for around 30 minutes.
3. Mix the mascarpone with the icing sugar, lime zest and juice in a bowl and beat well.
4. Top the chilled biscuit bases with the lime/mascarpone mixture. It should reach around three-quarters of the way up, depending on the size of the ramekins.
5. Chill the cheesecakes for at least 30 minutes before serving.
6. Decorate with whatever takes your fancy, e.g. grated chocolate, chocolate curls or a crushed Cadbury Flake. (You can eat the Flake if there's any left over!)

We do hope that you have enjoyed reading this large print book.

Did you know that all of our titles are available for purchase?

We publish a wide range of high quality large print books including:
**Romances, Mysteries, Classics
General Fiction
Non Fiction and Westerns**

Special interest titles available in large print are:
**The Little Oxford Dictionary
Music Book
Song Book
Hymn Book
Service Book**

Also available from us courtesy of Oxford University Press:
**Young Readers' Dictionary
(large print edition)
Young Readers' Thesaurus
(large print edition)**

For further information or a free brochure, please contact us at:
**Ulverscroft Large Print Books Ltd.,
The Green, Bradgate Road, Anstey,
Leicester, LE7 7FU, England.
Tel:** (00 44) 0116 236 4325
Fax: (00 44) 0116 234 0205

MAR.